THE **HUMAN MEGMADOR**

Edmantha Hall

Sagebrush Publishing
Canton, Texas

Edmantha Hall/Sagebrush Publishing
Printed in the United States of America
edmanthahallbooks.com

Publisher's Note: This is a work of fiction. Names, characters, places, and incidents are a product of the author's imagination. Locales and public names are sometimes used for atmospheric purposes. Any resemblance to actual people, living or dead, or to businesses, companies, events, institutions, or locales is completely coincidental.

The Human Megmador/ Edmantha Hall. -- 1st ed.

ISBN 978-1985859173 Print Edition

Also by Edmantha Hall

Destiny

Sacrificial Child

I am dedicating this book to my loving sister, Melissa Hall: 03/02/1942-09/15/2013, and to my wonderful brother, Edmantha Hall: 03/13/1948-4/22/2014, whose pen name I used for my book.

ACKNOWLEDGMENTS

Thanks to the Rocky Mountain Fiction Writers at
Southwest Plaza in Littleton, Colorado, who encouraged
me to write, AND to my editor.

CHAPTER 1

THE HUMAN CAPTAIN

Before the Galactic Committee collected humans from all over the galaxy and transported them to the human planet, Earth.

Captain Sadera Sedo was the only human living among the Beltese species.

She did not understand the surge of power that had been ripping through her body over the past two weeks.

Her heart rate had slowed by half, and her vision and hearing had sharpened. Her skin and sense of touch had become increasingly sensitive. When she neared her crew, she could hear their thoughts. Her body pulsed with energy, and her new powers excited and frightened her.

Her captain's living quarters on the *Volpus*, like those of the other crew members, were small. Her room simply contained built-in wall cabinets, a lounge chair, a table with four chairs, and a computer station.

Captain Sedo had searched the *Volpus's* database for evidence of the same physical and psychological anomalies she was experiencing in an effort to self-diagnose. Her changes were identical to those of the Beltese during their rare transformation into Megmadors.

But how could this be? She was human.

Growing up without other human contacts, Captain Sedo identified only with the Beltese traditions. Still, she struggled to fit in, because her adoptive species regarded humans as inferior beings. Of the known alien races, the Beltese were the most powerful and controlled much of the galaxy. Their physical appearance resembled humans, with the exception of their cat-like ears, skeletal structure, and genetics. They had pink complexions, gray eyes, and hair the color of the sun.

The Beltese did not believe in divinity, yet Megmadors were similar to gods. One Megmador evolved every two thousand years and contributed greatly to the Beltese's technological achievements. When a Megmador died, the mystery of its powers went up in flames, leaving only ashes. History proved that two never existed at the same time. They could walk through walls and build force fields around their bodies to protect themselves from harm, and they were telepathic.

Megmadors not only predicted the near future but also witnessed events that had occurred in the past.

Captain Sedo leaned back in her chair, stared blankly at her mother's colorful painting of her home planet, and pondered her situation. Sedo knew she was becoming a Megmador. Dr. Ohma, the *Volpus's* chief physician, held the key to her changes, and her medical records would detail the rate of her transformation. She felt it, envisioned it.

What had the Beltese done to her? An alien creature was taking control of her body, and she couldn't stop it. All crew members had access to their own medical records. Sedo's doctors had never given her a copy of her medical history

But then again, she'd never requested one.

That was about to change.

The captain left her room and headed for Dr. Ohma's office. Entering the infirmary in a rage, she rushed past the nurse's station.

"Captain ..." the nurse said.

Captain Sedo showed herself into Ohma's office without knocking and stopped in front of his desk.

He frowned. "Captain, is there a problem?"

"I want all of my medical records," Sedo requested.

The doctor gazed up at her. "You've never requested your medical records in the past. Why now?"

Sedo could read thoughts well enough to know that the doctor sitting before her could no longer be trusted. "Every crew member on this ship has access to their medical history except me. Why?"

His gray eyes beamed back at her. "You're human."

Sedo placed her palms on his desk, leaned in, and said, "Are human records are not compatible with the *Volpus's* database? I have a right to review my records.

I want everything from the time I was adopted until the present—and I want them now, Doctor."

"Sorry, but my orders are from a higher authority," Dr. Ohma said.

Sedo poked a stiff finger into the doctor's chest. She found it difficult to hold back her anger, as energy from the entity within her raged. Her voice rose an octave. "I'm the captain of this ship. You work for me." She grabbed him by the collar of his blue lab jacket and yanked him to his feet. Her new strength surprised her. She could have easily thrown him across the room. "Do I make myself clear?"

Dr. Ohma drew a ragged breath. His face turned a lighter pink, and his ears perked. "Let go of me, Captain. What's the matter with you? And why is this so important all of a sudden?"

He forced her hands from his collar and took a step back. "I've never seen you display such aggressive behavior."

Captain Sedo's heart pounded, and a cold sweat moistened her armpits. "I can override everything on this ship except my medical records. That makes me suspicious."

He held his arms up, his palms extended outward in front of his chest. "Calm down. My orders are from the fleet commander."

She stiffened. "My father?"

"Yes," Ohma said.

"If you don't provide me with my records, I'll relieve you of your duties on the *Volpus*."

Ohma's eyes darted around the room, as if searching for something. "But ... I can't. I have strict orders from the fleet commander. Relieve me of my duties if you must, but I will be severely punished if I disobey his orders. Only Dr. Fea and I can view your records, and we can't discuss them with you or anyone else."

A deep, profound terror stirred within Sedo. "Beltese genes are not compatible with human genes?"

"That's correct."

"So I can't possibly be part Beltese?" Sedo asked.

"Absolutely not," Ohma said. "You know it's impossible. Not only the genes but—"

"Why have you performed so many examinations on me over the years?"

Dr. Ohma smoothed out his lab jacket and tugged at his collar. "Because you're human. Your anatomy is different from ours, and my job is to ensure you're in good health. You were weeks old when you were adopted."

He calmed down, took a seat behind his desk, and motioned for Sedo to take the chair in front of him, but she remained standing.

Sedo licked her dry lips and glanced down at him. "You and Dr. Fea have been my only doctors, all my life. Why haven't I seen other doctors? And why have you both taken assignments on all of my ships?"

He shrugged, as if the reason was obvious. "Because we know your medical history. I must admit, you were an interesting subject."

"Interesting?"

"You are different from us. We needed to be prepared, just in case you became ill."

She stared at him. "Doctor, I need answers."

He scooted his chair farther under his desk. "Answers to what?"

"I'm not the same person today that I was a week—or even a day ago."

His mouth twisted. "What does that mean?"

Sedo's eyes went to the floor, and her stomach lurched. "I'll discuss it with my father."

He lowered his voice, as if speaking to a child. "Captain, don't leave here discouraged."

"I'm not discouraged. I'm confused." Sedo walked toward the door, then stopped in her tracks. Before she exited the room, she turned and gazed directly into Dr. Ohma's eyes. "Are you certain I have no genetic link to the Beltese species?"

His ears drooped, his nostrils flared, and his eyes shot into the distance. "Why, that's impossible."

She detected that the doctor was not only lying but was also nervous about the subject.

She needed her medical records, and she would do anything to get them.

***

Finding it difficult to sleep, Sedo spent most of the night on her computer. When she finally fell asleep, nightmares from long gone times surfaced and haunted her again.

Sedo lay on a tree branch, looking down at her clan. The sun stood high in the sky as bright rays filtered through thick leaves. She couldn't move, nor could she make a sound. Animals resembling humans were attacking her clan, ripping their bodies apart. Their deathly screams echoed below her. She heard sharp teeth crushing bones and saw blood running freely, staining the path it traveled.

Even closing her eyes, she still saw the attack. The dream repeated itself over and over for the remainder of the night.

A beeping alarm woke Captain Sedo the next morning, and she searched blindly above the bed with her hand and silenced it. Abruptly, she rolled onto her back, threw off the covers, and swung her feet to the floor. Brown, mussed hair fell into her face. She hugged herself tightly and closed her eyes.

A mechanical female voice announced, "Abnormal sleep study summary. Report to Dr. Fea prior to duty. Interrupted sleep patterns, erratic pulse rates, heavy perspiration, and high brainwave activity throughout this study. Total sleep time inadequate for duty."

Sedo slid back into bed and turned over onto her stomach. "Computer, I want to sleep without disturbance."

"You must report to the psychiatrist at once, Captain," the computer insisted.

Five minutes passed.

"You must report to Dr. Fea, Captain."

Sedo jumped out of bed, dropped to her knees, and opened the bottom drawer underneath her bed. She rummaged through the drawer's contents until she found a flat-headed tool. Then she removed the sleep monitor's cover and violently disarmed the device.

Dr. Fea's voice rang from her wall speaker. "Captain, come to my office prior to reporting for duty."

Silence.

"I know you're there," Fea said.

"I'll be down shortly, Doctor," Captain Sedo responded with a sigh.

Surrendering, she showered and donned a traditional dark gray, two-piece uniform. Looking in her mirror, she attached a narrow, red, stand-up collar with rounded edges and a center split to her uniform, distinguishing her captain's rank.

When Captain Sedo entered the empty waiting room, Dr. Fea peeked around the door from his office. "Come on in," he said, jerking his head.

Sedo entered and took the chair in front of his desk. Meanwhile, the doctor tampered with a control panel on the adjacent wall.

Seating himself in the chair behind his desk, he

rested his hands on its surface, interlaced his fingers, and gawked at her. "You disarmed your sleep monitor."

"Why do you monitor my sleep?" Sedo asked.

He glanced down at his desk. "Everyone's sleep is monitored."

"Not by you."

"You're human—"

"And you need to learn more about human sleep patterns," she snapped.

He took a deep breath and exhaled. "Why ... yes."

"You'll no longer monitor my sleep," she said adamantly.

"Dr. Ohma spoke to me concerning your request for medical records. Why are they so important now?"

"Both Dr. Ohma and you are hiding something very important from me." She viciously spat her words at him. "I feel it."

Dr. Fea changed the subject. "You're moving your arms and legs very erratically during rest periods again. Was it the same nightmare?"

Sedo calmed down but felt a void, her heart pounding with a sensation of emptiness. "I see my parents being eaten alive. I can't really see their faces, but I know it's them. I want to run away—save myself—but I'm paralyzed, and I can't move."

"You feel guilty because you survived and everyone else in your clan was killed, including your parents. Earlier, I didn't realize the psychological impact their deaths would have on you. The occupants on Pomptus were short creatures resembling humans, but the Trazods didn't analyze them. They were animals, carnivores with claws and sharp teeth. They—"

"I know the story," Captain Sedo reminded the doctor. "The creatures ate my entire clan. The next day, the Trazods heard me crying in a hollowed-out tree trunk. I'm grateful to live among the Beltese. I could be living as a human savage."

"You have dedicated your life to space travel, and you've received high honors from Fleet Command. You're the only officer who made captain's rank by the age of twenty-five."

She stared into his eyes. "And that concerns me. Humans are not intelligent beings, so why am I smarter than most Beltese?"

"You grew up with us."

"Don't insult me, Doctor." Sedo knew a genetic link existed between the Beltese species and herself.

How had they redesigned her genes?

Dr. Fea lowered his head and didn't respond.

Sedo stood. "Will that be all?"

"I thought we would sit and talk."

"We just did," Sedo said. "Good day, Doctor."

"Captain, tell me why you're so irritable lately," he called behind her back. "What's wrong?"

"Allow me to see my medical records and the irritation will cease," Sedo said.

"I'm not allowed to do that without your father's permission. I'm sorry."

"Then we have nothing more to discuss." She walked out.

Sedo had to control her vexation. Careful not to draw any more attention to herself, she concentrated on her 557 Beltese crew members.

After reporting to her workstation, Captain Sedo dropped into her chair behind an L-shaped desk and pushed a button. Her computer screen rose amid blinking lights. When she stroked a pressure-sensitive key on her desk surface, her computer screen turned from black to a soft blue. The keys had over a thousand functions, and Sedo had learned each from her father's computer by the age of six.

Lieutenant Bonuve shared the elevated platform with her. He had assumed his position when Sedo became captain, seven years earlier. His orange collar distinguished his rank of second-in-command, and he was taller and bulkier than most Beltese.

Sedo was reviewing the *Volpus's* budget, touching each key with speed and accuracy, until a humming sound interrupted her train of thought.

"Reporting for duty, Captain Sedo," a child's voice said.

Sedo swiveled her chair ninety degrees, puzzled by the contraption before her.

A machine, about half her height, made from nordon metal—lightweight, strong, and durable—stood at her side. Two blue electronic scanners glowed like nocturnal eyes, and its nose was clearly a motion sensor. The machine's mouth moved when speaking, and its joints imitated life. The android wore the same attire as most Beltese on Tandon: a long white robe and sandals to accommodate the warm climate caused by the planet's two stars.

"Reporting for duty, Captain," the android repeated.

Sedo shot a glance over at Bonuve.

"It's a science project for our younger generation," he responded. "Androids will be running all over the ship in the near future."

"Oh … yes." Sedo nodded. She had assembled her first android, Ange, at the age of six.

She leaned close to the machine and whispered, "I'm requesting that whomever is controlling this gadget remove it from Navigational Control."

The android turned to leave. "I'm sorry if I disturbed you, Captain."

"Why don't you and your project join me in the officer's lounge for lunch today?" Sedo called to the departing machine's back. "You can explain how it works."

"Thank you, Captain. We'll see you at lunch," the child confirmed.

Sedo smiled as the android moved through the sliding double doors and disappeared.

Bonuve chuckled. "I'll make certain it doesn't happen

again, Captain." Bonuve loved the little ones and had two of his own. Sedo didn't mind if he bent the rules a little when it came to the younger generation.

Chapter 2

Space

Captain Sedo had spent most of her thirty-two years in space, first with her parents and now as the captain of her own warship.

Space was vast and intriguing, and it held secrets she wanted to unravel. Her ambitions in life were to venture into the Forbidden Galaxy, find a permanent home planet for her fellow human, who were scattered all over the galaxy, and become fleet commander as her father, Celt Sedo, had.

Highly commended by the Beltese Fleet Command, Sedo piloted the great warship, the *Volpus*.

The *Volpus* was named after a furious beast indigenous to her home planet, Tandon. The *Volpus* was an enormous, cat-like creature. It was as tall as she was, with long, retractable claws and deadly fangs. The beast, extinct for thousands of years, was now the Beltese emblem.

***

Chief Engineer Chedzer's voice rang from the communication button on her collar.

"Captain, will you meet me in the engine room? I have something for you to review."

"I'm on my way, Chedzer," Sedo said.

Chedzer was the oldest crew member aboard the *Volpus* and had been chief engineer years before Sedo became captain. He was serious when he was on duty, but otherwise he exhibited quite prankish behavior.

Sedo had made it halfway through the double doors when Starco, her communications officer, called out to her. "Captain, the Velekans are armed with Rex-7s and have killed hundreds of Agoorons on Space Station M-9."

Starco had graduated from the academy three years earlier. He was young, smart, and aggressive. "The Velekans have overpowered them, infiltrated their main computer, and downloaded all pertinent files concerning their power source and protective barriers."

The captain moved back to her workstation. "The Velekans don't have the technology to overthrow the Agoorons." She turned her attention to Ferrus, the ship's navigator. "Get us there as fast as possible."

"It'll take two hours," Ferrus said.

Starco touched controls on his desk, insisting on a response from M-9. "Captain, I've been cut off."

Ferrus pushed the speed to a safe maximum. He and Nedra, a weapons engineer, occupied workstations in front of the captain's platform. The viewport covered the entire forward wall, and all workstations in Navigational Control faced it.

Sedo dropped into her chair and propped her elbows onto her desk. Visions of the destruction of M-9 flashed through her mind like sand in a dust storm. She shivered as the vivid apparition continued.

Becoming a Megmador was frightening, and she wasn't certain if she could deal with the pressure. The Agoorons should've used deadly force against the Velekans. Why hadn't they?

Starco said, "We're being contacted by a cargo ship, Captain."

"Put the subject on a vektren," Sedo said.

A life-size, three-dimensional projection of a grim-looking alien with a dark orange complexion, round nose, and sharp teeth appeared in front of the Navigational Control room. Excited brown eyes with nictitating membranes glared back at her, reminding her of the tree frogs that lived in the rainforests on Tandon.

Captain Amon and his crew had delivered cargo to the Agooron space stations for years.

Without preamble, Captain Amon rasped, "Captain, the Velekans threatened to annihilate M-9. They destroyed two Trazod cargo vessels that intervened and forced the remainder of us to leave. Where did they get such technology?"

"I don't know, but I'll find out," Sedo said.

Amon blinked his inner eyelids once and his outer eyelids twice. "Brainless Velekans."

"Captain, we have the space station coming up," Lieutenant Bonuve said.

A projection of M-9 appeared next to Amon, and he directed his attention to the substation, rather than Sedo.

"We'll warn other ships to stay away from M-9 until we can determine what's going on there," Sedo said.

The alien disappeared from the room.

Sedo focused on the other vektren and saw four dome-shaped warships circling M-9. A fifth, docked at one of its ports, sped away at maximum speed.

The space station was lit up like a small star with a blue beacon flashing on the top. M-9, one of five huge spheres, had multiple decks and resembled a small planet. It served space travelers seeking relaxation for months, and sometimes years, away from their home planets.

All space stations had protective barriers, but the Agoorons never used them. Cargo ships constantly docked there, and the species posed no threat to anyone in the galaxy.

The Velekan ships moved a safe distance, assumed a circular formation, and simultaneously fired pulsating blue rays. Multiple blasts whizzed toward the space station, creating a massive explosion in the main fuel system, ripping the station apart, and launching debris in every direction. Reddish-orange streaks of fire silently illuminated the surrounding area.

Captain Sedo flinched as she jumped to her feet, and her crew gasped in horror as they watched more than 2,000 Agoorons disintegrate.

"They killed everyone," Ferrus whispered.

Sedo had acquaintances who lived or worked on M-9. The Velekans were galactic pests, but—for the first time—she wanted to annihilate the entire species. Her heart felt as if a giant hand were squeezing it. She had never felt so powerful, yet so helpless.

Starco said, "Captain, we must do something."

"Contact Fleet Command and relay what has happened here," Sedo ordered. "We can't reverse history, Starco."

Sedo moved closer to the three-dimensional projection and concentrated on the scattered debris.

So many peaceful Agoorons had died in vain.

"Captain, the fleet commander," Starco announced.

When Commander Celt Sedo came into view, a scowl dominated his face.

He had assumed leadership of Fleet Command forty-seven years earlier. His projection stood next to the visual of M-9, and he concentrated on the debris from the substation, rather than on his daughter.

Other than in vektren projections, Captain Sedo had not seen her father in over five years. The age lines on his face looked more pronounced, his hair had thinned, and his face glistened.

"Commander."

"Captain." He returned her formal greeting, keeping his eyes on the vektren. "So, this is what remains of M-9. We're contacting the Agooron Council concerning this incident. Send me a visual of the attack. Rendezvous with the Velekan warships and obtain as much information as you can from them."

"They're usually pretty tight-lipped," Sedo reminded her father.

"Find out how the Velekans obtained such technology. Contact me after your meeting with them," he said.

"What if they attack other space stations?"

"We and our allies will send warships to protect them. Your ship shall guard M-7," the commander said before his projection disappeared.

"Although the Velekans have mastered advanced firing power," Bonuve said, "their warships are still primitive and their protective barriers are too weak to protect them effectively. It would be suicidal to attack more superior warships, like ours."

"The Velekans ignored all theories concerning black holes," Sedo said. "They claimed they had assembled a ship to withstand the force and deliberately piloted it into one's core, and then insisted they were in communication with it."

"Point taken, Captain," Bonuve said.

"Get a view of the attack to Fleet Command, Starco," Sedo said.

"It's done, Captain."

Ferrus worked at his computer. "The Velekans are headed our way. Assuming they don't change their course, we'll meet them in less than an hour."

***

"Captain," Starco announced, "we're within communication range of the Velekan warships."

The primitive Velekan warships approached the *Volpus* in a staggered formation—dwarfs compared to the huge, cubical design of the *Volpus.*

Sedo stood as the Velekan ships neared. "Put the one out front on a vektren," she ordered.

The Velekan captain sat in a high-backed chair and leaned forward with both arms draped over his armrests. His long, skinny fingers dangled freely, and he sat slanted forward. Bones resembling fish scales covered his hairless head and added protection to his skull. His cleft chin resembled buttocks, and his pale, gray skin was almost white. He wore an orange uniform with four black stripes on the left sleeve, indicating his captain's rank.

"I'm Captain Sedo of the Beltese Fleet."

From his chair, the Velekan captain sat taller than she stood. His red eyes met hers.

"I'm Captain Prog of the Velekan Fleet." A scowl covered his face. When he spoke, his thin lips barely moved.

Both captains studied each other for a moment.

"Are you insane?" Sedo's heart drummed wildly as she

clenched her hands tightly behind her back, her fingernails digging into her palms. If she had full Megmador
powers, she would have destroyed the Velekan warships
herself.

Prog's face wrinkled. "The Agoorons are our enemies.
We have a right to annihilate them at will."

"The Agoorons have no enemies," Sedo shouted. "You
only wanted their technology."

Prog leaned back in his chair. "And they refused to
share it."

"Where did you get such weaponry?"

Prog glared at Sedo and tilted his head to one side.
"We have friends, allies. Huh, only the Beltese would
make a human female captain of a warship. Humans are
savage. A female's only role is to bring comfort to males."

"You've just murdered over 2,000 Agoorons—and I'm
a savage?" Sedo said. "Your ignorant and belligerent policies regarding females are absurd."

Prog jumped to his feet, standing twice her height.
"I'll not take such insults from a human." He pronounced
the word slowly and with difficulty, as if it left poison on
his tongue.

"Your species will suffer dire consequences for what
you have done, Captain Prog."

"The Velekans have activated their protective barriers, Captain," Bonuve warned.

Sedo stepped closer to Prog's image on the vektren.
"Why did you activate your barriers?"

He responded as if the question was stupid. "To protect our warships."

"Bonuve, clear all outer decks," Sedo ordered. "They're going to attack."

Anger roared from Prog's voice. "Soon our technology will equal the Beltese's, and they will never look down on us again."

"You've just demonstrated why the Galactic Committee refuses to share technology with your species," Sedo said. "You Velekans need time to evolve, both technically and psychologically."

Prog ceased communication.

Sedo swiveled her chair in Bonuve's direction. "Have you cleared the outer decks?"

"We're doing so this moment, Captain," Bonuve said.

Sedo knew her crew was in danger. "You've had twenty seconds." She heard the emergency warning system, a beeping alarm that repeated every second with flashing red lights, directing the crew into the *Volpus's* inner protective barrier.

Nedra concentrated on her workstation. "The Velekans are revving their engines and assuming a formation, Captain."

"Are they insane?" Bonuve shouted.

Nedra studied her controls. "I've scanned their warships. They have acquired advanced weaponry—limited, but advanced compared to their old system. Their ships are now operating on crude engines—similar to ours."

Advanced warships like the *Volpus* operated on zircolon cores, producing an infinite quantity of neutrinos. The matter/anti-matter system operated by spinning the neutrinos, in opposite directions, through miniature accelerators.

"How did the Velekans advance so far, creating zircolon cores?" Bonuve asked.

Images of the Velekans attacking and damaging Sedo's ship flashed through her mind.

Was it a flawed premonition?

"Nedra, activate our barrier and destroy all five ships."

Nedra protested, "Captain, it's against Fleet Command regulations to—"

"They're close enough to damage the *Volpus*. Move away, Ferrus," Sedo urged.

As the *Volpus* moved, so did the Velekan warships.

Bonuve forced a dry chuckle. "They wouldn't dare."

Sedo yelled, "Nedra, activate our barrier and fire."

As Nedra hesitated, all five Velekan warships targeted the same area on the starboard side. Multiple pulses struck the *Volpus*, jolting Sedo and her crew out of their seats.

Sedo quickly recovered from her fall. Using her desk as leverage, she steadied herself, swiveled her chair around, and climbed up.

The Velekan ships immediately fired again, hitting the weaker top dome of the *Volpus*, jolting the ship a second time.

Nedra regained her composure and activated the barrier, but the Velekan ships had zigzagged away, in order to minimize their possibility of becoming targets.

Nedra fired at will and destroyed two escaping ships. When they exploded, flying debris crippled a third, sending it spiraling out of control and making it an easy target.

"They've damaged the outer hull, Captain." Chedzer, the chief engineer, blurted into the Navigational Control speaker. "I've sealed that section."

"They're returning, Captain," Nedra said. She fired on the damaged Velekan ship, and it exploded.

"There are two ships left, and I want them destroyed, now," Sedo demanded.

Nedra fired again, and multiple pulses of blue rays vanished into space—where her targets had been less than a second earlier.

Multiple strikes from the *Volpus* hit the last two Velekan warships, causing an incredible, dazzling explosion.

Captain Sedo contacted Chedzer in engineering. "How bad is the damage?"

He sighed. "The blasts breached the recreational area on Deck Five, and the top dome is cracked. Their weapons contain lethal radiation."

"High levels of radiation ..." Sedo mumbled.

Images of the damaged areas appeared before her on vektrens.

"I advise you not to visit this area, Captain," Chedzer

warned. "Most of the deaths are related to radiation exposure. Many of the crew members made it to safety, but others died trying."

Silence fell over the *Volpus* as Sedo and her entire crew viewed the remains of their fellow crew members. Sedo rose to her feet and examined the disaster before her.

Bonuve asked, "How shall we retaliate?"

Now enraged, Sedo walked to Nedra's station. "On your feet, Lieutenant." Heat flashed through her body like the flames that engulfed the space outside. Managing to control her temper, Sedo resisted slapping Nedra's face. "You disobeyed my order," she said between clenched teeth. "I make the rules. You follow them. I commanded you to fire. You hesitated to fire but activating our outer barrier would have protected us."

Beltese typically never cried, but Nedra appeared to be on the verge of tears. She stood at attention, staring into the distance as Sedo continued to lash out at her, almost nose to nose.

Sedo knew the entire crew would blame Nedra for the deaths of their fellow crew members and the devastation to the *Volpus*.

Sedo growled out her words. "I'll not tolerate insubordination on my ship. The Fleet Command Court-Martial Committee will determine your guilt and punishment when we return to Tandon." Sedo pointed a stiff finger at the door. "Go to your quarters and remain there until I decide what to do with you."

"Other than during war, Fleet Command forbids us to attack unless the other party is the aggressor," Bonuve said.

Sedo snarled at Bonuve and poked a thumb into her chest. "I make decisions on the *Volpus*, not Fleet Command. Get the other weapons engineer up here."

Bonuve headed toward Nedra's workstation. "He's one of the casualties, Captain, and so is our research physician. I'll take over."

"No, you have other duties. Nedra." Sedo stopped her weapons expert as she neared the exit. "Get back to your station. If you disobey my orders again, you'll spend the remainder of your life on Quandra-4. Do I make myself clear?"

Nedra's voice was almost inaudible. "Yes, Captain."

"I can't hear you," Sedo snapped.

"Yes, Captain," Nedra shouted. "It'll never happen again."

Sedo said, "You shall remain weapons expert until we reach Tandon. But you'll still face Fleet Command for insubordination."

Chedzer's voice rang loud and clear in Navigational Control. "We don't know how many casualties we have, Captain. I'm suiting up now." His voice was grim, heavy with sadness. "Sorry, but we didn't have time for a full-scale evacuation. The injured and burned victims are on their way to the infirmary."

Sedo stared through the viewport and pondered the issue at hand.

Her Megmador powers had warned her about the event.

The attack on the *Volpus* had been preventable.

Her heart grew heavy over her damaged ship—the dead and wounded crew members.

She snapped out of her reverie.

"Chedzer, can we use the students' androids to assist with radiation decontamination?"

"I believe so, Captain," Chedzer said.

"Take over," Sedo ordered Bonuve. "I'll help with damage assessment."

"Captain, the radiation level is too intense for you, even in a radiation suit. Beltese can withstand much higher doses, because over time our cells can repair themselves. Please, allow me," Bonuve requested.

"Captain," Ohma's voice vibrated from the Navigational Control speaker, "we're receiving wounded in the infirmary and more are coming. There are fatalities."

Sedo faced Bonuve. "All right, you take over the assessment, and I'll visit the infirmary. I'm on my way, Doctor." She turned to Ferrus. "Contact us immediately if you see anything out there, no matter what."

"I've completed a 360-degree scan. Right now, there are no ships within viewing distance," Ferrus said.

"Nedra, destroy any Velekan warships on sight. Do you understand?" Sedo said.

"Yes, Captain," Nedra replied.

The doors opened as Sedo and Bonuve exited

Navigational Control. Walking side by side, they rushed down the corridor and entered a vertical lift.

Sedo stepped off on Deck Seven to visit the infirmary. "I want to know everything that's going on down there, Bonuve," she yelled back at him before the doors closed behind her.

"I'll keep you updated, Captain," Bonuve promised.

Captain Sedo entered the infirmary and saw patients crowding into the area. The radiometer on her wristband immediately started beeping, and it registered critical. Rushing back into the hallway, she quickly opened a cabinet and donned a bulky radiation suit.

Reentering the infirmary, she saw Ohma and his medical staff buzzing around like bees but showing no signs of trepidation. She felt ridiculous being the only one wearing protective gear.

Bonuve's voice rang inside her suit. "Captain, we've started decontamination procedures. Using the androids was an excellent idea. Major repairs will have to take place back on Tandon."

"Thanks. Keep me posted," Sedo said, her suit muffling her voice.

She stood at the doctor's side and observed a severely burned victim.

A nurse, Bonuve's wife, assisted from the other side of the bed. She injected the patient with a clear liquid.

"Dr. Ohma, how are things going here?" Sedo asked.

Using his medical instrument, Ohma scanned another

severely burned patient. "Nine patients have radiation damage beyond repair, and another has a severe head injury." He shook his head. "All we can do is make them comfortable and wait for the inevitable."

Sedo saw the remains of another crew member and struggled to hold back her rage. "Can he hear us?"

"No, she's in a medically induced coma. Eight are females," the doctor confirmed.

"How long, Doctor?"

"Hours for some. Sixteen are already dead," Ohma said. "Their cause of death was not only radiation contamination, but exposure to zero atmosphere as well."

The doctor moved to another victim. Yellow blood soaked through the bandage that covered the patient's crushed head. "Minutes for this one. Part of the dome collapsed on him. These ten patients are not going to survive, and I suggest we end their suffering."

As captain, Sedo had made life-and-death decisions. It was the most difficult part of her job. A lump stuck in her throat, and a pain brewed in her stomach.

Dr. Ohma moved to another patient and tucked a skeletal hand underneath the covers. "My records will show they died in the line of duty."

Sedo trailed behind Ohma as he moved to another patient. "And the others?"

He said, "It'll take time for the radiation to purge from their systems, but with proper injections their cells will fully recover within a few weeks."

"I'll go through decontamination and wait for you in the conference room next door," Sedo said as she headed for the door.

Captain Sedo entered a chamber in the back of the infirmary that read: "DECONTAMINATION." After closing the door behind her, she tapped the button and remained under the spray wash for five minutes. A tingling sensation arose from the right side of her chest. Was it due to stress or her transformation? She stepped into a dry chamber and removed her suit, then entered the hallway and paced for a few minutes.

"Captain," Starco summoned. "The fleet commander wishes to speak to you. Are you available?"

Checking her radiometer, she responded, "Tell him I'll contact him shortly."

Starco's voice was firm but controlled. "I've submitted a report to Fleet Command. The commander wants to know how many are injured."

Sedo choked out her words. "Thirty-one injured. Twenty-six dead."

"I'll relay the message," Starco said.

Three crew members passed Sedo. "Captain," they acknowledged with solemn nods. She returned the salutation, and the crew members continued down the corridor, chatting about the attack.

Sedo entered the conference room and took a seat at the table. "Computer, activate a vektren inside the starboard side, Deck Five," she said to the ship's computer.

Other than during training, Sedo had never been involved in radiation decontamination or war.

When the projection came alive, Bonuve looked a head taller than the other three crew members. All wore white spacesuits for working in zero gravity. Multiple androids of various sizes shot a high-pressure solution onto the walls, ceiling, and other items, including chairs and tables. Long hoses vacuumed the spray wash into cylindrical radioactive waste containers that moved on four wheels. The contaminated wash circulated through a cryogenic solution that neutralized the radiation by absorbing a proton in the nucleus.

Sedo studied the process and waited for an inordinate amount of time. When Dr. Ohma finally entered the room, she stood.

Ohma held a palm-sized log in one hand and a radiation monitor in the other. "I'm sorry it took me so long, but I had to stabilize my patients first."

"I understand, Doctor." Sedo accepted the log and studied the names. "One of the dying is Lieutenant Ned. His son is in incubation. Which one is he?"

"The head wound," Dr. Ohma said. "He just passed away."

Her legs weakened. "Does his wife know?"

"She was at his side when he died," Dr. Ohma said.

Sedo gripped the log in both hands, her fingernails digging into its corners. "He had great potential, an excellent engineer. Are you positive these patients won't survive?"

Ohma squeezed her shoulder. "I'm certain, Captain."

Sedo scanned the remaining patients' names, pressed the approval button, and passed the log back to Ohma. She turned and left without saying another word. Sedo had lost crew members years earlier, and the current pain was just as devastating as it had been then.

"Captain, the commander wishes to speak with you," Starco said.

"I'll be up shortly," Sedo said.

When Sedo stepped onto the vertical life, Lieutenant Somgu was the only occupant.

Somgu had been on the *Volpus* for five years, and she ranked third-in-command. Sedo stood shoulder to shoulder with her, facing the doors. "Lieutenant, we'll be passing through the Negman Solar System in three days. Assemble and transport weapons to the Free Clan on Kodas."

"Captain, we have strict orders from Fleet Command not to interfere, but rather to allow the humans to resolve their own conflicts," Somgu reminded her.

"As long as the Velekans are involved, it's no longer a human conflict," Sedo said.

"Is this an order?"

"Yes, Lieutenant."

"I'll take care of it, Captain."

Sedo stepped off the lift and glanced over her shoulder. "Make certain their weapons give them an advantage over The Lords."

Returning to Navigational Control, Captain Sedo leaned back in her chair and focused on the ceiling that was ten times her height. She moved her head from side to side, trying to release the tension in her neck. Her mind stirred over the events that had happened within the past hour. She sat up straight when her father's image came into view.

"Commander, has Fleet Command determined where the Velekans obtained their technology?" Sedo asked.

"Not yet," her father responded. "We're still investigating. We believe they lost the data from M-9 when the *Volpus* destroyed their ships."

"We can't be certain. They may have advanced transmission technology as well," she added.

"I doubt it," the commander said. "I believe they were carrying the information back to their planet. This is a sad day for Fleet Command. I'll personally contact each family of the deceased."

"What've you decided to do about the Velekans, Commander?"

"We need to stop them before they modify their ships. I'm calling a Galactic Committee meeting."

"Shall we continue to M-7?" Sedo asked.

"No. Return to Tandon for ship repairs. I'll send another warship."

CHAPTER 3

PLANET TANDON IN THE PLATA SOLAR SYSTEM

The Galactic Committee

Commander Celt Sedo mingled with a crowd of eight high-ranking Beltese commanding officers and nine alien allies, preparing to discuss the Velekan attacks on M-9 and the *Volpus*.

He also served as chairperson of the Galactic Committee, which consisted of representatives from fourteen intelligent species who made critical war decisions and established galactic laws and policies.

The commander's voice rose over the mumbling crowd. "Attention."

Silence fell over the room, and the few standing guests took their seats.

"Five allies will participate remotely by the aid of vektrens," the commander said.

Commander Sedo felt his age: 173.

In less than thirty years, he would go through Naconda, a painful and inevitable dying stage during which the

Beltese's health deteriorated to a point that required eu-
thanasia. He and his wife, Mana, had lived better than the
average Beltese because of his high standing within Fleet
Command over the years. He had spent years traveling in
space prior to becoming commander of the Beltese Fleet.
Highly respected within the Galactic Committee, he had
almost as much power as the Beltese leader.

Various allies sat around tables with an assortment of
appetizers and wine.

Commander Sedo stood in front of the room. "I'd like
to thank you all for traveling this distance on such short
notice. We need to discuss two important issues today.
Primarily, the Velekan destruction of M-9 and their attack on the *Volpus*. We've not yet been able to confirm
where the Velekans obtained such superior technology."

A gentle Elgon, Commander Nowe, locked eyes with
Commander Sedo.

Nowe established the rules and regulations concerning the protection of inferior species from the technologically advanced. Like the rest of the Elgon species, Nowe
was short and stocky, with orange hair that spiked like
that of an angry cat. Nowe's gray eyes and pink complexion closely resembled the Beltese's, except for the short,
fine hair that sparsely covered his body. "Velekans are a
dangerous species, and we need to stop them before they
learn how to upgrade their warships."

Septa, the more vocal of the two attending Agoorons,
was only slightly taller than the chairs in the room. His

small ears resembled a human's, and his dark blue complexion complemented the small, blue pupils of his big brown eyes. "The Velekan warships have been spotted near M-7. They've already destroyed four of our cargo ships."

"Never allow your ships to travel without the escort of a warship, Septa," the commander said.

Over the years, Commander Sedo had tried to convince the Agoorons to assemble their own warships, but they had refused. Their rationale was that they had no enemies and posed no threat to any other species in the galaxy.

As Septa's upper lip protruded above his lower, he said, "Destroy the Velekans. Eliminate them all."

Commander Sedo shook his head. "To annihilate an entire species is immoral. Yet we've tried negotiating with the Velekans in the past—to no avail. Before adjourning this meeting, we'll determine how to cripple their war fleet—but not by obliterating them."

Rota was third-in-command and the youngest of the high-ranking Beltese officers. "This galaxy has been at peace for over a hundred years." Rota was smart, determined, and aggressive. The commander had even been considering Rota as his replacement when the time came.

Septa's face wrinkled. "With their new technology, the Velekans could disrupt continuity throughout the galaxy."

"We need a logical plan," Commander Sedo said.

Like a chameleon, the Camagon's skin changed to the color of the furniture, a dark brown. She waved a webbed hand in the air. "Order their warships out of space for the next 100 years, permanently if necessary. They may operate only cargo vessels. We'll destroy their warships and their production facilities if they don't comply."

Commander Sedo nodded at the Camagon. "Good plan. If they refuse to ground their warships, we'll destroy them on sight."

Septa jumped to his feet for emphasis, since he was half the height of most members. "I still say destroy them. My parents died on M-9."

"I'm sorry for your loss," Commander Sedo said. "What the Velekans did was an unthinkable tragedy. Why don't you have some wine? It may help calm you."

Septa's broad nose twitched in agitation as he slid back into his chair. "I don't need wine. I want the Velekans destroyed. They're savages—and always will be."

Nowe said, "We've all passed through aggressive stages before becoming more appreciative and understanding of different species in our galaxy, and the Velekans should have the same opportunity. In the future, they'll learn to settle conflicts and communicate with other species without being so hostile."

Septa jumped out of his chair again and faced the group, his eyes darting from one member to another, begging for their support. "Their technology has far surpassed their intellectual capabilities. They have no compassion for their own species, and I doubt if they'll be more civilized within the next 100 years."

"Please, a show of hands," Commander Sedo said. "How many agree that the Velekans' warships should be grounded for the next 100 years?"

The Camagon rubbed her chin with the tips of her crusty fingers. "That time period should be adequate."

The commander acknowledged that twelve allies agreed with removing the Velekans from space for the next 100 years.

The Agooron still insisted on annihilation.

Assistant Fleet Commander Colas spoke up. "When shall we contact them?"

"Now." The commander took a seat at a small table in front of the room. "Contact the Velekan commander," he said to Colas.

Septa fidgeted in his chair. "The Velekans won't agree."

The Trazod commander's small head didn't match his large frame. He leaned forward, took a piece of raw meat, and nibbled on it with small, sharp teeth. "Since the Velekans destroyed our cargo ships, we have declared war on them, and we'll destroy their warships whenever we meet them in space."

Commander Sedo's guests stood and helped themselves to wine and food.

Within seconds, the Velekan commander appeared on a vektren in front of the room. He sat behind a desk with a female standing at his side, serving him food. His brusque voice flooded the room. "Commander Sedo, why have you contacted me?"

"I believe you already know the answer. Your warships destroyed M-9, attacked one of our warships, and destroyed several cargo vessels. Members of the Galaxy Committee have come to a conclusion with regard to your punishment."

The Velekan commander waved his server away, his red eyes glaring. "Is that so, Commander?"

Commander Sedo stared sternly at the Velekan as he conveyed the verdict of the Galactic Committee.

The Velekan commander clenched his fists, and his face became white. "We will not remove our warships from space. We plan to destroy the Agoorons and any species that interferes."

Commander Sedo hit a button on the table, relocating the vektren so the Velekan commander could see the Galactic Committee in session. "What did the Agoorons do to the Velekans to provoke such an attack on their substation?"

"We tried to negotiate as allies, but they treated us like inferior beings. Even the Galactic Committee has denied us," the Velekan commander said.

Commander Sedo tried to remain calm. He took a sip of wine and cleared his throat. "You can't force other species to become your friends. Why did your ships attack the *Volpus*?"

The Velekan commander didn't respond, only stared at Commander Sedo.

"You have six months to ground the Velekan War Fleet," Commander Sedo instructed. "We'll consider the ones traveling anywhere other than toward your home planet a threat. If you don't comply, your warship production facilities will be destroyed."

"We'll attack again. That I promise," the Velekan commander shouted before ending the transmission.

Commander Sedo shook his head and sighed. "Give them time to consider our decision. Other than cargo vessels, destroy all Velekan warships on sight."

Nowe shifted in his chair. "They're a stubborn species."

Commander Sedo scratched the back of his neck. "Are there any questions concerning this matter prior to proceeding to the next subject?" He waited for responses but heard only silence. "That settled, let's move on to the Human Planet Project. The Galactic Committee had discussed, on numerous occasions, relocating all human clans to one planet. Humans are inferior creatures. They are scattered all over the galaxy, and many are enslaved by other species."

Nowe eyed the ceiling. "The question is where to place them. We don't know of any vacant planets that will sustain human life. We need to place all the human clans on one planet, where we can protect them from other species, like the Velekans and the Bugs, until they become more civilized."

Commander Sedo focused on the Trazod commander. "Are you still refusing to give up Pomtus? It's the best planet, when it comes to relocating the human clans."

Commander Sedo had met the Trazod commander thirty-five years previous. His crew had found his daughter, Sadera, on Pomtus, when she was just a baby. The Trazods were the second most intelligent species in the galaxy and maintained almost as many warships as the Beltese.

The Trazod commander's red skin glowed bright against his white uniform. "No, Commander," the shy creature said. "We have established quite a flourishing colony there, and I don't think it's fair to ask our citizens to leave."

"We have one other alternative, but it'll take a great deal of work—and extreme expense," Commander Sedo said. "Humans will be placed on a planet in a distant solar system that has no civilized beings."

"The remaining humans in the Zetta Galaxy must be moved," Rota said. "Maacon is losing its elliptical orbit faster than we expected, and the planet is moving dangerously close to its star."

"We have a ship in that area," Nowe said. "We relocated the first group, and now we'll move the others."

"Thank you, Nowe," Commander Sedo said. "We appreciate your help."

The Agooron commander was approximately the same height as Septa. She said, "We want the humans out of our solar system. They're pests who eat our fruits and vegetables."

The Camagon turned up her nose and wrinkled her brown face. "They're filthy, disgusting animals," she said.

Commander Sedo said, "My daughter is the most decorated captain in the Beltese Fleet. Humans are intelligent beings. We once lived as they do now."

Just then, the Sularous commander's voice came in loud and clear from one of the vektrens. "Perhaps we should educate them."

"I don't think we should interfere," Commander Sedo said. "Humans need to learn how to advance on their own. It might take thousands of years, but they'll prevail."

Nowe said, "They have been living like—"

"Commander." A lieutenant rushed into the room and stopped in front of Commander Sedo, standing at attention. "The Velekans just tried to attack M-7. They've destroyed Captain Amon's cargo ship."

"Thank you, Lieutenant. You're dismissed." The commander glanced around the room. "It's settled. We'll destroy the Velekans' warship production facilities. How long will it take to get the *Volpus* repaired?"

Colas rested his hands on his armrests. "The *Volpus* should be in port within six weeks, and it will take another two to complete the repairs, if we work around the clock."

"I'll allow the *Volpus* to destroy their production facilities. Members, contact your fleets immediately and inform them of our decision. Let's take a break and meet here after lunch."

***

The Galactic Committee resumed their meeting two hours later.

Commander Sedo said, "I'll have one of our scientists explain how we may obtain a planet for the humans." He punched in two numbers on his wristband. "Reiser, you may join us now."

A young Beltese rushed into the room, as if he couldn't wait to deliver his presentation. Like most non-military personnel, Reiser wore a white robe and sandals. He was tall and unhealthily skinny with huge ears and an eye tic. Most Beltese had fiery yellow hair, but Reiser's hair was brownish red.

"This is Reiser," Commander Sedo said. "He has many technical degrees. He and his parents crash-landed in a cargo ship on a desolate planet. Reiser contracted a virus that left him gifted, and it won't surprise me if he becomes our next Megmador. I'll turn this meeting over to him. Please tell this committee about the planet Captain Sedo has found for the humans."

Reiser's right eye twitched as he moved to the center of the room. He was the only known Beltese who spoke with the use of his hands. "Yes—ah, I mean—it's not ready yet. Computer, display the Alpha Solar System on a vektren."

Commander Sedo favored the prominent gaseous planets because they were colorful. He'd never ventured that distance during his voyages as the captain of the *Eliptus*.

The Trazod commander flashed a puzzled glance around the room as he repositioned his huge frame in his chair. "I'm not familiar with this solar system."

Rota shook his head. "Planets there are not habitable, especially for humans."

Reiser adjusted the vektren and focused on one planet. The pale glow of a lone satellite revolved within its gravitational force. "This will be the human planet: third from the star."

Through thick patches of hazy clouds lay barren land, and brown water covered two-thirds of the planet.

Rota gawked at Reiser in disbelief. "We trekked this system when I was captain. It's a seismic disaster—severe quakes and volcanic eruptions. Nothing can survive there. It doesn't have a crust and only has a limited upper mantle, causing extremely high temperatures."

Reiser held up his hands. "But we can make it habitable."

The commander detected a slight quiver in the young Beltese's voice as his fingers began to tremble. He wanted to intervene but knew it wasn't an option. Reiser had to convince the committee on his own.

Rota protested, "I disagree. It's impossible."

The Trazod's bluish-green eyes studied the sphere. "How do you propose to stabilize this planet? Show us a better view."

"I'm getting to that," Reiser said.

The Trazod commander shook his head in disgust. "This project will be a failure."

Reiser activated another vektren. "This is a planet in the Zetta Galaxy, believed to have been knocked out of its orbit by a huge asteroid. Its frozen pieces have been drifting in space for millions of years. It once flourished, with a multitude of plants and animals. Giant reptiles roamed this planet, both carnivores and herbivores, and creatures similar to humans lived there. I don't know how the humanoids survived among so many predators, but they did." The young Beltese cleared his throat and continued. "If we superimpose this planet's lithosphere on the newer planet and bring the ocean levels up to accommodate the added height, the atmosphere will clear, and direct sunlight will cause the brown water to turn blue."

Septa's brown eyes beamed curiously. "There's a large volume of water on this planet. Is there life in it?"

Reiser blinked several times, as if something was in his twitching eye. "Yes, but the *Volpus* scientists haven't analyzed its contents yet."

"Where will we find such huge volumes of water?" Nowe asked.

Reiser held onto the commander's table, as if he

needed it for support. "There's more than enough clean, fresh water on nearby planets."

The Agooron commander peered around Nowe. "And the atmosphere?"

"It has the correct proportion of oxygen and nitrogen for humans, and there are no poisonous gases. Once the planet is stabilized, the atmosphere will clear, and the oxygen content will increase, due to forestation."

"Reiser, how did the *Volpus* find this planet?" the Trazod asked.

"Captain Sedo has been searching for a planet for her human clans for years. Her crew analyzed it two years ago," Reiser said.

The Trazod commander frowned. "Do you expect us to move an entire planet?"

Reiser's hands danced about as he spoke. "Computer, enlarge Vektren One." Icy pieces of what resembled a broken egg came into view again. "We only need some of the lithospheres. We'll use lasers to separate them from the pieces you see here." Reiser glanced back at the commander. "Fresh water in the forms of lakes, rivers, and streams still exist on this planet."

"I see these pieces aren't near a star," Nowe said. "But ice can undergo sublimation, even in the middle of nowhere. Stray particles of radiation or cosmic rays can emit energy in the form of heat."

Reiser wiped a hand across his forehead. "I'm certain some water has evaporated, but 95% or more is still there."

Rota scooted his chair back from the table. "Is the gravitational force compatible for humans?"

"Yes, the gravity will slightly decrease after the lithospheres are added, but not much."

The Trazod leaned forward. "What's the radius of this planet?"

"With the addition of the plates, the new planet will have nearly the same diameter as this one." He pointed to the broken planet. "The only exception is that the new planet will have much more water."

"I counted twenty-one planets in the Alpha Solar System," Septa said.

Reiser hesitated and concentrated on the image, as if confirming the number. "That's correct. As you see, this planet has only one satellite, but others have as many as nineteen. An asteroid belt exists between the terrestrial, inner planets, and the outer gaseous planets." Reiser paused, gasped for breath, and pointed to an area on the second vektren. "Other planets once existed here but were pulled apart as a result of gravitational stress between the inner and outer planets. We may use some of these pieces to create islands on the human planet."

"Let's not get carried away, Reiser," the commander said. "Stick with our original plan."

"What about the radiation level?" Rota asked.

Reiser wiped his forehead again and rubbed his palms together. "Minor background, similar to the humans' natural habitats."

The commander intervened. "Each time one of our ships travels into the Zetta Galaxy, it can tow a piece back."

Reiser's hands continued to dance. "I assumed the human planet represented a perfect sphere, and I used space vectors to determine the most stable configuration for each piece of lithosphere. There'll be minimum seismic activity, but most of it will occur due to plates sliding against each other. They'll move constantly: 10 to 100 millimeters per year. This planet should have no more seismic or volcanic activities than a few other habitable planets. After the plates are in place, water and vegetation will be added." Reiser activated another vektren and rotated it, showing the final position of each plate.

"How many plates are there?" Rota asked.

"Thirty," Reiser said. "But I'm concerned with the seven largest ones, which will be the most difficult to position. The others are microplates."

"That's a lot of mass to move," Nowe said.

Reiser pointed at the vektren again. "The plates will separate most clans geographically, causing less friction between them. By the time humans learn how to move from one plate to another, they'll be more civilized. They may trade and learn different skills from each other."

The Trazod commander smirked. "Do you believe in magic, Commander Sedo?"

The idea amused everyone, with the exception of the Beltese and the Agoorons.

Septa crossed his short legs and leaned back in his chair. "I don't think it'll work. We should transport all humans to Pomptus."

Nowe sat straight up in his chair. "I agree. This project will take billions of galactic credits. Why put two planets together when we already have one to accommodate the humans?"

The Trazod commander was adamant. "We will not give up Pomptus."

"The committee can vote on it," Septa said. "Then the Trazods will have no choice."

"We're not leaving Pomptus," the Trazod repeated.

Septa smirked, "Then the Trazods can share it with the humans."

"I think we should vote on this matter," the commander said. "How many think we should force the Trazods to leave Pomptus and make it a human planet?"

The Camagon stuck out her chest. "I'm against it. I don't think the Trazods should give up their planet for savages."

"But Pomptus was intended to be a human planet," Septa argued.

"It was never intended to be a human planet," the Trazod interjected. "Only a temporary refuge."

"Let's vote," the commander said.

Eleven voted against the idea.

"Let's move on," Commander Sedo said.

Reiser regained his confidence. "I've completed all the

calculations. Both planets contain the same minerals and metals with the exception of two elements, atomic numbers 107.868 and 196.9665. These two metals are found on the planet in the Zetta Galaxy, not the proposed new planet."

"How long will it take this planet to thaw?" Nowe asked.

"A few weeks, depending on the season," Reiser said. "Unfortunately, the extreme north and south poles will remain ice. Nothing can survive there, but it's only a small part of the planet."

Septa glared at him, his blue pupils sparking. "What if these humans become civilized? A study of their planet's history will reveal false information."

Nowe slapped his palms on the table and raised his voice. "We're talking about humans. They've lived like savages for thousands of years with no technological advancements. The clan on Maacon has learned how to make crude spears from ore. Some have learned how to weave fabric for clothes."

"Even if they reach a technological age, they'll think their planet is billions of years old," the Agooron commander said. "They won't realize their lithospheres are from another planet. Remains of giant reptiles, radioactive data, and anthropology remnants will be false. They'll think they evolved from the humanoid creatures that once existed on the other planet."

Colas pointed a finger at the Agooron commander.

"Are we concerned about finding a planet for the humans—or facts about their past?"

Commander Sedo intervened. "We're giving them a planet. If they become intelligent enough, they'll figure it out in the future."

Reiser displayed the results of the blue planet, then a close-up of lush, green vegetation in its final stage. "We'll collect genetic compositions from every species of plant and animal in each clan's natural habitat. When the populations of herbivores flourish, we'll relocate the human clans, then add the carnivores."

"What about the humans living on Maacon?" Septa reminded him. "Most living things are dead."

Reiser stepped closer to the crowd. "Genetic materials there are still salvageable, and many plants and animals on Maacon are also found in other human environments."

"Carnivores won't know how to hunt," the Trazod commander said.

Commander Sedo grunted. "They will if they get hungry enough. There will be a few experienced hunters in each group."

Nowe took a sip of wine. "Is it necessary to introduce poisonous species and pesky insects back into the human environment?"

"We must place humans back into their natural habitats," Reiser said. "Removing some species may disrupt the entire ecosystem."

"It's a beautiful planet, but is it conceivable?" Nowe asked.

The Trazod folded his arms over his broad chest. "We can easily tow huge masses in space, but once ships enter the planetary atmosphere, we'll have problems with the gravitational force."

"We'll use anti-gravity lifts," Reiser said. "We'll need at least twenty warships for each of the seven largest sections. All we can do is decelerate the masses, so the final impact won't be destructive. That's why we'll add the first seven plates at the same nanosecond."

"This could take years," Rota said.

"Ten to fifteen," Reiser confirmed.

Commander Sedo nodded at Reiser. "Thank you for such a wonderful presentation. We'll discuss it and draw our conclusions."

Reiser stared at the commander with confidence. "I'm certain it'll work."

The young Beltese strode from the room, and Commander Sedo remained silent, giving the members time to consult among themselves before resuming the meeting.

When he felt enough time had passed, he made his position known. "This is the only way we can provide a planet for the humans. I trust this idea."

The Trazod shook his head. "I disagree with this theory. Are you expecting us to fund such a far-fetched notion?"

Commander Sedo picked up his glass. "Other scientists have reviewed this project, and they agree with Reiser."

"I trust you know what you're doing," the Camagon said.

The Trazod stared around the group. "The only way we'll agree to fund this project is if you guarantee it. If it doesn't work, we'll be requesting the return of our galactic credits."

Commander Sedo sealed the deal. "I agree. Commander Colas, relay this information to Captain Sedo."

Chapter 4

Planet Kodas in the Negman Solar System

The Revolt of the Saxons
Jason, a fifteen-year-old boy, lived in a valley surrounded by mountains.

He and a long line of slaves trudged up a narrow path along the ridge of the only mountain accessible by foot. At each dawn, his trip stretched up a long incline from the slave shacks at the base of the mountain to the mine.

Jason, as the other slaves, wore a long, tattered black robe covered with white dust from the mine. His leather water pouch hung over his shoulder. Rabbit fur covered his feet and lower legs, secured in place by wooden sandals with straps tied above his knees to provide warmth from the cold, damp cave where he toiled. His unwashed body reeked of rancid perspiration and the rotten-egg stench of the rocks he'd gathered.

Suddenly, Jason tripped and fell on his face, bringing the men behind him to a sudden halt.

"Get up," a fat guard growled.

Unlike the slaves, the guards wore white cloth that dropped to just above their knees.

A whip stung Jason's upper back, ripping strands of shoulder-length blond hair from his head when it recoiled.

The taller guard chuckled. "Stop it, Al. That one might be mine. Hey, slave, what's your mother's name?"

Jason kept his eyes focused on the path. He wiped his bloody nose with the back of his hand, ignoring the guard's question.

The fat guard coughed up mucus and spat. "I never remember their names."

Jason cursed the guard under his breath. He didn't know how to count but knew his age summed fingers on three hands.

The Lords had bred with Jason's once snow-white clan, creating a new race. Unlike The Lords' light-yellow complexion and brown hair, the slaves had a mixture of hair and eye colors and a diversity of complexions—fairer than The Lords but not as fair as their now-extinct ancestors. Jason's clan had once been the ruling lords—the superior and smarter race—but they were overthrown when the slave population outnumbered theirs.

Over generations, Jason's clan had lost its pure lineage and adopted the vernacular of The Lords.

Jason had worked hard all his life. He remembered only a few days of rest, all involving some kind of illness. Over the years, he had seen his clan perform long, tedious hours of labor, leaving their bodies thin and haggard early in life. When slaves became too old or permanently ill, The Lords took them away—and no one ever saw them again.

Jason entered the work area and began his daily routine. His good friend, Ian, appeared at his side. Tension rattled in Ian's voice, and brown curls fell to his eyebrows as he said, "Have you heard the latest?"

Jason welcomed any rumors, especially positive ones. "What?" He was just as slender as Ian but a head taller.

"Our clan, from the valley on the other side of the mountain, is going to free us. We'll fight The Lords and—"

"I've heard that rumor for as long as I can remember," Jason said, shooting Ian a sideways glance. "People can't exist in the mountains. Have you met anyone who has ever been there?"

Ian tied a cloth over his nose and mouth. "They're real, I tell you. They live in a valley like this one, on the other side."

"I still think it's just a rumor," Jason said.

Ian sniffed, his dark eyes gleaming. "We're running away, three of us. Will you come?"

Jason finished tying a rag over his mouth before answering. "Winter is not far away. We'll freeze or starve, whichever comes first."

Ian pressed his back against the rock wall. "I can't wait

to leave this place and live free. Can you imagine a day without working harder than horses?"

"Hey," the big guard hollered. "This ain't no social gathering. Get back to work. If I catch you two talking again, ten lashes each."

Using a well-designed mallet and wedge, Jason pummeled the wall of the mine, focusing on the rock rich in dark blue veins. He wondered where The Lords got such tools. The slaves certainly didn't make them.

For Jason's midday meal, the guards dished out warm soup and cold bread. Ian sat down next to him. Slaves could talk during short meal breaks, if they preferred wasting their time chatting rather than eating.

Ian turned and watched the nearest guard. "We don't need to carry much water. I understand there are streams everywhere up there. We'll have food, enough to last for a week. We should reach the other valley in less than two days."

"And if the valley isn't there?" Jason asked.

Ian moved closer. "We'll be free."

Jason shook his head. "If such a place existed, The Lords would've found it by now."

Ian stuffed his mouth with bread, gulped the last of his soup, and swallowed hard. "They've never reached the top. Look at them, lazy pigs. Are you coming or not?"

"If there's nothing there, we can't return here," Jason said. "We'll be killed."

"Eating time's over. Back to work," a guard growled.

"When are you leaving?"

"Any day now," Ian said. "Whenever we can sneak away. Food and warm furs will be waiting for us."

"And who will provide us with these things?" Jason whispered.

"I can't tell you. Are you coming?" Ian asked again.

Jason considered Ian's offer. "I'll let you know tomorrow."

***

Jason and the other slaves descended the mountain at sundown, burdened with heavy rocks—some carrying, others pushing crudely-made carts. When rocks fell from one of the carts, Jason struck up a conversation with a red-haired, bushy-bearded giant of a man with strange green eyes. Carriers had the hardest job, held by only the strongest men.

"What do they do with these rocks?" Jason asked the man. His eyes searched the area for guards, but he saw none.

The man stuttered, his hair flying in the wind. "They are dumped into a large pit at the edge of the village. In late summer, when it's full, the rocks simply disappear overnight. No one knows what happens to them."

Jason picked up the heaviest rock he could lift and heaved it onto the cart. "Have you asked the guards?"

The man grunted as he picked up another rock. "They

don't know either. You'd think they'd widen the path so we could use horses to move rocks straight from the mine to the pit."

Jason picked up another rock. "Why don't you suggest it?"

"I did and got fifteen lashes," the man replied.

"They're not very smart, are they?"

The man wiped sweat from his forehead. "The Lords overthrew our bloodline because they outnumbered them, not because they outsmarted them."

Jason stroked a rock with his fingers. "What's this blue stuff, and why is it so special?"

"I don't know and neither do the guards."

"You work at the pit. What do you think happens to these rocks?"

The man picked up another rock and glanced over his shoulders. "I saw an object land there three summers ago, around midnight."

Jason's eyes locked on the carrier's facial expressions to see if they gave anything away. "What did it look like?"

The man paused and sneezed. "Huge, like a rock lit with fire, but without flames. It sat on the ground, as gentle as a bird." Using his hands, he imitated the motion. "Strange-looking entities came out of the thing and spoke with Brye, the high councilman. Darkness prevented me from seeing clearly, but they didn't look like us. They were tall—with red eyes."

"What—" Jason gasped. He felt a shiver run through his body.

"And shortly afterward," the carrier said, "the thing flew away, headed for the stars. Now no one is allowed at the pit on the night the rocks disappear."

Jason shook his head in disbelief as the man's words echoed in his mind. "Things like that exist? The high councilman is communicating with evil spirits?"

"I believe the strangers took the rocks, because the next morning the pit was empty. Ssshhh, here comes a guard."

***

That night, as Jason fell asleep, distant images of a new world dominated his dreams.

He walked through the valley without the presence of The Lords restricting his every movement. He didn't have to work, and instead slept most of the day. He had plenty of food and joined his family in their own home. His mother smiled warmly at him, happiness radiating from her face.

***

At about daybreak, on the third morning after their discussion, Jason, Hugo, Ian, and Ben dashed from the line as they ascended the ridge. An inattentive guard, who was giving another slave a number of lashes, inadvertently facilitated their escape. The boys darted for cover behind rocks, rushed up the side of the mountain, and began their journey to freedom.

On their way, the group stopped abruptly a short distance above the mine, where a tall woman with a long nose stepped out from behind bushes and quickly passed out rations of food that were tied within four rags. She pulled furs from behind a large rock. "Take these. They'll keep you warm. It'll be cold up there, almost unbearable. Snow'll reach up to your knees. Step into these furs and tie 'em around your waist. They have feet sewn on the bottoms, so pull them up over your sandals and wear 'em only in the snow." Then she gave two fur pouches to each boy. "These'll keep your hands warm."

Hugo was the youngest and smallest in the group. His face turned as red as his hair, and his eyes were fearful. "Is it that cold up there?"

"Maybe you should stay here," Jason said.

Hugo's eyes grew wide. "Maybe I should."

"Come with us, Hugo," Ian said. "You can make it. We all can."

The woman's green eyes constantly scanned the area. "Even when you don't think you can bear it, keep walking. If you move steady, you should spend only tonight on the mountain. Once you reach the snow, rush through it as quickly as possible. You can freeze up there."

The woman seemed familiar to Jason for some reason. "Thank you so much," he said.

"Hurry, leave this valley," she urged. "Tell no one about me—or I'll be killed. Now off with you."

Jason, third in line, rushed to climb the massive mountain, but it didn't take long for his pace to slow. His heart pounded and sweat dripped from his chin. Shallow breaths turned into labored breathing, and his fingers began to swell. Steadily climbing, he placed one foot in front of the other. He stepped over rocks—some small, others large—as well as fallen trees and limbs. Dry twigs and leaves crumpled under his feet. The sporadic chatter of birds and chirps from rodents darting about the area were the only other sounds.

When the boys started their journey, the wind had stood still, but now puffs rose and fell, unsettling the leaves around them as the air grew colder.

Ian stumbled, fell to the ground, and hit his face on a rock. Jason helped him to his feet as blood trickled down the front of his chest. "How bad is it?" Jason asked.

Ian wiped his nose. "Not bad. Keep walking."

When the sun stood high in the sky, Ian stopped the exhausted group. He picked dried blood from his nose. "Let's take a break. Eat a lot. We'll need our strength."

Ben coughed. "After they took me to my first work camp, I never saw my mother again."

Frosty breath drifted from Hugo's mouth. "I saw my mother once. At least, I think it was her. She didn't recognize me."

Ben said, "I remember a little sister. The Lords should

allow families to stay together." He glanced at Hugo. "Do you have brothers and sisters?"

"Yes, but I wouldn't recognize them," Hugo said. "I saw my older brother once. After The Lords beat him, he didn't know me, and he mumbled when he tried to talk. I never saw him after that."

Ben gulped down his food. "I was told that my mother gave birth to me when she was twelve winters old and then had eight more babies by her lord. When my grandmother got too old to work, The Lords took her away."

"*Whenever The Lords take you away, you're never seen again.*" Jason didn't need to say the words.

Slaves knew it meant death.

Ian's nose had started to bleed again. "They treat their horses better than us."

"What about your family, Jason?" Hugo asked. "Do you know where they are?"

"I remember my mother's name—where she once lived. Over the years, her face has faded though." Tears welled up in his eyes. "I hate her master 'cause of the way he beat her. My grandmother told me how cruel he was to my mother. We went there once, and bruises covered her face where he'd punched her. I saw him hit her and throw her against a woodpile, just because we'd come to visit."

Ian spat food from his mouth as he talked. "Maybe someday you'll get a chance to make him plead for his life—as you kill him with your own hands."

"I doubt if she's still alive," Jason said. "I've passed the house where she used to work and saw no sign of her. The slaves there now have never heard of her either." Tears rolled down his cheeks.

Ian wiped his hands on his fur. "Jason, Hugo, eat more."

"I'm too afraid to eat," Jason said. He feared The Lords might be hiding in the shadows.

"Let's get moving then," Ian said.

The higher Jason climbed above the tree line, the harder the wind blew and the slower he moved. Other than the wind, nothing stirred except their deep breathing and the sound of their feet pounding against rocks.

Hugo whined, "I don't feel well."

Ian turned back and saw Hugo lagging behind the group. "I told you to eat more."

Hugo's voice became shrill and high-pitched. "I'm weak and tired."

Physical exertion had taken its toll on the group, and Jason now feared Hugo wouldn't be able to finish the trip.

"It's the height." Ian coughed. "I've heard that the mountain makes you tired and sick. Take deep breaths, and breathe through your mouth."

Hugo did, and his breath frosted the air in front of him.

Ben held up his hands. "At least the woman gave us furs for our heads and hands. How did she know we'd need them?"

"She knows the mountain," Ian said. "I didn't want to tell you earlier, but she's my aunt. Her brother is my Uncle Tito, who escaped to the Valley of Freedom years ago. That's how I know this place exists."

The wind blew harder, and Jason gripped his furs tighter. "Why didn't you tell us earlier?"

Ian glanced back at him. "I had to protect the clan in the Valley of Freedom. If you got caught and tortured by The Lords, you might've talked."

Hugo stumbled and almost fell. "So, why hasn't your aunt escaped if she knows about this place?"

"She has thirteen children scattered in different work camps. She doesn't see them often but wants to stay nearby."

"Why didn't you leave with your uncle?" Jason asked.

"Each time he returns, he takes slaves back with him. The last time he came, I was too young and sick to make the trip."

Hugo stopped and began weeping. His red face contorted in anguish, and his eyes were feverish, almost savage. He yelled at Ian, "I hate that I came. I shouldn't have let you talk me into coming up here."

Ian glanced over his shoulder. "Save your breath and keep moving."

Jason filled his water pouch from an icy stream and quickly stuffed his cold, trembling hand back into his fur. The harsh wind chilled him to the bone. Then he saw a stream of vomit squirt from Hugo's mouth. "He can't make it."

"Come on. You need to keep up," Ian yelled.

Hugo's sullen voice trembled. "I wanna go back. My face is so cold I can't feel my nose, and my hands and feet are freezing."

"We need to keep walking," Ian insisted. "The more we move, the warmer we'll be."

Hugo lowered his head against the strong wind. "I can't go any farther. We're going to die up here."

The group stopped and allowed Hugo to catch up. Ian's breath rose up in gray puffs. "We can't ever return. They'll kill us."

Ben started the group moving again. He walked ahead of the others, because he was older and stronger. "Let's go."

Jason climbed over boulders and loose rocks, stumbling often, and forged on through light, newly fallen snow. He saw snow drifts ahead. "Let's stop here for the night."

"There's still daylight left, and we're almost at the top," Ian protested. "We don't have much snow to cross during this time of the year."

Hugo bent over with both hands on his knees, taking deep, ragged breaths. "I want to stop too." His voice echoed over the mountain.

"We don't want to get stuck in deep snow tonight. Let's wait here until morning," Ben agreed.

Jason couldn't feel his hands or feet, and his face had grown so numb he could hardly talk. He studied the snowy landscape. "Hey, there's a hole in the rocks up there."

Ben climbed up the steep slope and peeked in. "Come on up. It's a cave."

Hugo was the last to scramble inside the shelter. "At least we're out of the wind."

Ben covered the small entrance with rocks.

The boys huddled together for warmth, shivering in the cold, their hopes of success fading in the night.

***

When Jason awoke at dawn, he found Ian standing at the edge of the snow, studying it. Jason was excited to be free but dreaded the uncertain trip ahead. "It looks deep."

Ian held up his footed furs. "That's why we have these."

Hugo had woken and now stood behind them. "How do they work?"

Ian demonstrated. "Put one leg in each side, pull it up to your waist, and tie it."

Ben glanced at Hugo. "Are you warm enough? Do you think you can make the rest of the trip?"

"My toes and fingers are blue, but I'm warmer."

"By midmorning we should be through the snow. The trip won't be easy, but you'll make it," Ian said.

When Ben entered the snow, he sank up to his knees, just as Ian's aunt had promised. He yelled back, "Step in my tracks."

Hugo's legs were too short to touch the bottom, so the others had to drag him along.

During the rest of their journey, Jason heard only grunts and heavy breathing. The boys slowly conquered the steepest slopes, meandering over one ridge, then another, and another. They climbed steadily until reaching the top, about midmorning. Towing Hugo had slowed their pace. The sun shone bright in the clear blue sky, but the rises prevented them from seeing what existed below.

Ben led the group, pulling Hugo down. He took a gradual decline on the right and tipped over, as his foot unexpectedly went through a hole in the snow. He stopped and studied the ground. "Hey, it's a trail. Look … footprints."

Snow partially covered the trail, but Jason saw faint tracks where others had stepped.

"People made this trail," Ben said.

Hugo whimpered. "Our clan?"

Jason took his turn dragging Hugo downhill, and it didn't take long to reach the end of the snow. Once they reached the timberline on the other side of the summit, Jason felt warmer, but his legs were still sore and stiff.

Hugo stood on shaky legs. "I can hardly walk, and I still can't feel my toes."

Ian turned and glanced back at the summit. "We're almost there. Let's keep following this trail."

Jason took the lead and hurried downward. Finally, he

came over a ridge, and a panoramic view of a lush, green valley sprawled before him. He gawked in amazement. His heart pounded so hard that he not only felt it but also heard it vibrating against his ribcage. "Look. Look." Hugo slid on loose rocks and sat on the ground. "There are people. The Valley of Freedom is just there." Ian gloated. "I told you it existed."

Jason helped Hugo to his feet. His eyes focused on homes, not clustered together, like those belonging to The Lords, but standing with distance between them. The village lay on a grassy plain similar to where The Lords lived, but larger and with more trees.

The boys stared at one another in utter silence, then glanced down at the village.

Hugo scrambled down the side of the mountain as Ben and Ian rushed him on either side.

"Slow down," Hugo yelled.

They came to a sudden halt when a group of men surrounded them: more than the number of fingers on both hands. They wore furs that looked thicker and warmer than theirs. Shiny, sheathed swords hung from their sides, and bows and arrows hung over their shoulders.

Seeing the men caused Jason to panic, and a chill ran through his body. He stood at a crossroads—between death and freedom. Jason clung to Hugo's arm, his fingers digging into the fur with all his strength. He felt Hugo's body tremble before he forced Jason's hand away.

If the men were The Lords, they were dead.

If they were his clan, it meant freedom.

A middle-aged man with long, graying hair spoke. "I'm Sax, leader of the Free Clan. Who are you?"

Jason was so relieved he almost wet himself.

Ian's voice grew with excitement. "We ran away from The Lords. My Uncle Tito lives here. Have you heard of him?"

Sax scrutinized the boys. "Yes, Tito is very well known here. He's a big man, with an even bigger heart. Are there any more of you?"

"Ah … no," Ian said.

"Were you followed?" the man asked.

Ian stammered, "No. I … don't think so. We ran away while a guard was—distracted."

A man standing behind Sax put his foot on a knee-high rock. "Do the The Lords suspect that our clan lives here?"

Jason glanced from man to man. "No. They think it's a myth among us slaves."

Sax's face turned red. "Never use the word 'slave' here. We're free men."

Jason jumped into the air and shouted, "We're free." He then ducked behind a bush and relieved himself.

Sax removed the fur from his shoulders and stepped closer. "How did you get past our guards? Did anyone stop you on the other side of the mountain? Did you see men there?"

"No one," Ian said.

The leader addressed his men. "This isn't good. They got past our men."

"They could've been The Lords," another man hissed.

"Do you remember traveling through a long, narrow passage?" the leader asked.

"Yes," Ian said. "It was the only way up."

Sax glanced at the man standing next to him. "Get up there and see what's happening." He then turned to the youngest man in the group. "Take them to our village."

Jason sensed that the leader was more concerned about his inadequate guards than them.

"Hugo can hardly walk," Ian said.

Sax pointed to the largest men. "You two. Help him down."

Two men stood at Hugo's sides. They picked him up with their arms under his buttocks and lifted him like a child. Hugo supported his upper body by wrapping his arms around the men's torsos.

The youngest man stepped forward. He looked about Ben's age. "I'm Elan. Welcome to our village. Let's go."

"I'm Jason. This is Ben, and that's Ian. Hugo's the one being carried."

"Glad to meet you," Elan said. "You're going to love it here."

Jason studied Elan's face. Unlike slaves of The Lords, he smiled and appeared happy. He had a stocky build and short, brown hair.

On the way down the mountain, Ben hurried in front

of the others. Elan yelled at his back, "What's your rush? You're free now."

As Jason slowed his pace, he told the men about their jobs in the mine and how they'd escaped. He also admired the men's weapons. "Where did you get those swords? I've never seen ones like those," Jason said.

The balding man on Hugo's right side pulled his weapon from its sheath, waved it in the air, and then replaced it. "The gods left them in the center of our village, as gifts for us to defeat The Lords. They're better than their weapons—and sharper too."

Jason turned to Elan. "May I hold yours?"

Elan handed his sword to Jason.

Jason held it, admiring the shimmer and sharpness. "I've never held a sword before. How do you know the gods left them?"

The man with long, black curls and teeth like a horse grinned. "Who else would've left them?"

The balding man laughed as well, exposing rotten, jagged teeth. "Maybe The Lords left them," he joked.

The black-haired man slid on rocks and almost dropped Hugo. "Now that we outnumber The Lords, we can easily defeat them, with the help of our clan on the other side. Are you willing to go back and fight?"

Jason didn't want to die, and fighting The Lords likely meant death. He stared at Ian in fright, then at the men. "Fight?"

"Sure, we'll train you well," one of the men said.

Jason's heart thumped faster. The thought of returning to the Valley of the Lords made him shiver. "Ah—"

The man with the horse teeth smiled. "We'll make guards of you all."

Onlookers stared when they entered the village. Some gawked from doorways, while others followed them. Murmurs echoed throughout the crowd. Close up, the Free Clan homes looked much better than those of The Lords, and nothing like Jason's crowded slave camp. Their valley seemed larger, but the village was smaller.

Elan led them to a house in the center of the village as the crowd of men, women, and children walked behind them.

Jason felt hundreds of piercing eyes. Attempting to ease his discomfort, he looked off at the livestock grazing in the distance and contemplated how this clan had gotten the animals over the mountain.

Unlike the children at his camp, the ones here laughed and played. Seeing them, his heart sank, and again he felt robbed of his childhood.

Elan stopped at the door of a well-constructed house with wooden block steps.

A burly man with brown hair and a red face walked around the side, coming from the back of the home. He was soaked with sweat and carried a bloody knife.

"Uncle Tito," Ian shouted.

Tito embraced his nephew, lifted him off the ground, and whirled him around in the air. "Hello, hello, Ian. The last time I saw you, you were knee-high to a goat. I expected you last summer. I thought you decided not to come. How's your aunt? Who are your friends?"

Ian made a brief introduction, and his uncle continued talking.

With a wave of his hand, Tito indicated the group surrounding them. "These people are your friends. I'll introduce them later. Welcome to our village. My wife and kids will be glad to meet you." He nodded at poor Hugo. "Hey, he got too cold up there, didn't he?"

"He lost all feeling in his toes and fingers," Ian said. "Can you help him?"

Tito pushed open the door. "Well, let's get him inside and see what we can do."

When Jason entered Tito's home, he found it more spacious than The Lords'. There, he met Tito's wife and three children.

The men placed Hugo on the floor in front of the fire, where Tito's wife was cooking.

Tito removed the furs from Hugo's hands. "Just relax, Hugo. Your hands don't look so bad. We're going to rub your fingers and toes, okay?"

"How does rubbing them help?" Hugo asked.

"We don't know, but sometimes it does." Tito demonstrated the process on one of Hugo's feet.

Jason worked on the other foot, while Ben and Ian rubbed his fingers.

After a short while, Hugo fell asleep.

Tito's wife placed food on the table. "Let's eat, boys."

"Shouldn't we wake Hugo?" Ian asked.

"No, let him rest," Tito said. "We'll save food for him."

Ian asked, "Will he get better?"

"Sometimes it works, sometimes it doesn't," Tito said.

"What if it doesn't?" Ian asked.

Tito glanced at him and shook his head. "The flesh rots."

Ian lowered his head. "It's my fault. He didn't want to come."

Tito put a hand on Ian's back. "You can't blame yourself for this. You had no way of knowing."

Ian's chin quivered. "He might die."

"We'll work on his toes again after he wakes up and eats," Tito said.

Jason remained seated on the floor. He picked up a toddler, bounced the baby on his knee, and stuffed a spoonful of mashed potatoes into the little boy's mouth. "What do we do now?"

"We always keep an empty house, in case we need it. You'll remain here until next summer. After we kill The Lords, you can stay in your own village."

Jason shuddered. Tito's nonchalant attitude frightened him.

Ian leaned back in his chair and stared at his uncle. "We're going to attack them?"

Tito shrugged. "Sure. The gods left us many weapons. They expect us to fight."

Ian spoke up for the group. "No, we don't want to go back there."

Tito slapped his nephew on the back, almost toppling him over. "Don't worry, my boy. You'll be ready by then. After you're settled in, we'll start your training."

***

Brye and six of the eight men of his council sat on rickety chairs covered with goatskin. Wooden plates, forks, and cups occupied two small tables.

Brye's stomach growled as he glanced over his shoulder, expecting the arrival of dinner at any moment.

Whenever Brye held meetings with his council members, he had the slaves set up tables with eight chairs in a cramped child's room. He had picked that room for privacy from his family and the slaves.

The house had a thatched roof, supported by exposed tree trunks and packed with rammed earth to keep it warm during the cold winters.

John, a fat, balding man took a seat at the table. "Who called this meeting?"

Brye ran his fingers through tendrils of thinning, shoulder-length hair. "I did."

An elderly man spoke through his nose as he slowly crept into the room, as if in pain. "Couldn't this have waited until our regularly scheduled meeting?"

Brye rubbed the scar that ran from his left eyebrow

to his chin. It reminded him of the runaway slave who'd taken his eye. "I had a dream last night, and it's not the first."

John scratched a large mole on his nose with a huge, hairy paw and raised a single bushy eyebrow. He lowered his head, squinted, and frowned at Brye. "A dream? We're here because you had a dream?"

"Yes, dreams come true, you know," Brye said. "There are too many slaves, and we need to dispose of most of them."

Huns, the youngest member, glared at Brye. "Dispose of them? Are you mad?"

"They outnumber us two to one," Brye said. "Let's keep only the number we need and kill the rest. I keep having dreams about them overpowering us."

John wiggled around, testing the strength of his chair. He bobbed his head up and down. "Brye is correct. That's how we got to be The Lords. We outnumbered their ancestors."

Huns shook his head. "They've no weapons."

The eldest man's voice was almost a whisper. "They could be doing the same thing our ancestors did—secretly making them."

Brye fingered his beard. "There are too many of them, and they consume too much food."

"Kill too many and we won't have enough slaves to do the work," Huns protested.

As leader of The Lords, Brye had to be smart and

ensure nothing threatened the future of his clan. "We'll work the remaining ones twice as hard. Some of them have it too easy anyway. The ones who take care of the livestock are idle most of the day. Alma, where is the food?"

A short, small-framed woman with salt-and-pepper hair tied back in a bun dashed into the room, loaded down with a large platter of steaming, roasted meat. She trotted back and forth, carrying vegetables and coarse bread, then placed a wooden pot of wine in the center of each table. She had been a slave in Brye's household for years and had given birth to four of his children. Now all worked in camps. He kept her because of her excellent cooking skills and patience with his six legitimate children.

Brye carved a piece of meat and placed it on his plate. He filled his cup with wine from the pot and dished out a heaping pile of potatoes, corn, and bread. He slid the food across the table to Huns, who helped himself. Then Brye dipped a piece of bread into heavy brown gravy and stuffed half of it into his mouth. "We need to pick the best workers and keep their numbers to less than half of our population," he said, with his mouth full.

Huns shook a fork at him. "I don't think it's a good idea, eliminating the slaves. Besides, they're confined and can't overpower us."

"Many have disappeared over the years, and we don't know where they went," John said. "They multiply like rabbits. Rumors are they're living in the mountains."

Huns licked gravy from his index finger. "That's just a slave rumor."

Another man filled his plate. "That's the only place they can be."

Huns swallowed a mouthful of food and chased it down with wine. "They can't survive up there. They've either starved or frozen to death by now."

The eldest man glanced at Huns. "Isn't it odd that our guards haven't found any remains? Many of the slaves know how to make swords, bows and arrows."

"Lazy guards," another man uttered. "Mason probably took his men above the mine for a week and then returned."

Brye guzzled from his cup. He felt pleased that all the men, except Huns, were in agreement with his idea. "If the runaways have been breeding up there like they have down here, there could be a whole village of them."

The old man's forehead wrinkled. "Another village?"

Huns wiped his greasy palm on his sleeve. "Impossible. Simply impossible. There isn't any game up there, nothing but rocks and snow. Our guards say the snow is too deep to wade through."

Brye burped and glanced around the table. "They could be living in caves or in a valley on the other side of the mountain. We've never been to the top because of the snow. I think we need to send men up there. Where's Mason anyway? As leader of the guards, he should be here."

Huns took a second helping of bread and gravy. "I don't know, but I told him about our meeting yesterday. Guards have been up there," he added.

Brye stared across the table at Huns. "Not all the way to the top. At least we'll know what's on the other side. What if there's another valley?"

Huns said, "If we're going to send guards up there, why not wait until next summer? What's the rush?"

Brye pounded a heavy fist on the shaky table. "We need to know now. I have a bad feeling about this, and it keeps gnawing at my insides."

Huns shook his head in disapproval. "The guards will need heavy furs. We don't know if they can make it through the snow or how long it'll take them to reach the top."

The elderly man held a hunk of bread in his crippled fingers.

"Two years ago, our guards had to turn back because of the cold."

Brye was adamant. "Not this time."

The old man's mouth wrinkled into a crooked half-smile. "Once we eliminate most of the slaves, we could spread out and have more grazing land for our livestock."

Brye nodded. "We could burn most of those awful slave camps."

"Excellent plan, but wood is getting scarce," another council member stated.

Leaning forward, Brye said, "Not in the mountains.

Let's move all the slave camps to the edge of the village. Then our families won't have to look at them."

John nodded in agreement. "Good idea. Think of all the food we could save."

"We could rearrange our village," Brye muttered through a mouthful of food.

"Slaves are pathetic animals ... dirty, ragged, and smelly," the elderly man barked.

Brye gazed around the table and smiled. "Then we won't have to deal with those Velekan demons."

John said, "We'll start eliminating slaves after they stockpile wood for the winters, concentrating first on the elderly and female populations."

"We could start as soon as the guards return from the mountain," Brye said.

"How shall we get rid of them?" the elderly man asked. "We don't want to alert the slaves, start a panic."

"Huh ... the guards can take them above the mine, a few at a time." Brye propped his elbows on the table, stared at his plate, and smiled. "There are many bottom-less pits up there."

John replied, "That'll keep Mason busy for a while."

Brye carved another piece of meat. "We could use some to rearrange the village during the winter and get rid of more next summer."

John raised his cup into the air. "Sounds like a good plan."

"Let's vote on it," Brye said. "All in favor of sending guards to the summit now?"

All agreed, with the exception of Huns.

"How about decreasing the slave numbers when the guards return?" Brye asked.

Again, only five out of six men agreed.

"Then it's settled. Ron," Brye shouted.

A short, skinny slave rushed into the room. His old but agile body bowed next to Brye. "Yes, my lord?"

"Fetch Mason and be quick about it. Then return to your camp," Brye said.

"Yes, my lord," Ron said, and the slave left as quickly as he had appeared.

The eldest man gripped the wine pot in his shaking hands and filled his cup. "Mason isn't going to like this."

Brye took another gulp from his cup and spilled some on his beard. "Well, he should've been here to express his opinion. Now he has to go to the top of the mountain."

"It'll be snowing down here within a few weeks," Huns said. "The mountains are already capped with snow."

"That's why we need to get the guards up there now. Do you agree with us, Huns?" Brye asked.

Huns's wide shoulders raised and lowered in a shrug.

"Alma, more wine," Brye shouted. He appeased his voracious appetite by stuffing his stomach with food and wine, as the other council members had. Remnants of his dinner covered his mouth and hands, caked his beard, and spilled down the front of his clothing, but he didn't care.

He licked his fingers, smacked his lips, and demanded more.

***

Around midnight, Brye paced under the moonlight at the edge of the pit.

The Velekans used the blue matter in the rocks for something they called "fuel," but Brye didn't understand the meaning of the word. The amount of wine he'd consumed made him sway on his feet. He made certain no one else was present—no guards or slaves.

The spooky Velekans claimed to be gods who lived and traveled among the stars.

He didn't know how "gods" looked or behaved, but these things didn't fit the image in his mind.

Only Brye and the other seven council members knew about the Velekans. A few slaves had spotted their ship a number of times, so they no longer landed there. Brye often wondered how they managed to move such huge herds of livestock. He gazed at the stars and thought about how the Velekans had helped his clan, by teaching them how to make swords, bows and arrows and how to handle the horses they had brought. They insisted the slaves cover their noses and mouths while working in the mine. If they didn't, the dust would eventually kill them.

Brye staggered in the dark until two Velekans appeared out of thin air. It no longer frightened him to see them appear or disappear. Their eerie red eyes glowed in the dark, reminding him of nocturnal animals. Like a herd of sheep, they all dressed and looked the same. The Velekans never smiled. Only one spoke, and his lips barely moved. He made strange sounds, but another voice came from something around his waist. In turn, each time Brye spoke, he heard the strange Velekan tongue, like an invisible third person. The Velekans were twice Brye's height and moved swiftly. Those strange fires without flames, that blinked on their arms and chests, were so mysterious. Sometimes they'd touch a light and disappear.

Evil spirits, Brye thought.

He was dealing with devils.

"Brye," one of the Velekan devils said.

Brye tilted his head. "Yes?"

Captain Mogayron never introduced him to the other Velekan. "We have the quantity of animals we promised. We need more ore."

"Ore?" Brye asked.

"Rocks, rich in blue matter."

"More ..."

Mogayron moved closer. "We need twice the quantity of ore ... rocks. In turn, we will provide you with twice the quantity of animals. Can you meet our demand?"

"The slaves will have to work twice as hard, and we don't know how long the blue rocks will last," Brye replied.

The captain glanced past him toward the village. "Start another mine opposite the one the slaves now work. We expect both pits to be filled by the end of next summer."

Brye reeled and almost fell. "But we have only one pit."

"You'll have two tomorrow."

Brye knew that meeting a two-pit quota would be difficult, since he had just swayed the council to kill half of the slaves.

Mogayron stared down on him, his eyes glowing. "Allow me to take you to my ship."

Brye turned and scanned the area. "Where is it?"

The devil pointed a long finger toward the starlit sky.

Brye looked up and trembled. "Why take me there?"

"I want you to have a closer look at the stars," Mogayron said. "See your planet from space."

"Planet?" he asked.

"Where you live," the devil said. "There are many planets like yours among the stars."

Brye stuttered, "Ah ... I don't ..." But before the words left his mouth, he found himself standing in a strange room. He had witnessed the Velekans appear and disappear, but never thought it could happen to him.

A tingling sensation ran through his body. His hands shook like trembling leaves on a windy day. He held out his arms and turned them over to determine if his body remained in one piece. The two Velekans stepped down from the platform they had appeared on, but Brye remained where he had landed. Slowly glancing around the area, he saw six other Velekans in the room. Two sat with their backs to one wall, and four others sat around two tables in the center of the room. They all gawked at him. He saw many colored lights on the tables where the Velekans sat.

Mogayron turned and looked back at him. "This is our ship's Navigational Control. You're standing on our transporter."

Staring down at his feet, Brye saw his knees shaking.

The Velekan stretched out his arm and waved a hand toward a clear wall. "See the stars? And there, that's your planet, what it looks like from here ... from space."

Squinting and blinking several times, Brye focused on a sphere, dark on the near side, lit on the far side. He eyed Mogayron and saw his small mouth turned up into a smirk of amusement—the first sign of a smile he'd ever seen.

"You have nothing to fear," Mogayron said. "Let me show you around my ship."

The Velekan claimed to have transported livestock, but Brye detected no animal odors, just the smell of blossoms.

The devil gestured toward the stars, with an arm still outstretched. "This is called space. Our planet is quite a distance from here, an expanse incomprehensible to you."

Brye's eyes froze on the scene. If not for the clear wall separating him from the stars, he felt he could reach out and touch them. He didn't know the word and couldn't pronounce it. "Incompre … ?"

The Velekan stepped in front of him and leaned forward. "It means that you wouldn't understand."

Still shaken beyond control, Brye's legs weakened to the point that they no longer supported his weight. He collapsed on hands and knees, then leaned back on his heels. He covered his eyes with his sweaty palms and felt his heart throbbing. When he removed his hands, he stared through the clear wall again. This time, he noticed another sphere in the distance. He gasped for air. "I want to return to my village."

Mogayron folded his hands behind his back and stood up straight. "But—"

"Please take me home," Brye begged.

"We have placed your animals at their designated location," the captain said. "We'll return at the end of next summer."

Brye closed his eyes again. The next time he opened them, he found himself kneeling at the pit, shaking in fright. He threw up his dinner and shivered, terrified by what he had just witnessed. He remained on his knees for a long time before standing up on trembling legs. He considered the fact that maybe he had never left the pit. The evil spirits must have put those images into his head. He knew man could never stand among the stars, and that his world was flat.

The devil had been toying with him—using magical tricks to confuse him.

Chapter 5

Battle with the Lords

In the early dawn, Ishka trailed the rear of a group of twenty guards and three other slaves on horseback. The party slowly ascended the mountain, carrying heavy furs and a week's supply of dried food. Ishka knew that Mason, leader of the guards, had strict orders to seek out and kill all runaway slaves. Equipped with swords, bows and arrows, the well-trained lords had another mission: to reach the top of the mountain.

The horse in front of Ishka's stopped, and his own animal skidded to a halt, nearly sending him sliding off.

"Stop," Mason yelled. "There's no way up from here. Turn around."

This put Ishka at the front of the group. He heard deep breathing, snorts, an occasional neigh from the horses, and the distinctive sound of hooves pounding on rocks. The animals were not accustomed to the altitude and had slowed their pace.

Mason's horse squeezed by the others and took first place in line. Ishka and the other slaves stopped and allowed the remaining guards to pass.

Light puffs of wind rose and fell around Ishka, chilling the air. Fallen trees and large rocks made it difficult for them to maneuver their horses. Rodents raced among the rocks, and birds chirped in the distance. Once the group passed the tree line, they couldn't ride any farther. Leaving one slave to tend the animals, Mason ordered Ishka and two guards to go ahead on foot, in search of a passage through the mountain.

Ishka and the two guards marched over one ridge, then another and another. He quickly became cold and exhausted and hugged himself under the fur that covered his upper body. He wanted to return to his camp, but he had no say in the matter.

The two guards had talked about eliminating slaves upon their return, as if Ishka weren't there to hear their cruel intentions. He knew he wouldn't live to see his camp again.

He followed the guards into a narrow passage with a high rock wall on either side.

Suddenly, Ishka heard the whizzing of multiple arrows, and within moments, the two guards lay dead. Covering his eyes with both hands, Ishka fell to his knees and cringed in fear.

When he felt the presence of others surrounding him, he peeked up. Men appeared from both sides of the rocks. They had better weapons than The Lords possessed and appeared ready for battle. He had never seen so many of his own clan in one place, absent of The Lords. Killing a lord brought death to not only the guilty slave but also to all known relatives. Tears ran down his cheeks and into his beard, and he began to have difficulty breathing.

"How many guards?" a lanky man with curly, graying hair asked. When Ishka didn't respond, the man repeated his question, this time louder. "How many?"

Ishka felt his lips quiver.

He held up his hands, opening and closing his palms twice. "This many guards." He then showed all fingers on one hand, except his thumb. "This many of us slaves."

"I'm Sax," the man said, "leader of the Free Clan."

Still shocked from the attack, Ishka couldn't respond.

Sax waved a hand at the men in his group. "Hide these bodies behind the rocks," he ordered.

"So, there really is a Valley of Freedom?" Ishka mumbled.

"Yes, it exists," Sax said.

"The Lords plan to kill most of us before it snows, because our population now outnumbers theirs. Many of my friends and relatives will be killed, including me," Ishka said.

Sax stepped closer to him. "Then we'll attack The Lords—and kill them instead."

Ishka wanted nothing more than to live as a free man. "I don't want to return to the Valley of the Lords," he pleaded.

Sax slapped him on his shoulder. "I'm sorry, but we need your help."

***

Mason kicked a rock. "Idiots. Where could they be? They've been gone too long," he growled.

A trail of frosty breath flowed from a guard's mouth. "They must be lost."

Mason instructed two more guards and another slave to search for the missing party. He pointed. "Study this area. Keep in mind, we'll be in the direction of that peak."

"We won't get lost," a big guard promised.

"All morning and no sign of slaves," Mason said. "No abandoned camp fires, no remains, nothing."

"It's madness sending us up here," a disgruntled guard muttered. "How do they expect us to survive in such cold and snow?"

Mason barked, "That's why we have heavy furs. Gather more firewood."

When the second party hadn't returned by sundown, Mason became leery. "Two parties couldn't have gotten lost. I want rotating guards all night. We'll start searching at daybreak."

The tallest guard scratched his head and surveyed the surroundings. "They must see our fire."

***

Mason woke cold to the bone from sleeping on the ground. His feet and legs were sore from the previous day's hike, and he still felt exhausted and restless. At daybreak, the remainder of his men and he started their ascent.

"I think we should turn around, get more men," the front guard yelled back at his leader. "Things are too strange."

Lagging behind his men, Mason stopped to catch his breath. "Stop your griping. Let's get this job over with. I don't want to return here next summer."

The men approached the snowdrifts and waited for Mason to catch up.

"See, Mason." The tallest guard pointed to tracks in the snow. "Four slaves have been through here."

"Maybe it's our men," another guard replied.

"These men wore furs on their feet." Mason squatted and studied a nearby rock. "Dry blood." He touched it with his index finger and surveyed the area, his eyes and ears alert. "This seems to be the only passage up."

Without warning, Mason saw several of his men cut down by a rain of arrows. Removing his bow from his shoulder as he stood, he yelled, "Get back."

Quickly loading an arrow, Mason shot it into the area above the rocks, in the direction the projectiles had come from. His arrow bounced off the rocks and landed on the ground. Strikes from above continued, and more of his guards fell to their deaths. Only two of his men and he remained standing, suffering minor wounds. He saw his last two guards face Sax, but within minutes, his men had lost the battle. One guard suffered an arrow through the chest. The last one dropped his weapon and surrendered—but received no mercy. Mason clutched his wounded arm and tried to wedge himself into a crack on the side of the wall.

Sax yelled to his men, "Stop. This one's mine."

Mason stood with his back to the rock wall. He no longer felt the pain in his arm. Instead, he concentrated on the man before him. His dry mouth couldn't utter a word, and a deep chill shot up his spine as he fingered the scar on his face. Sax was the man who had slashed Mason with a sword, taking his left eye and leaving him scarred for life.

Mason watched his ex-slave pull an arrow back on his bow and release it. The head and shaft penetrated Mason's chest, causing a burning, agonizing pain. His legs buckled, and he fell on his stomach, pushing the arrow through his body. Each time Mason exhaled, he wheezed and blood flowed from his mouth.

Rolling over on his side, the last thing he saw was Sax's cold stare.

It was as if he were counting down to Mason's last breath.

***

Sax approached a huge, blond-haired slave and slapped him on his back.

"You're a free man now. I'm Sax, leader of this clan.

Welcome." Gazing into the ex-slave's wild eyes, he saw only fear. The man scanned the results of the brutal carnage, his mouth agape and face frozen in shock, showing relief only when the two other slaves appeared.

Ishka approached the blond man and stood at his side. "This is our clan. They live in the valley on the other side of this mountain. They're going to free us."

"I expect you men to fight as well." Sax glanced around at his men. "Do we have any injuries?"

"I cut my finger on a rock," a clansman said, licking blood from a scratch.

Sax eyed the man's wound. "I've seen more blood after I bit my tongue."

The other clansmen burst into laughter, humiliating the man.

Sax questioned the blond man. "Are you sure there aren't any more guards?"

The man confirmed Ishka's story.

"How can you be sure?" Sax asked.

"We left my friend with our horses. His father serves in the house of the head council. He listens outside the room when they have their meetings."

"What happens when we don't return?" Ishka asked.

Sax concentrated on raiding The Lords' village. "We've been putting this battle off for a year. Now we have no choice."

The blond man stood frozen in his tracks. "The guards have lots of weapons."

"We also have many swords, bows and arrows. What we need is for every man, woman, and child to fight," Sax said. He clutched a dead guard under the arms and yanked. "Let's clear this area."

"They have horses," Ishka said.

Sax grunted. "We'll attack on foot and surprise them." The other terrified slave said, "It'll be hard to catch them off-guard."

Sax grunted again. "Not in the middle of the night. Don't just stand there. Help us move these bodies behind the rocks."

"Why were you here?" the blond slave asked.

Sax strained to heave a big man's lifeless body. "We watch this area in case The Lords try to come over the mountain during the summer."

The other slaves stepped closer to Sax. "You're not taking us to freedom?"

"After we kill The Lords, you can stay in either village," Sax said.

"If we return to the Valley of the Lords, we'll be killed," the blond slave protested.

Sax cleaned his bloody hands on nearby rocks. "You must return and help us fight," he said.

Ishka made eye contact with the other slaves. "Fight? But ..."

Sax turned to one of his men in haste. "Warn our village. We must attack now. Tell our people to bring all the weapons they can carry. Where are the horses?"

Ishka volunteered. "I'll take you there."

Sax told the slaves his plan. "My men will teach you how to fight. We'll attack The Lords tomorrow night."

***

Sax taught the ex-slaves how to shoot arrows and perform intense sword attacks, leaving them no excuse not to fight. He made certain they got plenty of food and rest, peacefully, within the comfort of a warm cave.

The next day, Sax watched his free clansmen swarm below the tree line on The Lords' side of the mountain. He couldn't guess the numbers in the dense crowd.

Sax had introduced Ishka and the three other ex-slaves to Jason, Ben, and Ian. Like Ishka's, he'd sensed the boys' fear. It glowed in their eyes, caused trembling in their voices, and made their hands shake when they handled the weapons.

Climbing onto the tallest rock in the area, Sax captured everyone's attention. Silence fell across the terrain as his deep voice echoed over the side of the mountain. "Our clan has killed twenty guards, and we have gained seven more clansmen. The time has come for us to enter the Valley of the Lords—and take back freedom for all."

A young man leaning on a rock frowned in confusion. "Why not wait until next summer, like we planned?"

Sax shifted his weight and coughed. "Next summer will be too late. The Lords plan to kill many of our clansmen before winter, and we need to help them defeat The Lords."

A high-pitched voice came from within the crowd. "Kill our clansmen? Why?"

"Our population is now greater than The Lords, and they fear us overpowering them. Remember, in order to win this battle, we must surprise our enemies," Sax said. "You all have done an excellent job toting weapons over the mountain. Women in this group have trained with our best men. I know they'll do excellent jobs."

"How do you expect women to fight?" questioned Ishka.

Sax said, "They'll watch the horses. If The Lords approach, they'll shoot them with arrows. We'll have a few men in the groups as well."

Tito stood next to Sax, his huge body covered in fur, with the exception of his head and hands. "The women will be protected. We need to make sure The Lords have no chance of survival."

Sax pointed at Tito, who was second-in-command. "He'll help me organize attack groups. We'll rest here until midday, move down the mountain, then stop at the base before dark. We'll be burdened with horses loaded with weapons, so take it slow going down."

A woman with long, red hair made her way through the crowd. "Will our clan fight? Since they've been enslaved by The Lords all their lives, they may be too afraid to stand against them."

"You were once a slave," Sax reminded her. "You're ready to fight."

A man shouted, "We'll soon find out."

Murmurs of agreement followed his words.

"We believe in our clan," another man said.

Sax bellowed, "We'll enter the valley during the middle of the night. Our clansmen should be in their own camps, so we won't have to be concerned about accidentally killing one of them when we enter the houses of The Lords. We'll arm and brief our clan, and they, in turn, will help us kill The Lords. Since we outnumber The Lords, they should be easily defeated."

Tito nodded in agreement.

The leader turned to Tito. "Free the miners first. They're the strongest men."

A distant voice shouted, "We should've done this last year."

Grumbling erupted.

Holding up his hands, Sax said, "We didn't have enough weapons then. Kill them all, women ... children too."

A sympathetic woman gasped and slapped both hands on her cheeks. "Even babies?"

"Shouldn't we keep some for slaves?" Tito asked.

Sax was adamant. "We'll not repeat the same mistake our ancestors made. We don't need slaves. Let's kill all of them. There'll be only one clan."

Roars erupted from the vicious and determined crowd.

"One clan."

"Kill The Lords."

"Kill them all."

"Freedom from The Lords."

"Collect your weapons. Let's get started."

Sax led his clan down the mountain. When the crowd stopped at the base, the sun hung low in the sky like a red ball of fire.

***

Around midnight, Jason entered the Village of the Lords with his Free Clan, his heart thumping out of control as silent, dark figures moved throughout the camp, like ghosts in the night. He and other men carried extra weapons to the miners' camp, watching and waiting from the shadows. He had never expected to see his old camp again. It stood just as it had a few days earlier. More shacks than Jason could count lined a rock wall. Fences, resembling livestock pens, made from tree limbs surrounded the site.

The stench of men's excrement lingered strong in the air.

Twelve guards always stood watch. Three stood talking outside the fence. Five sat slumped over on rocks, and four hovered and chatted near a small fire.

Men from the Free Clan rushed the alert guards, while another group focused on the sleeping sentinels. They overpowered all of them, instantly killing them with arrows. Two wounded guards screamed for help. Their cries of death echoed in the night.

Jason couldn't see the blood or wounds, but his imagination caused him to throw up.

Tito beckoned him. "Bring the weapons."

Rushing into the camp with the other men, Jason carried an armload of swords. His palms were sweaty, and his legs wobbled. He tripped, and the pile of swords slipped from his arms as he crashed face-forward onto the ground. The clinking of metal echoed in the silence of the night.

"Ssshhh."

Jason jumped to his feet and blindly groped around in the dark, causing more noise as he stacked the swords into a pile. He dashed into the camp and laid his load on the ground near Tito. Other slaves exited the shacks and grabbed weapons. Free clansmen whispered to groups of armed slaves.

"Remember Jason?" Tito said to the slaves. "He used to work here too."

A man in the camp whispered, "Jason, we thought The Lords ..."

"Let's get moving," Tito urged.

As Tito hurried the group toward the Village of the Lords, he explained their plans. "We'll kill them as they sleep. Remember, we outnumber them, and they don't stand a chance."

Jason wanted to protest but didn't dare. He gripped his sword with both hands, his heart pounding out of control.

"Four men will enter each house, with one free man as leader," Tito said. "Follow his orders."

"I've been waiting to kill The Lords all my life," a slave said.

At the edge of the village, the men split into groups of four.

Jason and three men entered Mason's home. The lead man carried a small torch and entered the first room. Jason entered last. He'd never killed anyone and didn't think he could comply with Sax's orders.

Mason's wife awoke and raised her head. "Mason?"

"Kill her, Jason," the torch man whispered.

Jason's hands shook so badly he almost dropped his sword.

The woman shielded her eyes from the light. "Who's there?"

"Now, Jason," the lead man urged.

When Jason froze, another man drove his sword through the woman's chest.

The image of the dying woman stayed with Jason as the torch man moved into the next room, which was separated by a cloth divider.

Four boys younger than himself slept, two in each bed. The men stabbed three of the boys, leaving one for Jason.

"Do it," the torch holder ordered.

Jason hesitated and stared into the sleeping boy's face. The child seemed so peaceful and innocent. Jason couldn't let his clan down, but he didn't want to kill either.

"Now, Jason," another man ordered.

Slowly raising his sword into the air, Jason clutched it with both hands. Then, closing his eyes, he stabbed his target in the side. The boy woke up, screaming in pain.

One of the men silenced the boy by covering his mouth with his hand.

"Do you want to wake the whole village? That's not the way we taught you. Aim for the center of the chest," the torch man scolded through clenched teeth.

Raising his sword again, Jason witnessed the pain and confusion on the young boy's face. This time he didn't close his eyes but plunged his sword through the boy's chest with all his strength. Blood spattered all over him, and the man who held the boy down. Jason wet himself and hoped no one noticed. With shaking hands, he yanked the sword from his victim's chest. Refusing to look into the boy's face again, he turned and left the room. If he hadn't already emptied his stomach, he would have thrown up again.

The torch man smiled. "Good."

Two younger children, almost toddlers, slept in the last room, but he couldn't kill them.

"Kill them, Jason," the lead man said.

Focusing on the blood dripping from the tip of his sword, Jason shook his head. His older accomplices showed no mercy and severed the children's heads as they slept.

When Jason reached Brye's house, a body lay outside the door, a sign that everyone within was dead.

Jason and his team moved from house to house. The more he killed, the easier it became, even children and babies.

It became a job to him, like working in the mine.

At daybreak, Jason's clothes, hands, and face dripped with blood. The thought of killing no longer haunted him. He reeked of the musty stench of death, but it didn't nauseate him anymore.

Jason helped his clan load the bodies into carts and dump their remains into the pits. The sun stood overhead when they'd finished the job. He had grown into manhood overnight. His stomach growled, and he needed to change his clothes.

Jason stood among the crowd, wondering what the rest of his life would be like without The Lords. He felt lost.

Who would feed him and tell him what to do?

Was his mother still alive?

Did he have other living relatives?

A redheaded woman cried out as she fell to her knees. "Please tell me again. Are they dead? All of them?"

"The Lords exist no more, not even a child," Sax confirmed.

"Let's have a feast, a victory celebration," another woman exclaimed.

"We'll slaughter some goats," one man said, then looked around for others to offer their help.

As other men nodded in agreement, Sax spoke up. "Listen up, everyone. We need a name for our clan."

"You're our leader, Sax," Tito said. "Your courage and bravery made this defeat possible. We killed The Lords and lost not one clansman. We'll name our clan the Saxons."

Everyone cheered.

"Then Saxons it is," Sax agreed.

Chapter 6

Returning to Tandon

Captain Sadera Sedo arrived home on a two-week maintenance leave.

The *Volpus* rested on a huge launch pad on Tandon for repairs: results of damage caused by the Velekan attack. Throwing the strap of her bag over her shoulder, she proceeded to the underground tram. Her crew had already departed, and fleet engineers had completed their assessment. Sedo walked through an underground maze of shops. Because it wasn't a workday, the place was crowded. Government offices, hospitals, restaurants, and living quarters all existed above ground.

Captain Sedo dropped her bag and hugged both of her parents at the same time. "Mother. Father." Like a child, she felt safe and secure in the comfort of their arms—their love. "You didn't have to meet me. I know my way home."

Her father hugged her again. "After five years, we weren't certain."

Her mother wore a short-sleeved white robe that danced around her ankles. "Sadera, you're so grown up."

"I grew up before I left home, Mother."

They had stopped in front of a play station. Bells and whistles sounded as kids laughed and squealed.

Her father wore his dress uniform with a black collar and the Beltese emblem on his chest. His skin had changed from dark to light pink, and his white hair hung on his shoulders, longer than the average Beltese's. He picked up his daughter's bag. "It's nice to see you in person. We're taking you to dinner."

"Father, I'm exhausted. All I want to do for the next few days is sleep."

"Rest," her mother exclaimed. "We've made plans—social gatherings and a trip to the beach."

Her father asked, "Remember young Jogen? He's meeting us at the restaurant."

A hot flash ran through Captain Sedo's body. "Father, no."

The mere thought of Jogen made her uncomfortable and being near him terrified her. He made her heart flutter, and—as captain—she couldn't be out of control.

Her mother took her hand. "He's the best doctor at the research center, and he's perfect for you. You're old enough to choose a lifemate."

The thought of Jogen brought back feelings she'd always hidden from him. Sedo sighed. "Not Jogen. Oh, why did I come home?"

"Because you have no other place to go," her father said.

Her mother threw an arm around her daughter's neck. "Now we go to dinner. Tomorrow you can rest half the day, if you'd like. With all the stress as captain, you need to relax."

Captain Sedo sighed again. "Mother."

"Your mother is correct," her father agreed. "You're becoming a stranger."

"More than you think," Captain Sedo mumbled.

"What did you say, dear?" her mother asked.

"Sorry, Mother. Just thinking aloud."

Her parents made eye contact with each other. They seemed edgy.

"We're going straight to the restaurant," her father said. "Jogen has changed so much. Why do you dislike him?"

"I don't dislike him. He and I were once friends," Sedo said.

"Perhaps you're afraid of getting too close to him," her mother said. "Give him a chance. He's very intelligent and responsible."

"I'm not afraid of him, Mother."

Her father turned and glanced at her. "He's seeking an assignment on a warship. Perhaps you'll consider him?"

Her mother's voice became soft and cajoling. "Sadera, you have a vacant position on the *Volpus*."

Captain Sedo threw her hands into the air. "There's an entire fleet of ships out there. Why mine?"

"He's like a son to us," her mother said.

"Do all parents try to match their sons and daughters?" Captain Sedo sardonically asked.

"You're not being reasonable, Sadera," her mother snapped.

"Father, have you already decided to assign Jogen to my ship?"

He shrugged. "Of course not. That decision is strictly yours. But I admire Jogen for trying to obtain a position in Fleet Command without asking for my influence."

Captain Sedo hesitated and glanced at him. "He never asked for your help?"

"No, but I wish he would," her father responded.

When they entered the restaurant, Captain Sedo saw Jogen seated at a table, sipping wine. At the site of them, he immediately jumped to his feet and waved.

She trailed behind her parents through the crowded place. Known for tasty, indigenous Beltese food and drinks, the restaurant attracted many aliens who visited Tandon. The transparent ceiling allowed lunar light from both moons and billions of stars to penetrate it. Four drunken Trazods played musical tunes with rubber instruments in the bar area. A boisterous group of Agoorons gurgled a song in a far corner—that wasn't far enough.

Jogen greeted her with a warm hug. "Hello, Sadera. Celt. Mana."

Captain Sedo's former admirer was handsomely dressed in a blue medical uniform with three scanners attached to his belt. He stood straight and tall, reminding Sedo why many Beltese females adored him. Her mother was right. She did fear getting too close to Jogen. As captain, she had to concentrate on her job, not finding a husband.

"Hello, Jogen. My parents have told me a lot about your accomplishments over the years."

Jogen responded with a broad smile and pulled back the chair next to his. "All good, I hope."

Her parents sat on the opposite side of the table.

Sedo's mother asked, "Are you on call tonight, Jogen?"

"Yes," he said. "I work at the Research Institute, but sometimes I double at the hospital."

"You look very competent. Smart," Captain Sedo said.

Jogen gazed toward the freckled sky. "I've read about your commendations. I can't wait to hear about your space travels and the Velekan ordeal."

Sedo's Megmador instincts caused her to change her mind. She had never allowed her personal feelings to interfere with making the best decision for the *Volpus*, and Jogen's research experience would be an asset to her crew.

Perhaps she should offer him a position on her ship. He'd spend most of his time in either the research laboratory or the infirmary, and she wouldn't see him often. She would continue to deny her feelings for him, although her heart told a different story.

Jogen gasped, "Chochu wine vapors are strong here. Perhaps we should choose another restaurant?"

Sedo glanced around the area. Red vapor lingered low and thick. "No need, Jogen. The vapors don't harm me."

"The vapors can make you sick. Humans—"

"In my case, it's not true," she interrupted. "My parents drink it, remember?"

For a moment, Jogen just focused on her. "Dinner is on me. Welcome home, Sadera."

Her mother pressed a button in the center of the table, lighting menus at all four place settings. "Shall we order?"

"I ate before I left the *Volpus*," Sedo said. "I'm really not hungry."

"How about dessert?" Jogen asked. "Have you ever eaten Mangellian love pie?"

Sedo cocked her head and looked sideways at him. "Yes, I have, and it doesn't make you fall in love."

Jogen ran fingers through his shoulder-length hair. "Foolish of me to ask."

Her father smiled. "We have a gift for you, my daughter."

Her mother eagerly placed a small black box on the table in front of her. "We hope you like it."

Sedo opened it and found a beautiful, rare tumok stone necklace in a shade of green, the color of her eyes.

She held the necklace up to the light. "It's beautiful, but jewelry isn't allowed on duty."

"Then wear it off-duty," her mother suggested.

"Thank you so much. I also brought gifts for both of you. They're in my bag."

A waiter placed a bottle of wine in the center of the table, and her father poured a glass.

Her mother smiled. "We've missed you so much."

Sedo's father took a sip of his drink. "Don't be silly, dear," he said to his wife. "We see her almost every week."

Her mother touched her father's hand. "Communicating over vektrens isn't the same."

Within minutes, the waiter served them.

Sedo dipped a spoon into her soup, emptied the contents into her mouth, and swallowed. "My parents tell me you're seeking a position on a warship, Jogen."

Jogen's eyes drifted to his plate. "It's been difficult finding an assignment, because I dropped out of the last stage of the Fleet Command program."

Sedo stared at him until his eyes met hers. "Why did you leave the program? You know how Fleet Command frowns upon that."

Jogen severed a piece of fish with his fork. "I want to be a research doctor. Now I realize that most of the research is up there, in space. I can complete the program if I spend a year in space."

"I need a research doctor," she said. "We encounter foreign viruses, some fatal. The *Volpus* has the best medical technology available, but sometimes that's not enough. Doctors must perform extensive and tedious analyses. Work is often trial and error. If you're interested, the job is yours."

Jogen gasped, and his fork stopped in midair. "But ... but you haven't examined my certificates and references."

Sedo took a sip of danberry juice. "Let's just say I trust my instincts. Congratulations. You already know the doctors, Ohma and Fea."

Her father flashed a broad smile. "Congratulations, Jogen. I'll contact Dr. Ohma tonight about your new assignment. Sadera, I'm so proud of you for considering him for the vacant position."

Jogen touched her hand. "Thank you, Sadera. I won't let you down."

Her parents gazed at each other. This time their eyes sparkled with admiration rather than dismay.

Sedo inhaled another spoonful of soup. "The *Volpus* leaves in two weeks."

Jogen's complexion changed to a light pink. "That soon? Don't you need permission from Fleet Command before bringing me aboard your ship?"

"I doubt the fleet commander will object," Sedo said.

"Ah … I need to give notices at the hospital and the Research Institute. Are you sure you want me on your medical team?" Jogen asked.

Sedo smiled. "I've kept up with your accomplishments as well. You're second-in-command at the Research Institute. Are you willing to give up such a prestigious position for a warship assignment?"

"Yes, I am," Jogen said.

His feelings for her showed on his face and radiated from him like a beacon. He still loved her after all these years.

Did she have the power to resist him?

"Remember, I'm your captain first, friend second," she warned.

Her mother eyed her daughter's body. "You should eat more. You've lost weight."

"Mother, I'm ten kilograms overweight."

Her mother placed a hand over her mouth and snickered. "Actually, you should gain a few kilograms."

Her father waved a hand at Jogen's plate. "Finish your meal."

Jogen said, "I'm too excited to eat."

After dinner, her parents departed, leaving Jogen and her outside the restaurant.

The wind remained still and the night silent. The moons and the distant stars lit the area.

They passed another couple who held hands, and Sedo hoped it didn't give Jogen any ideas.

They walked on sidewalks through a housing community connected by shared walls. Some occupants had their curtains drawn, Sedo viewed others through clear walls. The aroma of dinner and the smell of flowers filled the air.

A party at one house had overflowed onto the lawn, and guests flocked around a table covered with food and wine. Faint voices and low laughter filtered throughout the surroundings.

She took a deep breath of fresh air and slowly exhaled. "I love this planet. The weather is superb, always nice and sunny, and the moons are exquisite."

"But you've seen thousands of moons."

"You know you'll need a haircut," she teased.

"But … Celt doesn't trim his hair."

She faced him, walking backward. "When you become fleet commander, you can make the rules. Now, what do you think we should do?"

"I'd like to walk you to your door," Jogen said.

She turned and continued at his side. "I love walking, especially on my own planet."

"Your mother is wrong about your weight. Fitness charts are not accurate, because human body mass is denser than ours. I've studied a lot about humans."

"Why?"

"Because you're human. Do you dislike me?" Jogen asked.

"Would I offer you a position on my ship if I did?"

"Did your father influence your decision?"

She smiled. "Father had nothing to do with it."

He bowed, took her hand in his, and kissed it. "I'll be indebted to you forever."

"Jogen, you don't owe me anything. Dr. Ohma is an ornery old serpent, so don't thank me yet."

"I've worked with some of the worst doctors and staff on this planet. I can deal with Dr. Ohma. I can't believe it—meeting you again, getting an assignment on your warship, all in one night."

"You sound excited."

He stopped and stared at her. "You don't know what this means to me."

"Maybe you should think about it overnight. Concentrate on what you'll be giving up here," Sedo suggested.

"I have thought about it, and I'm resigning from my present positions."

"I mean it, think about your future. You may become the youngest administrator of a research institute in the history of Tandon."

"I've already decided. I want to work in space."

"Jogen—"

"I want to know about you," he said. "Do you have anyone special in your life?"

"No." She lowered her head.

"Have you thought about getting married?"

She gasped, "No."

"It's not a forbidden word, Sadera. You know how much I like you. I've made a fool of myself so many times in the past, and you've still rejected me."

"You've never made a fool of yourself."

He chuckled. "Remember the time an older student called you a human misfit? I tried to defend you, and he beat me senseless. Once, I tried to impress you by climbing a tyra tree, then fell and broke my arm. And the time—"

She threw her hands into the air. "All right, you made a fool of yourself."

He gently touched her hand. "Don't you get lonely sometimes?"

"If I think about it, but I've always been alone. Even as a child, you were my only friend. My crew respects me, because I'm their captain. Sometimes we dine together, and I play games with some, but we're not close. They never invite me into their rooms to just sit and talk."

He placed an arm around her waist and pulled her closer. "I've been dreaming of the chance to meet you again."

She stepped away from him, fearing he would ask her to become his lifemate. Most Beltese had spouses, and their families traveled together on either cargo vessels or warships like the *Volpus*.

They stopped in front of her parents' home, and he placed his arms around her neck. "You're beautiful."

She threw back her head, snickered, and blushed. "I'm not."

"I've always admired you."

She removed his arms. "I just got home. Let's not complicate things."

"Let's go on a hike tomorrow?" he suggested.

"I can't. Mother has made plans after lunch, but you're welcome to come with us to the beach the day after."

"If your parents don't mind …"

She said, "You're family, remember?"

"You've been in space for seven years. Do you still enjoy it?"

"I can't imagine doing anything else, at least not at the moment."

A young male jogged past them, breathing heavily.

Jogen asked, "As captain, what's the most difficult decision you've ever made?"

"Condemning ten crew members to an early death."

"You did? Why?"

She glanced up at the westward moon. "Sorry, I shouldn't have mentioned that. Jogen, space is unforgiving."

"I studied the story about how some of your scouting parties died after exposure to foreign microorganisms."

"That's why we need research doctors like you."

When she turned and walked toward the front door, she heard a faint but familiar sound that she wouldn't have detected weeks earlier. Quickly turning, she found Jogen scanning her body with one of his medical instruments.

Sedo rushed toward him and knocked his Z-2 scanner from his hand. She slapped his face and felt the burning impact on her palm. "What are you doing? You have no right."

Shock clouded his face as he fell backward and rolled over on his side.

Sedo kicked him in the shin. "Get up."

He sat up, gripping his leg. "Ouch, you didn't have to kick me. Sadera—"

She crossed her arms, dropped the friendly demeanor, and stepped into professional mode. "It's Captain Sedo.

You're not on my ship yet, and already you're creating problems for me."

Caressing the left side of his face, he stood. "Do you know how hard you hit me?"

"You're lucky I didn't knock your head off," she snapped. "Why did you scan my body?"

Jogen stood and brushed off his uniform. "I didn't mean any harm. I'm just curious about the human anatomy."

"That was an unofficial examination, and your actions might keep you out of Fleet Command."

Panic flashed across his face. "Please, Sadera. Don't do this to me. I won't tell anyone you're almost Beltese."

"I dare you to tell anyone. My parents and doctors don't think I know."

"But our chromosomes are not compatible with humans. Someone must have reengineered your genes."

She pointed a finger in his face and shouted, "Don't ever do that again."

He blurted, "Someone genetically experimented with you. Mixing our genes with other species is against the law. When did this happen?"

She took a few deep breaths and deflated; so did her anger. "As an infant, I'm sure. My parents probably thought they were helping me blend into the Beltese society."

He adjusted the two scanners on his belt. "So, that's why you're more intelligent than the Beltese. When did you find out?"

She turned her back to him. "I got suspicious two months ago."

He jumped in front of her and gently held her shoulders. "What alerted you?"

"Physical and mental abnormalities."

"I'd like to thoroughly examine you." His eyes grew wide. "There's a high-energy field within your body. I've never seen anything like it."

"No examination," she said adamantly.

"It's only a series of body scans, and no one has to know. My results will be strictly confidential."

"My parents, along with Doctors Ohma and Fea, did this to me—"

"They don't have the research technology. There must have been a third doctor."

"Can I trust you?" Sedo asked.

"Yes, of course," he promised.

Her eyes welled up, and she blinked back the tears. "I'm a mutant, not human anymore."

He placed his hands on her cheeks. "You must be part human. Beltese don't cry."

"As a child, I didn't want to be different ... human. Now I don't want to be even half Beltese."

"Sadera, you must allow me to examine you."

She picked up the Z-2 medical scanner and passed it back to him. "Did I break it?"

He turned it off, reactivated it, and pressed a sequence of buttons. A green screen lit up. "No, it's fine."

"My parents and the doctors could spend the rest of their lives on that desolate penal colony, Quandra-4, all because of me."

Jogen was appalled. "What they did to you is immoral."

"They didn't care about me. I could have been deformed or died at an early age. They didn't love me at all."

Jogen held her in the comfort of his arms and patted her back. "I'm sorry, Sadera. I scanned you because I care—not to be mean."

She mumbled into his chest, "I know."

***

The next morning when Captain Sedo rose, her parents' house stood silent. Like a frightened little girl, she crept down the hall and stopped in front of her father's office. It remained locked at all times and off-limits to everyone, including her mother.

"Computer, open door." It slid open. He had forgotten to lock it. She entered, closed the door behind her, and scanned the room. She walked to the desk and pulled on the handle of the top drawer.

"Drawers are locked," said a computer. "Please enter security code."

Standing at the closet door, she said, "Computer, open door." When the door opened, she focused on ten 10-by-20-millimeter electronic chips in transparent containers. They lined the shelf in front of her. Her fingers nervously searched through them. They dated back over a thousand years and were identified by century. Zooming in on the latest chip, she opened the container and shoved it into a portable scanner.

Sedo sat on the floor, crossed her legs, and began viewing the records. She muted the sound and watched images of herself as a baby, walking and talking with her parents at six months. She fast-forwarded and stopped when she saw one of Dr. Ohma's medical records, as well as some from another doctor she didn't recognize. The encrypted codes of the reports didn't hinder her from deciphering them. As she focused on one particular medical record, the office door opened and voices neared. She sat still, waiting. She'd forgotten to close the closet door.

The footsteps approached, then her father said, "I left my closet open?"

Dr. Ohma whispered in a panic, "Forget about the closet, Celt. I had to get you alone. Something's happening with Captain Sedo, and she no longer trusts Dr. Fea or me."

"Happening?" her father asked.

"When she requested her medical records, we referred her to you. She disconnected her sleep monitor and threatened to destroy it. She's behaving in a most peculiar manner."

"Sadera hasn't said anything to me. You're her doctor; examine her."

Sedo's heart pounded wildly, and the tingling

sensation on her right side intensified. Beads of perspiration appeared on her forehead, and she soaked them up with her sleeve. She had not only invaded her father's personal and forbidden space but also Fleet Command's secret documents.

She sat still, waiting for the inevitable. Sedo couldn't think of an excuse for being there, and she didn't know how her father would react to her intrusion.

"She's not cooperating with either of us," Dr. Ohma said.

"Force her to take a physical," her father urged.

"She doesn't work for us. We work for her. If we pressure her, she might consult with another doctor, and we can't risk that. Her physical isn't due for another six months. Perhaps you should tell her she's only part human."

"Absolutely not," her father said. "It'll only create more psychological tension for her."

"Once she realizes she's a part of yours and Mana's genetics, she may feel more like your daughter than an adopted human."

"She'll never know about that."

"Last year's examination results proved her to be 32% Beltese," Dr. Ohma warned. "Six months ago, she was 61%. She's evolving into our species, and if this continues, she may lose all of her human characteristics."

"You talk like she's an experiment."

"She is an experiment," Dr. Ohma reminded him. "Are

you forgetting that you took her in as a human pet? We've never mixed our genes with another species. We don't know what's going to happen. And whatever that may be, she needs to be prepared."

Captain Sedo's back became rigid, and her legs went numb. She clenched the scanner with trembling hands and placed it quietly on the floor.

"What we did could send us to Quandra-4," her father said. "You can't tell her."

"It's not my job to tell her; it's yours and Mana's. Humans are not that intelligent, but she's gifted, even for our species."

"Is this your way of telling me something could go wrong?" her father asked.

"What do you think I've been saying?"

"But she has never been ill a day in her life."

"My point exactly," Ohma said. "We've studied humans. They get coughs, fevers, and runny noses."

"She's thirty-two. If anything were going to happen, it would've done so by now."

Dr. Ohma lowered his voice. "She's growing a second heart."

Sedo's left palm immediately touched the right side of her chest, and she feared they would hear it pounding.

They had just confirmed her intuitions.

The tingling, itchy sensation was a second heart.

"So, she suspects something?" her father asked.

"Yes," Dr. Ohma said.

"Let me discuss it with Mana."

"Good decision," Dr. Ohma agreed. "Come, you can treat me to a glass of wine."

Sedo attempted to place the chips back on the shelf and accidentally dropped a container. She jumped and held her breath.

Footsteps approached.

She looked up as her father peeked inside.

He roared, and his body grew massive, as the Beltese's did when they became extremely angry. "Sadera, what are you doing in here? Are you spying on me?"

"Yes, Father," she replied.

He rushed into the closet, jerked her to her feet, and threw her into the office.

Dr. Ohma jumped between them. "Calm down, Celt."

"You've invaded my privacy," her father shouted. "You—"

"Pet?" she said. "Is that all I am? A pet."

Her father gasped, and his eyes showed a hint of savagery.

"I've known for over two months," she said.

"How?" Ohma asked.

"I don't want to talk about it." She shot past him.

"Captain," Dr. Ohma said. "Get back to the *Volpus* and let me examine you."

"No way." She hurried to her room, dropped onto the bed, and curled into a fetal position.

Her instincts alerted her that something more sinister lurked among her father's records.

She would return soon—to find out what it was.

Closing her eyes brought back memories of her childhood classmates teasing her for being human. When she was eight, she'd seen alien animals from other solar systems for the first time. Would she end up in a cage like them, a sideshow freak?

She heard a knock at her door. "Sadera."

"Yes, Father."

"May we enter?" he asked.

"No." Sedo resisted the urge to cry. She just let her mind drift through her past.

The door buzzed, but she had locked it.

"I'm sorry for the way I behaved," her father said. "We need to talk."

"Not now," Sedo said.

"Sadera, open the door. We can talk this through," her mother pleaded.

"Let's discuss it later," Sedo said.

"All right," her mother said. "We'll all have clear heads by then."

For the first time, she knew her parents didn't love her as they'd pretended. After thirty-two years, she realized they had experimented with her because they thought of her as a human savage, a pet. It proved her entire life was a lie. She lay in bed for hours thinking about her past, her future, and—above all—the alien creature taking control of her body.

She closed her eyes.

Captain Sedo stood in an electromagnetic cage that was shielded by closely spaced crossbars. A crowd of Beltese ridiculed her from the opposite side. Long, frizzy hair flowed across her bare breasts and down to her knees. Raw meat lay on the floor, along with feces and a child's toy. Fingers pointed at her as laughter erupted from the crowd. She could hear Bonuve yelling, "Look at the half-Beltese, half-human. What a savage."

Sedo woke with an unbearable throbbing pain in her head—the first headache of her entire life, and she wondered what had caused it.

Did it have something to do with her biological changes?

Soaked in perspiration, she rolled over and gazed at the ceiling. She needed to talk to someone, but she only had Jogen.

Wobbling into the bathroom, she gasped as glowing green eyes reflected back at her from the mirror. She placed a palm on either side of her face, blinked several times, moved her head from side to side, and then gasped again.

She didn't know if she could deal with her changes.

They were coming so fast.

They were too surreal.

***

That evening, Sedo slumped in a chair in the hospital waiting room, with her elbows propped on her knees and her face buried in the palms of her hands. She feared her future, what she was becoming. Jogen seemed to be in a rush. "Sorry I kept you waiting so long." He concentrated on the electronic instrument in his hands, rather than her. "I have an intoxicated and injured Elgon and very limited knowledge of his physiology. He fell quite a distance—onto his head."

"Why doesn't the Elgon doctor care for him?" Sedo mumbled.

"He is the ship's doctor." Jogen studied her face. "You look awful. Are you sick?"

"I have this pain in my head. It's throbbing, and I need medication."

"I must examine you first," Jogen said.

She shook her head. "Just give me some medicine."

"Examination first. That's the way it works."

A nurse buzzed the room. "Doctor, the captain of the Elgon's cargo vessel has summoned you."

"Excuse me, Sadera," Jogen said.

Sedo needed his help, but Jogen had matters that were more important on hand. "You're busy. I can do without the medication."

"Wait here," he said. "I'll be back shortly."

Sedo didn't wait, but Jogen had impressed her with his professionalism.

When she returned to her parents' home, the place was still quiet. Waiting in the darkness, she sipped chochu wine at the dining room table with two empty glasses. The pain in her head had ceased, and the absence of light no longer prevented her from seeing in the dark.

What would she tell her crew when they realized her eyes glowed in the dark like theirs?

When her parents entered, she had neared the bottom of the first bottle. She didn't see the door open but rather heard it—a swishing sound at her back.

"I'm against it," her father said.

"Let's think on it overnight and discuss it tomorrow," her mother said. "Lights."

The glow made Sedo's surroundings more colorful.

"Oh, my daughter, we're glad you're still up," her mother said. "Are you ready to talk?"

Her father gasped, "What is this? Chochu wine?"

"And I ... I've drunk al ... most an entire bot ... tle." Sedo chuckled proudly.

Her father shook her, as if awakening her from a nightmare. "Sadera. This wine is poisonous to humans."

"But I'm not human anymore, am I?"

"Mana, hurry, contact Dr. Ohma," her father said.

Sedo waved her glass in the air and glared through the transparent pink liquid. "There's a doctor ... next door, Fa ... Father. Don't ... bother, Mother. If I were going to die, I would've … by now. Don't know why … everyone makes such a big deal … about this wine. It doe … sn't taste good, and I don't … don't feel that impaired."

Her father grabbed her wrist and snatched the glass from her hand, spilling the wine. He placed the glass on the kitchen counter and turned to her. "Are you insane?" Fumes from the wine mixed with oxygen and generated a cloud of vapor, like a red rose melting in the air.

Within minutes, Dr. Ohma materialized in their living room with two medical instruments in hand. The white cloud of his silhouette appeared, followed by his body.

He hastily scanned Sedo with a Z-2 instrument, analyzing her blood content. "Captain, did you really drink chochu wine?"

"I'm not … not going to die, Doc … tor." Sedo grabbed the bottle and attempted to take a swig, but her father pried it from her hand.

"What made you do such a foolish thing?" Dr. Ohma scolded.

Sedo giggled. "I … don't … know. I just got the … urge."

Ohma gasped, "She has a very high quantity in her system. She should be dead."

Captain Sedo waved the doctor away. "Will … you stop … it?"

"How do you feel?" Dr. Ohma asked.

Throwing her hands into the air, Sedo chuckled. "Great."

Ohma scanned her body with another instrument and locked eyes with her father. "Beltese can't drink this much. How can she? I'm detecting a strange high-energy field within her body."

"Stop talking about me as ... as if I'm not here," Sedo demanded.

"You could have died," her father yelled.

"Everyone, calm down. Have some wine," she hollered, slapping a palm on the table.

"No more for you," Dr. Ohma ordered.

"A glass for you, Doc ... tor?" Without moving a muscle, Sedo mentally lifted a glass from the wall's shelf, willing it to land on the table in front of Ohma.

The doctor's eyes bulged and darted from Celt to Mana. "Did you see that?"

Her mother stared at the doctor. "See what?"

Sedo's glass left the counter, drifted in midair, and landed on the table before her. She giggled as everyone gawked at her, then at each other. The shock and confusion on their faces pleased her, and she felt powerful.

She could do things they couldn't—and feared.

The cork popped from the second bottle, bounced off the wall, and landed on the floor. Then, the bottle moved around the table, filling everyone's glasses, as if it had a mind of its own. Chairs moved back from the table, and Sedo indicated for them to sit.

No one moved.

"Did you do that?" Dr. Ohma asked.

"I'm sorry if I startled ... everyone." Sedo sensed their feelings: shock and surprise. All three had concentrated first on their own welfare, rather than her safety. She pushed her chair back from the table, stood, and wobbled into her bedroom.

Two months earlier, Dr. Ohma's whisper would have been inaudible. "She has powers."

"I can hear you," Sedo shouted from her bedroom.

Shortly afterward, the captain returned with her travel bag. "I've been called back ... to the *Volpus*."

When Sedo left, the room stood still, and she didn't look back.

***

Celt finally broke the silence. He took a deep breath and dropped into a chair. "She's a Megmador. What have we done?"

"It has been over three hundred years since the last one," Mana said.

Dr. Ohma fell into the nearest chair. "But she's part human. Can she manage such a gift?"

"We must tell no one," Celt said.

"We can't keep this a secret," Ohma protested. "She may become extremely dangerous."

Celt stood and sighed. "She's also a Fleet Command officer."

"Think of what could happen to her," Mana said.

"Beltese will fear her. Megmadors are powerful, immortal creatures. We don't know how they obtain or control their powers."

Dr. Ohma leaned forward in his chair, propped his elbows on the table, and rubbed his palms together. "Let's review all possibilities and options."

"Possibilities and options," Mana uttered. "We have none."

Celt glanced at Ohma. "Get Dr. Fea here at once."

***

Two days later, Captain Sedo returned to her parents' home. She pushed the button on the side of the door, and it opened.

Her mother was working in the kitchen, removing wine from a box on the floor in front of the wine cooler. "Sadera, are you here to stay for a few days?"

"No, I came to speak with you and Father," she said.

"Celt," her mother called, as if nothing had happened earlier, "Sadera's home."

Sedo took a seat at the kitchen table. An assortment of fruits filled a clear bowl in the center, and their aroma lingered in the air.

Her mother opened the door of the cold food storage bin. "Let me get you a drink."

"No, I'm fine, Mother."

Sedo's mother closed the door and took a seat in front of her daughter.

Her father entered the kitchen, his face haggard and hair mussed. "How've you been, my daughter?"

Sedo had never felt so uncomfortable confronting her parents. "Managing. I think we should talk."

Celt took a seat next to Mana. "First, let us apologize for what we did to you. We thought we were doing the right thing."

Her mother's eyes grew large as she nodded. "It seemed right at the time."

Sedo had trouble making eye contact with them. "I know you wanted me to fit into the Beltese society."

Her father pulled his chair in and rested his hands on the table. "And it worked. Linking our genes with yours gave you a superior mind."

"I've been nothing more than a pet to you; that's why you took a chance with my life. The effect could have been adverse. Deadly."

"We love you. You mean a lot to us," her father said.

Yes, like a pet. She scowled inwardly.

Her mother put a hand on Celt's. "Are you angry at us?"

Sedo sensed their tension. Her face wrinkled, and her eyes welled up, but she fought back the tears. "I thought you two loved me, but I didn't mean anything to you, otherwise I ... wouldn't have been an experiment."

"What we did was wrong, but we do love you, dear," Mana whined. "You're our daughter."

Her words didn't match her thoughts.

Sedo felt her parents' deceitfulness.

Thought signals indicated that they had discussed eliminating her before she gained her full powers.

She gazed from one to the other, wishing to find love in their eyes. "I feel like an idiot. I really thought you both cared for me."

Her father reached over the table and put a hand on hers. "Of course, we do."

Sedo felt his desperation. She moved her hands from the table and placed them in her lap. "Jogen knows I'm part Beltese. He scanned me without my knowledge. He doesn't know I'm a Megmador."

Celt locked eyes with Mana. "We trust Jogen."

"I trust him too," Sedo said.

"Do you have full powers yet?" her father asked.

Sedo knew the sole purpose of his question was to determine how difficult it would be to eliminate her. "Almost. I'm getting stronger each day. It's scary."

Her father said, "We fear you'll not be able to control your gift."

"I have three doctors to assist me. Don't worry," she responded coolly.

Her mother lowered her head and rubbed the back of her neck with a nervous hand. "Your becoming a Megmador has been a heavy burden on us."

"I won't allow anyone else to know about my powers," Sedo assured them.

Her mother said, "We could spend the rest of our lives on that dreadful penal colony for what we've done." Her father stared into space. "I've been there. It's an awful place to die."

"You both have my word. I'll keep my powers a secret."

"Just remember what will happen to us if the authorities discover what we did," her mother reiterated.

Sedo stood. "I must get back to the *Volpus*. I need to complete some medical tests."

Her father's head rose high above hers as they faced each other. "We want you to stay here with us."

She knew her life would be in danger if she remained with them.

"I'll visit again before I leave. I have captain's duties as well."

She had lived with strangers all her life.

No one cared for her except Jogen. She was just an alien, living among the Beltese species.

CHAPTER 7

CAPTAIN SEDO'S FRIEND

When Captain Sedo sprung another surprise visit on Jogen, he was working in his private laboratory on the *Volpus*, setting up his research equipment.

He wore a blue lab jacket over his Beltese fleet uniform. "Sadera, welcome. Is this a professional or friendly visit?"

"Both. I need a favor," she said.

Distillation units, ovens, electronic gadgets, containers, and an assortment of equipment cluttered the area.

"If it's professional, I must address you as Captain."

"You may call me Sadera when we're alone."

Jogen led her through the cluttered room and into the back of his laboratory. "This place is so spacious. I can't dream of a better setting. Sorry I can't offer you a seat." He beamed. "I'm impressed with all the advanced medical equipment here. Have you agreed to my medical evaluation?"

"Yes," she said.

He calibrated his medical instruments and scanned her body from head to toe.

"No permanent record of this examination," she reminded him.

"According to my instruments, you're 88% Beltese, and that unknown energy field is still there—now stronger."

He pricked her finger, sucked blood into a palm-sized instrument, and attached it to a computer. A colorful spiral conglomerate appeared on the screen.

He then scanned her with three other instruments she didn't recognize.

"I know exactly what happened. Someone isolated Beltese genes and injected you with them. Do you ever remember being sick?"

Sedo shook her head. "No, never. According to Dr. Ohma, they're my parents' genes."

Jogen displayed her genetic composition on a larger screen, showing two genes linked together. The smaller one was human, the larger one Beltese. He logged into the ship's database and found her parents' ZNA. "It's a perfect match, see? There is a covalent bond between the Beltese and human genes. The only thing it hasn't affected is your skeleton." He pointed. "This is where the phosphodiesters of your human DNA are attached to the Beltese lantadiesters, or our ZNA. You were injected with a catalyst."

She gasped. "An artificially induced chemical reaction? In my body?"

"That's the only way to bond the two genes. A research doctor did this," Jogen said.

She shook in fear. *What if I can't control my powers?* "Can this chemical bond be broken? I mean, if I want to terminate these changes?"

He held up his hands. "Never. I can't believe they experimented with you like this. You could have died or been permanently deformed. You're growing a second heart. Do you feel activity on your right side?"

"It's more like an itchy, tingling sensation. How about a blood transfusion? If we could get human blood—"

"No, Sadera." He took another sample of her blood. "The alteration is permanent. At this point, a transfusion would be poisonous to you. I must report this to Fleet Command and the authorities."

"You've already promised not to expose my parents or my secret," she protested. "I trusted you. You gave me your word."

His face grew stern. "But it's my duty to report this. I took an oath with Fleet Command, and it's my duty as a Beltese citizen."

Sedo stepped back from him. "Sending them to that dreadful Quandra-4 won't change my situation."

"I've always considered Celt to be a father figure. It's hard to comprehend his actions."

"Look, I know this puts you in a terrible position, but please don't do this. My parents, who once meant everything to me, can no longer be trusted. You are all I have left. Please, Jogen."

He tilted his head, staring at her for a long moment.

"All right, I won't report it. I will honor my word. You can trust me, Sadera. Always." He gave her a gentle smile before his device alerted him of an energy spike. "Huh. I wish I could figure out what's causing this strange energy. I'll need to research this."

"I can save you the trouble. I'm a Megmador," Sedo said.

Jogen locked eyes with her, then threw back his head and laughed hysterically.

For a brief moment, Sedo wanted to hurt him for ridiculing her. An empty feeling surged within, and Jogen's mockery worsened it, reminding her of when her classmates had teased her as a child.

With her mind, she cleared items on and around his desk so quickly his eyes almost crossed. The chair pulled out, and she dropped into it. "I repeat, I'm a Megmador, and no one must know."

He gasped and made a 360-degree scan, searching for his equipment. "But ... but you're human and Meg—"

"Part human," she corrected. "And I'm losing more of my human characteristics with each passing day."

A chair from the far corner drifted into the air and landed behind Jogen. He didn't sit but gazed at her in disbelief.

Her telepathy revealed the shock and confusion that stirred in his mind as he pondered the possibility of her having powers.

"You're shocked?" she asked.

"Of course," he said. "What a scientific mystery. This is fantastic. Unbelievable."

Jogen's statements irritated her. "I'm an experiment—and you're ecstatic."

"It's a gift. Do you know how many Beltese wish to become Megmadors?"

She lowered her head. "Well, it wasn't on my wish list. I've read that Beltese have trouble controlling their powers."

Jogen took a seat in front of her and held her hands in his. "I'll help you. Together, we can control it."

"I've studied a lot about Megmadors. Will I live up to two thousand years?"

He leaned back in his chair and folded his arms. "Honestly, I have no idea. Humans can live up to a hundred years with a proper diet. But with your Beltese bone marrow, there's no certainty. I couldn't even guess."

"They took me in as a pet," she nearly whispered.

His voice lowered. "What?"

"They took me in as a pet, an experiment. Now I'm a threat, and they want me to disappear."

"I'm sorry for what they did to you, Sadera."

"Remember when I asked you for a favor?" she said. "It's important to me."

"I thought the favor was a secret examination."

She stared into the distance. "You have friends, electronic experts."

"Yes, but such professionals are here on the *Volpus*."

"This can't be connected to Fleet Command. What I'm asking for is against regulations. It could cost me my career as captain, or worse, my freedom."

Jogen pondered the idea for a moment. "And if this person is caught?"

"That person will definitely lose his freedom, forever. The doors and desk have the most sophisticated locking devices."

"Where's this job? Not on the *Volpus*?" he asked.

"No, I'd rather not say. If we're caught, you won't be implicated."

"How long will it take?" he asked.

"Depends on the expert. I can get what I need in a few minutes, and the owners won't be present."

Jogen frowned. "But you're a Megmador. Why not do it yourself?"

"I can't walk through walls until I have full powers. I need to lock everything back up, as if no one were ever there."

He shrugged. "Just transport yourself in."

"Transporters leave traces, and I can't materialize inside a desk."

"This could be very expensive," he said.

"I know," Sedo replied.

He fanned a lock of hair from his forehead. "Meet me here tomorrow, same time."

She stood. "When I see you again, I want your hair trimmed."

"Yes, Captain," he said, rising quite a distance above her head as he stood. "Sadera, return my equipment." She turned and waved at him. "Things are exactly where you left them."

***

Two days later, Captain Sedo made certain her parents had boarded a civilian ship bound for the Agooron substation, M-5, to attend a galactic conference. In the early morning, she entered their house with an acquaintance of Jogen's. He was short and lean and kept inquiring about the information she sought.

"I know who you are. You're the only human on this planet. Whose house is this?"

"It doesn't matter. I have access, and the owners are traveling in space. Are you certain they'll suspect nothing?" Sedo asked.

He scanned the office security system with a palm-sized electronic device. A rapid beeping sequence occurred. "It does have an advanced locking system, but I'll leave no trace," he promised.

He studied the door's lock for a few seconds, pulled an instrument from the pouch on his belt, and punched some keys. The instrument's light blinked red. It had two leads, one black and the other white. He attached the two wires to the opposite end of the locking system, punched more buttons, and the red light turned green.

"Can you access it?" Sedo asked.

Without another word, he pressed the button and the office door yielded.

Once inside, Sedo walked to the closet. "Try this one first."

He performed the same procedure, and the closet door opened.

"Unlock the desk. I'll be done here shortly."

Using her father's portable scanner, she copied the data chips in less than two minutes. "Lock it."

The young Beltese hit a few keys on his instrument. "It's locked."

She found and downloaded three more data chips from her father's desk. Then her accomplice locked up, and they left.

Sedo gave him a chip with a generous supply of galactic credits. "Tell no one about this, or we're both doomed for Quandra-4."

***

Back aboard the *Volpus*, Sedo locked herself in her quarters and spent hours searching through hundreds of years of family history. She watched her genetic Beltese grandparents and their grandparents, both maternal and paternal.

As she narrowed in on the latest records, she viewed herself playing on the beach with Jogen. Each time waves rolled in, she ran away until they receded, then followed them out again.

Jogen, on the other hand, ran into the water, and it rose to his neck. His father rushed in, picked him up, and carried him ashore.

Sedo followed her life through various schools and higher learning academies. Jogen was always there. He had been her only friend all her life. Viewing the records made her realize how lonely she had actually been—and still was. Now estranged from her parents, she needed Jogen more than ever.

Sedo saw copies of her medical records, verifying the genetic alteration of her genes shortly after adoption. She was now a prodigy among the Beltese species.

She observed her father and five other Fleet Command officers standing among black, hairy beings with green faces, yellow eyes, and four arms. The records proved that he'd lied to Fleet Command. Rather than being marooned on the desolate side of the planet Cypus for three years, he'd been living on Neptus, a planet in the now-forbidden solar system in the next galaxy. He had convinced Fleet Command that the species on Neptus was more technologically advanced and too hostile to encounter, claiming they had destroyed his warship, the *Eliptus*, and his crew.

Due to his accusations, the Galactic Committee had declared the next galaxy off-limits.

The beings on Neptus had experimentally mixed their

genes with the Beltese, in an attempt to create more superior beings, and the results had been devastating for the hosts. Some grew extra limbs, resembling spiders. Other deformities created mounds of flesh, restricting the hosts' mobility.

Sedo cringed and shook her head. Such deformities could've happened to her.

Perhaps they still could.

Was this what her future held?

How did Father get this information past security, and why would he keep such incriminating evidence?

She studied Fleet Command's secret records, which she would later incinerate.

She tilted her head back. Her neck felt weak, almost paralyzed.

When her door buzzed, she almost jumped out of her chair. Sedo displayed another screen on her computer, tapped a button on her desk, and unlocked the door.

Lieutenant Bonuve entered, walked to her side, and folded his arms. "Your parents are waiting to speak with you, Captain."

"You came all the way to my room to tell me this?"

"Actually, the crew is worried about you ... being locked in your quarters so much."

She focused on her screen. "I appreciate their concern, but I'm working on an engineering project."

Bonuve eyed the pile of data chips on her desk.

Sedo gazed up at him. "Anything else, Lieutenant?"

"No, Captain," he said but remained at her side.

Sedo placed her hands on the armrest of her chair, leaned back, and continued staring up at him.

Bonuve reluctantly left the room, and she locked the door behind him.

Captain Sedo had dreaded this moment. She wasn't certain if she ever wanted to see her parents again. "Computer, vektren."

When her parents came into view, her mother beamed. "Hello, Sadera."

Her parents sat next to each other, with a beach view in the background.

"Hello, Mother. Father. How's your visit on M-5?"

Her mother waved a hand and flashed a fake smile. "Great. We've spent the entire day on this private beach."

"And you, Father?"

The commander's face was pale and gaunt, and his eyes were red, as if he lacked sleep. "The meeting didn't go as well as I'd expected." His voice was scratchy and hoarse. "That's all I can say."

Captain Sedo knew her transformation had caused his grimness.

"I'm scheduled to leave for the Velekan planet tomorrow. Shall I continue as planned?"

"Yes, and destroy any Velekan warships you encounter," her father said.

"Do you think this is necessary? Perhaps we should

reconsider the situation and deal with them in another manner," Sedo suggested.

He raised an eyebrow. "Are you questioning my orders?"

"No," she blurted.

"This decision has been handed down by the Galactic Committee. Proceed as planned," her father instructed.

"We're leaving for M-7 in a few weeks," her mother said.

Sedo shook her head. "Don't go, Mother. I see death."

Her mother maintained her smile. "Don't be silly, Sadera. We're traveling on a civilian ship."

"If I attack the Velekans' planet, they'll retaliate. Promise me you'll travel only on warships until the Velekan ordeal is settled."

"Then we'll take a warship," her mother agreed.

"I'll contact you after I take care of the Velekans. Goodbye, Mother. Father."

Images from Sedo's past created visions, taking her to places she didn't want to visit. Through her powers, she mentally saw Beltese slaves living a dreadful life in an alien environment. They were skin and bone and dressed in rags. Their pain and misery were like knives in her chest.

They beckoned her.

She had to defy Fleet Command orders and rescue them from the Forbidden Galaxy.

CHAPTER 8

THE *VOLPUS* ATTACK ON THE VELEKANS

Planet Numus in the Spartis Solar System
Numus hadn't changed since Sedo's last trip, four years earlier. It was 85% water with plentiful, thick vegetation and limited rock formations, forcing the Velekans to mine other planets, such as Kodas, for ore.

Sedo sat in her chair and watched a dozen Velekan warships in orbit. Four approached the *Volpus* head-on, while eight others following at a distance.

"I've scanned the Velekan warships," asserted Khyla, her new weapons engineer, "and their firing range is still limited, Captain."

The closest ships continued their paths, but the others split up and tried to surround the *Volpus*.

"Destroy the warships first, then their production facilities," Sedo instructed.

Khyla fired and reduced the four closest ships to rubble.

"Three are approaching from the starboard side," Bonuve said.

"I see them." Khyla fired immediately. Pulses of blue rays destroyed the three ships on the starboard side, then the aft.

Bonuve activated two more vektrens. "Here come ten more."

The Velekan warships maneuvered closer to the *Volpus.*

"They've started their zigzag pattern again," Bonuve said.

Khyla destroyed two more ships. "They're moving away."

Bonuve said, "We're coming up on the nearest production facility."

"Put it on view, Lieutenant," Sedo said.

Bonuve pressed a key on his desk, and a huge facility came into focus on a vektren. "There's one on each side of the planet, if my source is correct."

Sedo didn't like the idea of killing so many Velekans. "Get a closer view."

Through scattered clouds, Sedo saw a series of large, white structures clustered together. About fifty warships sat outside the compound. "I want everything down there destroyed."

"Coordinates have been established," Khyla announced.

As a series of rays hit the huge complex, Sedo sat up straight in her chair. Flying debris hurled into the air. Sedo's body tensed as she watched the devastation her ship had caused to the Velekan species. She'd killed thousands—many more than the number on M-9. She hated the Velekans, but her instincts warned her that the Galactic Committee had made a hasty decision, rather than taking a more logical approach.

"Mission completed, Captain," Khyla acknowledged.

Captain Sedo stared at the dust and rubble. "I can't see anything down there. Did you destroy all of those warships on the ground?"

Khyla glanced back at her. "Yes, according to my instruments."

"Bonuve, what happened to the other ships?"

Bonuve leaned back in his chair. "They're still out there but keeping a safe distance. They're no match for us."

"They've damaged us once," Sedo reminded him.

"We have a more efficient weapons engineer," Bonuve said.

Sedo spoke calmly. "Ferrus, get us to the other side of the planet, fast. I want to get this job over with and leave here before the Velekans plan something drastic."

They encountered a cluster of Velekan warships on the other side of the planet, but the warships sped away. Scattered clouds thickened, but they didn't hinder the *Volpus* attack.

"The second facility is coming into view, Captain," Khyla said. "The target has been located, and I'm firing."

Sedo crossed her legs. "I don't see any warships outside this facility."

Bonuve zoomed in on another vektren. "Look, Captain, a new and larger production facility."

"Destroy it," Captain Sedo ordered. "With their new technology, they're planning to upgrade their warships."

Sedo watched Velekans working like ants, moving parts between facilities. Within seconds, the *Volpus* had left no trace of the structures that once stood there.

"Let's do another scan of this planet to make sure we got every facility," she said.

Bonuve concentrated on his workstation. "Captain, their warships have left. I'm searching for them."

"Starco, contact Fleet Command and confirm that our mission here is completed."

"Yes, Captain," Starco said.

Bonuve swiveled his chair around and faced the captain. "I can't understand why they had so many warships circling their own planet."

"Maybe they were expecting us. Contact the Velekan commander," Sedo said.

"We don't have to. He has summoned us," Bonuve said. "This must be a bad day for him."

"Put him on projection," Sedo said.

The Velekan commander's complexion had turned from gray to white, veins on his temples and the sides of his neck bulged, and his red eyes glowed with fury. He stood, gripping the back of his chair, his long fingernails digging into the headrest.

"You've destroyed our warship production facilities

and murdered thousands of our citizens. I'm declaring war on the Beltese. We'll rebuild our structures and with our new technology, we will destroy the Beltese Fleet."

Sedo remained seated and kept a firm voice. "The Galactic Committee made this decision, not just the Beltese. If you rebuild your facilities, we and our allies will simply destroy them again. Velekan warships will not operate in space for the next hundred years. We can ground your fleet indefinitely if necessary. All Velekan warships will be destroyed on sight."

The Velekan raised a fist and pounded air. "You'll not get away with this. We'll retaliate, I promise."

His image disappeared.

"Well, I think we got his attention," Khyla said.

Bonuve sighed. "Now that we've completed our mission here, where are we headed?"

"Set course for the Mondumos Solar System, Ferrus."

"Mondumos?" Her navigator gasped, "But that's near the Forbidden Galaxy. It'll take us at least six months to get there."

Bonuve turned his attention to her. "What mission do we have there?"

"It's a surprise," Sedo said.

She envisioned images of the deaths of her parents and others who had traveled on the civilian ship with them. She felt a conflict between sorrow and relief concerning their demise. Her mother had lied and boarded the later ship from M-5.

The Velekan commander said he would retaliate, and he had kept his promise.

"But, Captain, we'll be out of communication range from Fleet Command," Starco said. "Shall we inform them of our flight plan?"

Starco's voice sounded like a whisper, mixed with the chaos in her head. She heard him but didn't respond.

"Shall I contact Fleet Command?" Starco repeated.

Bonuve raised his voice. "Captain, is there a problem?"

When Sedo turned, everyone in Navigational Control was staring at her. "The commander is aware of our voyage. We have six months to contact Fleet Command."

"Captain, Velekan warships are surrounding us," Khyla warned. "Shall we outrun them?"

"No, attack. Get the other weapons expert in here, Lieutenant Bonuve."

Bonuve activated six vektrens that displayed all sides of the *Volpus*. He rushed to the workstation next to Khyla. "I'm counting forty-five warships. Where did they appear from so fast?"

Warships circled around Sedo's ship, like vultures over a fresh kill. The *Volpus*, like all Beltese warships, could attack from all sides.

Sedo felt excited and competent approaching her second battle. "There's a group approaching the aft."

Khyla said, "I see them, Captain. Protective barrier has been activated."

Bonuve and Khyla destroyed eleven ships as others kept coming.

"Focus on the clusters. In order to damage the *Volpus*, they must concentrate their forces."

One of the Velekan ships fired on the dome but caused no damage.

"Take out the closer ones," Sedo urged. "Put yourself in their heads. Where would you maneuver next?"

Khyla continued to punch buttons at her workstation. "They're making a series of sharp turns in alternating directions."

"I've figured out their flight pattern," Sedo said. "I just logged it into the database. Communicate with them, Starco."

"They've blocked all communications, Captain," Starco announced.

"Keep trying."

The second weapons engineer relieved Bonuve.

"There's a cluster of four—too close to us," Sedo warned.

Multiple laser strikes eliminated all but one of the closest Velekan warships, which quickly joined others and came after the *Volpus* again. Two other ships got close enough to hit the *Volpus*. One struck the starboard side and another smashed against the stern. Neither hit penetrated the ship's protective barrier.

Khyla turned to the other weapons expert. "The

captain has entered their maneuver pattern into the ship's computer. Follow it."

"Captain, they still refuse to acknowledge," Starco said.

Sedo tightened her fist as half of a burning vessel drifted and exploded near the viewport, jolting her ship.

"Fifteen other ships have just joined in the battle," Khyla said.

Sedo scooted to the edge of her chair, her body tense. "The Velekan commander must be insane." She stood and stared at the rubble surrounding the *Volpus*. "Why don't they give up?"

"Their radiation level is still lethal, Captain," Bonuve said. "It'll probably take them years to master it."

The weapons engineers concentrated on another cluster of ships, annihilating them all. With every movement the Velekan warships made, the *Volpus* destroyed more of them.

The battle continued until only nine enemy ships remained, and they sped away, disappearing into space.

Carcasses of Velekan vessels glowed orange over Numus, littering space.

***

"Captain Sedo, Assistant Commander Colas would like to speak with you," Starco said. "It's urgent."

Colas sat at her father's old desk, with an animated

Volpus emblem on the wall behind him. He was half her father's age, short and thin with a narrow face and a pinched nose.

He first lowered his head, then stared straight into her eyes. "Hello, Captain. I have some sad news for you. The Velekans destroyed the ship that Commander Sedo and his wife traveled on from M-5. You have our deepest sympathy. We never expected them to attack a civilian ship."

Sedo froze in her chair, unable to move or blink, not only because of her parents' deaths but also because images of the destroyed vessel flashed through her mind again. Sedo heard violent screams of death as the ship exploded into mangled pieces. She saw bodies ripping apart, flesh tearing, and limbs severing. Charred flesh floated in space among the rubble. "They promised not to travel on a civilian ship until after we settled the Velekan matter."

"Captain?" Colas asked. "Are you all right?"

"Yes ... yes," Sedo said.

"There were over three hundred other passengers of various species aboard, including the Trazod commander."

"When did this happen?" Sedo asked.

"After you destroyed the Velekan production facilities."

"How did they find out so fast?" Sedo asked. "I didn't think they had the capability to communicate at such a distance."

"Probably ship-to-ship communication, but they may have acquired advanced communication techniques," Colas said.

"Thank you for informing me. I assume you'll be commander now?"

"Until a permanent commander is assigned, yes. Will the *Volpus* be returning to Tandon?"

"No, I'm going on a mission I discussed with my father during my leave on Tandon."

Sedo knew he wouldn't question her lie. Unlike her father, Colas didn't react well under pressure.

"It'll take me a few weeks to sort out all of the commander's projects. I'll get back with you later."

He signed off.

Captain Sedo remained seated at her workstation and overrode all ship-wide communication systems. She saw herself on a vektren in Navigational Control. "This is the captain speaking. The Velekans attacked and destroyed the civilian ship that Commander Sedo and his wife were traveling on ..." Her voice flowed, stronger and under control, showing no remorse or compassion. But inside, she was crumbling. As captain, Sedo could only show strength.

She was becoming a Beltese, and they didn't mourn their dead.

"Assistant Commander Colas will assume Commander Sedo's position until a permanent commander is assigned. End of message."

Instant death relieved her parents from the humiliation of spending the remainder of their lives on Quandra-4, living through Naconda, without medical assistance.

***

At her workstation, Sedo tapped two buttons on her wristband. "Jogen, where are you?"

His voice sounded off on her collar communicator, and her heart warmed. "In the laboratory. Come on down."

When Sedo entered the room, Jogen stood in front of a distillation unit. Through a glass door, she could see a green liquid boiling under a ventilation system. On a workbench behind him, a red light glowed on an oven, and laboratory dishes littered the area.

Jogen ran his fingers through Sedo's shoulder-length hair and placed his arms around her neck. "I'm sorry, Sadera. Celt and Mana were like my own parents. I can't believe they're gone. Remember when I lost my mother and father?"

Sedo pressed her cheek against his and savored his warmth. "You were only six when your father was killed."

He hugged her tightly and caressed her back, making her spine tingle.

"My parents and I became estranged," she whispered into his ear. "When they realized I had powers, everything changed. I didn't trust them anymore."

"They feared for their freedom. When they reengineered your genes, they never suspected you'd become a Megmador."

"I knew they'd be killed. Mother promised to take a warship," Sedo said.

Holding her shoulders, he stepped back at arm's length. His eyes narrowed, and he frowned. "You told them?"

"They knew of my powers; still, they didn't listen," she said.

"That doesn't make sense."

The laboratory door opened, and Sedo and Jogen jumped apart.

A chemist entered, picked up an electronic log, and left.

Sedo heard a series of nearby beeps.

Jogen turned off the distillation system and adjusted the oven temperature. "Do you think she saw us?"

"Of course," Sedo said. "What are you working on?"

"The last research doctor kept some of the tetrad microorganisms responsible for killing fourteen of your crew members. I'm trying to determine what makes them so deadly."

Sedo wrinkled her nose in disgust. "He never told me he kept some. Jogen, I want them destroyed. I can't have another epidemic."

"We know one way to kill them, and they're isolated in four consecutive safety containers."

A clear liquid dripped from the side of a distillation column.

"What are you doing, cooking them?" she asked.

"No, I'm making a series of compounds to determine how the organisms react to each. I'm studying other ways to destroy them, in case we come into contact with similar ones." Jogen opened the oven's door and removed a small, clear container. "You need a research doctor, and that's why I'm here."

She turned to leave. "I'm sure you're familiar with our decontamination procedures by now."

"I've completed all the necessary training. Are we having lunch together? Same time?" he asked.

"I'll be there," she said.

For the first time in Sedo's life, she had a close friend and admirer aboard the *Volpus*. She longed for his touch, his smile—or just his voice. He filled the void in her life, and she wanted him with her forever.

She knew he felt the same about her and would soon ask her to become his lifemate.

***

Captain Sedo entered the officers' lounge and joined Jogen at their usual table in a far corner. Everyone gazed at them, then diverted their attention, resuming their conversations.

Jogen touched a button that lit up the menu. "You know the crew has started rumors about us."

Sedo scanned the room for curious eyes. "Yes, I've known for quite some time. Ignore them. We don't need their approval."

Jogen read the menu. "I've been on the *Volpus* for two months and already I miss Tandon."

"If you're planning to spend the remainder of your life in space, forget about home."

"Why are we going to the Mondumos Solar System?" Jogen asked.

Sedo crossed her legs at the ankles. "To correct my father's mistake."

"What did he do there, and how do you know about it?"

"Remember your friend who did me the favor?" she whispered.

"Who? Oh, yes, him."

"I copied some of my father's old records."

His mouth gaped open. "That's why this trip's a secret."

"My father did things in the Second Galaxy."

"What kinds of things?" he asked.

"Everyone will know at the end of our voyage, and the Beltese will hate him," she said.

"Sadera, you can trust me."

"I can't risk having anyone else involved—"

Dr. Ohma intruded, taking a seat next to Sedo. "May I join you two?"

"Of course," Sedo said.

"I'm sorry about your parents, Captain," Ohma said, studying the menu. "They were my friends. Perhaps you should visit Dr. Fea."

"I'm not having any emotional problems," she said. Dr. Ohma gently touched her shoulder. "See him anyway. Let him decide."

Ohma should have known that she no longer possessed strong emotions, such as grief.

"I'll visit him after lunch," Sedo promised.

The doctor placed his order. "You two sit here every day."

"Dr. Ohma, we're just having lunch," Jogen said.

Ohma looked around the area. "Well, rumors are there's love between you two, since you spend so much time together."

Sedo was adamant. "We're friends, and my crew should mind their own business."

"You two exercise together. And you, Capatin, spends lot of time in Dr. Kaen's laboratory."

"I never thought you'd participate in such gossip, Doctor," Sedo scolded.

"Oh, I'm not participating, just repeating it exactly the way I heard it." Ohma changed the subject. "Did Dr. Kaen tell you about his breakthrough with his Naconda experiment?"

Sedo smiled. "It's excellent."

"I'm excited," Ohma said. "Glad you brought him aboard."

Jogen took a sip from his glass, swallowed, and cleared his throat. "We have three crew members going through the stage, and I asked Dr. Ohma not to euthanize them yet. Naconda has slowed 50% in one patient. Two others received different treatments but showed no progress. They're in too much pain. We have no choice but to terminate their suffering."

***

After lunch, Sedo sat under the dome and took in the view. Watching objects speed by the *Volpus* always relaxed her. After all her years in space, she still found it intriguing.

For hours, she leaned back in an adjustable chair and fixated on the thousands of stars that littered the galaxy, shining as single bright lights or in clusters—some near, others thousands of light-years away. An immense cloud of dust and gases blurred a pageant of stars on the starboard side. In the distance, a neutron star pulsated at random intervals, and the nebulas varied in color from blue-green to yellow.

Sedo closed her eyes and watched Beltese prisoners living on Neptus, held captive by an inferior species.

"I'm coming to rescue you," she said aloud.

CHAPTER 9

THE VELEKAN ALLY

The Crustan commander sat in one of two high-backed chairs in a small room, directly across from his host. A female stood behind the Velekan commander, staring into space, her face submissive. She was almost as tall as her master. Unlike most rooms he was accustomed to, this one did not simulate natural, bright sunlight. Rain pounded on the only window and displayed a gloomy scene of the weather outside.

In the sealed room, the two commanders smoked safrez roots, grown only on Onupa. The Velekans used it, as well as a few other species, but the Crustans treasured it more. The smoke was soothing.

A bowl of atfridazan worms—large, fresh, and wiggly—occupied the small table between them. They were scarce on most planets but plentiful on Numus, due to its high-water level. The Crustans and two other species in the galaxy consumed them. The worms were a delicacy of the Crustans, but the most popular were the huge fireflies on Numus that were available only two weeks a year.

The Velekan commander leaned his huge bulk back in his chair. "Like us, your species is considered outcasts by the Galactic Committee. They consider us inferior beings." The Crustan commander sat on the opposite side of the table, drinking wine. "They refer to us as 'Bugs' behind our backs," the Crustan commander said. "Our technology lags behind them, but only by a few generations. We are working hard to catch up, and the Velekans should do the same. We have been working on the creation of a wormhole for over a century now, and we've had a very promising breakthrough."

"With your new technology, the Galactic Committee will beg your species to join them," the Velekan commander said. "More wine?"

The Crustan commander held up his glass, and a female servant rushed to his side and filled it.

"Leave us," the Velekan commander said to her.

"We don't want to be accepted by the Galactic Committee. Let's join forces," the Crustan commander said when they were alone. "We can help you upgrade your warships, especially your communications technology."

"We lost all the data we obtained from M-9 when the Beltese destroyed our warships," the Velekan said.

"The Velekans put fear into this galaxy. The Agoorons are still shaking in their boots."

"They refused to be our friends or share their technology, and worst of all, they laughed in our faces."

The Crustan adjusted the shell that covered his genitals. "The first thing we will do is upgrade your communication abilities. You will no longer rely on ship-to-ship communication, and you will transmit just as well as the Beltese."

"When do we start?" the Velekan commander asked.

"Now. We have engineers aboard our ship who can begin the process. We can teach you everything you need to know."

The Velekan nodded. "Good. We would like to upgrade our zircolon cores, but we lost most of our ships during the Beltese Invasion. A hundred years is a long time to be forced from space and killing Commander Celt Sedo didn't even the score."

"Set up a production facility on planet Onupa. There are many caves there where you can produce zircolon cores in secrecy. The complete assembly can take place on our planet. The Beltese are not monitoring our operations."

A wide grin spread across the Velekan's face. "The Crustans are our only true friends," he said. "Thank you for your help so far. Does the Galactic Committee suspect us to be allies?"

"No. They haven't a clue where you received your new warship technology."

"Together, we can defeat the Beltese and others who interfere. Are we friends?" the Velekan asked.

"Yes," the Crustan commander said. "We are willing to be your ally—on two conditions."

"Conditions?"

"Yes. We purchase 70% of the fireflies from the Velekans."

"If you share your technology with us, we'll sell you 100% of the fireflies."

"We are not greedy," the Crustan said. "70% will suffice."

"Your other request?" the Velekan asked.

"Educate your females and make them equal to males. This is for your benefit."

"What?" The Velekan leaned forward in his chair.

"Females are great contributors to our technology, and Velekans should consider the important roles of females as other species have. Our wormhole data has been greatly contributed to by females."

"Females," the Velekan shouted.

"We will only share our technology with you if you are willing to incorporate females into your educational society."

"But that's none of the Crustans' concern."

"Those are my leaders' demands. The Velekans can start them out on computers. How hard can it be?"

"I can't make such a decision."

The Crustan crossed his legs, his huge feet almost touching the Velekan's leg. "But as commander, you can greatly influence your leaders. Trust me, with educated females in your society, your species will become twice as smart. Our females lead the zircolon mining process on Onupa. They can improve your technology greatly. You can trade the quartogolite crystals you mine for zircolon."

"We will consider it," the Velekan commander said as he lowered his head.

"We are tired of the Beltese dictating to us. They are trying to force us to leave Onupa, because we have human slaves there who mine zircolon. With the creation of the wormhole, we will be the galactic leaders." He raised his glass and toasted his new friendship. "To a new beginning."

The Velekan laughed, then hesitated. "But what about Captain Sedo? She could be of great concern."

"She is not on Tandon most of the time. Even if she's there, she will be just as surprised as the other Beltese citizens."

"A new beginning." The Velekan nodded. "With a wormhole, they won't know what hit them. We can appear above their planet without warning. But what about other galactic members? They will retaliate."

"Once they learn what happened to the Beltese, they will not dare attack us. The wormhole is still in the developmental stage, but we hope to perfect it within the next two years."

The Velekan nodded again.

The Crustan's feelers detected excitement from the Velekan.

"We will become the most feared leaders in this galaxy."

CHAPTER 10

THE EASTERN DYNASTY

Planet Onupa in the Quadra 6 Solar System
Lin, a young girl of fifteen, rushed down a wide path that meandered along a river and through the forest, separating two villages.

Nervous about being recognized, she hesitated and glanced from side to side. Peasants sometimes took shelter in the forest, and she didn't want anyone to see her. Her customs forbade women from meeting men without chaperones. Nonetheless, she continued to meet with Ming.

Like her mother, Lin was short and petite with a pretty, round face. A long, black braid with a string tied at the end dangled down to her lower back. She gripped the handle of an empty basket with her left hand and secured a shawl around her head and shoulders with her right. A long, shapeless dress, wet with dew, danced around her bare ankles. Moving like a windblown leaf, she dodged the oxen and pig manure that littered the path and jumped over puddles, remnants of the night's rain.

Willows grew along the river. Branches from giant redwoods creaked and swayed overhead like green clouds, dripping water as their leaves trembled in the gentle breeze that cooled the early summer morning.

Lin lived in Gong Ho, a small village in the Eastern Dynasty, and her soon-to-be groom, Ming Chi Chang, lived in an even smaller, nameless farming village. Their fathers had arranged their marriage at her birth.

Tossing a glance over her left shoulder, Lin saw the back of a peasant whom she'd just passed fade into the swirling fog. The fear of someone catching her with her lover terrified her, but the desire to hold him was overwhelming. Quickening her pace, she ducked into dense foliage where she found Ming leaning against their tree, a large redwood. A thicket of bushes and smaller trees surrounded the area.

"Ming," Lin whispered. Rushing forward, she graced him with a warm smile. "I can't stay long."

Ming's eyes sparkled with lust, and he beamed at the sight of her. "My beautiful butterfly."

Ming had a slender frame, a lean, honest face, short bangs, and shoulder-length raven hair. Like his brothers, he had inherited his height from his maternal grandfather and was taller than the other men in both villages. A baggy shang, secured around his waist with a tie, covered the lower part of his body. A long-sleeved V-neck yi covered his chest and fell below his waist.

Lin would move in with Ming and his family after

their wedding. His two sisters had moved in with their husbands' families in Gong Ho, and his two brothers had taken their wives into Ming's family house.

She ripped off her shawl, threw it into the basket, and dropped them onto the wet leaves that blanketed the ground. Then they swiftly embraced, with Ming's masculine chest pressing against Lin's face. The closeness of their bodies excited her, and she savored his warmth. On tiptoes, she wrapped both arms around Ming's neck, kissed his cheeks, and passionately rubbed her face across his narrow chin.

With hands around Lin's waist, Ming picked her up and pressed her back against the tree. He groped her small breasts with both hands, then he fumbled with her dress and managed to lift it to her waist. Ming untied his shang and let it drop to the ground.

Lin grasped his erect male part and caressed it, enjoying its size and stiffness.

His calloused fingers climbed up the soft skin between her thighs and ended in her velvet hair. He gripped her buttocks with both hands, squeezed hard, and penetrated her.

With her back pressed against the tree, Ming ravished her with raw passion. Lin groaned as Ming buried his face into her neck, biting it softly. They kissed each other's lips, and she ran her hands across the broadness of his back, caressing his shoulders. Within the safety and security of his arms, she didn't want their lovemaking to end. Ming's touch was sensuous, his masculine desires exhilarating. The intensity of their passion magnified until he wet her, emitting a series of groans.

"We need to get married, and soon," she whispered.

Ming snuggled his chin in her hair. "We can continue to meet like this until we do," he suggested.

"What if someone catches us?"

"No one knows about us," Ming said. "Don't worry."

"You know what will happen to me if we're caught?"

He held her tighter. "Nothing is going to happen."

She felt the rhythm of their hearts. "You promise?"

"Yes."

Lin abruptly jumped, breaking away from Ming's arms. "I must go."

He eyed the empty basket on the ground, pulled up his shang, and tied it at the waist. "Where?"

She straightened her dress. "To your village for eggs and vegetables. My father told me not to trade with yours, because they're not speaking to each other. I heard my parents whispering this morning, something about our wedding."

"Could you make out anything?"

"Not really." She retrieved her shawl, wrapped it around her head, and tied it under her neck. "I heard your name, your father's name, and 'marriage.' Father was very angry."

Ming laughed. "They're acting like children."

"They'll have to get along once we're married," Lin said.

Ming placed a hand on the small of her back. "Let me walk with you."

"We can't be seen together without a chaperone. Wait here. Give me time to reach your village."

He leaned his head against hers and whispered into her ear.

"We'll be married soon and won't have to sneak around. Can we meet here in five days, the same time?"

"Yes, I'm sure I can find a way, but now I must go."

Ming held her hand in both of his. "Please, stay longer. Tell your mother you met your friend, Gea."

She pulled away. "I've told her that story four times already."

"Make up another one."

"Next time," Lin said.

He released her hand. "Goodbye, my beautiful butterfly."

She grabbed her basket, peeked through the bushes, and dashed away.

Both families would honor Lin and Ming's wedding, a wondrous festival. Lin loved Ming and would do anything he wished. She would marry him and later give birth to his child, fulfilling her life as a wife and as a woman.

***

Ming lingered around the swollen river, giving Lin enough time to reach his village.

The muddy brown stream had overflowed its embankment and spilled onto the marshy grassland. He stood at the edge of the rushing water and watched a fish leap above the surface in an attempt to feed on something he couldn't make out. A raccoon left the water on the opposite side, a mother bird fed her young from a nest in a nearby tree, and white water surged around impeding logs and rocks.

Ming walked slowly back to his home, knowing his chores would be delayed until near sunset. He saw nature as never before and enjoyed its beauty. He whistled a tune and skipped a few steps along the way. He returned to a typical home, identical to peasant dwellings, only larger. The house consisted of rammed earth with a thatched roof and a single door at the front. After removing his muddy wooden sandals, Ming dipped them into a large bowl of water just outside the door. He then stepped inside and stood on a dirt floor covered with straw.

"Ming, you missed your meal." His mother escorted him into the kitchen lit only by the sunlight shining through an open shutter. "The food is barely warm."

He took a seat on the floor at the edge of the table and his mother served him a rice dish with chicken and vegetables, millet soup, and green tea. Securing two small sticks between his fingers, he began to eat.

"We didn't know where you were," his mother said. "Have you been with your friend?"

He smacked his lips. "No, I just went for a walk."

"Your father is out back. He needs to speak with you when you've finished."

It didn't take Ming long to gulp down his food and slurp the last of his tea.

He walked into the backyard, where he found his father cleaning a rabbit under a nearby tree.

Ming's father, Yu Fong, was balding and shorter than Ming, with weathered skin. He sat on a soggy bench made from tree branches. A rabbit's fur and intestines lay on the ground on one side of him and a bowl of water sat on the other. Fine gray rabbit hairs littered the carcass. He had removed the feet but not the head, because he liked to eat the eyes and brain with steamed rice or eggs. His father wore a simple yi and shang like Ming's, but his clothes hung loosely on his small frame.

"You asked to speak with me, Father?"

"Where have you been?" Yu Fong asked.

"Walking in the forest along the river, thinking about my wedding day."

Yu Fong turned his head and sneezed. "I'm sending you to Trong to barter for me while we prepare for your wedding. We need fabric, tea, and bamboo leaves. The children need sandals, and your mother needs herbs. You must leave the day after tomorrow at dawn."

Ming couldn't believe what he'd heard. "But, Father, that's a two-day journey."

The old man exposed his rotten teeth in a wide grin. "You need more experience and responsibilities, since you're becoming a married man. After all, this farm will be part yours one day."

Hearing that, Ming was overjoyed. "I'll make you proud, Father."

His father peered up at him, squinting through sunrays that filtered through the tree leaves. Dirt was wedged under his worn fingernails, and his hands glistened with blood. He dipped the rabbit into the bowl of water and washed it. "I've found you a new bride, a more suitable girl."

Ming's mouth dropped, and he stood frozen for a moment. "But ... but ... Lin and I are to be married."

"That wedding is off. I informed her father this morning. Cong has been most untrustworthy. He cheated me out of many eggs and three chickens, and this is not the first time. He's no longer my friend, and his daughter is not welcome into our family—our home."

"But, Father—"

Yu Fong smiled. "Your new bride is not as pretty as Lin, but her family has plenty. She shall come with a most handsome dowry."

"But, Father, I must marry Lin."

"No, you can't marry her. Your bride-to-be lives near Trong. Her family has a farm like ours with much more land, and they own four peasants. They know we're not wealthy, but we're proud and honest."

"But ... but Lin?"

"No. Not her. You'll marry your new bride in ten days."

Ming couldn't move his limbs. "No, Father. I'll not marry this new girl. You promised me Lin. We love each other, and I'll marry only her."

His father rose. "Don't use that tone of voice with me." Ming stomped closer and glanced down at his father. "I'll marry Lin, and you can't stop me."

"That family has bad blood," his father said.

"You and Lin's father have had a disagreement, but that has nothing to do with us," Ming protested. "Lin is a wonderful girl, and I'm marrying her."

His father shook a finger at Ming. "You'll marry the girl I pick. It's the father's decision, not the son's. If you marry Lin, you'll no longer be a part of this family. Do your chores and think about living with her as a peasant for the rest of your life."

Ming didn't respond but walked away to think about his future without his family's support.

As he dumped food for six sows and multiple piglets into a hollowed-out tree trunk near the forest, his father's words echoed in his mind. Marrying Lin meant immediate expulsion from his family, and he would end up a peasant for the rest of his life, scrounging through the forest for food or working long, hard hours for two meals a day. He couldn't reason with his father. He had no choice but to forget Lin and learn to resist his feelings for her. She didn't exist anymore. That part of his life was over.

He needed to be strong, prove he was a man, move forward, and marry his new bride.

***

The next afternoon, when Lin met her lover in the forest, the sun beamed brightly in the clear blue sky. Muddy puddles had disappeared, and everything seemed greener and livelier than the day before.

Gasping for air and trying to catch her breath, she rushed to Ming. "Gea said you have an urgent message for me? We're not supposed to meet today. I'm sorry I took so long, but I had a hard time getting away." On tiptoes, she reached up, cupped his chin in her hands, and tried to kiss him. "My mother—"

Ming stepped back and forced her hands away. "Lin, Lin."

She first noticed his eyes, cold and distant. When she touched him again, he withdrew. A grim expression clouded his face, and he didn't attempt to embrace her. Ming nervously shifted from foot to foot. His eyes focused on the ground, the forest, the sky, never meeting hers.

"What's wrong?" she asked.

"Our wedding is canceled. Didn't your father tell you?"

She backed up and studied his face, trying to read his expression. She gasped and shook her head. "No. It can't be. You must be my husband."

"I can't ever see you again. I have a new bride, and we're to marry in nine days."

She stared into space for a moment, letting the impact of his words sink into her mind.

Taking his tensed hand, she squeezed it, and for a third time he pulled away. Her gaze never left his distant eyes. She shuddered and couldn't utter a word. Her stomach felt queasy, and she tasted bile. "You can marry me if you wish. We can leave this village." Her face wrinkled as tears flooded her eyes and tumbled down her cheeks.

"If we defy our fathers, we'll be outcasts, peasants for the rest of our lives," Ming said. "I can't support a family."

"Marry me anyway," she begged through nervous sobs.

He shook his head. "I can't."

Weeping, she said, "Ming, I'm with child. You must marry me."

He hissed out his words and stepped away from her. "Child? How ... how could this happen?"

Her body stiffened. "Where do you think babies come from?"

His eyes focused on her stomach. "Are you sure?"

"We must marry right away," she persisted.

"How long?" he asked.

"Two months. I planned to tell you after our wedding."

During the silence between them, Lin didn't hear anything but the sound of the rushing river and her father's raucous shouts, calling her a whore. Realizing the predicament she now faced alone, her legs became so weak she could hardly stand.

"Father won't allow it," Ming said. "I can't be a peasant for the rest of my life."

Lin stood transfixed. "You know what will happen to

me, being with child and no husband?" Profound fear chilled her like the icy water flowing through the nearby river. "I have dishonored my family. I … I will be beheaded. Your child grows inside me, and I can't stop it. Please, marry me."

Ming's voice was flat and adamant. "There's nothing I can do."

When his eyes finally met hers, his gaze appeared stern and cold. To her astonishment, his love had disappeared. She detected no empathy or sorrow on his face.

She cried out in a wretched voice, "You don't care if I'm killed." She could no longer restrain her fury. "Even if we are peasants, we'd be together. Maybe our parents will learn to accept our marriage and allow us to return."

He squinted his narrow eyes. "You knew our customs forbade meeting without a chaperone. You should never have allowed me to touch you until after our wedding."

Lin growled through sobs, her anger sharper now. "You're blaming me?"

Ming stared at her with icy eyes. "It was your idea."

She shook her head in disbelief. Who was this person? Not the man who had loved her yesterday and couldn't wait to get married. How could his feelings change overnight? She didn't know him at all. "I did it because we were getting married. You can't do this to me."

Ming turned and lumbered away, then stopped and glanced over his shoulder at her one last time. "Goodbye, Lin."

Her outstretched hand grasped air, her stomach lurched, and her knees buckled. "No, Ming, no." She stared at his back through floods of tears as he disappeared through the bushes.

She had submitted to him, given him marital privileges, and now he had abandoned her—condemned her to death. She had to find a way to save her life, protect herself. With both hands, she dug her fingers into her stomach. She wanted the baby to disappear.

She wanted it dead.

***

When Ming returned home, he found his father on a bended knee, filling the bottom of a pushcart with vegetables.

"You disappeared yesterday, now today. We must get the rabbits, chickens, and eggs ready for delivery. Where have you been?" Yu Fong snapped.

Ming swallowed hard and lowered his head. "I'm sorry, Father, but I met with Lin."

His father used a hand to support himself on the cart as he stood, his eyes wild and furious. "You went to her house?"

"No, I met her at a secret place to say goodbye."

Yu Fong shouted and approached him with a raised hand. "Without a chaperone? How long have you been seeing her?"

Ming turned his head and flinched, waiting for the blow that never came. When he faced his father again, his hand remained in midair. "Just a few times to discuss our wedding."

"I forbid you to meet her again. Do you understand?"

"But ... Father."

"Lin no longer exists, and I don't want to hear her name again," his father said.

When Ming didn't respond, his father dropped his hand and stared up into his son's eyes. "Do I make myself clear?"

Ming eyed the ground. "Yes, Father."

"Now, help me get everything ready for your journey tomorrow. Spend the night at Heng's house and leave the cart there. Do you remember the places we stopped during our last two trips?"

Ming responded with a solemn nod.

***

Late the next night, a persistent pounding on Yu Fong Chi Chang's door sprung everyone in the household to life.

Yu Fong reluctantly answered, standing in the doorway, wearing only his shang. He became fully alert when he saw Cong and his three sons standing before him with a crowd of about fifty men, all carrying torches. He blinked several times to clear his vision. "Why are you waking us at this time of night?"

"Where's Ming?" Cong roared.

"He left at dawn, bartering for me. The wedding is off, and you have no business with my son. Why did you bring these men here?"

The stone-faced crowd made him shiver. Yu Fong had witnessed two such gatherings in his lifetime, and each meant death to the families they visited.

Cong approached Yu Fong, holding a stick. "Ming forced himself on my daughter, more than once," Cong bellowed. "She's with child, and no man will ever marry her now. When the child is born, I'll kill it."

Yu Fong's eyebrows arched into a deeper frown. "Ming wouldn't do such a thing. Your daughter is not allowed to meet him without a chaperone."

He thought about the secret meeting place Ming had mentioned and the times he'd thought he detected the scent of a woman on him.

Cong stepped closer. "You've already accused me of being a thief. Now you're calling my daughter a whore?"

Yu Fong opened his mouth to speak, but before he could respond, Cong hit him in the face with the stick he carried. Yu Fong landed on the floor, staring up at three strong men who stormed in and jerked him to his feet.

"Bring 'em all out," yelled a man from the group.

Cong's voice echoed through the night. "I'll avenge my daughter's honor."

As the men forced Yu Fong into the yard, he coughed and spat blood that ran down the front of his bony chest.

Gaining his balance, he fought against the men, but they firmly held him.

When Yu Fong's two sons rushed outside, the vicious mob attacked them too. They were beaten, kicked, and dragged into the center of the crowd.

His wife's small frame hovered in the doorway. "What's happening?"

Yu Fong watched as two men approached her. One grabbed her by her hair and slammed her head into the side of the doorway. They clutched her under both arms and dragged her outside.

"Don't hurt her," Yu Fong pleaded as tears welled up in his eyes.

Cong raised his torch high into the air. In the flickering light, his eyes grew wilder as he spoke. "Your son has committed a crime, and your entire family will pay. Ming's crime is punishable by death."

Yu Fong's wife gasped, holding the side of her bloody head. "What?"

"Cong claims that Ming took advantage of Lin," Yu Fong said to his wife. "She's with child."

Yu Fong's wife yelled, "It's a lie."

"Men who take advantage of girls must die," Cong said. "So must the parents of such an evil child, and your bad blood flows through all of your children."

Yu Fong saw the fear on his wife's face. He wanted to comfort her and protect his family. He had never felt so helpless in his life, so he lunged at the nearest man and grabbed him around the neck. "You can't take matters into your own hands. Summon our elder."

"You mean your friend, Manchu," Cong corrected.

"My daughter told us what Ming did to her, and she doesn't lie. She wasn't good enough to marry, so Ming abused her."

The men from Cong's village would obey his orders without question. Over the years, he had become a man of great stature.

"No honorable girl would meet a man without a chaperone," his wife shouted. "You and your whole family are liars, crooks, and thieves."

Cong punched her twice in the face, and she collapsed onto the ground while the mob restrained Yu Fong and his sons.

Several men forced his two daughters-in-law outside, along with all five grandchildren. Both women clutched infants and fought against the controlling mob that pushed them along with their family.

Neighbors in the distance must have seen the burning torches that lit the night and heard the screams and loud voices.

But still, no one stirred. If his friends didn't rescue them, the Chi Chang family would be doomed.

The mob forced the accused family deep into the forest, barefoot and half naked. Staggering blindly in front of the crowd, they tripped over branches, fell over logs, and plowed through thick bushes, ending the journey at the edge of a huge, freshly dug pit. The flickering torches revealed an incredible sight. Yu Fong's eyes bulged at the ghastly horror before him. Flies swarmed over the bodies of his two daughters and their children, who lay criss-crossed in the bottom of the pit.

Screams erupted from his wife and daughters-in-law. His wife threw up. "My daughters, my grandchildren." She fell to her knees, hugged herself, and touched the ground with her head.

Yu Fong's sons-in-laws, Sheng and Jun, sat on a mound of dirt, their tattered clothes stained with blood.

A dozen men stood guard over them with sticks.

***

Sheng's newborn son lay on top of his wife's body with his skull caved in, his skin tinged gray.

Her hair covered the lower half of the infant and was caked with blood from both her and the baby. His heart ached, and a pain of hatred stirred from deep within.

"No." Sheng heard his mother-in-law cry. "Please, let the children go."

He had already witnessed the killing of his wife and children, and now Yu Fong. Men in the group bashed his head with rocks and sticks. One by one, he saw the entire Chi Chang family's lives end as the mob slaughtered them and threw their bodies into the pit. His mother-in-law had watched the murder of her husband, sons, and grandchildren.

She didn't struggle but surrendered to death.

One of Sheng's sister-in-laws jumped into the pit with the bodies of her husband and children.

Two peasants passed Sheng, crept to the edge of the mound like frightened dogs, and hesitated before peeking in.

Cong yelled from the other side as he stepped into the light. "You two. Finish covering this hole, and I'll reward you with plenty of food for you and your families. Do you know who I am?"

Both peasants gave a submissive nod.

"Be at my home tomorrow, when the sun is directly overhead," Cong said. He then turned his attention to Sheng and the other remaining in-laws. His face showed no remorse. "I'm sorry you married into such an evil family."

Sheng heard his own voice croak, "You murdered my family."

Cong didn't reply but turned and walked away.

One of the peasants pointed a shaky finger. "But ... a woman is still alive."

"Bury her," Cong ordered over his shoulder.

The crowd gave the peasants a few torches and disappeared into the night.

Sheng helped the peasants remove his sister-in-law from the pit before they covered the bodies.

He had to warn Ming before he returned.

***

Ming heard someone call his name and turned at the sound of Sheng's voice.

Dry blood covered the front of Sheng's yi and matted the left side of his head. Scabs covered his face, neck, and hands. He had two swollen shut black eyes, and Ming wondered how he could see.

"What happened to you?" Ming asked.

Sheng paused to catch his breath. "Lots. I've been walking half the night, trying to catch up with you."

"What's wrong? Is it Mother?"

"It's your whole family."

"What? What?" Ming asked impatiently.

"Lin … she accused you of forcing yourself on her. Cong and members of our village killed your entire family—even my wife and children."

"What?"

"They killed everyone in your family and buried them in the forest."

Ming stood motionless, his heart throbbing out of control, making it difficult to breathe. "Killed?"

Tears squeezed through swollen eyes and rolled down his brother-in-law's face. "They're all dead. Cong convinced our village that your entire family had to pay with their lives, because it's our custom." He coughed several times to clear his throat, then continued. "There were too many of them."

Ming screamed and dropped the load from his back. "No. My family."

"The men obeyed Cong," Sheng said.

Ming wiped tears from his cheeks and stared into oblivion. His legs weakened, but he still managed to stand. Bile rose and erupted from his mouth. He coughed and threw up again, staggering and reeling from shock, his body melting to the ground. He rolled over onto his side, his chest heaving.

Sheng dropped to his knees. "They forced us to watch."

Ming sobbed for a long time before speaking again. "I'm going back to kill everyone who helped Cong murder them." Sitting up, he raised a fist and pounded air. "Cong and his family will be the first to die. And Lin, I'll make her suffer."

"You'll be killed if you return."

"Did you recognize them, all of them?"

"Yes, even the old man who used to make us wooden toys."

Sheng conveyed the events that had taken place during the night.

He spared no details.

Ming lowered his head and continued to sob. "I'll kill them in the middle of the night while they sleep," he vowed. "I'll kill a different family every night."

"No, Ming," Sheng pleaded. "You must keep traveling to a place where Cong can't find you."

"Our elder, Manchu allowed this to happen?" Ming asked.

"Your village knew nothing about it. All the men came from mine, and they came in the middle of the night."

Ming covered his face with both hands and mumbled, "My entire family, gone. I didn't force Lin."

"I know," Sheng said. "I saw you and her together in the forest once."

Ming crawled to his feet, grabbed Sheng by his yi, and viciously shook him. "And you didn't defend me? You allowed them to murder my family and yours?"

"Cong called me a liar. Said he would kill me if I repeated it again." Sheng lowered his head. "Don't you think I wanted to save my own family?"

"You could have."

"If you were there, you would've done the same thing."

"Save myself, you mean," Ming said accusingly.

Sheng nodded toward the bundle on the ground. "You still have things to barter with?"

Ming blinked tears from his eyes. "Yes. I—"

"Use what you have left to start a new life. You can get a better bargain in the City of the Dynasty."

"Lin said I wouldn't get away with refusing to marry her, but I never—"

"Your father was right about her family. They're untrustworthy. Now killers."

Ming blew out an exasperated breath. "I don't have any place to go."

"You must keep traveling."

Ming shook his head. "It can't be true. It just can't be."

Sheng stood. "If I can find you, so can Cong. Good luck, Ming."

"But the house, the farm?"

"My brother and I will take care of it," Sheng said.

The men hugged each other farewell.

"Thanks for warning me," Ming yelled at Sheng's back.

His brother-in-law turned and waved goodbye.

Ming spent the remainder of the day sitting under a tree, gazing across the landscape, but his eyes captured nothing. He spent the night there as well, never sleeping, just concentrating on his sad life and trying to collect his thoughts. He suffered a vague detachment—an emptiness that nothing could fill. He had caused the dishonoring and death of his family. He remembered the pride on his father's face the morning he had left. At seventeen summers old, he had no home or work. If he had married Lin, his family would still be alive.

Ironically, he would end up a peasant after all.

***

The next morning, Ming continued westward.

Weary and dazed, he trudged forward, passing numerous travelers, peasants and commoners like himself. He saw an entire family of eight moving their possessions toward the countryside. A beautiful wedding occurred in one village. Later, he pushed his way through a cluster of people and stopped near the front. A man approached his victim and raised his pike high into the air, ready to dismember a thief's head. A woman's scream ripped through the early morning as she fell to her knees, clutching a baby. Before the weapon made contact with its target, Ming pushed back through the crowd.

At nightfall, he made a bed of leaves near the main trail. Exhausted, yet restless, he tossed and turned most of the night.

On the third day, at around dusk, Ming was walking along a desolate trail at a slow pace, his thumbs hinged under the straps of his load to prevent its weight from digging into his shoulders. The sun had dipped below the horizon, and the sky had turned a dark orange under a full moon. Fatigue had overwhelmed Ming. He could hardly keep his eyes open.

He had become so weary that he hardly reacted when leaves crunched, bushes rattled, and four men stormed out of the forest and surrounded him. Long, ratty hair hung down the men's backs. They wore tattered clothes and exuded the stench of rotten eggs.

The shortest and oldest man whacked a stick in the palm of his left hand, blocking Ming's path. He cocked his head and studied Ming. "Hey, what are you carrying on your back?"

"I have nothing," Ming replied. "I'm just a peasant."

The man smiled, exposing rotten teeth. "You're not dressed like a peasant. Do you take us for fools?"

"I have nothing of value," Ming repeated.

"Let's see what he's carrying," the man said.

The other three men rushed Ming. Knocking him to the ground, they forced the roll from his back.

The one holding the stick laughed but kept his distance. "Open it."

Ming jumped to his feet and struggled with the three men, in an attempt to retrieve his belongings.

He punched one in the face with a powerful blow, sending him to the ground.

His fist sank into another's gut, and the man let out a loud groan. The man holding Ming's possessions tried to run, but Ming jumped on his back, forcing him into the dirt as well. As Ming turned on his side, a dark figure loomed over him, holding a stick in the air. Ming rolled over as the stick crashed to the ground. He grabbed the stick and hit the man on the head, causing him to collapse in a heap. He gored a recovering man in his stomach and hit another in the face, and he and the fourth man tussled over the stick until Ming drove a knee into his assailant's groin, making him howl out in pain.

The men were small and wiry, and their strength was no match for him, even in his depleted state. After he knocked two to the ground, the others fled.

Ming beat the remaining men with the stick until exhaustion forced him to stop.

Ming didn't have to kill them, but he did. Their bones cracked, and warm blood spattered all over his body. Killing the thieves brought relief, as if he were somehow avenging the murder of his family. His heart raced as he caught his breath, and he shook in disbelief at what he had done. He'd killed two men yet felt no remorse. He had never hurt anyone in his life.

Now everyone in the world infuriated him.

One of the men had been carrying a rabbit-skin pouch with two divided sections. He opened it and found dried vegetables and chopsticks inside one section and a wooden bowl and a dirty rag in the other. He kept the pouch and discarded the rag.

Walking into the forest in the direction the thieves had come from, he found their campsite, where meat roasted over a small fire. He took the rabbit and ate it as he walked.

He traveled half the night, then left the trail and fell asleep against a tree in the forest.

When Ming sputtered awake the next morning, he winced from a headache. The sun stood high in the sky. Dizzily, he staggered to his feet. He had overslept, but then he remembered he had no place to go, and the pain in his head forced him down again.

He slept until midday and started his journey again, his head still throbbing.

***

Days later, Ming reached Mongu, the village where the emperor of the Eastern Dynasty resided.

The trail led into the middle of the village. It was larger and filthier than Gong Ho. Traders of roasted rats, insects, chickens, eggs, and vegetables of every kind crowded both sides of the passage. The stench of fish and human excrement filled the air, and Ming wrinkled his nose in disgust. He had expected the City of the Eastern Dynasty to be clean and elegant.

A woman opened a door and threw dirty water from a pot onto his feet. She didn't apologize but simply walked back inside and closed the door. Ming approached another woman, with a painted white face, standing near a passage. "Can you tell me where I can barter things?" he asked.

She turned her back to Ming. "Go away."

Looking around, he saw groups of men squatting around in four different circles, chatting and sipping tea.

He stopped at the nearest group. "Excuse me, but—"

"Don't interrupt our game," one of the men snapped.

Ming walked around in search of a promising shop and found one. He entered a small room stocked with valuables. It contained clothing and other items he could never afford. Most things he recognized, others he had never seen before.

A well-dressed woman, plump and short with the glow of wealth, was trading rare stones for a fine comb and other goods.

Standing just inside the doorway, afraid to move or touch anything, he waited for the woman to leave.

The woman threw an inquisitive glance at him as she departed.

The old shopkeeper beckoned Ming forward. "Bring your things here and put them on the table, my son. If they have been stolen, you'll be put to death."

The man reminded Ming of his father. He was short and thin, and walked with a slight limp.

"They're not stolen. I swear it," Ming said in an honorable tone.

The old man helped him remove the contents. "Let's see what you've got."

The man scrutinized each piece. "Uh-huh. Good."

Ming didn't want strange women wearing his mother's elegant shawls, but he had no choice but to part with them. Painted fans, bowls, and chopsticks, made by his sisters-in-laws, would be lost but not forgotten.

The owner examined the needlework. "Yes. This is very good. Excellent. Can you bring me more?"

Ming shook his head, and his eyes welled up. "They were my mother's. She's dead."

The man never took his eyes from the items. "Sorry for your loss."

Ming kept two painted bowls, two pairs of chopsticks, and one of his mother's shawls.

He would marry one day and pass them on to his wife.

His heart sank when he left the shop. He had used his family's work to move forward in life. The old man had traded him bartering stones, which he had heard of but never owned until now. They filled the small side of his pouch.

With the stones, Ming acquired a new yi and shang and discarded the bloody ones.

Then, glad to leave Mongu, he continued his journey westward.

Three days from Mongu, he stopped at a farm where a man and three young girls tilled the land.

"I'll work for food," Ming said.

The man, drenched in sweat, glanced at him and started working again.

Ming raised a sleeve and flexed the muscle of his right arm. "I'm strong and a good worker."

The farmer turned, frowned, and nodded toward a stick attached to leather straps. "All right, help move the soil."

The man's wife brought Ming a bowl of soup, and he greedily guzzled it down and went to work. That evening, he received a generous portion of food.

***

He slept with the chickens and remained there for three days.

"Stay," the man said on the morning of Ming's departure. "You have no home. You're a good worker, and as you see, I have no sons. You and I can make this farm prosper. Three years from now, you can marry my oldest daughter."

The girl was ugly, with eyes like a frog, and Ming wanted no part of her. "I must go, but if I return, I'll consider your offer."

The family gave him dried fish, rice, and vegetables for his journey.

CHAPTER 11

PLANET KODAS IN THE NEGMAN SOLAR SYSTEM

The Return of the Velekans

Sax felt sunlight on his face. "What," he yelled and sat up in bed.

His wife rose beside him.

Three tall creatures with gray skin and bald heads stood in his room, their bodies bent over to prevent their heads from hitting the ceiling.

One of the things pointed a long finger at Sax. "You're the leader of this clan?"

The thing's voice didn't come from its mouth, but from its side.

A small sun in the palm of the creature's hand lit the entire room, giving Sax more than enough light to make out the thing's features. "What are you?"

"I am Mogayron: a Velekan god," the thing answered. "We made a deal with Brye. We trade livestock for rocks from the mine. With the exception of skeletal remains, the pits are empty, and we need the rocks."

Sax didn't answer, only stared back in shock.

The thing stepped closer to his bed. "We need answers."

"The Lords are dead," Sax said. "That clan no longer exists."

"We have livestock to exchange for rocks," the thing said again.

Sax jumped to his feet. "We don't need livestock."

"You shall continue mining," the intruder said.

"We're not slaves anymore," Sax nervously blurted out. "We don't work the mines. We have no need or desire to—"

"Meet with your councilmen," Mogayron said. "You must start working the mine tomorrow."

"My clan is asleep," Sax said.

The door flew open and the other seven council members tumbled into his small bedroom.

Burle, second-in-command, shielded his eyes as he stared at the bright light. "What's happening? What are these strange things? What's he holding: a small sun?"

Sax pointed to the intruders. "They call themselves Velekans. Brye traded them the rocks we collected each summer. I don't know what makes the light."

"You'll mine rocks for us," the creature insisted again. "Both pits shall be full—and soon."

The bare-chested Sax pointed a shaky finger at the door. "Get out. We're not slaves anymore, and we refuse to work for you."

"We are gods," the thing offensively blurted out. "I dare you to defy us."

"You're not gods, but devils," Sax yelled. "If you were gods, you wouldn't need us to collect the rocks. The mountain is just there. Get them yourselves."

Sax's wife scooted near the edge of the bed and clutched his arm. "Go away. Leave us alone."

"Your clan will start working tomorrow, or you will all be killed," the Velekan said.

"We have guards," Sax warned. "We killed The Lords and can defeat you—whatever you are—as well."

***

Burle, second-in-command to Sax, saw a Velekan pull an object from a pouch on his side.

The Velekan gripped the bulky part and pointed the round end at Sax, and a green light hit Sax in the chest. Sax fell backward onto his bed and jerked with pain.

"Sax. Oh, Sax." his wife screamed when she saw her husband slumped over, trying to sit. She sat beside him and held his cheeks in her hands.

The strangers covered their ears with their hands.

A Velekan yelled, "Stop that noise."

Sax's wife continued screaming until a Velekan struck her with the light.

Burle cowered in fear when the three things faced him.

As Sax recovered, he grabbed his sword from the side of his bed and plunged it into the chest of the nearest Velekan. One of the creatures quickly turned and hit him in the torso with a red light. Sax grasped his chest and slithered to the floor.

The sword remained in the creature for only a moment, until both disappeared.

Sax's wife stirred on the bed. When she screamed again, a red light struck her in the chest, and she collapsed on top of her husband, burn marks on her clothes.

Burle's whisper was almost inaudible. "They killed them, didn't they?" he said, more to himself.

The Velekan showed no remorse. "These two no longer exist. If you refuse to work, we'll kill you and all of your clan."

The shock sent Burle reeling backward into the group. "But ... you didn't have to kill them."

Now leader of the Saxons, he didn't know what to do or say. Realizing the Velekans would kill his clan left him no choice but to comply with their demands. He had never been so frightened and confused in all his life. Burle trembled, and his head buzzed with uncertainty. The Velekans had weapons he had never imagined. Killing with lights—without flames—petrified him.

The Velekan's red eyes glared at Burle. "We'll remain here to oversee your work."

***

Overnight, Jason and his clan had once again become slaves. At sunrise, men, women, and children worked the mines, performing long, tedious hours of hard labor. Even the elderly loaded the carts.

Jason resumed his old workstation and chiseled away at the rocks, as he had last summer.

"What are these strange things?" Ian asked. "Have you taken a good look at them?"

"A carrier told me about them last summer," Jason said. "They live and travel in something that looks like a rock, and it can move faster than the eye can see."

Ben threw a large stone into a heaping pile. "I've heard rumors, but—"

"They claim to be gods, but Burle doesn't think so," Jason said. "Sax stabbed one before they killed him, and Burle thinks he died. His body disappeared—with Sax's sword in his chest."

Ben gasped, "If they have such powers, they must be gods."

Ian heaved a rock and threw it on the pile. "We must find a way to defeat them."

Ben removed his sweaty mouth cloth and wiped dust from his face. "The Lords used to trade them rocks for livestock. Why would they want rocks?"

Ian took a gulp of water from his pouch and swallowed. "So, that's where all the livestock came from every year. They didn't want us to know about the devils."

"The Velekan told Burle we must have the pits filled by the end of each summer or they'll kill us all," Ben said.

Jason tripped over Ben's foot and held on to the wall to stay upright. "They've killed all but three councilmen," he said.

"Why?" asked Ian.

Jason glanced over his shoulders. "I don't know, but they've killed everyone who refused to work the mines. Maybe they refused to be slaves again."

Ben shook his head. "Even The Lords weren't so cruel."

Ian scooped up the rocks at his feet and threw them into a cart. "Somehow, they widened the path so horses can pull the rocks directly from the mine to the pits, leaving the strongest men to work, rather than carry rocks all day."

"The Velekans have allowed Burle to decide how to rotate the shifts, as long as the mining operation never stops." Ben placed a finger to his lips. "Quiet, one's coming."

The Velekan approached Jason and motioned him with a hand to get back to work. If Jason didn't obey, he knew the Velekan would punish him with a green flame. The thing wore black shiny shoes that came up to his knees. A yellow flame flashed on his left arm, and a square box glowed orange on his chest.

As the Velekan walked away, Jason stared at the magical weapons he carried on his side.

Ben whispered to the others, "A green flame causes awful pain, and a red one means death."

The dusty mine made Ben cough, and he immediately covered his mouth and nose with his rag. "They touch the fires on their arms a lot. Maybe that's the way they communicate."

Ian saw the Velekan walk around a corner. "Other than the one, they never speak, even to each other."

Ben coughed again. "At least we can do whatever we like when we're not working the mine."

Ian locked eyes with Jason. "Let's go to the next valley, like we did last summer."

"He's close enough to hear you," Ben whispered.

Jason's laugh attracted the Velekan's attention. "If he understood our tongue, he would speak to us. Hey, you big ugly Velekan. See? He didn't understand a word I just said."

"Yes, let's do it again," Ben said.

"Does everyone still have the furs my aunt gave us last summer?" Ian asked.

Ben hugged himself and shivered. "Yes, and this time I'm bringing extras. I almost froze up there the last time."

"Let's leave next week," Jason said.

"It'll be snowing up there soon," Ian said. "We might get trapped in heavy snow. We'll leave in two days. That should give us enough time to hide our furs."

"All right, bring them tomorrow," Ben said. "I know a nearby cave where we can hide them."

"We're taking extra furs, and we know where the caves are," Ian said. "We could stop there and rest. We can get there sooner, if we travel day and night."

"Are we all going?" Jason asked.

They all nodded.

***

Armed with extra furs, Jason escaped to the mountain with Ben and Ian, as he had the summer before, but this time without Hugo.

Just above the timberline, thick flurries fell around him, and he knew the snow would be deeper than last summer's. They stopped at their clansmen's old cave, expecting warm shelter, but it was empty and cold.

Jason helped build a fire near the entrance with wood left from the previous summer. "What if the Velekans are here as well?"

"They don't know about this valley," Ian stated.

Jason asked, "How do you know? They could be everywhere in our world."

"Forget about the Velekans." Ian sat on the ground. "Let's huddle together and try to stay warm."

Jason stood at the cave's entrance, watching heavy, falling snow. "It looks pretty deep out there."

"Tomorrow we'll reach the valley," Ian said. "We have nothing to worry about. Let's travel to the top as fast as we can."

***

The next morning, Jason headed toward the summit with Ben out front, but he became hampered by deep snowdrifts. Exhausted, Jason waded, just as he had last summer. His teeth chattered, his body shivered, and his feet throbbed as he continued. Huffing and puffing, he slowly took one step, then another.

It was nightfall when Jason stormed into the nearest house at the edge of the village. Like his two friends, he was covered with snow and shivering. The same man, woman, and small children sat at a table, eating. The family turned and stared at them but didn't seem surprised.

"We're so sorry to intrude on you again, but we're from the next valley," Jason said. "We were here last summer. This time we came to escape the strange Velekans. They've made us slaves again."

"We can stay with Uncle Tito tonight," Ian said. "As soon as we warm up, we'll be leaving."

They removed their furs and left them near the door. The house was just as Jason remembered it, warm and cozy. He stood in front of a stone fireplace, absorbing the heat.

The starry-eyed family still didn't utter a word. The woman brought them bread, potatoes, and roasted meat.

Jason sat on the floor near the fire with the other boys and greedily gulped down his meal.

Ian forced out his words through a mouthful of food.

"We need to talk to your councilmen about these strange things in our village."

The man finally spoke. "The Velekan devils are here as well. We, too, are slaves."

Ian sat straight up. A dark veil of fear shaded his face. "They're here?"

"They've killed many and forced the rest of us to work harder," the man said. "Our clan fought the Velekans on several occasions and lost. Young men, you should've remained in your own valley. At least you would've been with your families and friends."

No one spoke for a while.

"Flee back over the mountains while you can," the man said. "We only get a few hours of sleep here."

"We just came over the mountain. The weather is too harsh," Ian said.

The pale-faced man eyed his plate. "I'm sorry, but Tito and his family were killed by the Velekans."

Ian sat his bowl on the floor and jumped to his feet. His eyes welled up, and Jason knew he was fighting hard to hold back the tears. "Why did they kill them?"

"Tito helped fight the Velekans, and they eliminate such people to set an example for the rest of us."

Jason stood and put a hand on his friend's shoulder. "I'm sorry about your uncle and his family."

Ian dropped his hands at his sides, clenching and unclenching his fists. "Why his wife and children?"

"To set an example," the man said. "They have no remorse when it comes to killing children."

Ian lowered his head. "My little cousin would have been two this winter."

"We're like insects to them," the man said.

"We all miss Tito," the woman said.

"You must work the mines," the man said. "They're higher and colder than those near your village. Stay here tonight, then return to your village. The Velekans are not yet aware of your presence here."

"But it's snowing so hard," Jason said.

The man took a sip of his drink. "You can make it back over the summit before it worsens. If you don't, it may be difficult for you to leave. It'll be snowing in the valley soon. The Velekans have tripled their guards here, and they watch us closely. We don't know how long they'll be here."

"We'll have to stay," Jason said. "How did you know the Velekans were in our valley?"

The man said, "Six others came over the mountain, seeking freedom as you did, only to find things worse here. They tried to return, but the Velekans stopped them, and here they remain. No matter which valley you live in, you'll be slaves."

Ian sighed.

"By the time the Velekans leave, it may be too difficult to travel across the mountain," the man suggested. "You may stay here for tonight and then move into Tito's house tomorrow. Your friend Hugo now lives there."

"Hugo's alive?" Ian asked.

"Yes," the man said. "He survived the cold from the mountain, but he walks with a limp."

"I'm going back," Ben said.

Ben's willingness to cross over the mountain again surprised Jason. "When are you leaving?"

"As soon as I warm up," Ben said.

"You should wait until morning," the man suggested. "It won't be as cold."

Ben tied food into a rag and stuffed it under his fur, next to his chest. "Thank you and your wife for helping us, but I must be going." He turned to Jason and Ian. "I'll see you two next summer."

***

Ben stirred about midday and started his final descent down the mountain. He entered the village at the livestock area and went in search of Burle, but he was working in one of the mines, so Ben went home to rest and later returned to Burle's house.

"Where have you been, and where are the other two?" Burle scolded. "We had to work harder because of your absence."

"We went over the mountain," Ben said. "Jason and Ian stayed."

"Fool. Why did you return?" Burle asked.

Ben folded his hands behind his back and stared at

him. "The Velekans are there as well. They've killed many, including Ian's uncle and family."

Burle's jaw dropped. "They're there? How did they know about the other valley?"

Ben shifted his weight. "We don't know."

"Rest now. Tomorrow you'll return to the mine and work twice as hard." Burle turned and stomped away.

***

After working in the mine all day, Ben met at Joss's house with Kurt to discuss the Velekans.

Kurt and Joss had grown up in the same slave camp. They sat around a table in a small kitchen. Joss's family was working in the mines, leaving the group alone to discuss their plans.

Ben considered Joss the leader of the group because he was almost twice his age, husky and tall with brown hair and a matching beard.

Joss folded his arms on the kitchen table. "Let's capture a Velekan."

"No, they're too powerful," Kurt said. "We don't understand what those flames on their arms and chests do. But we know the sticks on their sides can kill."

"If we learned how to use their weapons, we could defeat them," Joss said. "We can do this."

Ben shook his head in disagreement. "What about

the huge object sitting near the pits? We don't know how many are in there."

Joss pounded a fist on the table. "We must try."

Kurt leaned back in his chair. "They appear and disappear. Maybe they really are gods."

"Devils," Joss corrected. "Gods wouldn't kill us, and they wouldn't be interested in blue rocks."

Ben rubbed his haggard face and yawned. "Maybe they just need us to collect them."

Joss stared around the group. "If gods put the rocks there, they wouldn't need us to collect them."

"We may be killed," Ben said.

Joss was persistent. "Let's overtake the one at the mine tomorrow morning. If we manage to hold his hands, so he can't reach the lights, I believe he'll be harmless."

Ben scooted his chair back from the table and crossed his legs. "We don't know how to work those lights."

Joss said, "We'll force him to show us."

Ben leaned in closer to Joss. "The one who speaks is not there. This one doesn't understand our tongue."

Kurt moved his hands, as he had seen the Velekan do. "We could use signs, the same way he communicates with us."

Joss pounded a fist into his palm. "We'll beat him, then he'll understand."

Ben's voice quivered. "What if the lights hurt us? It's too dangerous."

"We need to try," Joss urged. "I can't be a slave for the rest of my life."

Ben's stomach growled. "I don't think we should try it."

"Let's do it," Joss said. "When we enter the mine, there's only one, and he's usually close." He held his hands over the table with fingers spread. "We'll act as if we're going to work, then we'll grab him." He then made a fist.

Ben still wasn't satisfied with the idea. "He's so tall. He must be strong."

Kurt stood. "I'm starving. Let's discuss it on the way to the mine tomorrow."

Joss jumped to his feet. "No. We'll decide now. How about it?"

Kurt scratched the back of his neck. "They're too strange—too frightening."

"Are you with me or not?" Joss demanded.

Kurt eyed the table. "I ... I'm not sure anymore."

"I need to know now," Joss insisted.

"I ... or ... yes," Kurt said.

Joss then focused on Ben. "How about you?"

"No," Ben said. "I want no part of it."

Joss stood, walked around the table, and stood in front of Ben. "So, you're going to stand by like a coward and let us risk our lives?"

"It's too dangerous," Ben said.

Joss glanced back at Ben, shaking his head as he left the room. "With or without your help, we'll proceed as planned. What a child."

The next morning, Ben and the others entered the mine as usual, replacing men from the night shift.

When the Velekan motioned them to their workplaces, Kurt and Joss grabbed his hands and twisted his arms behind his back. Kurt jumped on the Velekan's back and choked him. Because of his height, they had a difficult time wrestling him to the ground.

Long fingernails dug into Joss's wrist, but he held on tightly.

Kurt grabbed the weapon from the struggling Velekan's side and hit him on the head with a rock.

The Velekan lay motionless. An orange, gooey liquid oozed onto the dirt.

Ben shook his head. "What have you done?"

Kurt panted. "I didn't hit him that hard."

Ben said, "I told you not to do it."

Kurt took a step back. "Is he dead?"

Joss viciously shook the Velekan, but he didn't stir. "I think so."

Ben squatted beside the Velekan's head. "Is that blood?"

"Not red like ours," Joss said. "I told you they aren't gods. We couldn't kill a god."

Kurt grabbed a nearby rock. "Hurry, let's smash these lights."

Joss grabbed the Velekan's weapon from Kurt. "No, let's see if we can make this thing work."

Using both hands, he pointed it at the side of the cave.

He squeezed it, shook it, and tapped it on a rock, but nothing happened. But then he gripped the bulky end and a red light hit the cave's wall, scattering rocks in every direction.

Kurt exclaimed in utter bewilderment, "Wow. Did you see that?"

Joss shushed Kurt and randomly touched the lights on the Velekan's arm and chest.

Suddenly, images appeared on the square object in the center of the Velekan's chest. It displayed six creatures. One stood out front, with five directly behind him. The images were small but distinct.

Ben retreated in disbelief.

Kurt's startled expression grew wider. "Oh no, they're devils after all."

"They're in there, staring at us," Joss gasped. "They saw what we did."

"What shall we do?" Kurt asked.

"Destroy these lights," Joss commanded. "Quickly."

The flames without fire made loud beeping noises, and no matter how hard Joss smashed them, the sounds continued.

Ben stood frozen in his tracks.

Kurt shouted, "Help me move him, Ben."

Ben grabbed the Velekan under his arms and yanked. "He's so light. How can he be so tall and so light?"

Joss tried to silence the noise without success. "Throw him into the pit. Hurry."

Ben pulled the body to the other side of the wall, pushed it into a bottomless pit, and no longer heard the beeping sound.

Kurt scurried around on his hands and knees, raking rocks and dirt over the wet area with his fingers. "Help me cover up the blood … or whatever this stuff is."

Then six Velekans appeared in front of them.

"Joss," Ben yelled. "Use the weapon."

As Joss froze, a Velekan hit him with a green light.

Ben backed away, but he felt the results before he saw the flash. He let out a deathly scream as an unbearable, paralyzing pain penetrated his body. He jerked uncontrollably and fell to the ground, unable to move. Something landed on his back, but he couldn't see what.

Ben didn't know how much time had passed before his arms and legs started to recover. He pushed Kurt off his back and rolled over. He still had little control of his body, but he sat up and glanced around at Kurt and Joss as they stirred.

"You will all die for this," a voice from the Velekan's waist device snapped. "Get up."

Ben tried to stand. "I … I can't."

The Velekan who had spoken followed the drag marks around the wall and returned shortly. "Get up or you'll be punished again."

Using a rock to support himself, Ben stood on weak legs.

Slowly, his two accomplices stood as well.

***

Burle helped a group of men break up a fight in the center of the village.

"What's the problem here?" Burle asked. "We have enough problems without you two fighting."

"His kid attacked mine." The smaller of the two men wiped blood from his mouth with the back of his hand. The man pointed at a boy. "He's a bully, just like his father."

The larger man said, "Your kid's a wimp, just like you."

"We've got company," one of the men said.

Six Velekans marched Ben, Kurt, and Joss before Burle.

The one calling himself Mogayron spoke. "Three of your clansmen have killed one of us, and your village will pay dearly for their crime."

Burle gasped and stepped forward. "Ben, is this true? Did you three kill a Velekan?"

Ben wrung his hands together, on the verge of tears. "I didn't have anything to do with killing him. It was Kurt and Joss. I just happened to be there."

Burle's eyes grew excited. "How did you kill him?"

"No more questions," the Velekan snarled. "100 of your clansmen shall give their lives for their mistake."

"I don't want to die," Ben yelled at Burle. "I had no part in it."

Burle stared into the unblinking eyes of the Velekans.

"No … no. If they killed one of you, why should many of us die? It's not fair. And Ben didn't participate in the killing."

The devil stood tall and powerfully, and his voice flowed with resonance. "We're the masters and you're the slaves. Slaves don't kill masters."

Burle became frantic. "But Ben is innocent."

"He stood by and did nothing to stop the killing," the Velekan said. "He's just as guilty as the others."

"Please, take the lives of the men who killed him," Burle insisted. "Leave the others in peace."

The Velekan glanced around the area. "We'll kill these three plus 100 others. Their bodies will decay in the center of your village. The stench shall remind your clansmen of what happens to killers."

Burle dropped to one knee. "No, please," he begged.

"Will you call these villagers forward, or shall we decide?" the Velekan asked.

Burle wiped sweat from his forehead with a shaky hand. "I can't choose who shall live and who shall die."

Ben wept and shook his head. "I told them not to do it."

The crowd grew larger. Passersby had stopped to watch, and others came from nearby homes.

Burle cringed when the Velekans pulled their weapons from their side pouches.

Red lights hit the three accused, and they fell dead.

Burle couldn't prevent the Velekans from marching so many of his clansmen into the center of the village and slaughtering them. They killed the old, the ill, women, and children not old enough to work, then forced other Saxons to throw their bodies into a heaping pile.

The Velekans disappeared.

Burle's heart felt heavy with pain and sorrow when he spoke to a now small group. "I'm leader of the Saxons. Yet I cannot protect my clan. I'm certain now that Sax killed the Velekan he stabbed. They can be killed, just as we can."

A man wrinkled his nose. "Winter is almost here. At least the stench won't be so bad."

A young man limped toward Burle. "I don't care what the Velekans said. I'm going to bury them. The only reason I'm still alive is because I live beyond the lake."

A group of men volunteered to help the man.

A woman wiped tears from her eyes. "We may be able to defeat them now."

Tavin, second-in-command, kicked dirt into the air. "Fools. We don't know how they killed him or how they caught him off-guard."

Burle's weary eyes glanced from one slave to another. "Did they tell anyone of their plans?"

Tavin said, "I'll visit the mine and ask around."

Burle gritted his teeth. "So many Saxons dead—for nothing."

"They're going to increase their guards now," said Otto, the third council member. He gawked at the pile of bodies and sighed. "This gives us hope."

"How much rock can they want?" Tavin asked. "There must be an end."

Burle said, "As long as the blue rocks exist, they'll never go away."

***

It was winter when Burle stood with two Velekans, while onlookers watched.

Mogayron said, "We will take our ore and leave. When we return here at the end of next summer, both pits shall be full or we will kill half of your clan, forcing the remainder to work twice as hard."

Burle lowered his head like a whipped dog. "We'll have the pits full."

The Velekan peered down at him. "Just remember, you humans are our slaves—forever."

"Aahh," the crowd murmured when the Velekans disappeared.

Burle stood before the Saxons. "We have two choices: death or slavery. We don't have to work as hard now."

"We can't be slaves for the rest of our lives," a woman whined.

"We've done so in the past, and we shall again," Tavin said.

Burle felt hopeless. "We can work a few hours per day during the winter, then harder during the summer months."

"Did you ask the Velekans what they did with the

rocks?" a young boy asked.

Burle squinted. "Yes, but he used words I didn't understand, something about fuel."

"What's fuel?" the boy asked.

Burle shrugged. "I think they burn them."

"They burn rocks instead of wood?" a man asked.

"I told you I didn't understand. He used other strange words as well," Burle said.

"Did they say where they came from?" the boy asked.

"Another world," Burle said. "He called the huge object they live in a cargo ship."

"What's a ship?" a girl asked.

Burle stared toward the white clouds. "The thing they travel in among the stars. He told me where their world is, but—"

A woman's eyes went up to the sky. "Traveling among the stars."

Burle stared into the haggard faces in the crowd. "The Velekans will no longer try to convince us they're gods. They realize we don't believe them, now that we've killed one of them."

"Two," Tavin corrected. "Sax killed the first. They're powerless without their weapons."

Otto pointed toward the sky. "He said there are other clans like ours, up there." They all looked up to where he pointed.

"Can we really trust their words?" a woman asked. "They're demons."

"I don't know," Burle replied.

CHAPTER 12

THE WESTERN DYNASTY

Weeks later, Ming's bleary eyes scanned the horizon that exposed a daunting expanse of an arid, rocky terrain.

Snow-capped peaks loomed under the clear blue sky and sparkled in the bright sunlight. Back at Ming's village, the terrain was mostly flat, but the farther he traveled west, the more pronounced rolling hills and ridges became.

Ming witnessed sights that, until then, had been only myths in his mind. Families lived in caves on hillsides, walking around naked and begging for food. Children stood at the entrances, skin and bones. They didn't play or smile but stared down at him. Their stomachs were empty, but his was full. He reached into his pouch and tossed a rag full of food up to them. They scrambled for its contents like starving ants. He had never seen people living such desperate, degrading lives, like scavengers without a fresh kill in months.

A toothless man with white hair waved from a ridge above, trying to get Ming's attention. A dirty cloth covered his genitals. "Hello."

Ming didn't respond but slowed his pace. He cast his eyes up and down, from one side of the ridge to the other. Rumors were that some people lived so poorly they ate their neighbors. Curiosity turned into fear as he sped up, almost running.

Could these people be flesh eaters? Was his life in danger?

"Up there." The elderly man pointed.

Ming eyed the early morning sky as a gigantic, imposing shadow blocked the sun. It passed overhead at a slow speed. Its wings didn't move, but remained bent downward, as if broken. "A dragon." He cowered beside the rocks with no place to hide. He had heard stories and seen drawings of dragons all his life.

The huge black beast dropped over the top of the second mountain, and then Ming lost sight of it. He remained frozen in his tracks, his heart pounding and sweat dripping from his chin.

When he finally started walking again, he cast his eyes to the ground. His mind churned. Then, startled by the sound of pounding feet, he glanced up and saw a group of soldiers approaching.

The lead man was shorter than most of the others: thin with a single graying braid dangling down his back. "You saw the dragon, as we did," he said.

Ming shivered. He couldn't control the excitement in his voice. "How many dragons have you seen?"

The man shook his head and wrinkled his face, making his chin dimple more pronounced. "I can't count them."

Ming stared at the mountain. "Maybe it's the same one."

"They're not the same colors. Their wings are different—and so are the blinking eyes that are all around their bodies."

Ming glanced up to where the dragon had disappeared. "Have you ever seen one swoop down and take someone as a bird takes prey?"

The leader wiped sweat from his forehead with a dirty rag and pointed. "Many of our men went in that direction. We never saw them again. Others searched for them, but they never returned either. Soldiers from both dynasties have lost men to the dragons."

Ming trembled. "Do you think the dragons ate them?"

"Sure," the man said.

"How long have they been living there?" Ming asked.

The man shrugged. "Forever. A man ventured into the mountains and claimed he watched devils enter a dragon. He said the dragons weren't alive but hollow like a cave. Now he wanders around the countryside mumbling about demons living in the mountains. Strangest thing though, the elders around here said that one of the mountains has disappeared over time."

"Over how long?" Ming asked.

The man wiped his forehead again. "Twice the lifetime of my grandmother."

Ming spread his arms like a bird about to take flight. "Maybe the dragons tore down the mountain. But how can it fly without moving its wings? The one I saw didn't look alive."

The man squinted. "Don't know."

For the first time, Ming noticed the soldiers' clothes, dusty and tattered. Blood-soaked bandages covered some of the men's arms and legs. Many walked with the support of sticks. "What happened to them?" he asked the leader.

"We're at war with the Western Dynasty. They've claimed villages that once belonged to us."

Ming had never known a conflict existed between the two dynasties.

"Where are you going, young man?" the leader asked.

"To the next village," Ming lied. "My sister lives there."

"That village has been taken over by the West," another soldier replied. "If you enter, you will not be able to return. Where are you from?"

"Near Gong Ho," Ming said.

The man gave a weary shake of his head. "Never heard of it. Join us. You can't do anything for your sister now. To the south," the man said, pointing, "are flesh-eating families that run in packs, like animals. North, over the mountains, is the land of the dragons. Go either direction and you'll never return."

Ming moved from the trail, sat on a rock, and allowed the soldiers to pass. "I must find my sister."

The soldiers trudged past Ming, as if each step were their last. He thought about the dragon with blinking eyes around it. He turned and glanced up to where the dragon had landed. Curiosity beckoned him to go there and see it with his own eyes. He felt the pouch around his waist. It contained enough food for two days.

He changed direction and headed toward the land of the dragons.

Near dusk, Ming reached the summit of the smallest peak.

Fiery red and orange colors of the setting sun dipped below the mountains. From the top, he saw nothing below. He continued down, as darkness fell, and slept in a small meadow.

He rose at dawn and ascended the taller mountain. Before reaching the top, at about midday, Ming heard loud humming and crushing noises. He peeked over the side and saw two dragons at the base of the mountain. He'd seen the black one the day before, and a gray one sat next to it. He watched in amazement as an object as large as a house rolled along, on many rotating wheels. It moved not only back and forth but also up and down. The thing ate at the base of the mountain, pulling away piles of rocks. It crushed them with four giant claws, then rotated and dumped its contents onto a long, moving bridge.

Dark brown, bug-like creatures with two legs, but taller than men, stood on clawed feet. Shells covered their bodies. They had two sets of arms. The pair in their mid-section contained claws, and the upper pair had large hands like men. The backs of their heads protruded downward. Their faces were as crusty as the side of a mountain, and their lips were black. They had long feelers where their noses should have been, and the creatures had huge, glossy eyes that resembled those of bugs Ming had played with as a child. The insects watched over men who wore glowing green rings around their necks—slaves, no doubt. The slaves left some rocks on the bridge and tossed others aside. The remaining rocks went straight into the side of the dragon, and both men and bugs went inside.

Why would bugs collect rocks?

Finding it difficult to move his legs, Ming crouched low to the ground and moved down the side of the slope, wanting to see more. He couldn't run away from this mad world even if he wanted to. Stepping close to the activity, he watched the bug things in horror. No matter how he tried, he couldn't control his shaking. He feared that stepping on a twig or setting off a rockslide could attract their attention.

Ming kept glancing back, fearing that one of the Bugs might be standing there. The sun shone brightly and hot, and he had no shade. His hands trembled as he wiped sweat from his face and neck. He'd lost his appetite, but thirst had taken its toll.

His attention again locked on the scene below him.

The thing on wheels stopped moving, its side opened, and a Bug jumped out.

A slave dashed from the worksite and ran up past Ming. Two Bugs chased the fleeing man and pointed an object at him that caused red lights to strike his shoulder. The man abruptly stopped and screamed in pain. He turned and saw Ming as two more lights hit him in the chest. The slave fell to his knees, his face contorted in pain, with his mouth open. His eyes glazed as he fell onto his back.

Ming smelled burning flesh, covered his mouth with both hands, and gagged. As the Bugs neared, he eased to the opposite side of a rock, lay on his stomach, closed his eyes, and silently sucked in air through his mouth. He listened to the heavy thumps of his own heart beating in his chest. The wind stood still, and he wondered if they could detect his odor. He heard strange screeching sounds between the two and guessed it was their way of communicating.

Once their footsteps retreated, Ming took his original position and watched the Bugs motion for the slaves to get back to work.

Ming sat on the ground and wet himself. He felt just as helpless as he had when he'd learned about his family's death. The world as he knew it no longer existed. If he got out of there alive, he'd never venture into the mountains again.

Looking over at the dead man, he saw that deep burns

covered his chest and blood oozed from his wounds. His eyes stared vacantly toward the sky, and the ring around his neck had vanished.

For a long time, Ming sat with his back against a rock, knees to his chest and feet on the ground. Sweat broke out in beads and ran down his forehead as the unrelenting sun beamed down on him.

What are these things? Do they really eat men?

The Bugs had left the man's water pot secured around his waist. Ming had watched the slaves and Bugs use them. They were round and twice the length of his hand. He wanted to dash for it but couldn't risk the chance of being seen. He had no choice but to remain hidden until darkness.

At sunset, the Bugs created their own suns that lit the work area. Another crew of slaves replaced the day shift.

Ming crawled on his stomach toward the dead man, hoping the beasts were either too busy to notice him or couldn't see him in the dark. With his head so low to the ground, Ming inhaled dust and sneezed. He tightly pressed his hands over his mouth and nose to muffle the sound. He didn't want to die—didn't want to end up burned to death. Men he could defeat, but not such powerful monsters.

Ming lay silent, relieved that they hadn't noticed his presence. He groped at the man's waist for his water pot. Ming couldn't see how to remove it, so he held his head to the ground, pulled out the nipple on the end, and guzzled the cool water that had been sitting in the sun for half a day.

A loud humming noise caused him to focus on the gray dragon as it lifted into flight and rose to the top of the mountain, creating a thick cloud of dust. Once the dragon cleared the mountain, it headed toward the stars at a tremendous speed. He blinked, and it was gone.

A shouting woman drew his attention to the worksite again. She had pale skin and rounded eyes, not slanted like his. A male-looking creature stood beside her and they wore the same strange clothing. He couldn't understand their conversation, but the woman showed anger.

Now the Bug's feelers and arms were moving fast and the screeching sound became louder.

Ming watched the Bugs load the strange working things and the rotating bridge into the dragon.

The Bugs freed the men, and then they scrambled blindly into the darkness.

Ming didn't fully comprehend what had happened, but he knew the dragons were not alive and the woman had power over the Bugs.

The furious Bugs killed the sunlight, and the dragon sped away, as the other one had.

Ming's fingers gripped the rock as he peeked around at the dark site. If the woman and the male-looking thing were still there, he couldn't see them. The place reminded dark and silent.

As Ming struggled back the way he had come, he

couldn't see where to step. He cautiously made it to the other side of the first mountain by dawn, guzzled from a stream, washed his soiled shang, and continued on the westward trail.

As Ming walked, he didn't notice who passed or in which direction people traveled. Images of the strange creatures strongly remained in his mind, as he tried to understand what he had witnessed.

How had they killed a man with lights, never touching him?

Things other than man lived in his world. People wouldn't believe him. Even his own family would have called him insane.

He'd allow the ex-slaves to tell their stories.

***

Ming ended his journey in the village where the emperor of the Western Dynasty resided.

It was smaller than Mongu and better off. Shops, food, and vegetable traders were rare. The passage was clean and absent of any stench.

The people seemed kinder. They greeted Ming on sight. A woman and her pretty daughter passed. The girl turned and smiled at him. She made him feel warm inside, as if living was worthwhile again.

Then, as Ming wandered the area, a group of five soldiers surrounded and detained him. One circled him with a strange smile on his face. He was not quite as tall as Ming but stocky and older. "Are you a peasant?" the man asked.

Ming tried to hide his fear. He was tall and lean and not dressed in rags, which indicated that he was well-fed but not from nobility. "I ... no."

"I'm the leader of this group," the man said. "Where are you from?"

"The eastern countryside that now belongs to the West," Ming answered.

"Do you live with your family?"

"No, I had to leave because I refused to marry the girl my father picked for me," Ming said.

"So ... you have no family, no home, and no work?"

"Yes," Ming agreed.

"Then you're a peasant, you idiot," the man said.

The group erupted into laughter.

"We're your family now." The leader turned to one of his men. "Get him some food and clothes."

A soldier beckoned Ming to follow him. "My name is Tao. You're a tall man. You'll do fine in our group. My job is to train new soldiers to fight."

Ming shivered, and his muscles tightened. "Fight?"

Tao glanced back at him. "That's what soldiers do. We keep the peace, and sometimes we must use force."

"You mean invade?" Ming said.

Tao flashed a broad grin. "If necessary."

After a hearty meal and a bath, Ming received a new

yi and a shang with a red tie, the color of the Western Dynasty. Not only would he have food and shelter, but also one day he'd return to the East and kill those responsible for the murder of his family.

A grin slowly spread across his face.

CHAPTER 13

The Forbidden Galaxy

It had taken the *Volpus* almost six months to reach the Mondumos Solar System, but Captain Sedo's destination was beyond, in the Forbidden Galaxy.

"Captain, we need to let Fleet Command know our flight plans," Starco urged. "We'll be out of communication range within minutes."

Sedo approached Starco, removed a memory chip from a pouch around her waist, and handed it to him. "Transmit this data directly to Commander Rota and tell him it's urgent. There are Beltese slaves living on Neptus, and we're going to rescue them."

Starco held out his hand, and Sedo dropped the chip into his palm. He stared at the chip, then squinted up at her. "The next galaxy?"

Bonuve hopped out of his chair and rushed to the captain's side. "The Second Galaxy is off-limits. The species on Neptus have overpowered us once."

Captain Sedo chuckled and moved back toward her station. "Overpowered us? The occupants on Neptus

239

have primitive technology not nearly as advanced as the Velekans.'"

"How do you know?" Bonuve asked.

"I just do," Sedo said.

Bonuve stiffened as he stepped closer to Sedo. "I object, Captain. You're putting the *Volpus* and our crew in great danger, and this is an unauthorized trip. Starco, contact Fleet Command."

"You're not going over my head," Sedo snapped.

Bonuve raised his voice. "You're violating Fleet Command regulations. I've the right to oppose you. Starco, contact—"

"Sorry, Lieutenant," Starco said, "we're now out of communication range."

"Ferrus, continue," the captain ordered.

"Captain, you can't do this," Bonuve said in an ominous tone.

"Lieutenant, a word with you in private," she said.

Sedo left Navigational Control as Bonuve strode past her. When they entered the nearest conference room, Bonuve turned on her like a wild beast. "You haven't been yourself lately. I've witnessed changes in your behavior over the past few months. I'm recommending that you consult our psychiatrist prior to taking us on this suicide mission. Where are you getting these ideas, Captain?"

"Calm down, Lieutenant," Sedo said.

He opened his mouth to speak, but not a word came out.

She sat at the only computer in the room and accessed the data Starco had transmitted to Fleet Command. "Have a seat and review this. These are my father's records: the true version of what actually happened to the *Eliptus* and its crew."

Sedo stood, and Bonuve took control of the computer. With him being second-in-command, she needed his support.

His eyes bulged and his mouth tightened as he scanned the records. "This can't be true. Where did you get this?"

"From my father's office. The species on Neptus tricked him out of his crew and ship."

"Are you certain? I mean ..."

"He made up that story about a more superior being on Neptus to keep us away," Sedo said.

"Beltese are still there?" Bonuve asked.

"Some. There's no way to know how many. After all, it's been a hundred years. Based on their ages, I've calculated that over a fourth have passed through Naconda."

"We should turn back and get authorization from Fleet Command," Bonuve demanded.

"If Colas were still acting fleet commander, I would. But Rota is now the permanent commander, and he's strict on regulations."

"This could cost you your career. Your father will be considered a coward and a traitor," he said.

"Getting the Beltese slaves off Neptus is more important," Sedo said.

"Give me time to study this more," Bonuve said.

"Take as much time as you like." She exited the room. When Bonuve returned to Navigational Control, he sat silently at his station and stared through the viewport. Ferrus glanced from Bonuve to Sedo. "Look, straight ahead is the Zone. We'll be the first ship to visit this galaxy."

"The second ship," Sedo said. "The *Eliptus* was the first."

According to her father's data, the bluish-purple cloud was made of a permeable electromagnetic membrane, unfamiliar to her, that separated the two galaxies. It simulated a lightning field that extended as far as she could see.

"We'll penetrate the membrane in less than an hour," Ferrus said.

"We must enter slowly," Sedo said. "At our present speed, it'll be like hitting a giant asteroid. Increase speed after we enter it."

"Where did you get this information?" Ferrus asked.

"Data from the *Eliptus*," Sedo said.

"But that ship was destroyed." Ferrus stressed his words.

"The *Eliptus* still exists, I assure you."

Sedo contacted the lead scientist from the communication device on her workstation. "Jetra, I want to know what this electromagnetic membrane consists of—what makes it work."

Jetra's voice held a hint of excitement. "Instruments are ready, Captain."

Prior to entry, the *Volpus* decelerated to minimum velocity. When the ship entered the Zone, it rolled through the entity like an object in water. Turbulence shook the ship, and everything outside glowed a serene white.

"Captain, I've begun to accelerate, but our instruments have not changed," Ferrus said. "I'm not detecting anything out there."

"We know some type of energy field exists because we've seen it. We're in it," Sedo said.

Khyla said, "We may be vulnerable in this area. Our protective barriers are not registering. I have probes out front. Let's just hope there's nothing to collide with."

"How do we know when we'll exit the Zone?" Starco asked.

"Use the *Eliptus* data," Sedo said.

Sedo saw confusion on Starco's face. "Captain, we don't have that ship's data."

"Of course, we do. You just transmitted it to Fleet Command," Captain Sedo said.

They had been in the Zone for ten minutes when Sedo contacted the lead scientist again. "Jetra, how are your analyses coming?"

"They're not. According to our test results, there's nothing there. No matter, energy, particulates, gases, or liquids."

"Analyze your samples again," Sedo said.

"We have, Captain. Our probes came back empty."

"Take several samples and store them. Analyze them after we exit," she said.

Navigational Control remained quiet for the next hour. Everyone stared ahead, as if mesmerized by the light through the viewport.

Sedo was now 100% Megmador, and she knew the outcome of most things before they happened. "Decrease the speed to a minimum, Ferrus."

"Decreasing speed ... or at least I think I have," Ferrus said.

Within minutes, the *Volpus* erupted, as if spat out by the Zone. The ship shook and accelerated into the Second Galaxy.

"Our instruments are working again," Ferrus said. "At our present speed, we should arrive at our final destination in five days. It took the *Eliptus* almost two weeks."

Sedo contacted Jetra. "Have you received results for those samples?"

"We've analyzed our probes, and they contain nothing," Jetra said.

"That's impossible," Sedo said.

"Maybe the membrane contains things our instruments are not programmed to detect," Jetra said.

Ferrus interrupted. "Captain, we're headed toward an unidentified object. It's twice the size of the *Volpus* and camouflaged like an asteroid."

Sedo leaned forward in her chair and studied the

entity. It displayed no flashing lights or identification. "It's like some type of ship."

"It is a ship," Khyla acknowledged.

Starco sat straight up. "Maybe it's from Neptus."

Sedo leaned back in her chair and crossed her legs. "That's not possible."

"Captain, are there things you're not telling us?" Ferrus asked.

"Yes," Captain Sedo said. "You'll find out when we reach our final destination."

Khyla tapped away at her computer. "We're not close enough for a thorough analysis, but I can't detect any threats. I think it's some sort of a research vessel. So far I haven't been able to determine what powers it."

"Get the language expert up here, Starco," Sedo ordered.

Zanta entered Navigational Control, dropped into her chair, and started working at her computer. "Remember, we're in a different galaxy, Captain."

"It doesn't matter," Sedo said. "Intelligent beings should easily decipher our codes or language differences."

After a few moments, Zanta reported to Sedo, "I'm not receiving a response. They either don't understand or they're refusing to acknowledge."

"I have a visual of their Navigational Control room," Bonuve said. "Coming up on a vektren. Humans in this galaxy?"

Sedo stared back at a blonde female. Her face was

young. Her body was thin and vibrant. The alien stood before her captain's chair and appeared to be about the same age as Sedo. They just stared at each other while the language translator tried various communication links.

"I've completed an analysis of her," Bonuve said. "She's not human, but a species of an unknown origin. I'm detecting no other life aboard the ship."

Sedo's instincts warned her that the alien captain was friendly, but the ship could be a great threat—even to the *Volpus*—if provoked. "Are you positive you've detected no danger?" Sedo asked Bonuve.

"If weapons exist, I can't find them," he said.

"Zanta, what's the problem with the translation?" Sedo questioned.

"I think I have a break, Captain. Hail her," Zanta said.

"I'm Captain Sedo of the Beltese Fleet," Sedo said.

"I'm Captain Zee of the Betta Force. You're not from our galaxy, and your ship is built for war."

"Yes, this is a war vessel. How do you know we're not from this galaxy?" Sedo asked.

"Your ship came through the Zone. Our ships are not designed to travel through it."

"What species are you?" Sedo asked.

"We call ourselves Tewils. We're scientists, seeking other intelligent life-forms."

"I'm human. My crew is Beltese," Sedo said.

"Do all humans possess such powers as you?" Zee asked.

Sedo was at a loss for words. "All humans are the same. You must have a crew, but we haven't located any."

Zee flashed a smile. "I have a crew."

The *Volpus* kept its distance from the alien ship. "How many?"

Zee twirled her hair behind an ear. "I cannot disclose that information."

Sedo was leery of Zee's ship. "Are you familiar with the species on the planet Neptus? It's the fourth planet in the first solar system."

Zee nodded and took a seat. "They are in the Mantus Solar System. Mantus is our word for 'large.' All the planets in that solar system are huge, and the fourth planet is the smallest."

"You've met the species who live there?" Sedo asked.

"Yes, they're an untrustworthy menace, aggressive—with primitive technology. They are the only species that pose a threat in this solar system."

Sedo slid back into her own chair, no longer trusting her Megmador instincts. Perhaps her powers were useless in this galaxy. She couldn't read the other captain's thoughts. The alien didn't ask about her civilization or how the *Volpus* crossed the Zone. Zee also didn't ask why she wished to travel to Neptus.

Sedo placed both hands on her armrests. "Our probes came back empty during our voyage through the Zone. Do you know what it consists of?"

"Our probes also came back negative," Zee said.

"Perhaps we'll visit your planet during our next voyage, Captain Zee."

"Captain Sedo," Zee acknowledged.

Sedo maintained a visual on a vektren as the alien ship sped away.

"That's no ordinary research ship, Bonuve," Sedo said. "I believe it poses a great danger to anyone who challenges it."

Bonuve turned to her. "I've completed a thorough scan of their ship and downloaded its technology into our database. I've detected no danger. She is the only living thing on the ship. Her entire staff is mechanical. What was her comment about humans having powers?"

Sedo shrugged. "I have no idea. Ferrus, set the same course as the *Eliptus* did a hundred years ago."

***

The first three planets in the Mantus Solar System were huge and rocky, and they orbited too closely to the star to support most life-forms. At a distance, Sedo saw Neptus. It was small compared to distant planets in that solar system. She zoomed in on a deep green ocean and lush purple vegetation.

When they neared Neptus's orbit, Ferrus gasped. "That's the *Eliptus*."

The ship was an elliptical design, not cubical like the *Volpus*. A few of this old type remained in the Beltese Fleet.

"Is anyone aboard?" Sedo asked.

"No," Ferrus confirmed. "It's just drifting in orbit."

Sedo summoned Chedzer from her workstation.

"I see it, Captain," Chedzer acknowledged.

"Transport a crew of engineers over and see what you can find. Make it quick. We want to get out of here without a confrontation."

"This planet has a polar radius of almost double the size of Tandon, and its gravitational force is too heavy for Beltese," Khyla said.

Sedo studied the planet through the viewport. "Bonuve, scan this planet. How many Beltese are here? Don't consider half-Beltese."

Khyla gawked at Sedo. "Beltese ... here?"

Bonuve gave Sedo a startled glance. "137."

"There were almost 500 aboard the *Eliptus*," Sedo said.

"That's all I've located," Bonuve said.

"Transport them aboard the *Volpus* immediately," Sedo demanded.

Khyla gasped, "Captain, these aliens have primitive technology. They're no threat to us."

Chedzer stood in the *Eliptus's* engine room. The area was a maze of wires and tubes. "The zircolon core is still intact, but the engineers cross-wired and entangled everything. It could take hours to unravel it. Push the wrong button, or cross the wrong cable, and the ship will self-destruct."

"How's the solar power system working?" Sedo asked.

Chedzer's eyes went to the ceiling. "Excellent condition, Captain. It's been keeping this ship's life-support system in operation for a hundred years."

"We have alien communication," Starco announced.

"Chedzer, this conversation may prove beneficial to you," Sedo said.

Sedo stared into the green face of one of the monsters responsible for the pain and suffering of the Beltese prisoners on Neptus. He had savage yellow eyes, a narrow face, and a thick, black, hairy body that reminded her of a beast. She gripped her armrests and twisted in her chair.

The lower pair of the alien's arms rested on his desk, and the upper pair made vivid hand gestures. "Who are you, and why have you invaded our space?" he asked.

Sedo saw nothing in the background except for a white wall. The species didn't wear clothes, and he wasn't bashful about displaying his genitals.

"I'm Captain Sedo of the Beltese Fleet. We've been in your space for almost an hour. I advise you to update your security."

The alien viewed her officers in the background. "Your crew is Beltese, but you are a Tewil."

"I'm human. We only resemble Tewils in appearance," Sedo stated.

"I've never heard of such a species," the strange creature said.

Sedo released her grip on the armrests of her chair. "Humans exist in our galaxy," she replied.

"You don't have permission to enter our space. Leave immediately," the alien commanded.

Unable to control her rage, she growled out her words. "Not until we recover our ship. The remainder of our crew has already been transported aboard."

Khyla interrupted, "Seven primitive explosive devices are approaching us from all directions, Captain. They're electronically guided missiles with nuclear warheads, propelled by exothermic, oxidized solid fuel."

Two objects approached the *Volpus* head-on. Five others appeared on different vektrens, and all were closing in on the *Volpus*. A plume of white smoke trailed behind the nozzle of each weapon.

"They're traveling slowly, Captain. Time of impact, twenty-two minutes," Khyla said.

Sedo stood, walked closer to the viewport, and warned, "If your weapons come any closer, we'll retaliate with deadly force. We have the power to obliterate Neptus."

"This is our planet, and we'll protect it from all threats," the alien snapped.

"You've held our military personnel and our ship prisoner for a hundred years," she exclaimed. "We don't care about your territorial claim."

"They're closing in, Captain," Khyla said. "I can destroy them by using their own electronic codes."

"Do it," Sedo commanded.

Khyla punched a series of keys at her workstation, and within seconds, all the missiles exploded at the same time.

The creature jumped to his feet and stared at the remnants of his weapons.

Sedo saw a smirk on Chedzer's face. "I think he got the message."

"What happened to the remainder of the *Eliptus* crew?" she asked.

"They're deceased," the alien said.

"How?" Sedo asked. "Did you experiment on them?"

"I don't recall how they died," the alien said. He then quickly left the room.

"He never introduced himself," Bonuve said. "How unprofessional."

***

When Sedo entered the dining area, it was crowded with weak and undernourished Beltese prisoners from Neptus.

She focused on the pathetic Beltese citizens. The crew was just as she had envisioned: skin and bones and dressed in dirty rags, their faces haggard. Their long, frizzy hair lacked grooming, and their light pink complexions seemed unnatural, even for the Beltese. They stopped eating, and all eyes focused on Sedo.

She heard their thoughts: *How could a human savage become a captain in the Beltese Fleet?*

Lieutenant Bago, chief of security, stood and met her. "Sicker crew members are in the clinic. If we double up, we can have quarters for all of them."

"Chedzer is restoring the *Eliptus's* engine. They can return to their old quarters. Give them time to rest and restore their strength before questioning them."

"But some want to talk now, Captain, especially Dr. Marcom." Bago said to the crowd, "This is Captain Sedo, Commander Celt Sedo's adopted daughter."

A female gasped, "Commander? He's a commander now?"

The *Eliptus* crew froze and stared at Sedo in disbelief. As she stood before the group of half-starved Beltese, hate radiated from them like heat from a sun. She felt their disgust, their loathing for her because of her father's actions.

Dr. Marcom gripped a wooden stick at his side, and his hands shook as he rasped, "Where is Captain—er—Commander Celt Sedo?"

She knew there was nothing she could say to ease their hatred toward her father. "My parents were killed in a Velekan attack months ago."

Marcom's eyes narrowed in on her. "Velekans. They have such technology now?"

"A great deal has changed over the past hundred years," Sedo said.

"You are a human alien," Dr. Marcom said. "How did such an inferior species as you become a captain in the Beltese Fleet?"

Captain Sedo's skin tingled. She hated the word "inferior."

"That's a long story, Doctor."

Marcom growled at her, his eyes twitching and his face pinched in anger. "Your father left us to die on that awful planet. The gravitational force was twice as that on Tandon, and its food lacked the proper nutrients for us."

Captain Sedo couldn't block the negative feelings emanating from the group. Nor could she ever find the words to express her sorrow or remorse for her father's actions.

For the first time in her life, she felt ashamed to be Celt Sedo's daughter.

"When I learned of what my father had done, I disobeyed Fleet Command orders to rescue the *Eliptus* crew. You all can't imagine how I feel about his betrayal of you and the Beltese Empire."

"Why didn't Fleet Command want to rescue us?" a female croaked.

"My father claimed that the *Eliptus* had been destroyed by a more hostile and technologically advanced species here. He stated that, prior to the *Eliptus* exploding, three others and he escaped in a small craft that crash-landed on Cypus. He claimed to be the only survivor. Since then, the Second Galaxy has been off-limits. Lieutenant

Bago will take your statements and submit them to Fleet Command."

Bago took his seat and resumed his interview. "What happened after you arrived on Neptus?"

Dr. Marcom spoke for the *Eliptus* crew. "The Giltons— that's what they call themselves—had very primitive weapons, and our captain didn't think they posed a threat. After talking to the Gilton commander, Captain Celt Sedo, four officers, and I transported down to the planet. We discovered later that the *Eliptus* crew couldn't communicate or detect our position on the ship's scanners. It seemed that we had disappeared. An hour later, we reappeared."

"Where were you?" Bago asked.

Marcom locked eyes with Sedo as he spoke. "In an underground facility."

Bago squinted. "I don't understand."

"The rock formations had metal that prevented our ship from locating us." The doctor shifted in his chair. "Later, we discovered that it must have been an experiment."

Bago perked his ears. "An experiment?"

"To determine if our ship scanners could locate us. The Giltons wanted our technology. They used their only weapon. First, they gained our trust. Then they deceived us."

"What did the captain do after he discovered your party couldn't be located?" Bago asked.

"We remained on Neptus for another four hours. The next day, he gave the entire crew leave on the planet. I guess, due to their limited technology, he still didn't think they posed a threat to us."

Bago gawked at Captain Sedo. "Totally against Fleet Command regulations."

"The first lieutenant strongly disagreed, because we knew nothing about this Gilton species. He and a few other officers refused to leave the ship." Dr. Marcom paused. "The aliens wanted to know all about the Beltese civilization and technological accomplishments. They were most interested in our Megmadors and how they could live up to 2,000 years."

"They were intrigued by all of this?" Bago asked.

"Yes. Their life span is only about eighty years."

"Did your crew carry weapons down to the planet?" Bago asked.

Marcom laid his walking stick across his legs. "When we took leave, only a few of the crew carried weapons, but as soon as we transported down to Neptus, we were overpowered and our communication devices were confiscated."

"How did the aliens transport to the *Eliptus*?" Bago asked.

"I don't know. When Captain Celt Sedo disappeared, we assumed the Giltons had killed him." Marcom wheezed and cleared his throat. "Our weapons were located at their stations, so the remaining crew members were defenseless. The Giltons must have somehow over-powered them, killing all but one. When the chief engineer realized what was happening, he locked himself in the engine room and cross-wires everything." "It's a good thing he did," Bago said. "How do you know this?"

"Our language expert concealed a communication device. When the aliens found the device, they smashed it and then killed her. That's when the reality of our predicament hit us. The Giltons didn't know how to reassemble the core without destroying the ship, so they tortured and killed all the engineers, even those who had no knowledge of the ship's engine and weaponry system."

Dr. Ohma entered the room. "Excuse me." He injected Marcom with a clear liquid. "This will make you feel better. Eat again within two hours." Dr. Ohma moved to the next patient.

Marcom continued, "They had a worthless piece of technology on their hands, so they punished us, made us slaves."

Bago shook his head. "Unbelievable."

Marcom's eyes shifted around the room. "If this galaxy has been off-limits, what made you come now?"

"After Captain Sedo's father's death, she found information that contradicted his story," Bago said.

Marcom coughed out his words. "That coward. We don't know how he left the planet. If the Giltons let him go, he gave them something in return."

"His crew," Bago said.

Marcom leaned back in his chair. "Our genes were used in genetic experiments, and the results were devastating. Most of the Gilton hosts had to be euthanized."

"You said you were slaves," Bago said. "What were your duties?"

Marcom closed his eyes. "We did whatever they required but mostly tended crops and livestock. We slept on the ground, and some of the crew died from snakebites. Once bitten, the poison took four days to kill the victims, and the Giltons refused to administer anti-venom. We dug holes and buried our dead. Some of our crew died while going through Naconda without medical assistance. I joined the *Eliptus* crew at thirty-eight. Now I'm 139."

Captain Sedo sensed that a disaster was about to occur on the *Eliptus*.

Strong signals jolted her brain like static electricity. She left Bago and the ailing *Eliptus* crew members and rushed down the corridor, punching in the chief engineer's communication number.

"Yes, Captain," Chedzer said.

"Stop all engine operations at once. Don't touch another thing."

"Why?" he asked.

"Just do it. I'm on my way. I repeat, stop all operations," Captain Sedo commanded. When she transported into the *Eliptus's* engine room, the engineers had reattached everything, with the exception of two cables. The *Eliptus*, like the *Volpus*, had a secondary backup core. Its diameter was three times Sedo's height, dark, and inactive. Standing side-by-side, Sedo and Chedzer stood on the second level. A bench in front of the cores contained tools and instruments.

Chedzer placed both hands on his hips. "We're almost finished here. Is there a problem, Captain?"

She had rarely seen a core in the off position. "I can't believe the solar power system kept this ship operating for so long."

Chedzer picked up one of the two thick cables with eight prongs and attempted to attach it to the primary zircolon core. "All we need to do is connect these."

"That's the wrong cable. Review your diagrams again," Sedo warned.

Chedzer took a step back and gawked at her in disbelief. "Captain, I've been chief engineer for almost a hundred years. I know every aspect of this engine. Are you accusing me of being incompetent?"

Captain Sedo pointed to the second cord and asked Chedzer to confirm it a second time. "I've never been chief engineer, but you're about to make a deadly mistake."

Chedzer reviewed the diagrams again, smacked his forehead with the palm of his hand, and sighed. The color drained from his face as he stood there, studying the two cables. "I can't believe I made such an error, Captain.

I … could've killed everyone on board." He reversed the two cables, causing the auto-destruct warning light to go off. The primary coil came alive, emitting a dim blue glow. The engine's purr was low and soothing.

"How did you know, Captain?" Chedzer still seemed baffled. "I apologize for my error. I—"

"Your misjudgment could have killed everyone on the *Eliptus*. I'll document this incident in your record. Make another mistake, no matter how small, and you'll be relieved of duty. Do I make myself clear?"

"Yes, Captain," Chedzer said.

"Perhaps you're getting too old for this position," she added.

Chedzer lowered his head. "Yes, Captain."

Sedo transported back to her ship and asked Bonuve to navigate the *Eliptus* back to Tandon. He sped off in front of the *Volpus*, headed for the Zone.

"Careful, Bonuve," she said. "Don't overload the engine. Its speed is not comparable to the *Volpus*."

He stared back at her from a vektren and flashed a broad grin. "This ship is fine. I'm requesting promotion to captain."

"Why haven't you applied already?" she asked.

"I was waiting for the right time," he said. "I feel that I'm ready."

"Bonuve, you've done an outstanding job over the past seven years, and I'm certain Fleet Command agrees."

Both ships entered and exited the Zone at the same time, with the *Eliptus* on the starboard side of the *Volpus*. Sedo felt victorious as she reentered her own galaxy.

***

Sedo relaxed in a secluded area under the dome with Jogen at her side. Watching the planets and stars zoom past always took her mind off her problems.

"Look." Jogen pointed. "A red planet. I've never seen one that large."

Sedo caressed his hand. "We've passed many. You need to get out of the laboratory more often."

He placed a arm around her neck. "They glow like embers."

"Metallic gases make them glow," she said.

"Living in space is different from just passing through it," he said. "I still miss Tandon."

She felt his passion as he pulled her closer.

"I love you," he said. "We're perfect for each other." He kissed her lips, and his warm tongue caressed hers. She felt his right heart pounding against her chest. "Will you be my lifemate? I think we're the only two on this ship who are not united."

"I know of one other." Sedo pulled away. "Ask me again when this ordeal is over. Rota will be difficult to deal with."

"Are you sure?" he asked.

"Yes. I see him sitting behind my father's old desk. He's aggressive and arrogant, and he wants to become a Megmador. He's strict and plans to make many changes within Fleet Command. I defied Fleet Command orders, and Rota will hold it against me."

"You should receive a medal for what you did. You're the most decorated captain in the fleet. Rota wouldn't dare punish you."

"It doesn't work that way," Captain Sedo said.

"If Colas were commander, he wouldn't punish you," Jogen said.

"Probably not. I'll have to inform Rota that I'm a Megmador," she said.

"Why?" Jogen asked.

"I took an oath when I became captain. Fleet Command has a right to know."

"Regardless of what happens, I want you to be my mate," Jogen said.

"I'll be reprimanded, but not demoted."

"You said Commander Rota will be furious with you."

"He'll be concentrating on a much more serious problem than my defying Fleet Command."

"You mean you being a Megmador will sidetrack him. Shake him up a lot," Jogen said.

They both chuckled.

"I know you want a son. What if I can't conceive a child?"

He laughed. "Then we'll find a human pet."

Sedo elbowed him in the side. "That's not funny."

"You're Beltese now. I believe we can have a child."

She sat up straight in her chair. "What if it's a Megmador?"

He threw his head back and chuckled. "A baby—"

"We can't be sure," she said.

"There has never been such a thing as a baby Megmador," he added.

"At least I won't have to carry it to fullterm, like females in my clans. I can't imagine having something growing inside me for nine months."

"Six," he corrected. "After the first two weeks, it goes into incubation."

For the first time in months, Sedo's powers didn't stress her. She didn't feel the pressure and anxiety felt by the previous Megmadors she'd studied.

***

Sedo joined Jogen for lunch again at their usual table. He reached across the tabletop and took her hand in his.

She quickly withdrew. "Stop it. Crew members are watching."

"I don't care," he said.

"It's not proper. You know the crew has spread rumors about us."

He smiled and touched her foot with his under the table. "They're not rumors anymore."

After lunch, Sedo went back to Navigational Control. Somgu, her new lieutenant, smiled. "Captain, you seem to be in a good mood lately."

Sedo smiled back. "I am."

***

As soon as Sedo was back in communication with Fleet Command, Commander Rota contacted her.

"Captain, the fleet commander has requested to speak with you," Starco's voice rang through the wall speaker in her quarters.

Sedo sat at her computer. "Put him on a vektren."

When Rota appeared, his eyes were cold and stern.

"Hello, Commander. Did you review the data I transmitted?" she asked.

"Yes, our team reviewed it thoroughly," Rota said.

"My father created quite a story to keep us away from the other galaxy."

Rota tugged at his collar. "I understand the *Eliptus* is on its way home, and the aliens didn't know how to reassemble its core."

"That's correct. We also have what's left of the crew, 137."

"How's the *Eliptus's* crew recovering?" Rota asked.

"Those who could recover have. Three are nearing Naconda."

Rota rested his hands on his desk. "Send me their statements."

"I'll get this information to you immediately," Sedo said.

His nostrils flared. "When you return to Tandon, have Doctors Fea and Ohma meet me in my office. I'll deal with your insubordination later."

"Please, remember the doctors only did what the late Commander Sedo instructed when they reengineered my genes. They know my medical history, and I need them."

"Captain Sedo, you disobeyed Fleet Command orders."

She knew that Rota wouldn't understand her logic. "But I knew Neptus posed no threat to us. The information I transmitted to Fleet Command proved it."

"You didn't contact Fleet Command concerning your intentions until you were seconds away from communication range," Rota scolded. "You had six months to inform us."

"Tell who? My father?"

"When you disobeyed orders, Commander Sedo was already dead. You took matters into your own hands, Captain."

Sedo felt as if her hearts were crumbling. "I have no excuse for my actions."

"Where will you be stopping on your way back to Tandon?" he asked.

"I plan to spend a week on Marcus, in order to give my crew time to relax."

"Give Nowe my compliments regarding his decision to help fund the Human Planet Project."

"I'll see you in six months, Commander."

The vektren image disappeared.

***

When Jogen rushed into Sedo's room, she was staring at her computer screen.

"Sadera," Jogen said. "It's all over the *Volpus* that you'll be punished for what you did."

"I expect to be disciplined," she said.

He paced before her, ranting, "But it's not fair. The crew has started rumors about you being kicked out of Fleet Command."

"I have three degrees in advanced engineering. I don't think I'll have a problem finding another position."

Jogen squeezed her shoulders. "We can't be separated. I want to complete my research in space with you. I'm making great progress with my experiments, and I wish to remain on the *Volpus*."

"I doubt I'll lose my job, Jogen. Relax."

"How would you know?" Jogen asked.

"I'm a Megmador, remember?"

"You can't know how Rota will react. We're too far from Tandon for you to read his thoughts. You must convince him to let you remain captain."

"I'm not worried about it," she said. "Once he realizes I'm a Megmador, everything will change."

He stood at her side and turned her chair around to face him. "Well, I don't share your confidence."

Chapter 14

The Human Slaves

After traveling for two months in space, Captain Sedo gave the *Volpus's* and *Eliptus's* crews a week's leave on Marcus.

The ships remained in orbit, maintained by minimal crew members who rotated taking leave. Nowe invited Captain Sedo to visit his rural home. When she transported down, the sun stood high in the sky. A small spacecraft occupied a launch pad on the left side of a two-story home. The wraparound porch had numerous hanging basket plants. The area looked like a jungle, and Nowe was nowhere in sight. The huge garden had a variety of fruits and vegetables. Various species of lush grapes hung from vines that mingled on wooden fences. There were plants both indigenous to Marcus and from other planets.

She envied Nowe, because she wanted to live as he did, surrounded by nature, but with all the comforts of modern technology.

Commander Nowe stepped from behind a bush

burdened with fruits and waved a straw hat at her. He wore gloves and knee-high boots. "Over here."

Sedo laughed and hurried in his direction. "Hello, Commander." She threw her hands into the air. "This place is amazing, gorgeous."

He led her around, proudly showing off his lush stock.

Surprised, Sedo gawked at a young black male with a shaved head. "Human? You have a human here?"

"Yes, Hammon and his wife. I pay them well," Nowe said.

The bare-chested male knelt on the ground. Using a metal rake with a wooden handle, he tilled soil around a wide plant. When they approached, he never looked up. His hands were calloused. He wore dirty blue pants, and perspiration dripped down his face and torso.

Sedo glanced askance at Nowe. "Are there any more humans on Marcus?"

"No, just two." Nowe laughed. "You can't believe how happy they are here."

"He doesn't look happy. Where do they live?" Sedo asked.

Nowe pointed at a structure resembling a storage facility. "There."

"Is it equipped with modern conveniences?" the captain asked.

Nowe's face showed no compassion. "They're protected from the elements, and they like the heat."

Captain Sedo folded her arms and gawked at Nowe. "And how did they tell you this?"

He struggled for words. "Well ... ah. They refused to live in my house."

"Do they have children?" Sedo asked.

Nowe cleared his throat. "No."

"How long have they been here?"

He punched a button on his wristband and coughed. "Two years tomorrow."

"Hammon," Captain Sedo said.

The male stopped working, peered up from bended knees, and sat back on his heels. His dark eyes darted from her to Nowe, and he grimaced. He opened his mouth to speak but didn't utter a sound. For the first time, Sedo noticed his youth. He looked to be somewhere in his late teens.

Sedo ventured into the young man's mind and realized that Nowe had tortured him. He hated Nowe but feared him too much to defend himself. Hammon lived in a strange world with no way out, surrounded by things he would never understand, which left him miserable and lonely for his tribe.

"They know a few words in our language," Nowe said. "But they mostly speak gibberish in their native tongue."

"Do you have a language translator?" Sedo asked.

"No. We get along fine without one."

Sedo challenged Nowe with a stern gaze. "Did you bring them here against their will?"

Nowe waved his hand in a half circle. "Look at the good life they have here. They don't walk around naked, killing animals with crude spears in order to survive. They have more food than they could ever eat."

She hated the nonchalant demeanor Nowe had revealed concerning her species. "Freedom means more than available food. How can you be so cruel?"

Nowe placed both hands on his chubby hips and bent backward with his eyes skyward. "It's a hot one today."

"You didn't answer my question. Are they from one of the tribes you removed from Maacon?"

"Yes," Nowe admitted.

Her heart rate increased. She sucked in humid air, trying to control her temper and maintain professional composure. "They're slaves. You're no better than the Velekans."

Nowe spread his arms and opened his palms to the sky. "They're free. Both can go anywhere they wish. They're not in bondage."

"And how will they leave here, Commander? On their own ship?"

"They want to remain here."

"How did they relay this message to you?" she asked again.

Nowe mumbled something inaudible. Sedo didn't ask him to repeat it.

Sedo didn't listen to his words that followed but thought of the cruel, surreal side of Nowe. He had taken advantage of her trust, enslaved her species, and showed no remorse.

At a distance, she saw a young, skinny black girl carrying a basket on her head. She wore a long green dress with a matching head wrap.

"Let me treat you to lunch," Nowe said after the grand tour of his garden.

Sedo trailed behind him, thinking about what to do with the human slaves. Because of their exposure to space and alien life, uniting them with their tribe could prove deadly.

She entered Nowe's plush home, which he had decorated with fine art and artifacts from extinct civilizations.

He turned his back to her and poured two glasses of wine. "Have a seat."

"None for me," Sedo said.

She sat on furniture made of soft kamatton fur. For centuries, the Galactic Committee had forbidden killing the cats for their coats.

"At least taste it," Nowe insisted. "I have quite a variety, made right here."

"All right, just a sip."

She noticed a probe near the kitchen table used to immobilize animals. It alarmed her, because Nowe had no livestock.

He tapped an intercom button and spoke a few words in his own language.

Shortly afterward, a girl appeared with a serving tray

carrying two meaty sandwiches and spongy desserts with a brown topping.

Sedo was too nauseated to eat or drink anything in Nowe's house. She turned the food down, claiming she'd eaten prior to leaving the *Volpus*. She accepted the wine, lifted the glass to her lips, but didn't take a sip.

"Superb stock, isn't it?" Nowe asked.

"Excellent," she agreed.

The female slave appeared to be a few years younger than Hammon. Her eyes never met Sedo's, and a scowl dominated her face. She worked like a robot trained to do special duties.

Sedo sensed signs of lingering oppression and resisted the urge to torture Nowe. She had promised her parents and herself that she would never use her powers except during life-or-death situations.

Nowe took a bite of his sandwich, chewed a few times, and swallowed. He dabbed the corners of his fat mouth with a napkin and took a sip of wine. "I'm sorry about your parents' death and the scandal concerning your father. Although Beltese Fleet Command tried to conceal it, the truth is all over the galaxy." He held up a hairy paw. "I'm sorry, I shouldn't have mentioned that."

Hairs rose on the back of Sedo's neck. "It's perfectly all right." She deliberately changed the conversation. "Where's your wife?"

"She doesn't care for rural life," Nowe said. "She's strictly metropolitan."

After four hours of total boredom, Sedo transported to the *Eliptus*.

Bonuve sat smartly in the captain's chair. "Captain Sedo, I hope you have good news for me," he said.

"Well, the good news is Rota approved your promotion to captain. The bad news is the *Eliptus* is now your ship. Congratulations, Captain Bonuve."

A broad smile spread across his face. "Thank you, Captain."

"We have a reception for you on the *Volpus* in an hour. Rota will perform the ceremony over a vektren."

He smiled. "I wouldn't miss it."

***

During the crew's last day on Marcus, Sedo declined Nowe's donation of fruits, vegetables, and wine for her crew. She sat in her captain's chair in Navigational Control. "Somgu, are all crew members aboard and accounted for?"

"Yes, Captain," Somgu said.

"There are two humans on this planet, maybe more. I want them transported aboard the *Volpus*."

Within seconds, Somgu announced, "I've located two, and they're being transported."

"Ferrus, take us home," Sedo said.

"What are we going to do with the humans?" Somgu asked. "And why did Nowe have them?"

"Slaves," Sedo said. "Contact a language officer. Find out which tribe they're from and how Nowe treated them."

Somgu gasped, "Slavery is against the Galactic Committee's rules, established by Nowe himself. Superior species don't take advantage of the inferior ones."

***

When Zanta entered the transporter room, the two humans were huddled together on the floor at the back wall.

The bare-chested male's head was bald, and his arms swelled with muscles. Dirt covered his pants and bare feet, and perspiration dripped from his body like rain. The girl wore a long brown dress with a matching head wrap.

Zanta eased down onto her knees next to them, but the humans scooted away. "Hello, my name is Zanta."

The male placed an arm around the female's neck, perhaps as an act of protection. They stared back at her with cold eyes. She not only witnessed their fear but also felt it.

"This," Zanta said, "is a language translator. You speak, and your language is translated into ours."

She punched in Sedo's personal communication

number on her wristband. "Captain, the humans are huddled against the wall, frightened to death and trembling."

Sedo's voice rang loud and clear on Zanta's collar communicator. "Can you get them into living quarters?"

"They're not going anywhere. They're too afraid," said Zanta.

Bago entered the transporter room. "Any progress?"

"No."

"Just send them to Altaur," he said.

Zanta looked back at Bago. "If we transport them to the wrong tribe, they'll be killed." She poked a thumb at her own chest. "Zanta. My name is Zanta."

Then she pointed a finger at the young girl, but she didn't respond. She did it again with the male—still no results.

"Let's take a walk and leave the machine on," Bago suggested. "They'll talk to each other."

Zanta touched buttons on the language translator. "There are only two languages on their planet. Let me try one."

Zanta spoke, translating the language into Zulu, and the humans grew tenser. The girl's face wrinkled, and her mouth opened, as if she wanted to scream.

Zanta adjusted the translator. "Let me try the Womba's language. Hello, my name is Zanta."

The humans relaxed and their eyes squinted.

***

Anan, the female human, had witnessed so many strange things, like traveling among the stars.

She feared her surroundings more than death. Without Tamba, she would have ended her life long ago. Her eyes froze on the small talking box, like the one she had seen on Nowe's ship. "My name is Anan." She felt her own voice quiver when she spoke to the thing named Zanta. "This is Tamba."

"My name is Tamba," he confirmed.

Anan felt not only her body shaking, but Tamba's as well. Would this thing make them slaves as Nowe had? Would their lives become better or worse? The future frightened her. The thing called Zanta was female with short, yellow, limp hair, pale skin, and strange gray eyes.

"We're taking you back to your tribe," Zanta said. "Would you like to go home?"

Anan clasped her hands together. "Yes, please, take us home."

"It'll take two seasons, but I promise we'll get you to your new home."

"New home?" Anan became even more shocked.

"Yes, your village moved too close to the sun—"

"No, the sun moved closer to us," Anan corrected.

"We've relocated your tribe to a new place, temporarily, of course, until we can find them a permanent home." Zanta paused, as if waiting for a response. "The alien you lived with, his name is Nowe. What did he force you to do?"

"He made us work," Tamba said. "He hurt us with a strange stick if we refused or didn't do things his way."

"Slaves? You were slaves?" Zanta asked.

Tamba removed his arm from around Anan's neck but remained close. "Yes. In our world, only the Zulus take slaves. I wanted to kill him, but he had such strong powers. At first, we thought he was a god."

"I'm sorry for what Nowe did to you," Zanta said. "That's not our way of life."

"Nor ours," Tamba said.

Zanta picked up the talking thing. "When you traveled on Nowe's ship, didn't they talk to you through a translator like this one?"

"Yes," Anan said. "But we thought it was a spirit." She studied it. "How does it work? We talk, but another voice answers."

Zanta bounced to her feet, attached the talking box at her waist, and pulled the strap tight. "This is called a language translator. We use them to communicate with different species if we don't know their languages. Most species speak our language, Beltese. It's sort of the galactic language."

"What is communicate?" Anan asked.

"Communicate means to speak. It's how we talk to others," Zanta said. "Sometimes our translators don't use the exact word meanings in your tongue."

Anan repeated the word. "Communicate."

"I'm assigning you to living quarters. Nowe said you two are married. You are too young."

Tamba stood next. "We live as husband and wife, but we would like to be married, and soon."

"How old are you?" Zanta asked.

Tamba held up fingers. "I'm this many summers, and Anan is this many winters. In our village, we're old enough to marry."

Zanta frowned, and she used her fingers to count. "Beltese are not allowed to marry until after our thirty-first birthdays."

Using the wall, Anan held down her dress and climbed to her feet. "That's our parents' age."

"You have nothing to fear on this ship," Zanta said.

"What are living quarters?" Anan asked.

Zanta said, "A room where you rest, sleep."

"Like on Nowe's ship?" Anan asked.

"Yes. Was Nowe on the ship with you?" Zanta asked.

"No, but we understood that it belonged to him," Tamba said.

"Are you hungry?" Zanta asked.

"No," they said in unison.

"I know you're afraid, but you must eat something. I'll take you to your living quarters first." Zanta led the way, glancing back at them. "We eat in a 'dining room.'"

Anan followed her down a hallway and into a vertical lift with Tamba at her side, just as she had long ago on Nowe's ship.

The doors closed behind them as Zanta spoke. "There'll be others like me, but they won't harm you. We have a captain who is human like you. Her skin is light and her hair is brown, but she's from one of your tribes. She saw you at Nowe's home and she brought you here."

"What's a human?" Anan asked.

Zanta cocked her head and squinted. "Human is a species. You are human, I'm Beltese, and Nowe is Elgon. Not only do we speak different languages, but also our physiologies are different. Like, we have two hearts, and humans have one."

Zanta's words fogged Anan's thoughts. She didn't fully understand what they meant.

They stepped off the lift and walked down another hallway.

Each time they passed a Beltese, Anan recoiled toward the opposite wall.

Zanta pushed a button on the wall and a door opened. "Don't be afraid, they're just passing crew members. Here we are. Anan, this is your room."

Anan peeked inside but remained with Tamba.

Zanta walked to the room across from Anan's and pushed another button. "Tamba, these are your quarters. Just push the button and the door opens. It automatically closes."

Anan didn't understand much that Zanta said, and she was certain that Tamba didn't either.

Zanta opened the door, and they entered. "See these

two buttons?" she said. "Press the red button if you don't want any visitors. It locks the door. The green button is an invitation to anyone who wants to enter. Red light locks, green button welcomes," she repeated.

***

When Captain Sedo entered the room, she noticed that a conversation was transpiring between Zanta and her two guests. The humans sat on the bed, and Zanta occupied a seat at the desk.

Leaving the translator on, Zanta informed Sedo of what had transpired.

The humans gawked at Sedo curiously.

Zanta introduced them. "This is Anan and this is Tamba. They're from the Womba tribe."

Sedo addressed Tamba first. "Nowe called you Hammon."

He said, "Nowe didn't like our names, so he gave us new ones."

Sedo faced Anan. "Please, do not fear us. You're welcome here."

"We've never seen a tribe like yours," Anan said.

"I'm Captain Sedo. I'm human like you. A Beltese couple adopted me. I'm the leader of this ship, like a chief. So, if you need anything, just let me know."

Anan gasped, "A female chief?"

Tamba's eyes drifted from Sedo to Zanta. "In our world

females are never chiefs. They're not equal to men, because they don't know how to hunt, fight, or be leaders."

"In our world men are physically stronger than women," Sedo said. "But here, we're judged by our minds, rather than our strength."

Sedo turned off the translator and made a ship wide announcement. "This is the captain speaking. We have two humans aboard the ship from Maacon. These humans were enslaved and tortured by Nowe and are frightened of all beings. They'll be dining with the crew. Please be courteous and show friendly gestures toward them. Thank you for your cooperation."

***

When the door closed behind Zanta and Sedo, Anan rushed into the bathroom while Tamba bounced on the bed.

"We have a washroom like on Nowe's ship. It's painted blue," Anan said.

"This room is nicer, and this bed is softer," Tamba said.

"We've never seen anyone like this Sedo," Anan said. "Her hair is straight and the color of her eyes is strange."

Tamba walked to the desk and studied the blinking lights. "There was one of these on Nowe's ship."

Anan grabbed his hand. "Don't. Remember what happened when you touched the other one. It came alive and spoke to us."

"Maybe Captain Sedo will show us how it works," Tamba said.

She pointed. "Look. This room also has a thing on the wall that controls the air."

Tamba pulled out each drawer from underneath the bed. "They're all empty."

Anan whispered, "How do we know this Sedo is of one of our tribes? Zanta invited us to eat with them. Perhaps it's us who are on the menu."

Tamba took a seat on the bed again. "Don't speak of such things."

She sat next to him. "Remember what we saw outside this ship—darkness. There's no sunlight to grow fruits and vegetables. Herds cannot survive here."

"We survived on Nowe's ship. You thought they would eat us, but they didn't. They fed us well."

"I don't trust this Sedo," Anan wept. "We'll never see our village again."

Tamba took her hand and squeezed it. "We must believe."

Anan focused on the gray fabric that covered the floor. Tears ran down her cheeks. "I don't think so, Tamba. I miss my sister, our tribe."

Tamba gently patted her on the back. "I miss our tribe too."

"We're trapped in a world where women cannot bare their breasts and men must wear clothes," Anan said.

"Anan, I don't mind wearing clothes. These things

would stare at us if we bared ourselves, as we did in our village. We must respect their traditions and accept their world."

"I don't want to fit in. I want to go home, no matter where it is," she said.

"Back to what? Many of our family members died on the plains. If Sedo does belong to one of our tribes, she'll take care of us," Tamba said.

"She can't look after us all the time."

Tamba said, "I don't think I want to go back to our world. Look at the way they live here. Just push a button and you get whatever you want."

"What if we end up slaves again?" Anan asked.

"I trust Sedo. I believe in her."

"Tamba—"

"You'll never have to carry wood, build a fire to cook food, or spend days making your own wraps."

"We don't know their tongue."

Tamba's voice was pleading, demanding. "We can learn, like Sizwe. He was born Zulu, and he learned our customs. We even learned some of Nowe's words."

"On Nowe's ship we didn't eat with them. Zanta said we could move freely here. I'm afraid to walk around here," Anan said.

"When the time is right, we'll ask Sedo if we can stay here, on her ship."

"If they don't eat us first," Anan said.

Tamba sighed. "Are you still thinking about that?"

***

"Captain, Commander Nowe is coming into view," Starco said.

From her captain's chair in Navigational Control, Sedo's gaze left her computer and focused on Nowe's wide gray eyes. He sat at a desk, his back facing the wall, rather than his plush furnishings.

He took deep, raspy breaths, as if both of his hearts were pumping at maximum speed. Sweat ran down his face and dripped off his chin. "Captain Sedo, my humans are gone. I'm reporting you to the Beltese Fleet Command."

"You mean your slaves." Sedo spat her words at him. "We've questioned them, and we know how you treated them."

"You had no right to take them away," Nowe bellowed.

Sedo folded her arms. "Report me to the commander. He'll confirm I did nothing wrong. From your own mouth, superior species shouldn't take advantage of the inferior ones."

"Because of your actions, I'll no longer help finance the Human Planet Project."

She propped her elbows on her desk and gawked at him. "I promise that everyone in this galaxy will know that you were a slave owner."

Nowe jumped to his feet. "Are you threatening me, Captain?"

"Yes, Commander, I am."

He raised his voice. "Don't get smug with me, Sedo. You've violated the galactic codes by taking away my workers."

She spoke in a calm voice. "You violated galactic codes by forcing an intelligent species into servitude."

"I provided them with food and shelter," Nowe yelled.

Sedo stood, her eyes scrutinizing him. "They shouldn't have been on your planet in the first place. Did they ask to be tortured as well?"

"I—" Nowe couldn't get his words out.

"You took them from a primitive environment and transported them into our world. Now they're afraid and confused."

Nowe wiped sweat from his wrinkled forehead with a napkin. "Go on, take them to Altaur. They'll no longer fit in with their tribe. If they repeat what they've witnessed, they'll become outcasts—considered demons—even killed."

Sedo took a seat. "Computer, cease communication."

***

When the door opened, Sedo and Zanta entered the room. Anan wasn't as frightened now.

"You both look refreshed," Sedo said.

Anan had showered and changed into a white robe, exactly as Tamba had.

Sedo glanced down at their bare feet. "We're taking you to dinner. Where are your shoes?"

"We don't like them," Anan said. "Nowe said we didn't have to wear them."

Sedo picked up sandals at the foot of the bed and gave each a pair. "You'll need them here. They're so comfortable you won't know they're on your feet."

Like Tamba, Anan stepped into her sandals and followed Sedo. They did feel like a part of her feet.

Zanta walked behind them, making Anan nervous.

When they reached the eating area, Anan stopped at the entrance and slowly scanned the room. At her last home, she'd only seen Nowe. Here, a herd of the cat-like things crowded the area. The males all looked the same, and so did the females.

Anan couldn't force her feet to move forward. Tamba had, likewise, stopped behind her.

"Captain," Zanta called out.

The captain turned and approached Anan and Tamba. Sedo motioned with a hand. "Come on in. No one is going to harm you."

She had no appetite, and the cats still frightened her. She felt Tamba's trembling hand on her shoulder.

Every now and then one of the cats would glance in their direction, but they didn't stare as a predator would at prey. Many were involved in conversations among themselves. Some focused on the tabletops in front of them. Anan walked slowly, her eyes searching the room for an attack she feared would come at any moment.

Sedo took Anan's trembling arm and led her into the room. When they reached the table, Sedo pulled back the chairs, inviting Anan and Tamba to sit next to each other. Then she pushed their chairs close to the table. Unlike at Nowe's place, the chairs moved only backward or forward.

Zanta pressed a button in the center of the table, and it lit up. "This is a menu. We order our food from it."

Anan saw squiggly black lines on a white background. She rolled her chair backward, but Tamba remained at his position.

"Nowe's tables didn't have menus," Tamba said. "How can a table come alive like the thing in our room?"

Sedo smiled. "You have a computer in your room. This is similar to one. It only lights up when you touch it."

"When you traveled on Nowe's ship, didn't you eat with the crew?" Zanta asked.

Anan glanced around the large room again. "No, we ate in our rooms."

Sedo's eyes went from the menu to Anan and Tamba. "Please move in closer so I can demonstrate how it works."

Anan feared the living table and remained where she was.

"It's written in Beltese. I'll read it to you," Sedo said.

"We'll start with fruit or soup. Which would you prefer?"

"Fruit," Tamba and she said in unison.

"Always ask a server to explain the menu," Zanta said. "We'll provide each of you with a language translator. Keep it with you at all times."

Sedo explained everything on the menu. "With your main dish, you get vegetables. They're not the same as the ones in your world. You'll just have to try them. How about danberry juice? I'm sure you'll like it."

Sedo and Zanta talked, but Anan wasn't listening to the voice box. She kept glancing around the room at the cat-like things.

When the male brought their meals, he flashed a courteous smile. She intensely studied his face, expecting sharp teeth.

Tamba pointed to his eating tools. "Nowe wouldn't allow us to eat with our hands. We had to use these."

Sedo dug one into her food. "We eat with them as well. After two years, you must have mastered their use."

"Yes, we have," Tamba said. "What kind of work must we do?"

Sedo threw back her head and laughed. "You're my guests. I don't expect you to work. Study and learn about space and our language. I'm entering you both in an intense educational program."

Anan asked, "If we're going home, why would we learn your way of life?"

Tamba shook his head.

Sedo took a bite of food. "There's nothing wrong with learning."

CHAPTER 15

JOBS FOR THE HUMANS

Midway through the voyage, Sedo stopped at M-5 to purchase supplies, affording her crew five days of relaxation. Warships like the *Volpus* were too large to dock at the substations, so her crew transported over. She always allowed her second-in-command to take leave first.

Once her crew was aboard the substation, Sedo visited the research laboratory. She stood behind Jogen and looked over his shoulder as he entered data into his computer.

"Jogen, I've taken a few bottles of chochu wine from supply, and I need to replace them."

He continued punching keys on his computer. "Isn't that wine for celebratory occasions and guests?"

"Yes, that's why I need to replace it," Sedo said.

He faced her. "How could you do something so obvious? Only you and Somgu have access to that supply room."

"Here, take my galactic card. Buy as much as you can and keep it in your room."

Jogen grinned. "Why don't you tell everyone you're a Megmador and have cravings?"

She punched him in his side with a fist. "Stop joking."

***

Sedo waited for Jogen for over five hours. He took his time, probably shopping for ancient artifacts from all over the galaxy, she imagined.

When he finally returned, he had sixteen bottles of wine with him. "That's all I could get. It's a popular brand."

"What took you so long?"

"I had personal shopping to do as well."

Sedo went straight to the supply room with six bottles of wine in a bag strapped over her shoulder. She had replaced four bottles when the door opened and her second-in-command entered.

Somgu moved closer, staring at the two bottles of wine in Captain Sedo's hands. Her eyes narrowed in suspicion. "Are you removing them or replacing them?"

Sedo felt like a thief. She paused, her mind scrambling for a reason. "Are you questioning me, Lieutenant?"

"Of course not, Captain. It's just odd, seeing a human with chochu wine."

"Replacing them. We had a special occasion. Jogen and the doctors."

"Oh. What special occasion?" Somgu asked.

"That's none of your concern. Somgu, why is it that every time I turn around you're standing there?"

"I didn't realize I was crowding you, Captain. From now on, I'll try to maintain my distance."

Sedo placed the last two bottles on the shelf and left. Somgu remained in the storage room.

Jogen was lying on her bed when Sedo returned to her room. "Somgu caught me replacing the wine."

He stared at the ceiling. "What did you tell her?"

"That you and the doctors had a special celebration."

"Did she believe you?" he asked.

"No," she replied.

"You're the captain. You don't have to answer to her."

Sedo picked up a bottle and moved to the table. "I'm sure Rota has her spying on me. She's really getting under my skin. How about some wine?"

Sedo twisted the cork from the bottle, retrieved two glasses from inside her desk, and filled them. She turned at the sound of her door opening. Once again, Somgu appeared.

"Captain, I found your door unlocked. If I'm intruding—"

"Do you want something, Lieutenant?" Sedo asked sharply.

Somgu didn't respond but gawked at the glass in Sedo's hand.

Sedo felt like she did the time her mother caught her peeing behind a bush in the park when she was a child.

"Oh, this." Sedo raised her glass. "Well, my parents used to drink lots of it, and the fumes never harmed me."

Somgu stood frozen. "Chochu wine is deadly to humans."

Sedo had never been good at lying. "Jogen gave me an injection to make me immune to the poison. That's one of his research projects."

Somgu still concentrated on her glass, mesmerized.

"Your reason for being here, Lieutenant?" Sedo snapped.

Somgu turned to leave. "I … I see I'm intruding."

"Lieutenant, don't mention this to anyone, and that's an order."

"Yes, Captain," she said as the door closed behind her.

From her desk, Sedo locked the door. "Do you think she believed me?"

Jogen laughed. "Not a word."

"Well, I'd better not hear about it or she'll be serving in the dining room."

Jogen took a gulp of wine. "Somgu isn't an idiot. She senses something is happening. That's why she's always spying on you. I suggest you behave more like your old self."

"Have I … changed?" Sedo asked.

He shrugged and lowered his head. "Somewhat."

Sedo's glass paused midway to her mouth. Suddenly, she didn't crave the wine anymore. "What does that mean?"

He rubbed his chin and licked his lower lip. "Well, you ... I can't explain it. I feel a radiating superiority from you. Invincibility. Your personality is stronger than before."

Her glass hit the table with a thud. "Why haven't you mentioned this before?"

"Don't worry, only the crew members closest to you will notice, like those in Navigational Control and the doctors. It's normal for Megmadors."

"And you still want to marry me?" she asked.

"Of course. You're the Sadera I grew up with, and I love you."

***

From Navigational Control, Sedo punched in Zanta's communication code. "How are the human educational programs going?"

"Fine, but I don't understand why we're teaching them. Aren't you transporting them back to their village?"

"Drill them twelve hours a day if necessary. Teach them everything they need to survive in our world. When we reach Tandon, I expect them to speak Beltese."

There was a long pause before Zanta spoke. "What are you planning to do with them?"

Sedo sighed and gazed into space. "I don't know yet, but they won't be going back to their tribe."

"Have they told you they wish to remain here?" Zanta asked.

"They've been exposed to advanced civilization, and I doubt that they'll want to return to their primitive lifestyle." She felt proud that her species had learned the destinations of all vertical lifts and horizontal trams. They no longer feared the Beltese. Both had learned how to swim and had discovered new clothing. Her humans had no choice but to live among aliens for the rest of their lives, as she had.

Sedo leaned back in her chair and stared through the viewport. Billions of kilometers away, she saw an immense black hole lurking within the beauty of the galaxy, mysterious and dangerous. Surrounded by a vortex of gases and asteroids, it slowly vacuumed in and digested everything that entered its powerful gravitational force. To escape the critical zone, the scary black spherical center, required a velocity greater than the speed of light.

On the port side of the *Volpus* beamed Altus, the largest gaseous planet known to space travelers. The uninhabitable sphere enveloped thick clouds of turbulent gaseous vapors that created 132 spectacular dust bands of various colors. Probes sent into its atmosphere stopped transmitting and never returned.

Only future technology would yield the secrets of this planet.

***

Captain Sedo had just retired when her door buzzed. She donned a pink robe, ready to scold a crew member for interrupting her privacy. "Computer, open the door." Since Somgu's unexpected visit, she'd been keeping her door locked.

Anan's eyes made contact with Sedo's, and her voice quivered in broken Beltese. "Sorry for disturbing, Captain, but we have request."

Tamba stood at her side, hands behind his back.

Sedo stood aside. "Come in. Have a seat."

Since space was dark, her guests couldn't distinguish the time of day. Neither did they know that Somgu and she rotated duties.

Anan took a seat at the table opposite Tamba and studied the room.

Sedo sensed their disappointment. They thought the captain would live better, like Nowe. Apart from personal effects, their rooms were identical.

Anan sat stiff and straight in her chair, knotted her hands, and twisted them in her lap.

Sedo sat opposite her.

Tamba scratched his head and appeared to be focusing on the painting on her wall.

Sedo waved a hand. "That's what Tandon looks like from space." She glanced from one to the other, waiting for them to speak. Neither did.

Sedo didn't like intruding into others' thoughts, but she invaded theirs. "You don't want to return to your village."

Anan blurted out in broken Beltese, "Here you cook food without building a fire—"

"You have no dangerous animals," Tamba said. "Is this how you live on your planet?"

"Yes," Sedo said.

"We wish to remain here with you," Anan said.

"My ship is for Fleet Command crew only. Regulations don't allow having civilians onboard, other than in special circumstances such as yours. However, I might find work for you either on an Agooron space station or on Tandon."

"Where will you be?" Anan asked.

"Traveling in space," Sedo said.

"What's Agooron?" Tamba asked.

"The Agooron is another species. They are very friendly, and their space stations are a relaxation place for travelers," Sedo explained.

Anan's face brightened like a star. "In return for our work, we get galactic credit?"

"You learn quickly, Anan."

Tamba nodded. "And we trade with credits?"

"Yes, the exchange of universal credits for items is called a purchase."

Anan lowered her head. "We may not like these Agoorons."

"I understand that you both are excellent swimmers." She saw their eyes brighten. "The space stations have huge beaches, much larger than the swimming areas here on the *Volpus*."

Tamba flashed a cheerful smile. "No snakes, crocodiles, or hippos. The water is a clear bluish-green."

"Not muddy like in our world," Anan said.

Sedo glanced at the clock over her bed. "The Agoorons are very pleasant. You'll feel comfortable with them. You'll meet other aliens, different from the Beltese. Some are extremely tall. Another species looks like bugs with four arms. You must be willing to continue learning our language, because most species in our galaxy speak it. We don't expect you to speak other languages. That's why we have translators."

"What if the Agoorons treat us like Nowe did?" Anan asked.

"No, they won't. I'll stay in contact, stop there from time to time. Remember how afraid you were when you first came aboard my ship? You'll probably feel a bit uncomfortable at first."

"I have question, Captain," Tamba said in broken Beltese. "Why we are considered primal?"

Sedo cringed at the thought. "Oh." How could she explain it without insulting them? "You're considered primal because you lack technology or the ability to read and write in your language. It means you're uneducated."

Anan's eyes welled up. "We understand that monkeys are primal. Is that how other species see us?"

"No," Sedo said. "We consider monkeys are primates."

Anan scooted to the edge of her chair, her eyes excited. "Have you been to other planets where our species lives? Have you seen many?"

"I've seen a few," Sedo said. "I'm trying to find a planet to transport all of our clans to."

Tamba relaxed his body and crossed his legs. "That's the reason we study so much?"

"You must learn our way of life in order to survive here," Sedo said.

Tamba frowned and tilted his head. "Can we become as smart as you?"

"If you're willing to learn," Sedo said.

Sedo punched in Somgu's communication code from her computer station. "Just a minute, Tamba."

"Yes, Captain," Somgu said.

"Contact Septa. Put him in my room."

Agoorons slept only a few hours per day, so Sedo guessed that he would probably be awake.

Within seconds, Septa appeared on a vektren. He sat at a small table in his quarters. He wore a green robe and held a glass in one hand. He took a bite out of something brown and placed the remainder on a dish. He stared at her with big brown eyes, their blue pupils sparkling.

Both of Sedo's guests rushed to the door and frantically groped for the control button. When the door opened, they stumbled into the hallway and fled.

Sedo stood. "I'll get back with you, Septa."

When Sedo caught up with Tamba and Anan, they had stopped quite a distance down the corridor, their faces etched with fear.

Tamba gasped, "What was that thing?"

"How did he get into your room?" Anan asked. "Did he transport?"

"No," Sedo said. "He's not really there, just his image. That's how we communicate with each other at a distance. He seems to be there, but he's not."

"But he was alive," Tamba said. "He was looking at us."

Sedo placed her arms around their waists. "It's just a three-dimensional image of him. I know you don't understand, but we create them by using mathematical space vectors in time. Engineers can create them anywhere on this ship. Come back to my room and just watch."

She felt Anan shiver. "Can he come into our room?"

"Only if you invite him," Sedo said.

Reluctantly, they followed Sedo back to her room but remained near the door.

Septa dabbed the corner of his mouth with a white napkin. "Captain."

"I need a favor," Sedo said.

"What?" Septa asked.

"I have two humans from the planet Maacon. Rather than being transported to Altaur, a commander, whose name I prefer not to mention, enslaved them. We've been teaching them the Beltese language."

"You mean the two who just bolted from the room?" Septa asked.

"They need jobs. They'll fit in well on one of your space stations. I prefer M-7 because it's closer to Tandon."

He took another bite. "How well do they speak Beltese?"

"Broken Beltese, but they're young and fast learners."

"I don't know. How old are they?"

"She's fourteen, and he's seventeen."

Septa adjusted his view and focused on the two humans in the background. His forehead wrinkled. "What's in it for us?"

"How about if we help rebuild M-9?"

Septa took another sip from his glass. "You don't have the authority to make such a decision. The Galactic Committee will probably help us rebuild anyway."

"What if I can get additional funds from Fleet Command?"

"What percentage?" he asked.

"Ten," Sedo suggested.

"Thirty," he countered.

"Septa, let's not play games. Twenty percent—and that's final. You can use them in your beach areas."

He shook his head. "I don't know."

"We destroyed the Velekan warships and production facilities. I'm talking about work for two humans. Remember, most of your substations and cargo ships were protected by us."

"I've heard that humans are savages," Septa replied.

In a calm voice, Sedo asked, "Are you calling me a savage?"

"Ah … no. Are you headed our way?" Septa asked.

"We'll be there in three days. I'd like for the humans to

participate in an extensive training program on Tandon before I release them to you."

"Then I accept your proposition," he said. "Let's talk about salary."

"There's nothing to discuss. They'll make as much as your average staff."

Septa gasped, "And what'll my other workers think?"

Sedo said, "I suggest you don't tell them."

"We'll talk about this in more detail later, Captain."

When Septa disappeared, Sedo turned and found Tamba and Anan frowning.

"Are you sure he can't come in our rooms?" Anan asked.

"I'm sure," Sedo promised.

"He looked strange," Tamba said. "But you said lots of them will be different from us."

Anan's face lit up like a child's. "Our chief said gods live up here. Did they make space?"

Sedo hesitated. "Gods?"

"Yes, gods," Tamba said.

"Well, if there are gods, we've never met ... them," Sedo said.

"So, gods not exist?" Tamba asked.

Sedo shook her head. "I don't think so. Your chief believes in gods, because we transported down to your planet and offered him advice. You've transported, and you're not gods."

"Will you explain how transporters work?" Tamba asked.

"Someday, but it's too soon now," Sedo said.

"Where did all these species come from?" he asked.

"Thousands of years ago, we had a theory that all beings evolved from animals. We have no proof of this. In other words, we still don't know."

CHAPTER 16

THE HUMAN GUESTS

When the *Volpus* arrived at M-7, Sedo gave her crew a week's leave.

The space station, identical to M-9, was a sphere that resembled a small planet.

Sedo arrived at Septa's large office with Tamba and Anan in tow.

They took seats at a table with six chairs near the back wall and waited.

Septa's office had limited furnishings. It was almost empty. The walls were a dull blue and a darker blue carpet covered the floor. Only one computer workstation occupied the room. There was another door, perhaps an exit or a closet.

As they waited, Sedo explained why the space stations existed and how they worked. "The Agoorons manage space stations like M-7. It provides a place of relaxation for space travelers from all over the galaxy. Much of the space stations simulate home environments for travelers, like the Beltese, and they offer food and various supplies."

Septa panted as he rushed into his office. "Sorry, I had an errand that couldn't wait."

Sedo introduced her humans to Septa. "This is Tamba. And this is Anan."

Septa repeated the names. "Tamba and Anan."

"This is Septa. He's the one you saw in my room. He manages all Agooron space stations. You'll be working for him."

Neither Anan nor Tamba said a word. Both just gawked at Septa.

Septa moved closer to Anan, and she took two steps backward. "You've been traveling for months, Captain. Why don't you relax and let me show them around?"

"I'll tag along, if you don't mind," Sedo said.

Sedo spent the entire day introducing them to other species. Tamba and Anan seemed amazed by what M-7 had to offer. They loved the beaches and the variety of food and games.

Neither Tamba or Anan talked on the way back to the *Volpus*.

***

Three days had passed since Captain Sedo had introduced Tamba and Anan to Septa. When the door of her private quarters buzzed, she knew who was on the other side.

Tamba flashed a broad smile when Sedo answered her door. "May we talk to you?"

Sedo stepped aside. "Of course. Come in."

Both took a seat at the same table as their last visit.

Tamba held Anan's hand. "We would like to marry."

Sedo took a chair at the table with them. "That can be arranged."

Anan leaned forward in her chair. "We want to marry on M-7, and we would like to remain there. We spent the entire day there yesterday and today."

"I know," Sedo said. "I'm proud that you know how to travel on your own."

"We speak enough Beltese, and we're getting better every day," Tamba said.

Sedo felt the excitement in Anan's voice. "We're no longer afraid of Septa or other aliens. We like the jobs he found for us, and we would like to start working as soon as possible. Septa showed us our room, and it's much larger and nicer than the one we have here."

Tamba asked, "Can we get married tomorrow?"

"Yes," Sedo agreed. "I'll make arrangements with Septa."

He smiled at Sedo. "Thank you."

"We know you wanted us to travel to Tandon and learn more before we start working," Tamba said. "Are you angry at us for remaining at the space station?"

Sedo laughed. "Of course not. I'm glad you wish to

remain here. It means that you're becoming very educated and independent."

Anan said, "In our village, newlyweds have wedding ceremonies."

Sedo smiled and nodded. "Just describe the ceremony, and I'll see what I can do."

Anan lowered her head. "We know we can't have babies, because Nowe had us steri ..."

"Sterilized," Sedo said.

Tamba squeezed Anan's hand. "But we have each other."

***

Sedo stood in her dress uniform in a grand room on M-7.

The Agoorons had decorated it with flowers, ornaments, and ribbons. A variety of foods and appetizers covered many tables. Most of the *Volpus* crew attended, and many other aliens found the occasion interesting. Since Sedo didn't have goats' blood, Anan and Tamba settled for wine.

Sedo had ventured into their minds and imitated their native attire for such an occasion. Anan's red, yellow, and green dress resembled her native costume, with the exception that she had to cover her breasts. Tamba couldn't go naked, but Sedo managed to find him comfortable clothes. Sedo read their vows in Beltese. Tamba and Anan drank from each other's glasses at the end of the ceremony, and everyone applauded.

Anan held their marriage certificate stating their real names, ages, and birth planet. "Captain, thank you so much. This is the happiest day of my life."

Sedo smiled. "We tried to make it as close to your village customs as possible, and both of you look so wonderful."

"Everyone wore their dress uniforms, just for us," Tamba said.

Sedo hugged Anan and then Tamba. "Of course. This is a very special occasion."

"Our wedding here was much better than the ones in our village," Tamba said.

Sedo gave Anan a small chip. "This is your wedding present, from all of us on the *Volpus*. Don't lose it, because it contains many galactic credits."

"Thank you so much, Captain," Tamba said.

"You both may purchase whatever you'd like, within reason." Sedo chuckled.

Tears rolled down Anan's cheeks. "I don't know what to say."

"Promise me that you and Tamba will continue with your education and obtain advanced degrees in science or engineering. Learn all you can."

"That's our goal," Anan said.

"Whenever I'm in this area, I'll stop and see how you are. I won't forget you," Sedo promised.

"Nor we you," Tamba said. "Thank you, Captain. You've done so much for us."

"I'm proud of you both," Sedo said.

Music started playing, and Anan and Tamba demonstrated their native dances. Sedo was shocked at how well they fit into the society on M-7. Both took turns dancing with other aliens.

Anan danced with a male of the Crustan species, often referred to as "The Bugs." His four arms swayed with the music, and his protruding head wobbled from side to side. His wide claw feet didn't miss a step.

Sedo didn't want to lose them, but now they had their own lives. They seemed so happy.

***

Prior to the *Volpus* leaving M-7, Sedo and Somgu transported to Deck Twenty-Eight near an unidentified cargo vessel that was attached to the outer wall.

They stood in the dimly lit corridor that ran the entire perimeter of the substation. Various transport containers stood against the inner wall. Sedo glanced into the open door of the vessel and saw no crew members.

"This is a Velekan ship," Somgu whispered. "Look at how tall the chairs and controls are. They must be nearby."

Sedo quietly alerted her crew of the situation, asking them to come prepared to overpower the Velekans. She peeked around a storage container. In addition to Zanna side arms, the Velekans carried bulky Rex-7s. Both weapons used the same deadly pulses, but the Rex-7s were 100 times more lethal.

"There are four of them, and they're armed," Sedo whispered.

The Velekans faced the door of the lift, chatting in their native language.

Sedo stopped behind the Velekans with Somgu at her side. "Why are you here? Weapons are not permitted on this space station—and neither are you."

The doors of the lift opened, but the Velekans abruptly turned their attention to Sedo and her lieutenant.

Two Agoorons were on the lift when the doors opened. Their huge eyes grew wide.

"Level One," the female Agooron said.

The doors closed and the lift descended.

The Velekan captain moved closer to Sedo. "We have a right to take leave here."

All Velekans were tall, but this captain was taller than average. Sedo's head reached his waist.

"You're the Agoorons' enemy," Sedo said. "You're not welcome here."

The Velekan stepped closer. "We secured a dock space and were not refused."

She stared up at him, never taking her eyes off her target. "That's because you falsely identified your vessel. The Agooron security system wouldn't have allowed your ship to dock here and traveling in an unidentified vessel is against the Galactic Committee rules. I demand that you and your crew leave here at once."

"We're not a member of the Galactic Committee. Such rules do not apply to us," the Velekan captain said.

"The rules apply to everyone," Sedo said.

The alien towered over her, as if trying to intimidate her with his bulk. "So, I finally meet the great Captain Sedo. You destroyed many of our warships and devastated our production facilities."

"I'm the one," she said.

The Velekan captain made a fist and pounded it into the palm of his left hand. "I used to be a warship captain ... now demoted to a cargo vessel."

A voice blurted from M-7's intercom system. "Attention. There are armed Velekans aboard this substation. Everyone got to your quarters and lock your doors."

When the Velekans took a few steps back and drew their Rex-7s, Sedo's Megmador powers automatically kicked in. She pushed Somgu behind her and bounced backward, putting more distance between the Velekans and them as a green force field surrounded her like a second layer of clothing. An electrifying tingle caressed her skin, and her hair felt as if someone had yanked on each strand.

The Velekans hesitated a few seconds, their eyes wild with amazement. They fired their weapons, and Sedo remained in front of Somgu, taking two powerful blasts to her chest. The impact threw her backward. Her force field hit Somgu and knocked her against the back wall, where she bounced off and slid on the floor.

Sedo glanced over her shoulder. "Stay down, Lieutenant."

With her mind, she threw the Velekans against the other wall with such force that their Rex-7s fell from their hands and they lay unconscious. Before they regained their composure, she removed their Zanna side arms, opened an empty cargo container, tossed all but one weapon inside, and locked the lid.

She picked up a Rex-7 and tossed to Somgu. When her lieutenant didn't catch the weapon, it slammed against the wall.

Somgu sat on the floor, breathing hard, her eyes glazed. Standing, she stared at Sedo, as if seeing a monster.

Sedo whispered, "Get up and stay behind me. There may be others."

Two more Velekans rushed from their ship and immediately drew their weapons. Before they could fire, green pulses hit them like lightning from an invisible force, killing both.

Sedo enjoyed the adrenaline of the moment, the rush. This was the first time she'd gotten to use her powers for defense, and it was a learning curve.

The lieutenant leaned against the wall for support. She didn't respond but stared at Sedo as if hypnotized.

"Somgu, get the weapon," Sedo shouted.

After a short hesitation, the lieutenant grabbed the Rex-7.

Sedo's crew flooded the area and quickly overpowered the four Velekans. After rounding up their unwanted guests, they escorted them from M-7.

***

When Septa arrived at the dock area, he eyed Sedo from head to feet. "You look strange, and your skin is so pale."

Captain Sedo combed fingers from both of her hands through her tangled hair. Powers still surged within her. "How could your crew allow the Velekans to dock here?"

"Somehow, they had a permit," Septa stated.

"You never updated your computers to prevent the Velekan ships from taking leave here?" Sedo asked.

He held up both hands. "Calm down. What happened to you?"

Sedo took several deep breaths before answering. "We had an encounter with them."

Septa shook his head in disgust. "We've never had to deny ships here and didn't expect the Velekans to show up."

"Now would be a good time to take care of this problem," Sedo said.

Septa walked away. "How could they dare dock here?"

Sedo turned to Somgu. "I need to speak with you in private."

Somgu stood rigidly, her face a pale pink and her eyes distant. As they walked to the transporter, neither spoke.

On the *Volpus*, Sedo led her lieutenant into her quarters and locked the door.

Sedo motioned to the table. "Have a seat. Wine?"

"Yes, Captain," Somgu said.

Sedo poured two glasses of chochu wine and joined Somgu at the table but remained silent.

Her lieutenant's facial expression didn't relax.

"I know you're confused about what happened during the Velekan attacks," Sedo said to her.

Somgu threw her head back and gulped the entire contents of the glass. "I am," she said, barely audibly.

Sedo refilled Somgu's glass. "I feel that you've been spying on me for months now."

"Yes, I have," Somgu admitted.

"Why?" Sedo asked.

"The chochu wine and other things."

"My parents altered my genes during my childhood. Other than physical appearances, I'm 100% Beltese."

"Does Fleet Command know you're a Megmador?"

"No, but they know I've been transformed into a Beltese."

"A human, female Megmador," Somgu said. "It's unbelievable."

Sedo took a sip of wine and placed her glass on the

table. "Promise me that you'll never tell anyone about this, Lieutenant. I'll inform Fleet Command about my transformation in person."

"Yes, Captain," Somgu said.

"You've been trained to react under stressful conditions, yet you froze during the Velekan attack," Sedo said. "I'm disappointed in you."

Somgu said, "I hesitated because of your actions, not because of the Velekans. I'm sorry, Captain. I … was thrown off guard for only a few seconds."

"It takes less than a second to die," Sedo snapped.

Somgu took a sip of wine and swallowed hard. "It won't happen again. Those blasts from the Rex-7s were enough to kill 100 crew members. How do you feel?"

Sedo shrugged. "Fine."

A frown wrinkled Somgu's forehead. "You must feel some pain."

"No, no pain. It's as if it never happened."

Somgu said, "Thank you for saving my life."

"I need to find Dr. Fea."

"He's on M-7. Does he know?" Somgu asked.

"All the doctors know."

"What about Lieutenant—ah—Captain Bonuve?"

Sedo stood. "He doesn't know. You may stay and finish your drink, but I must go."

Somgu patted the top of her own head. "Captain, take care of your hair first."

CHAPTER 17

A DYING WORLD

Planet Maacon in the Zetta Solar System

Thabo lay on a cured antelope hide and gazed into the serene darkness of his cave.

Bright light filtered through holes in the animal skins that covered the entrance. He crossed his ankles and watched faint water reflections flickering on the ceiling above him as thoughts about his dying world raced through his mind. Other than working nights, he had to remain within the confinements of the cave.

With each passing season, the sun came closer to the Womba's village. Its radiant glow blinded him, and the intense heat made breathing outside difficult during daylight hours.

Boys Thabo's age shared jagged ledges ascending the wall. Parents with younger children occupied the sandy floor below. The only sound came from a multitude of snoring men. Thabo sat up, dropped his feet onto the ledge below, and stood on a bed of small rocks. Walking down the incline toward the cave's entrance, he saw two guards slouched on boulders on either side, their backs against the veined wall. Their malnourished bodies resembled black skeletons.

They were barefoot and naked. One guard was perched on a rock with his feet propped up and a spear in his lap. The other sat with his feet resting on the floor and his weapon leaning against the wall. Both slept with their heads drooping over their laps. Thabo thought first of waking them but instead, he turned and headed toward the back of the cave.

Blazing heat had scorched all the vegetation to a crisp, and the once bountiful lake had evaporated into a muddy puddle.

Most of the tribe's nightly chores consisted of hauling pots of water from the nearby lake to water their garden, located a short distance from the cave, that hardly survived. The tribe grew grass for the goats and a limited supply of potatoes, beans, and leafy green vegetables. They had assembled rock barricades around the edge of the tract to prevent flooding. Shade made from dead limbs and dry grass protected the plants from direct, sizzling sunlight and prevented deluges of rain from washing away the crops.

Between dawn and dusk, the sky raged a bleeding crimson and glowing jaundice, and the moon shone dull in a bright night sky.

Thabo's desolate world had reduced him and his tribe to nocturnal troglodytes, who slept through dour days and performed tedious nightly chores under the apparition of the ominous sky.

At the age of thirteen summers, he stood almost as tall as Kobe, his father, the tallest man in his tribe. His charcoal skin, almost bluish-black, was identical to all the other members of his tribe. Bored and thirsty, he walked toward the source of the reflections and stood at the edge of a deep, dark hole near the back of the cave that contained eel, shrimp, fish, and precious water for drinking and washing. He picked up a small bowl, filled it with water, and gulped it down.

Infrequent runoffs from a mountain stream flowed through an underground passage and into the pit where the water level dwindled until the next rain. Stalactites hung from high ceilings and sharp stalagmites sprouted from the floors. Sticks marked a maze of winding tunnels, in case someone became lost.

Thabo heard a toddler, the youngest of the tribe, squealing. The women shuffled and mumbled as they attempted to prepare food.

Just then, Chief Imoo's screams echoed throughout the cave, springing everyone to life. Thabo rushed back to the entrance, where the chief stood before the two guards, his arms folded across his chest and his feet spread wide apart.

"Sleeping. While on guard." The furious chief's nostrils flared, and the veins under his neck bulged. "Since you've slept all day, both of you will work all night and stand guard again tomorrow. And if I find you sleeping on duty again, you'll be put to death."

The two humiliated guards stood facing the chief. Neither spoke.

Thabo felt the imminent demise of his tribe, and the threat implied by killing two men only worsened the situation. Small bumps covered his skin, and a chill flowed through his body. His heart dropped as he backed away. When Thabo returned to his resting place, he still heard Chief Imoo's screams.

After the chief had severely berated the guards, he called a tribal meeting. Adolescents Thabo's age usually didn't attend the coming-together-of-men, but the chief had changed the rules during their time of peril. Every six days, a meeting took place in an adjoining cave that was occupied by single men and the tribe's six scrawny goats.

Like other tribesmen, the chief's drudging existence and lack of proper diet, had drained years from his life. He hardly resembled the man he'd been three summers ago. His stature had shrunk, and his graying hair and matching, stubby beard put him years beyond his actual age. He sat on the ground and crossed his legs with his feet tucked underneath him like the other men in the esoteric circle.

The chief roared, "This evening, I found our guards sleeping. I'll not tolerate this. Guards sleep nights so they'll be alert all day. Kobe, you and Thabo shall not stand guard tomorrow." His voice lowered to almost normal. "The same two guards will stand duty, and I better not catch them sleeping again."

Kobe, now second-in-command, sat next to the chief with Thabo at his right side. Directly across from Thabo sat Sizwe.

Sizwe had joined the Womba tribe before Thabo was born. The shabangu had accused him of being too unsociable, and the Zulu king had expelled him from the tribe. However, the real reason for his expulsion was his interest in the same girl as his best friend, who was the king's son. The Zulus exiled Sizwe to the plains without even a spear to defend himself against predators. He was two heads shorter than Thabo, and his body was permanently scarred from a lion attack he'd suffered when he was a young boy.

The Womba tribe never mixed with the Zulus, but Chief Imoo had made an exception. Sizwe brought the Zulus' advanced skills in making pottery and beads.

The chief lowered his head. "If the lake dries up completely, we'll have no water for the crops. If the gods don't save us, we're doomed."

"We can take water from the cave," Thabo suggested.

"It can't provide enough water, Thabo," Kobe said.

"Crops are hardly surviving, and we need more grass for the goats," Sizwe said.

Thabo leaned in. "Maybe Buru and the chief's son, Bakko, have found a better place for us."

Until recently, Buru had been the long-time second-in-command. He had resolved conflicts and disputes within the tribe, led the men on hunting parties, and taught limited fighting skills. Two summers ago, he had defied Chief Imoo by joining Bakko and following the migrating herds.

The chief shook his head. "All summer the western sky has been blackened with smoke. Those lands are on fire. Nothing could have survived there, and the rest of the world is a barren desert. Like the lions, my son chose to follow the migrating herds. A son should never defy his father or his chief. My son, Bakko, defied both."

Thabo thought he would meet his best friend, Matata again—but the chief's words destroyed his hope. He enjoyed the story about how the chief met the gods and wanted to hear it repeatedly. "Did the gods really tell us to move here, Chief?"

"Three summers ago, two gods appeared to me when I sat at the spring," the chief said. "They had foreseen that our world would get hotter with each passing summer. The gods told me to keep my tribe near the mountain where it was cooler, and we would always have plenty of water."

"What did they look like?" Thabo asked.

"Thabo Abubakar, don't ask so many questions," Kobe scolded. Thabo's father only used his middle name when he was displeased with him.

The chief's eyes became distant. "The female god's

name was Sedo. She claimed to be from one of our tribes, but her skin was so pale. The other was male, but not a man. Bonuve was his name, and his ears were like those of a cat. His skin was pink, and his hair was yellow, like the sun."

Imoo coughed and cleared his throat. "Both wore the same strange clothes. Sedo's eyes were green, and the male had gray eyes. When I spoke to Sedo, another voice answered from a strange black object attached around her waist. I didn't know where they came from, but when they left, they simply vanished. Disappeared."

"If they were gods, Chief, wouldn't they look like us?" questioned the other young boy in the group.

"I've always thought they would," the chief admitted. "But these gods … they looked strange."

"Maybe they weren't gods, Chief," the young boy replied. "They may have been demons. I've heard that they exist too."

The chief squinted at the boy and shook his head. "No. Demons wouldn't have saved our lives."

"We thank you for taking their advice, Chief," Sizwe stated. "If we had followed the migrating herds, we would all be dead."

The chief glanced around the circle. "Any other concerns?"

"My wife is getting sicker, and I fear the worst," Kobe said. "She now has difficulty doing daily chores."

Kobe had married again, shortly after Thabo's mother

and baby brother died during childbirth. That was the last time snow had covered the mountain.

A somber expression clouded the chief's face. "I'm sorry, we no longer have any herbs."

"How could we have known they would die so quickly?" a tribesman asked.

A young girl with woolly, ungroomed hair ran into the cave and disrupted the meeting. "The wind is blowing."

Thabo hurried outside the cave with the other men, his eyes searching the sky, studying black churning clouds that blocked the ominous glow. He welcomed the threatening rain, savoring the breeze that cooled the air, and watched leaves rustle across the barren land. Dead trees swayed, and their branches trembled in the strong wind. The dark sky reminded Thabo of what night used to look like.

Kobe stared down at the small garden surrounded by a tawny world, bereft of life, in an inhospitable land. "We won't have to water tonight."

"Not for a few days," Imoo agreed.

Sizwe braced himself by placing a hand on the side of the cave. "This is the first storm this season, and flooding will be worse than ever."

"The rain will replenish the lake and the pit in the cave," Kobe said.

Thunder roared, and lightning danced perpetually near and far, crackling and flashing across the sky in random strings of light.

Thabo pointed. "Look, look."

They all turned their attention to the direction of his gaze. Small, blurred figures slowly advanced toward them, wavering in and out of sporadic heat mirages.

"Could it be our men?" Thabo asked.

Kobe squinted. "I can't tell."

Thabo glanced from his father to the chief. "Shouldn't we meet them?"

"No." The chief was adamant. "They may be animals."

Thabo said, "But all the animals are dead, aren't they?"

"Let them get closer," the chief ordered. "Everyone, get your spears."

Since the chief's interlude with the gods, Thabo had noticed an increase in his paranoia about the tribe's safety. Imoo stated that all other living beings were dead, yet he posted guards day and night. He had also created an obscure hiding route to access a clandestine fissure above the water source, by carving vertical foot holdings.

A bolt of lightning struck a dead tree near the edge of the garden and created a huge explosion of fire that sent embers flying in every direction. Within seconds, a graveyard of dead grass and shrubbery surrounding the area caught fire and abruptly burst into flames. Blazing tree branches and grass shelter on top of the vegetables became a floating inferno.

"Our vegetables," a woman screamed.

Thabo helped his villagers collect pots of water from the cave, but they couldn't reach the garden. A woman's wrap caught fire around her ankles, and he threw a pot of water on her clothes before she suffered a severe burn.

Imoo cupped both hands over his mouth and yelled, "The fire is too intense. We can't put it out."

Tears ran down the woman's face as she ran toward the cave. "Now we shall starve for sure."

Most of Thabo's tribe rushed back into the cave, as if lightning would seek them out. Surging winds continued to carry the fire in a multitude of directions, and the cave became tinged with smoke, burning their eyes and making them cough.

Thabo and a few men rushed back outside. In the distance, he saw four diminutive figures, now distinctive human forms. "There. It's our men, the scouting party."

"Get some water," the chief ordered as the struggling men approached the cave.

Thabo and another boy ran into the cave, filled two bowls with water, and trotted toward the scouts as others followed.

"Water, water," the thirsty men begged.

The youngest of the four had almost collapsed. He staggered with the support of two others.

The men greedily gulped. "Water. More water?"

"That's enough for now," Imoo warned. "Don't drink too much."

One of the scouts studied the lost garden as he walked up the stone passage and into the cave, barely avoiding a sudden downpour. "Our garden?"

"It's gone," Kobe said.

Thabo lit another torch and joined the group of men.

"What did you find?" the chief coughed out. "Is anyone else alive?"

"No," the lead scout said breathlessly. "We passed the remains of about fifty Zulus, half a day's walk on the other side of our old village. Their flesh had decayed. Like sleeping rugs, their skin was stretched over their bones. They had been carrying spears, pots, and other personal things."

"Perhaps the gods told them to move here as they told us, but they waited too late," Imoo said.

"When we arrived at the Zulus' village, it was empty." The scout paused and took a swallow of water. "There were signs that the village had flooded in the past, but we saw no recent footprints. Dust covered many pots and personal items. Some spears left behind had started to rust. We believe most left the village, but a few remained."

"As Buru and Bakko, they must have followed the migrating herds," Imoo stated.

The man said, "We brought back four spears, but left about twenty near our old village."

The chief gasped. "You took their things? If they return and find that we raided their village, they'll slaughter us for sure."

"That village is dead," the scout said. "I don't know where the Zulus went, but they exist no more."

"The Zulu village must be dead," Sizwe confirmed. "If

most of the tribe followed the migrating herds, they've most likely perished. But the remaining ones wouldn't have left their weapons behind."

"No, they wouldn't," Kobe agreed.

One of the men pulled pouches from his bag. "We found herb seeds. They were in covered pots, protected from the weather."

Imoo examined the seeds. "They still look fresh. We'll plant them as soon as the storm passes."

"More water now?" the younger scout asked.

"Yes, then eat and rest," Imoo said. "I'll send men to retrieve those spears after the storm passes."

Thabo longed for a spear of his own. "What are you going to do with the extra spears?"

The lead scout tossed a spear to Thabo, and he caught it in mid-air. He smiled and caressed the weapon, as if it were alive. "I'll always keep it at my side."

Rain blew into the cave, saturating the lower level and forcing the tribe to higher ground.

"The storms have never been this bad," Imoo said.

Lightning struck the side of the mountain, and the cave shook, creating a rockslide that roared louder than thunder. Gigantic rocks tumbled down and covered the entrance, bringing a cloud of dust into the smoky cave.

"We're blocked in." Sizwe jumped to his feet, waded through rocks, and stopped where the entrance used to be.

"We're going to die in here," a woman sobbed.

"No, we won't," Kobe said. "Calm down."

"Let's start moving these rocks," the chief said.

Thabo helped others move the smaller ones a short distance inside the cave. Each time they cleared the passage, more rocks fell into their places.

"Bring another torch," the chief said.

The struggling men combined their forces and pushed. Kobe grunted. "Chief, the rocks outside are too heavy to push away."

Sizwe said, "In one of the back caves, I've seen light. We may be able to climb up and widen the hole large enough to pass through."

The chief nodded. "Once outside, it should be easier to move the rocks."

With both hands, Sizwe wiped the dust from his face. "That may be our only chance."

The chief said, "Let's rest. We'll dig our way out after the storm passes."

The tribe huddled on the dark ledges as the storm raged outside.

Thabo sat in silence for hours before falling asleep.

Chapter 18

The New World

Planet Altaur in the Dantus Solar System

Thabo woke from a calming sleep.

Before he opened his eyes, he heard shuffling and murmurs. Glints of sunrays shone through tree leaves and branches. Birds and crickets chirped in the background, and the gentle wind caressed his naked body. He wrinkled his nose and sniffed, inhaling the aroma of roasting meat, which enhanced his hunger. He discovered not the dark comfort of his cave, but soft, warm daylight, as vague images of people and huts surrounded him. He swiftly sat up and stared into the familiar faces of his lost tribe. His friend, Matata, stood among them. An endless beauty of life surrounded him. Lush, green grass and sprawling trees with branches swayed lazily in the gentle breeze. His tribe from the cave slept in the center of a strange village. Spears, personal items, and cooking pots were also there, and their scrawny goats grazed in nearby grass at the edge of the village.

Frightened out of his mind, Thabo climbed unsteadily

to his knees and absorbed the whole scene before him. "Chief. Chief, wake up," he shouted.

The rest of his tribe stirred, and they appeared to be just as shocked as Thabo. Moments passed without a word. He stared at the people before him, and they, in turn, did the same. Chief Imoo slowly sat up, reeling from fatigue. He broke the silence. "Where are we?"

***

Buru gawked at the man before him. "Chief Imoo. Is it you?"

Imoo glanced around at his tribe before responding. "Yes, yes, it is I, Chief Imoo. How ... did we get here?"

Buru dug his long, calloused fingers through his thick, woolly hair to scratch his scalp. "The gods must have moved you here, as they did us. We have been here for more than eight seasons." He stood like a giant, bulkier and taller than other men in the tribe, with brawny shoulders and a broad neck that matched his immense and powerful frame. He had a friendly face with sleepy, dark brown eyes and carried no excess fat on his body. Buru had a gentle demeanor and always seemed to be in a good mood.

The chief turned and looked at the jungle. "Where is this place?"

Buru said, "We're in a different world."

The chief tried to stand. "What? We're in heaven?"

Buru helped the chief to his feet. "No, we're not dead—just moved."

Imoo took a step. "Moved ... to where?"

"We don't know," Buru said.

Imoo said, "Maybe we're still in our world, just a different place. Our world is vast and—"

Buru shook his head. "No. This place has two moons and the star patterns are completely different. There are no predators here, and there's plenty of food."

Like his other tribesmen, Imoo had difficulty moving. "If this place is better than our old world, then it must be heaven."

"We're alive. We bleed, and we can die," Buru said.

The chief took a few steps. "We thought your group perished on the plains."

Buru smiled. "We also thought you were dead."

A woman's frantic voice rang out. "Chief. My baby and all of the children are older. Yesterday my son was four seasons old. Today he's at least six or seven."

The chief looked at Buru for an explanation. "Older?"

"The same thing happened to us. We had been on the plains for days. We went to sleep one night, woke up here the next day, and the children were all older, as if we had slept for two seasons. We were so weak, we had difficulty moving about. The gods left us food. Everyone had a small puncture inside their left arm at the elbow, even the babies. That area was sore, swollen, and bruised, as if a thorn had been there for some time, then removed."

Imoo's tribe studied their arms and erupted into low murmurs.

Thabo caressed the inside of his left arm with his fingertips. "I have one too. Did you find out what caused it?"

"No, but it'll heal within a few days," Buru said.

"How long have you been here?" Imoo asked.

Buru replied, "Eight seasons."

"But you've been gone longer," Imoo insisted.

Buru said, "We've been here for eight."

"My wife is not here, Chief," Kobe said. "Everyone's here except her."

"Was she sick?" Buru asked. "Three of our tribesmen didn't come with us. They were extremely sick, and we think they died."

Kobe had discussed the possibility of his wife dying, so the news didn't shock Thabo. "She's dead?"

"I'm sorry, Kobe. Thabo," the chief said. "You have my deepest sympathy."

"I knew she would die soon." Kobe lowered his head.

Chief Imoo saw strangely dressed women before him. Their clothes covered their breasts. Some wore white, while others were dressed in bright, colorful patterns. Most of the women had their hair braided in various designs and styles, decorated with beads and small wooden sculptures. One woman's bushy hairstyle resembled a giant bird's nest.

The chief gawked at the unfamiliar men in the crowd. Patches of animal skin covered the tops of their heads. Unlike his people, with bluish-black skin, this tribe's skin color varied from light to dark brown. Their lips were thicker and their noses broader. "Who is this tribe?"

"What's left of the Zulus is a two-day walk from here. They no longer outnumber us," Buru stated.

"But—"

"Their tribe defied the gods as we did, and most perished on the plains," Buru said.

"But this tribe is not Zulus," Imoo said.

"No, Chief," Buru replied.

"Who are these strangers?" Imoo asked again. "Where are they from?"

"Many of these women are our wives," Buru said. "We don't know where they came from, but they're not from our old world—or this one."

The chief squinted at Buru and shuddered. "Another? How can you be sure?"

"The star patterns in their old world were not the same as those in ours. Many of our women and children perished on the plains, and this new tribe had many available women, so we married them. Since we didn't speak each other's tongue, we produced our own, and a new tribe." Buru pointed in some unknown direction. "Their old village is half a day away. We call ourselves, our new tribe, Yorubas."

Imoo's heart dropped, and he felt weaker. "A new tribe? Well, I—"

"Your tribe will love it here, Chief," Buru continued in his good-natured manner. "We're the largest meat-eaters here. There are no snakes or crocodiles. No irritating insects like ticks, flies, mosquitoes, or scorpions. And the season never changes."

"If the seasons don't change, how do you know how long you've been here?"

Buru flashed a broad smile. "I've had two sons since I've been here."

The chief studied the robust bodies around him that were in superb health. He couldn't ignore the hunger pangs in his stomach. "What food do you have?"

"The same as in our old world, only more. We don't need gardens here. Fruits and vegetables grow wild everywhere, and the water is clear and clean. Our women are preparing food for your tribe. You must be starved."

"But this is my tribe," the chief corrected him. "Everyone here, even if you have new wives."

"Chief, we're no longer Wombas."

Imoo glanced up at him. "You're the chief of this new tribe?"

"Yes," Buru said.

Chief Imoo's mind raced like the storm he remembered from last night—or some other night. He wasn't certain about anything anymore. He no longer listened to Buru's words. He felt a void, an emptiness, like never before. Rather than joy, he felt misery. The hope of re-uniting his village looked gloomy, and he envied Buru for claiming much of his tribe—no, he hated him.

Imoo's weary eyes searched through the crowd. "Where are my son and my grandchildren?"

Buru lowered his head. "I'm most sorry, Chief, but your son is dead. The dust was so thick on the plains, we could hardly see. A male lion charged from nowhere. After we exhausted all our spears, the animal disappeared with Bakko in his mouth and faded into the dust."

Imoo took a deep breath and stared into the distance. His eyes welled up, but he managed to fight back the tears. "My last son, dead. I gave him up seasons ago but seeing the remainder of my tribe again gave me new hope. The gods punished him for defying them. Where is his family?"

"Conditions were too harsh. We had no food or water," Buru said. "Your daughter-in-law and newborn grandson died during childbirth. Your two other grandsons are dead as well."

The chief's legs became so weak he almost collapsed. "All dead? I have no males to take my place as chief of the Womba tribe. My first daughter has four girls, and the second is barren. My lifeline is dead."

"You need to eat," Buru said. "Gain your strength. Then we'll leave you to grieve."

Imoo followed him to the center of the village, where women dished out food they'd cooked over a shallow burning pit. The Wombas swarmed around the area like hungry ants.

The chief stopped, faced Buru, and gazed steadily into his eyes. "You'll remain chief of this new tribe, the Yorubas?" he asked, pronouncing each syllable with difficulty.

"Yes, the men made that decision," Buru said.

Something blocked the sunlight. Imoo searched the sky and saw a huge object passing overhead at a tremendous speed. It was many times larger than the village. He ducked. "What's that?" Struggling to run, he wobbled like a baby. The chief took shelter in a nearby hut, as did the remainder of his tribe.

"Chief," Buru called. "It won't harm you. They fly over all the time."

Chief Imoo peeked out of the hut, his knees knocking together. Buru's tribe remained calm, staring at him, as if he were mad. Gripping the side of the hut, Imoo stepped out. "What was it? Not a bird?"

"No," Buru said. "Trust me, we're in no danger."

The frightened Imoo and his tribe returned to the cooking area, their eyes scanning the sky.

"They never land here, and we don't know what they are. You'll get used to them," Buru said.

Imoo glanced over at the jungle in the direction the thing had headed. "It didn't look ... alive."

"We don't think it is either. Come and eat," Buru said.

"After seeing that thing, you expect me to eat?"

Buru took him by his arm. "There are many strange animals and things in this world, Chief. You must quickly get used to them or they'll drive you crazy." He pointed a finger at his head and twirled it.

After his meal, Imoo sat under a nearby tree to think. He stared at the jungle as children laughed and played and men and women spoke in a strange tongue. He didn't know what to make of it all. Even before the sun moved too closely to his old world, it was not like this new one. He now lived in a world where life was easy and food was plentiful. Everyone had aged.

If the gods had such powers, why didn't they save the sick?

And why not move them all at the same time?

What was the strange thing in the sky?

Nothing made sense. Now that he had found his lost tribe, he couldn't lose them again, even if it meant fighting Buru. Imoo was once a strong and respectable chief, and he would be again. He planned to regain the support of his old tribe and prove he was the better chief. Yesterday, his worry was keeping his tribe alive. Today, reuniting his village was of utmost importance, and he had a plan.

***

At midmorning the next day, Thabo lay on his back under a tree with his friend, chewing on a piece of herb grass with his eyes closed.

Matata told him stories about his life on the plains of their old world, and Thabo told him about how his tribe had survived in the cave.

Although two summers older, Matata was shorter than Thabo. His muscular body had lost its slender, boyish build.

Matata sat up and kicked Thabo's foot. "Let me show you where all the fruits and berries are. First, I'm taking you to my special hiding place, where three fallen trees lie crisscrossed in a small clearing in the jungle. It's a short distance from here."

Thabo turned on his side, his stomach stuffed from his early morning meal. "Do we have to? I prefer to rest."

Matata stood and coaxed him with a wave of his hand. "Come on. It'll be our secret place. No one else knows about it."

Thabo had never been in the jungle of his old world but had heard rumors of dangers that had lurked within. "It's not safe to go there."

"It's not like the jungle in our old world. I go there all the time."

"Alone?" Thabo asked.

Matata threw his head back and laughed. "Of course, alone. There are no dangerous animals here." He took a few steps, then stopped and glanced back at Thabo with a mischievous gleam in his eyes. Sharp, crooked teeth enhanced his devilish grin. "You're not afraid, are you?"

"No." Thabo couldn't let his friend sense his fear. He retrieved his spear and reluctantly followed.

At the jungle's edge, a colossal undergrowth of ferns, creepers, and bushes tickled and caressed Thabo's nude body as he plowed down a narrow trail. Tree trunks were as wide as his height. Roots sprouted up and gnarled over the ground. He stumbled over one, but his spear helped him regain his balance. Drooping vines whipped his face and neck and burned his skin. He heard squawking and whistling from flocks of exotic birds. Butterflies of every color fluttered away from disturbed vegetation. Crickets fell silent as he neared, and noisy bees swarmed around succulent blooms.

When he entered the perennial shade, a cloud of trees created a dark and eerie world. The most frightful of all was an unearthly hissing from a distance. Thabo jumped over gorged streams that flowed to and from nowhere. He saw fresh water springs bubbling up from the ground and tramped through moist areas of putrid peat.

Thabo stopped and studied purple birds while Matata walked ahead. "I've never seen birds like those."

His friend said, "Sometimes they fly into the village, but they mostly stay near the jungle. Come on, you'll see more."

Thabo turned and saw a hardly visible trail behind them. "You said it wasn't far."

"Come on, we're almost there," Matata coaxed.

Thabo heard annoying hoots and chatters from small monkeys that lived in the canopy of trees above the jungle floor. Upon closer inspection, he also saw wings. He pointed up at a group of orange monkey-like animals with pink faces and floppy red ears. Their wings resembled those of huge bats as the flock flew from tree to tree. A few babies clung to their mothers' backs.

Thabo couldn't keep his eyes off them. "Monkeys can't fly."

His friend chuckled. "They do here. Come on, you have lots to learn about this place."

"I've never seen such large bees, and they're white." Thabo stopped to take a closer look.

Matata grabbed one from a flower, then let it go.

"They don't sting either. Catch one."

Thabo expected to be stung when he caught the bee, but he wasn't. "I can't believe it." He gazed in the direction of a sudden hissing sound but saw nothing. "What's making that sound?"

"We don't have a name for them. Don't worry, they're not dangerous," Matata bragged.

"What do they look like?"

Matata gave a nonchalant shrug. "A small, hairy crocodile."

When Thabo reached the secret place, his thoughts swirled about—like the mystery surrounding him. "So, what do you do here?"

"I just come here to be alone."

"And do what?" Thabo asked.

Matata grunted as he struggled up the huge roots of the first tree. "I watch animals, listen to the jungle. I lie on this top tree and just think or sleep. Come on up."

Thabo didn't follow him. "I don't like it here. It's too dark and distant."

"You're afraid."

"No, I'm not. I'll find a better hiding place," Thabo said. He heard crunching leaves and breaking twigs.

"Ssshhh." Matata held a shaky finger up to his lips, jumped down off the tree, and darted from the area with Thabo at his heels.

Thabo didn't know what danger approached, but Matata's actions intensified his fear.

Thabo's knees sank into the moist ground next to his friend. He gripped his spear, his heart pounding. He expected a big cat or worse, but instead he heard voices. A Zulu was talking in his native tongue. "How much farther is it?"

"Not far. Just follow this trail," another said.

They continued without stopping, and Thabo followed Matata farther from the trail and waited for them to pass through again.

Long after the Zulus had left, Matata still insisted on whispering. He quietly told the story about the Zulus.

"You brought me here knowing I could be killed," Thabo accused.

Face pinched in fear, Matata said, "Quiet. They usually don't come this far into the jungle."

"How do you know?"

Matata lowered his head.

The hissing noise came closer. Bushes rustled, and a

hairy, green animal with eight legs appeared, its tongue lolling. It stopped and stared, moving its head from side to side, as if sniffing them out. Thabo couldn't see its feet. It's large black eyes blinked several times, and it exposed sharp, jagged teeth that resembled a crocodile's. He clutched his spear with his arm back, his muscles tensed.

"No," his friend whispered. "It only eats insects and small rodents."

Thabo rapidly sucked in air. "I've never seen an animal with eight legs. What is it?"

"We don't know. There are many strange creatures here."

***

When Thabo woke, it was near sundown and darkness had already fallen over the jungle. He heard the Zulus chatting as they passed through again.

When he no longer heard them, he shook Matata awake. "They're gone. Do you know the way back?"

Matata rubbed his eyes. "I've never been out here this late. We take a right at the large spring. The trail leads straight to our village."

Thabo followed him, but they never found the spring, and the trail was no longer visible, so he plunged through the brush behind Matata. The trip back took twice the length of time.

When they exited the jungle, Matata pointed. "There's a fire. It must be our village."

As Thabo trudged closer to the village, his father, Kobe, approached him with a torch as a crowd followed. "Where've you been, Thabo?" his father asked.

Buru stepped forward, his face wrenched in anger. "We've been searching for you two for half the day."

"We went into the jungle." Thabo's voice was almost inaudible, now that he knew the seriousness of the situation. He had never seen Buru display anger, until now.

Buru scolded Matata. "You know you're not supposed to leave this village. We thought the Zulus had gotten you."

Thabo lowered his head. "We saw five in the jungle."

"What?" Buru snapped.

Matata whined and shook his head. "They didn't see us. We hid."

Thabo glanced at his father. "We think the Zulus spend most of the afternoon near here."

Buru said, "I know this is your second day here, Thabo, and you don't understand our problems, but never leave this village again. The Zulus will kill you."

"Come with me, son," Matata's father said. Matata and his father walked a short distance from the others and engaged in a short, one-sided conversation.

Thabo knew his friend was in trouble, because Matata held his head down and lagged behind his father when they headed back to the group.

***

When dusk gave way to darkness, the Zulus' drums attracted Sizwe and three Yoruba scouts to the old Nubian village. Two fires blazed opposite each other, and a crowd mingled in the center. Shadows flickered across the area as warriors tossed spears in skill contests.

Sizwe and his scouts carefully crawled through tall grass on their hands and knees, maneuvering as closely to the party as possible. His eyes darted slowly through the crowd, trying to find his four brothers. He saw two. He perhaps recognized the third but had doubts, and he didn't see the youngest at all.

Sizwe recalled participating in the same war games when he was a Zulu warrior. If his parents were still alive, what did they look like? Were his three sisters still alive? He hadn't seen the Zulus since his expulsion from their tribe, and it brought back both good and bad memories.

A Yoruba scout broke Sizwe's train of thought. "We should've burned this village."

"Ssshhh," Sizwe cautioned. If the Zulus discovered them, it would mean instant death for the men in his party, but Sizwe would be tortured slowly, to prolong his suffering, because he had been born Zulu. He concentrated on the experienced warriors who trained the younger fighters.

"Kill," a warrior said.

"You're dead," another bragged.

"Excellent," the king praised the group.

A leopard headband with woven ostrich feathers

pricked in a gray halo crowned the king's head. He stomped about the crowd, wearing a leopard-tooth necklace, intimidating the warriors with great charisma, like the beast he worshipped. A leopard-claw bangle gripped one wrist, and an mkhokha bracelet loosely hung on the other. The animal's skin covered his groin, and another covered his buttocks.

The Zulu king held up a leopard skin, shaking it high in the air. His voice roared across the village, vigorous and mesmerizing. "Leopards are not in this new world, so you know how sacred this kaross is. Every warrior shall have a piece of this skin after killing at least ten enemies in battle. Concentrate on the leopard when fighting. It represents power and strength."

Sizwe recognized his once closest friend and wondered how he had become the king, since he was the youngest of four sons. He knew the importance of the leopard to his old tribe. The animal possessed physical and spiritual powers believed to strengthen bones and muscles and promote good health and prolonged life. Only the king and his family wore parts of this sacred animal.

Sizwe had once worn bushy bands above his elbows and knees, made from white deer tails, as the Zulus did. These added the appearance of great bulk to their bodies. Sharp plaits known as amagodas, smeared with a protective medicine, showed their determination to fight to the death and to prevented the enemy from killing them too soon in battle.

Sizwe recognized the old shabangu, the spiritual leader, who entered a white circle on the ground. He wore an astrological robe, an old lion skin that was turned inside out, with colorful beads in patterns of circles and stars. His visage held a world of inscrutable wisdom and secrets. Wrinkles scored his forehead. Large bags drooped below his eyes, and folds of loose skin hung from his cheeks and neck. The old man danced around in a circle, unable to keep up with the rhythm of the pounding drum, loudly panting and chanting as he performed his ceremony.

The shabangu clutched a small bowl with tapered, bony fingers, shaking it as he went. The spiritual leader gave the bowl one vigorous shake, mumbled words in a mystical tongue, and then threw its contents into the center of the circle.

The drumming stopped, and the night fell silent.

Several bones landed crisscrossed in the sand. He picked up the bones and placed them back into the bowl. The old man repeated the ritual, took a step back, and shook his head. "I see death. We shouldn't attack our enemies. We're outnumbered, and we'll lose many warriors. I see death," he repeated.

The king shouted at the old man. "What? Are you out of your mind?" He grabbed the spiritual leader's arm and led him away from the warriors, with the shabangu's younger assistant at his side.

They stopped so close to Sizwe, he could smell the acid

of their sweat. Trembling in the grass, he was too afraid to breathe. His chin rested on his folded arms, and his chest moved with each breath. He hoped they couldn't hear his heart throbbing. He was too short to outrun the enemy, and the Yoruba scouts were too sluggish.

The Zulus were such fast runners; they regarded their speed like that of a cheetah.

The king poked a finger at the shabangu's chest. Rage barked from his voice, and his eyes shrewdly focused on the old man. "We're about to attack, and you've just broken their spirits. This ceremony makes even cowards fight like lions. How do you expect them to win when you've just destroyed their courage?"

"I advise against this attack, my king," the old man said.

"It's your job to protect us from evil spirits, especially during battle. Lately, your judgment seems crippled. You've turned into an idiot, and the children laugh at you. Two days ago, they saw you squatting behind someone's hut for a long time. If you have to relieve yourself, please leave the village."

"My king, I'm in good health for my age," the shabangu said.

"It took you over half a day longer than the rest of us just to reach this place," the king scolded. "I think it's time for you to pass shabangu over to your assistant." The king pointed his thumb at the younger man, who stood next to him.

"My king, my spiritual powers and wisdom grow stronger with age. I survived the unbearable conditions on the plains of our old world when younger men died. I—"

"Now, you get back there and throw those bones again, and this time you better see victory," the king demanded.

"Attention," the king yelled out as he reentered the milling crowd, his arms outspread like a bird about to take flight.

The crowd fell silent.

"The Nubians outnumbered us and we beat them. The gods will protect us if we fight bravely. We have already won one battle. Now we shall get ready for our final victory. We need our enemy's spears. We shall keep the women we desire and kill everyone else."

A voice bellowed from the crowd, "Women and children?"

"Everyone," the king yelled. "I want them all gone."

Murmured agreements exploded from the warriors as the king's voice resonated over the village and echoed into the empty night.

The old man shook the bowl a third time and threw its contents on the ground. "I see victory," he said weakly.

"Now, give them the muti," the king ordered.

The warriors formed a line in front of the old man's boiling pot. Each dipped his bowl into the liquid and took a swallow of the hot broth.

The king thrust a fist into the air. "Now, let's do our

maneuvers again, this time quicker. Speed is important. It makes the difference between life and death. Don't give your enemy time to think, to react. Remember, always aim for the chest or the stomach. War," the king yelled.

"Li-li-kee-keeee." The men's bloodthirsty shrills echoed in the night.

Sizwe shivered as the warriors were stirred into a fiery rage by the pounding drum. Their chants sounded, as if they came from a thousand throats. They participated in vivid war dances, lithely imitating the movements of wild animals. Their bodies moved in unison, twisting, curving, and leaping high into the air. Feet vigorously pounded the ground in ritual rhythms, and white bands of deer hair danced below their knees with every movement, throwing columns of dust like a stampeding herd of wildebeest.

The drummer pounded faster and faster, his body dripping sweat. Bands of white deer tails above his elbows moved so quickly they appeared like one dancing cloud.

Sizwe and the three scouts left as quietly as they had come, crawling back through the tall grass. He was glad to be done with his mission.

***

Chief Imoo and his tribe slept in the center of the Yorubas' village until they could build their own.

When he roused from his third night of restless sleep in his new world, he found Buru standing over him, holding a fistful of huge blackberries. Buru's widely spaced teeth caged a blue tongue. "Greetings, Chief Imoo. How did you sleep?"

Imoo glanced up at him, squinting in the early light. "Not well." He frowned as he scanned the village, embarrassed that he had slept longer than everyone else in his tribe. He scratched the back of his neck and sat up on his sleeping rug. The women in his tribe mingled with the Yoruba females around the cooking area, dishing out food to the children. The men squatted around in a circle, eating and chatting.

Green treetops and bushes fused together over the alien landscape before him. Blades of lush grass rolled like waves over a lake. The jungle stood behind the village, a bulky green mass that floated on the horizon and drifted into infinity. A vaporous haze of cumulus clouds billowed in the rich blue sky, and the chief's new world exploded with a multitude of sounds from an abundance of life.

Chief Imoo bellowed a yawn and rubbed his eyes, itchy from fatigue. "What were those drums pounding all night?"

Throwing two large blackberries into his mouth, Buru chewed and swallowed. "It's those stupid Zulus. Sometimes they beat those drums from dusk to dawn, then back to dusk again."

Imoo staggered to his feet. "You said the Zulus are a two-day walk from here. Those drums sounded close."

Buru smacked his lips. "They use the Nubians' old village to practice war fights."

"War against who?" Imoo asked.

"Us, Chief. That's why they practice so close—to intimidate us. Our plain is surrounded by this jungle, and the gods placed the Zulus as far from us as possible."

"What dispute do you have with them?" Imoo asked.

"None," Buru said. "Their king died on the plains of our old world, and their new leader is more hostile than the last. His mind is on war, fighting and killing, like a disease. We married most of the available Nubian women. The remaining ones rejected the Zulu."

"Can you blame them?"

"The gods brought the Zulus here without spears, so they tried to trade us a few of their young girls for some of ours."

"They actually thought our men would marry those wenches?" Chief Imoo asked, his mouth agape.

Buru extended a hand of berries to Imoo. "They insulted us, so we insulted them by stating that they had nothing worth trading."

Imoo took four large berries. "Why don't the Zulus just make spears?"

"This new world only has material for making wooden spears. They're not as powerful, because they have a shorter throwing distance."

"This is a strange world." Imoo tossed two berries into his mouth.

Buru added, "I didn't want to worry you yesterday, but the Zulus later raided the Nubian village and killed most of their men. They took childbearing women, leaving the children and older women behind. That's why their village is abandoned. They sacrificed some of the young boys, even babies. They cut off their arms and legs and their male parts while they were still alive. The Zulu shabangu brewed muti with the parts, and he thinks the more the victims scream, the more potent the medicine."

The chief slapped his cheeks with both hands. "No. The Zulus abandoned that tradition long ago."

"This new king has started it again. Most of the remaining Nubian men joined us, but some are still hiding in the jungle."

"You said the Zulus have only wooden spears."

"They took most of the Nubians' spears," Buru said.

"If the Nubians outnumbered the Zulus, shouldn't they have won the battle?"

"The Nubians are gentle, peaceful people, Chief Imoo. They're not warriors, and the Zulus attacked them in the middle of the night."

"Their women remain with the Zulus?" Imoo asked.

"They hunt down and kill runaway women, so most are too afraid to leave."

"They're fearless fighters." Chief Imoo lowered his head. "Can your—ah—our tribes survive an attack from them?"

"Our scouts watch them engage in their war games. We've learned to imitate and improve their tactics. We have also taught our women and children how to fight."

Chief Imoo gasped, "Women and children—"

"We think they're planning to attack us as we sleep."

"But women and children?" Imoo protested.

Buru said, "We may need their help. They'll attack the Zulus only if they enter our huts or if they're near the entrance. They won't enter into battle."

"Good," Imoo said.

"They want our spears, our women—and they'll certainly want your goats. We post guards day and night and keep our spears nearby, and we also have many stick spears."

"Do you know where the rest of the Nubian tribe is hiding?"

"They're scattered. The last time our scouts ventured into the jungle, they brought back twenty-three, mostly men." Buru continued, "The Zulus are dangerous and unpredictable, worse than wounded animals. We'll have to fight them, and very soon. We must become warriors, if we are to survive here."

Imoo searched Buru's eyes for answers. "Maybe there's another place across the jungle far from the Zulus."

"Many days ago, our scouts ventured into the jungle but found no end. Four men are there now for a second time. They've been gone for fifteen days and shall not return until they've reached the end."

"They may have met the Zulus during their trip," Chief Imoo said.

"Maybe, but we don't think they travel far into the jungle. Our men may find land so distant that the Zulus will never find us."

CHAPTER 19

THE ZULU ATTACK

After traveling more than sixteen days deep into the dense jungle, Nkosana and his three scouts found an end.

He saw a floating wall of what appeared to be a clear liquid that contained light blue bubbles the size of his thumb. It could only be seen close up, and he couldn't tell how thick it was. It rose from the ground, extended upward without end, and blended into the sky.

Nkosana hesitated and glanced at the other men, then again at the mysterious wall.

Ayo, the youngest of the four, whispered, "What is it?"

"I've never seen anything like this," Nkosana whispered back. "It's alive. It's moving."

On the other side of the wall, Nkosana saw formations taller than any mountain he'd ever seen, some clusters stood taller than others. They reflected sunlight, like water on the surface of a lake.

On top of one structure, Nkosana saw a yellow and green cloth flying in the wind. "People must live there."

Ayo was only nineteen summers old, but he was taller

than Nkosana. "Look at how straight they are. I think they have four sides. Look," he pointed. "There's a round one."

A prominent scar over Haben's left eye distinguished him from his twin brother, Jafaru. "They must be mountains?"

Nkosana stared long and hard, shaking his head. "No, mountains don't look like those."

"We need to go back to our village and report what we've seen," Jafaru said. "There's too much magic here."

Haben agreed.

Nkosana's skin tingled, and hairs on his body stood up as he moved closer to the wall. "It's our duty to learn more, determine what this strange thing is."

Picking up a stick longer than his height, Nkosana took two steps forward and then stopped. He turned and glanced back at his scouts, who had moved farther away.

Ayo danced in his tracks. "No, Nkosana. Don't."

"Please, let's leave here," Haben begged.

Nkosana crept closer and stopped again. Looking from left to right, he saw no end. As leader, he couldn't let the men see his fear. He placed his hands on his knees, bent forward, and stretched his neck for a better view. He straightened and thrust the stick into the wall, expecting it to burst. Instead, something resembling a bolt of lightning ran through the stick and up his arm.

For a brief moment, the wall and his arm became one. A sharp, burning sensation like fire raced up his arm, paralyzing it. He heard his own painful scream echo across the jungle. Nkosana pulled away, but the wall held his arm firmly. He tried to release the stick, but his hand wouldn't open, so he dug his heels into the ground and leaned back with all his strength. At last, the wall released its grip on him, and he landed on the ground with the stick at his side. His frightened tribesmen moved even farther away.

Haben called out but didn't come to his rescue. "Nkosana, Nkosana."

Placing his wounded arm between his knees, Nkosana squeezed it. Clenching his teeth, he rocked back and forth. "It's ... so painful ... hurts." He rolled over on his side, gasping for breath. Tears squeezed through his tightly closed eyes and rolled down his face. He bit his bottom lip and tasted blood. Staggering to his feet, he struggled toward his men with his right arm dangling limp at his side.

Haben and his twin raced to meet him. One stood on either side to assist him.

Jafaru's voice quivered. "Come on. We'll help you walk."

When he stumbled, both men grabbed him under his arms and yanked him swiftly to his feet.

The men took the same path back toward their village. Broken bushes and vegetation clearly marked their trail.

After Nkosana had traveled half a day, his pain became too severe. "Let's stop. I can't travel any farther." He found a level place to rest and dropped his sleeping rug.

Ayo unrolled his own rug. "I'll stay with you while Haben and Jafaru hunt for food."

***

Nkosana felt a hand on his shoulder and something warm pressing against his side. He opened his eyes and found Haben kneeling beside him. "We found another plain here in the jungle. Tonight, we can sleep there."

Nkosana rubbed his eyes. "Another plain? How did you find it?"

"Chasing a small pig. We can't tell how large this area is, but we saw no end," Haben said.

"How long did I sleep?" Nkosana asked.

"A long time," Ayo said. "We should spend a few days scouting this land. Give your arm time to heal."

Nkosana stroked his injured limb. "I'm not sure it will."

Haben helped Nkosana sit up. "You'll have to walk a short distance. This plain is a great place for our new village."

When Nkosana reached the grassy area, he lay down on his rug. Waking to the aroma of roasted meat, he caught the rays of the sun, just as it dipped below the horizon.

Ayo carved a piece of meat with his spear and placed it in Nkosana's bowl. "How is your arm?"

"It still hurts, and I can't lift it," Nkosana said.

"Eat this," Ayo said. "I'll stay at your side tonight."

***

During his fourth and last day on the plain, Nkosana's arm throbbed less. When the sun was directly overhead, he saw a strange object fly across the sky, this time lower, and he got a better view of it. It was huge and black, clearly not a bird. It had no wings and made no sound. Using a hand to shield his eyes from the sun, Nkosana said, "Look."

"What is it?" Ayo asked.

Nkosana watched the object go down behind the trees. He had never seen one so close up. A short time later, it flew high into the sky and vanished past the clouds within two blinks of an eye.

***

Nkosana and his scouts returned to their village with fifteen Nubian men they'd found living in the jungle. He noticed that most ex-Womba men had silently acknowledged Imoo as chief again. They reported to him, as if the tribe had never separated.

Nkosana attended Chief Imoo's meeting with all the men in the village. He knelt in the center of the circle and drew crude diagrams on the ground with his left hand, indicating the distance they had traveled and the location of the strange, powerful wall. His dark eyes drifted from man to man. "The things we saw were taller than a mountain, and the huge thing in the sky flew lower."

"Only the gods have such powers," Imoo said. "And you think we're surrounded by this wall?"

Nkosana shook his head. "I'm not sure, but I believe so."

"We walked along it for two days," Jafaru said. "We're prisoners, caged like animals."

"Maybe they're planning to raise us like goats and eat us," a man in the group said. "Why else would they fence us in?"

The chief held his palms skyward. "They're gods. They won't eat us. This place is heaven."

Thabo said, "Chief, you said the two gods you met looked strange. Maybe they were demons."

The chief was adamant. "They haven't eaten any of us yet."

"The Nubians are scattered throughout the jungle," another man said. "How do we know some haven't been eaten?"

Chief Imoo shouted, "Stop it. The Zulus are our enemies, not the gods. With all the food here, why would the gods eat us? Our main concern is how to survive an attack from the Zulus. The only way to avoid them is to move, very soon."

"Beyond the wall is forbidden," Kobe said. "Because the gods themselves live there."

"Yes, that must be the land of the gods," Imoo agreed. "The strange things we see in the sky must belong to them."

The chief's statement appeared to have a calming effect on the men. "You said the wall will only attack if we touch it."

Buru asked, "How large is this new land?"

"We saw no end," Haben said. "It has the same types of animals, fruits, and vegetables as we have here."

Nkosana caressed his wounded arm. "I don't think we should move there."

"How's this injury that left no mark?" the chief asked.

Nkosana made a fist and pumped his arm up and down. "The pain is gone, but it still tingles. It's slowly returning to normal."

"You men rest for a few days," Chief Imoo said. "Then we'll gather our things and move."

***

When Sizwe woke Thabo the next moonlit night, he whispered, "Get up and follow our plan. The Zulus are coming."

Imoo's tribesmen rushed into the huts with their spears and sleeping rugs in hand.

Thabo picked up his spear but then dropped it. He retrieved it with a shaky hand. Grabbing his sleeping rug, he ran into Buru's hut.

Buru stood just inside the entrance, gripping his spear, with his wife at his side. Both had their backs against the wall, waiting.

Buru whispered, "Remember how we taught you to fight, Thabo?"

Thabo nodded, his palms sweaty and his heart pounding.

Buru's two sons slept in the back of the hut. Thabo manned the other side of the entrance, clutching his spear. Although trained to fight, he wasn't looking forward to his first battle. Death frightened him, but suffering scared him even more. He peeked outside and watched two Zulus standing at the entrance of each hut. Thabo couldn't see the ones outside his own hut, but he felt their presence. He caught a quick glimpse of the Zulu king and his witchdoctor standing at the edge of the village. The king held up a hand, then quickly dropped it to his side.

The first Zulu who stormed in was the same height as Thabo, but bulkier. Thabo jumped in front of the intruder and thrust his spear with a mighty force, stabbing the warrior in his chest. He heard crushing bones and felt warm blood spatter across his face and chest. Thabo grunted as he pulled his weapon from the falling man.

When the second Zulu stormed in, Buru speared him.

The Wombas and the Yorubas surrounded the remainder of the Zulus in the center of the village, leaving them no way to escape. The enemies' white arm and leg bands distinguished them in the night, allowing the two tribes to slaughter them within the arena of their village.

Thabo heard screams of pain, grunts, and panting

from the men in battle. Cries of death filled the night like the darkness that covered the land. Thabo fought hard and fast. His tribe expected him to be a man, and he wouldn't disappoint them.

Buru shouted, "Quicker, Thabo, use all your force."

Thabo stabbed one Zulu in the side, another in the chest, and a third in the back. He should have been exhausted, but adrenaline kept him going. With tensed muscles, he attacked each enemy as quickly as he met them.

Then he found himself face-to-face with a more muscular warrior.

His father, Kobe, killed the Zulu, but not until after Thabo had suffered a cut from a spear between his left underarm and ribs. His injury didn't slow him down. He continued fighting, now harder.

A few Zulu warriors fled into the night.

Buru ran to the edge of the village and hurled his spear with a mighty force, bringing down the witchdoctor.

Quickly, and without mercy, Thabo helped his men slaughter the remaining, incapacitated Zulus. He smelled the scent of musty, humid blood and hated it.

After the raid, Thabo stood outside, horrified at the number of bodies that littered the arena. He wanted to sit, but blood saturated the area. He slipped in a pool of it and almost fell.

Thabo didn't sleep that night but listened as women mourned their dead and tended to their wounded.

***

In the early dawn, Thabo held his bandaged ribs, mesmerized by the carnage. During the night, the battle seemed like a dream, but in the early morning light, reality shook him. Women wrapped the bodies of the dead, while the men held a tribal meeting in the center of the village.

Buru said, "Seven members of our tribes are dead. We have a severely wounded man, and we don't expect him to survive. Chief Imoo is among the dead. My brother died attempting to save his son. Now both are gone."

Kobe's body was drenched in blood, as were those of the other men. "You have our deepest sympathy, Buru."

Buru said, "I'd like to thank our guards for doing such a great job of warning us. Tonight could've been the end of both tribes."

A man with a deep cut on his cheek stepped from the crowd and faced Matata's father. "I saw your son's death. Two adolescents attacked him, one from the front and another from the side. His side attacker killed him. Sizwe was too late to save Matata, but he killed both boys."

"My only son is dead," Matata's father said.

"He died bravely," Buru said.

"Chief Imoo fought his best," Kobe said, "but he was no match for the big Zulu. He speared the chief in the stomach."

Nkosana wiped tears from his eyes and sniffed. "My

son and daughter saved my life. My wife rescued our children, and now she's dead. I wish the Zulu had killed me instead. My children ... now my children have no mother. I don't know how I can manage without her."

Kobe placed an arm around Nkosana's shoulder. "We're sorry."

Buru asked, "Did anyone see how Sizwe died?"

"No," several men replied.

"I did," Thabo said. "Sizwe called the man 'my brother.'"

Buru shook his head. "Killed by his own brother."

"I don't think the Zulus will return," Kobe said. "They're no longer a threat to us."

Nkosana gave Kobe a menacing scowl and moved closer to Buru, his jaw clenched. "We must raid their village and finish them off."

"Yes, yes," roared the men. "Let's kill them all."

Just thinking about attacking the Zulus made Thabo's stomach queasy. He had escaped death once and might not be so lucky the next time.

Nkosana's eyes were wild and furious. "The Zulus are like wounded beasts. If we don't kill them now, our grandchildren will have to fight them."

Kobe forced his way through the crowd and stood at Buru's side. "If Chief Imoo were alive, he'd agree that we shouldn't attack the Zulus. After our dead are buried and our wounded have healed, we shall travel to this new land, live in peace, and forget about the Zulus."

Buru shook his head. "We'll not attack the Zulus but leave this plain and move to the next."

Nkosana stormed toward his hut.

Jafaru let out a dry chuckle. "Did everyone see how fast the Zulu king ran? He fled like a scared rabbit. Rather than stay and fight, he saved himself."

Thabo didn't find humor in Jafaru's comment, neither did anyone else.

The men stood in silence.

"How's your cut, Thabo?" Kobe asked after a few moments.

"It's just a scratch."

The men talked, but Thabo didn't hear them. Scenes from the dramatic battle raced through his mind. He still heard screams of pain, and the stench of death nauseated him. Dry blood from his kills caked his face and body. His friend, Matata, had once returned from the dead, but this time Thabo would never see him again.

Buru snapped Thabo out of his reverie. "Imoo was a good and faithful chief. He was the leader since his twenty-fourth summer. He did great things for our tribe and tried to keep us together in times of peril. If we had listened to him, many of our tribesmen wouldn't have perished on the plains of our old world."

Kobe glanced down at the chief's body. "We'll miss him."

Thabo stood next to his father. "Since the chief has no sons or grandsons, you'll become chief of the Wombas, Father."

Kobe gasped and jerked his head in his son's direction. "Thabo Abubakar, this is no time to discuss such matters."

***

Thabo helped the other men move the dead Zulus quite a distance from their village and left their bodies for small scavengers.

Like the other tribesmen, Thabo touched each of the dead, so his body would forever have their spirits. He then helped the men lay Chief Imoo's body in a shallow grave near the village. The other bodies shared one grave. Imoo was the only one wrapped in animal skin. His wife and daughters wept at the foot of his grave, as other tribe members showed their respects.

***

"Now that we've taken care of our dead, let's cover this blood with dirt," Buru said.

Thabo washed his body in a nearby stream. When he returned to the village, he found women already preparing a victory feast. He didn't wish to participate in the singing and dancing but would attend the ceremony, because it would acknowledge his father as chief of the Wombas and celebrate his marriage to a Nubian woman. He felt proud that his father had actually become the Wombas' new chief. He loved his father and never wanted to see him die, but one day he would succeed Kobe as the chief.

***

As during the previous night, Thabo and the tribesmen waited in the darkness of their huts, listening to the sound of approaching voices. Nubian women appeared, rather than Zulu warriors. A crowd of runaways appeared in the center of the village, half with young children. Most were with child.

Once they learned of the Zulus' defeat, the Nubian women had grabbed whatever they could and fled the Zulus' village. Most of their unwanted husbands had died during the battle, and the few remaining warriors hadn't pursued them.

Buru's wife squealed, greeting her sister. "Enu." They hugged and refused to let go. "You're expecting."

"Zola." Enu broke her sister's hold and shoved a toddler in front of her. "This is my son, Amadi."

Zola took the toddler from her sister and stood him on the ground. "Amadi, that's a wonderful name. It suits him fine." She squatted to his level and placed her hands on the boy's cheeks. "Hello there," she said in baby talk.

The cute little boy just made baby noises and swayed about gleefully.

"Zola, will you ask Buru if we can stay?" Enu asked.

Zola turned at once and called to her husband. "Buru, Buru. You remember my sister, Enu."

Buru approached his wife and sister-in-law. "Hello, Enu. You look well."

"You must stay. We'll be moving to the middle of the jungle," Zola said, pointing. "I understand it's a long distance, and the Zulus will never find us there."

The men in the crowd frowned at their leader and shifted about.

Buru lowered his head in guilt and embarrassment. Other Nubian women welcomed their relatives and chattered in front of Buru's tent.

***

Thabo attended the mid-morning tribal meeting to discuss the future of their new guests.

Buru glanced back at the women. "I've never seen so many big bellies at one time."

"They can't come with us," Haben said. "We won't have Zulu children in our tribe."

Nkosana said, "We either leave the Zulu children behind or kill them."

Buru's voice roared through the crowd. "These women are our wives' relatives. We can't kill their children."

Jafaru faced Buru. "Now we must take them with us. Thanks to you, they know the direction we're headed."

Kobe asked, "Are you suggesting we kill their babies as they're born?"

Nkosana said, "They can't live with us. They don't belong. The Zulus killed my wife."

"We don't need to kill them," another tribesman said. "Just leave them in the jungle. Let nature take its course."

"Let's think about it. Discuss it with our wives," Buru said.

Nkosana waved a hand. "We're not like you, Buru. We don't discuss such things with our wives."

Buru's tall, menacing figure approached Nkosana. "Do you think our wives will willingly come with us after we've killed their relatives? I'm chief of this tribe, and I make the final decision. There will be no baby-killing here."

Thabo didn't understand why the men hated the children. "They're babies. They don't need to know who their fathers were. They can grow up to be respectable members of our tribes. After all, they're only half-Zulu."

Nkosana quickly turned to Chief Kobe. "What? Is this how you raised your son? He wants Zulus in our tribes."

Kobe said nothing concerning his parental shortcomings.

Thabo said, "If the Nubians accept the Zulu children, why can't we? Their women were taken against their will."

"Chief Kobe, where's your son getting these silly ideas?" another tribesman asked.

Thabo put a hand on Kobe's shoulder. "Father, can we keep them in our tribe?"

His father wore a proud look on his face. "Yes, we'll accept them."

Most of the men disagreed. "Never."

Kobe said, "Sizwe was born Zulu, but he died a Womba. Until the Nubians can reunite their village, the women shall remain with us. When we move to this new place, we'll invite their tribe to share it with us. Our three tribes can live in peace."

More murmurs erupted among the men.

Nkosana pointed a finger at Kobe. "As long as you keep them in your tribe."

Kobe said, "I now have a Nubian wife. They're gentle and forgiving people, and we should be too."

"And look at what it got them," Nkosana shouted. "Most of their men were slaughtered, their women were taken against their will, and the rest are hiding in the jungle like scared monkeys."

"I'm chief of the Womba tribe," Kobe stated. "I've decided the Nubian women and their children will remain with us until they can reunite with their people."

"A tribe of women and children," Haben said. "Who will hunt for them?"

Kobe pointed a thumb at Buru. "There are Nubian men in his tribe."

"And they'll remain in my tribe," Buru said.

Kobe twisted his face in disgust as he walked away. He yelled over his shoulder, "Let the Nubian men decide."

A few days later, Thabo helped burn the two villages, and they left in the foggy dawn, taking the Zulu offspring with them.

Chapter 20

The Megmador

Captain Sedo and Dr. Jogen Kaen stood at attention before Commander Rota and eight high-ranking Beltese officers.

The committee consisted of five females and three males. The Fleet Command members sat around an oblong tyra wooden table, with Sedo and Jogen at the table's head.

The brightly lit room had a vase of fresh-cut white roses on a stand next to a transparent cabinet that contained six bottles of wine and glasses. Two computer stations faced the back wall.

Rota's voice took on a menacing tone. "At ease, Captain. Dr. Kaen, why are you here?"

Sedo took a seat, but Jogen remained standing.

Jogen said, "To explain the captain's medical history."

"And what does her medical condition have to do with this meeting?" Rota snapped.

"I—" Jogen said.

Rota's eyes remained cold and penetrating. "Dr. Kaen, you're excused."

Jogen's controlled words flowed fast. "But you don't understand. Doctors Fea and Ohma forgot to mention that Captain Sedo is a Megmador."

Rota gawked at Jogen, as if he were insane. "Humans can't become Megmadors."

Jogen placed both hands on the back of Sedo's chair. "She isn't human anymore—but Beltese."

Rota frowned. "We are aware of this."

"Captain Sedo has powers," Jogen said.

Rota rubbed his chin. "We had a meeting with Doctors Ohma and Fea yesterday. They admitted to their knowledge about altering Captain Sedo's genes—but nothing about powers."

Jogen's tension grew as he spoke. "The doctors falsified her medical records."

Rota asked, "Do you realize what you're saying?"

Bewilderment sparkled in the Fleet Command members' eyes as they glanced at Captain Sedo.

"Compare these images," Jogen said.

A giant, colorful, three-dimensional spiral molecule materialized and revolved slowly, as if moving from the table and into the ceiling. "This is human DNA. I'll not go into the chemical composition. This is our ZNA." Another spiral complex appeared. "Now, a combination of the two." He paused to allow the committee to examine the three structures. "Genes undergo mutation when human DNA, in our case ZNA, changes on a specific location on the chromosome. The cluster is quite complex and unique."

"Who's the research doctor responsible for this?" Rota asked.

"He went through Naconda fifteen years ago," Jogen said.

Rota stood, reached out, and touched the nearest compound as it floated in midair. He dropped back into his chair. "It's real. Dr. Kaen, how did you do that?"

Kaen motioned a hand toward Sedo. "I didn't. She did."

"Captain Sedo, do you have powers?" Rota asked.

"Yes," Sedo said.

"Can you do something else to prove that you're a Megmador, Captain?" Rota stuttered.

Sedo sensed his fear, his inability to deal with her powers. The floating images above the table vanished. She pulled Commander Rota's chair from behind the table, lifted him into midair, and sat him on the table, all with her mind.

Rota jumped out of his chair. His skin changed to a lighter pink, and his eyes bulged.

"Commander, I'm not going to hurt you. Please sit," she said.

Rota didn't respond.

Sedo moved the chair back to its original position.

Rota jumped off the table like a cat and stood behind his chair but remained silent, pondering the situation at hand.

Captain Sedo mentally opened the door of the nearby

wine cabinet. Glasses drifted into the air and landed in front of each member.

Dr. Kaen held up a hand. "None for me."

Everyone's eyes focused on the two bottles in disbelief as they moved in space from person to person.

Most of the committee members sat, their mouths agape, frozen in their seats.

The captain sensed vibes from the committee. They thought about eliminating her the way her parents had.

She moved away from the table and activated a green force field around her body. She touched a vacant chair, and it propelled away from her and crashed into the opposite wall, terminating the force field. "Once I realized I was becoming a Megmador, it took me months to reach my full powers."

"How long?" Rota asked.

"A year," Sedo answered.

Rota's voice faltered. He pushed his chair under the table but remained standing. "Are you certain you have full powers? Beltese Megmadors have trouble controlling their powers, and you—"

"My powers don't dominate me. I can control them at will," Sedo said. "That's what former Megmadors couldn't master."

Rota asked, "Did your parents know?"

Sedo nodded.

Rota's face changed from shock to anger. "Fleet Command should have been informed."

"My father was commander at the time. He and my mother would have suffered legal consequences for what they did," Sedo said.

"Indeed, they would have—and should have," Rota said.

Sedo said, "With my background in advanced engineering, I can tremendously enhance the Beltese society. I've redesigned our ships' engines, so they can travel at twice the present speed. I have the data here." A chip floated from a pouch around her waist and landed on the table before Rota.

Rota sighed and took a seat.

"I can work on the Human Planet Project with Reiser. I've reviewed his analysis and have ideas for improvements."

Jogen's lips quivered. Addressing Sedo, he said, "No, Sadera. We must stay together." He stared at Rota, who in turn gawked at the chip.

Rota rubbed his throat with his hand. "I'll allow our engineers to review your data."

Colas's forehead wrinkled. "Megmadors are always males."

Sedo said, "Maybe the covalent bonding between the two genes accounts for the inconsistency. I'm not a threat to anyone, and I'm asking Fleet Command to never disclose my secret."

Rota asked, "Do you know what we're thinking right now? I understand that Megmadors' heads are preoccupied with so many thoughts, they're near the point of insanity."

Sedo leaned forward in her chair. "I can read minds, but only if I desire to. I don't want to know what crew members are thinking, because it invades mental privacy. I've total control over my telepathic abilities."

Rota cocked his head. "What about the incident on the *Eliptus,* when you were in the next galaxy? You were far from the other ship."

Sedo said, "I sensed danger. It was like a beacon, summoning me. My powers are somewhat different from past Megmadors. Some things I can't explain, because I don't fully understand them myself."

"Captain, I'm sending a security team with you to retrieve all of Commander Sedo's data."

"I've submitted everything I have."

Rota said, "Not the originals. How did you get the commander's information?"

"My father left his office unlocked when I was on leave. I only copied my medical records and family history."

Rota had a distinct I-don't-believe-you look in his eyes. "How long have you had this information?"

"Prior to submitting it to Fleet Command: seven months," Sedo said.

"Did you obtain this information illegally?" he asked.

She knew he couldn't prove a thing. "Ah ... no."

"Most of the records in your father's possession were highly secret documents, secured at all times. If you illegally obtained this information, you could spend years on Quandra-4."

Yes, punish me.

"He forgot to lock up, Commander. Military and civilian laws state that as long as I'm considered a resident, I'm privileged to anything that's not locked."

Rota said, "*If* it was unlocked. You're dismissed, Captain. Doctor. Be at my office early tomorrow morning, Captain."

The committee waited silently for them to leave.

On her way out the door, Captain Sedo turned, glanced over her shoulder, and saw multiple keen, gray eyes glaring back at her with indignation.

A smile dented her cheeks.

***

Commander Rota walked to the front of the room, his stomach in a knot.

He had never felt so defenseless. Captain Sedo was now the most powerful being in the galaxy, and Rota didn't know how to deal with her. For the first time since becoming fleet commander, he had a problem he couldn't deal with.

Lola, the third-ranking officer in Fleet Command, was nearing Naconda. "This human Megmador presents a serious problem for us."

Murmurs of agreement filled the room.

Rota shook his head in disbelief. "The doctors will be severely punished for their role in this matter. Their duties are to protect Fleet Command and the Beltese military personnel."

"This occurred under Commander Sedo," Colas said.

Rota leaned over and placed his palms on the table, with his head down. "I'll accept no excuses from the doctors."

Colas's voice rose to almost a shout. "She may be sensing our thoughts at this very moment."

A chill of fear ran down Rota's spine. Fleet Command affairs he could deal with, but not a Megmador. "Since we can't terminate her, we can only hope she can truly control her powers."

"A human Megmador?" Colas said. "I still can't believe it."

Rota stared around at his commanders. "Well, you'd better believe it, because she could change our lives, the future of Tandon, and this galaxy—for generations to come."

Lola sighed. "How frightful. Did you see that astute smirk on her face?"

Rota pushed a button on his wristband.

A female voice answered, "Yes, Commander."

"Contact Doctors Ohma and Fea. I want them here at once," Rota said.

The doctors materialized, one and then the next, first their silhouettes, then their solid forms.

Rota motioned with a hand. "Have a seat, Doctors."

Rota remained standing after the doctors took their seats. "I understand that we have a human Megmador on our hands. Do you care to explain why Fleet Command wasn't notified?"

Dr. Ohma twisted in his chair. "That incident occurred under Commander Sedo."

"Incident?" Rota repeated. "Is that what you call it?"

"Ah ... yes," Dr. Ohma said.

Rota swiftly turned from the doctor and walked back toward his chair. "Expect a much greater punishment than the one I gave you two yesterday."

"I falsified her medical records," Ohma said. "Dr. Fea found out later."

Rota focused his attention to Fea. "You attended to her psychological issues, so you're equally guilty."

Ohma's voice trembled. "We complied with Commander Sedo's orders."

Commander Rota took a seat. "Fleet Command is responsible for military actions, not political. You both could've taken this matter to a higher authority, but you did nothing to stop this experiment."

Ohma's face turned pale. "Commander—"

Rota pointed a finger at him. "You have nothing to say, Doctor. And now you have implicated Dr. Kaen in this ordeal."

"Dr. Kaen is a research doctor. He understands areas in genetics that we don't. It was Captain Sedo who confided in him, not us," Ohma said.

"We don't want anyone else to know she's a Megmador," Rota said. "Can she detect our thoughts at this moment?"

Dr. Fea said, "She can't read our minds from the *Volpus*. She would have to be within close proximity to this room."

"If this is true, then explain how she realized the mistake the chief engineer was about to make on the *Eliptus*?" Rota asked.

Fea lowered his eyes to the table. "I don't know."

Colas said, "It wouldn't be wise to involve new doctors at this point."

Rota rolled his eyes toward the ceiling. "So, we must be content with these two traitors."

"I'm afraid so," Colas said. "They've kept it a secret so far."

Lola slid to the edge of her chair, her frail hands gripping the armrests. "You're not allowing her to remain captain?"

Rota took a seat and shifted his weight. "No matter what position she holds, she's still a Megmador and may be a great danger to us. What do you suggest we do with her?"

When Lola didn't reply, Rota reverted his attention back to the doctors. "Thanks to you two, she's now impervious to death. If you had warned us after her father's death, we could've euthanized her."

Lola's nostrils flared. "What if she can't be controlled? She has already disobeyed Fleet Command's orders once."

"You make a very good point," Rota said.

Fea said, "She already knows the committee finds her dangerous."

"Did she tell you that?" Rota asked.

Fea said, "She didn't have to."

Dr. Ohma squirmed in his chair. "She hasn't done anything abnormal, compared to other Megmadors."

Rota snapped, "When did you become an expert on Megmadors?"

"We know this one," Fea said.

Lola voiced her opinion again. "Perhaps we should transport her to a desolate planet in the other galaxy."

Rota wiped a hand across his forehead. "Computer, decrease the room temperature by five units. Other than the beings on Neptus, we have no knowledge of the species that exist there. We—"

Dr. Ohma held up a hand. "What if an alien species finds her? With her knowledge of our space technology, she could become our deadliest enemy."

"We have no choice but to keep her," Fea said. "She won't be a danger to us—unless we give her a reason to."

Rota pounded a fist on the table. "What you doctors think and reality are two different things."

"Are you going to punish her for disobeying orders?" Dr. Fea asked.

Rota said, "Are you insane? Punish a Megmador?"

Colas addressed the committee. "I think we should

retain her as captain of the *Volpus*. We don't want to infuriate her. So far, her intentions have been good."

Rota tugged at his sleeve. "I'm not as optimistic."

***

Captain Sedo spent the remainder of the day at her parents' residence.

Late that evening, the front door buzzed, followed by rapid pounding. When she opened it, four Fleet Command security officers forced their way in.

A young, female security captain walked past her. "We have orders to search this house, and you must leave."

"What are you looking for?" Sedo asked.

"All Fleet Command data that was in the late Commander Celt Sedo's possession," the security captain growled.

Sedo said, "You've had months to search this place. Why now?"

"We've searched this house once. Now we must do it again," the officer said.

"But—"

"Spend the night on the *Volpus* and return tomorrow," the security captain said. She stormed into Sedo's bedroom. Two officers entered her parents' room, another started searching the living room.

Sedo entered her room and started packing her bag.

"I need to witness what you're taking," the security captain said.

A male officer stood in the doorway. "Captain, Commander Rota would like to speak with you."

Sedo stepped back into the living room. "Computer, activate vektren."

Rota glared back at her. "I'm sorry for any inconvenience I may have caused you, Captain. We found other information in the late Commander Sedo's possessions that you didn't give us. I don't know if you missed this information or just refused to turn it over."

Sedo felt her body temperature rise. "I transmitted everything I had to Fleet Command months ago."

"I'd like to inform you that your quarters on the *Volpus* are being searched, as we speak," Rota said.

Sedo didn't like losing control of her emotions, but she snapped. "What are you searching for?"

Rota was calm. "Don't be annoyed, Captain. I'm using the same procedure as I would with any other officer."

Captain Sedo was glad she had destroyed the Fleet Command data months earlier. "Just tell me what you want."

"I'm not obligated to discuss it. I'll see you in the morning."

Rota disappeared.

***

The next day, Captain Sedo visited Commander Rota to determine her future.

She rode the vertical lift to the top floor of the Fleet Command complex, with Jogen at her side. They stepped off and walked in silence down a long corridor past other high-ranking Fleet Command officers, ending their journey at the last office.

Sedo stopped in front of Rota's open door. "Commander."

Rota sat behind her father's old desk, working on his computer. "Come in and take a seat, Captain. Dr. Kaen, this meeting doesn't concern you."

"I'll wait outside," Jogen said.

Sedo seated herself in a firm chair on the right side of Rota's desk.

The fleet commander's office ceiling stood higher than other offices in the complex to accommodate the life-size projection of the *Volpus* beast in its natural habitat, which covered the wall behind his desk. Sedo had feared it as a child because of its illusionary movement, especially its head and blinking yellow eyes.

Captain Sedo had never realized how spacious the office was without all of her father's personal belongings. The name outside the door had changed, and it now smelled like the sweet nectars of a variety of flowers that Rota had cultivated.

The commander stood and closed his door before speaking. "Your father had secret information in his personal possession that was against regulations. We don't know why he had this information or what he intended to do with it."

Sedo shook her head. "I have no other data."

She felt fear beaming from Rota, like radiant heat. His complexion had changed to a light pink. He never looked her in the eyes, and he shifted nervously in his chair. She fought hard to block his thoughts, but she couldn't resist.

The pale-faced commander said, "The data was hidden in a secret compartment in his desk, and I had to make sure that you didn't have it."

"Are you now convinced I don't have whatever this mysterious data may be?" she asked.

"I'm convinced that you don't physically possess it." Rota poured a glass of water from a pitcher and gulped down half of it. "My staff and I have discussed your defying Fleet Command orders by venturing into the next galaxy. I've noted a permanent record of your insubordination. You'll remain captain of the *Volpus*, for now."

Sedo then did something that surprised her, completely out of military context. She placed her hand on his. "Please don't fear me. I promised my parents I'd never use my powers unless absolutely necessary."

His eyes met hers. "I appreciate that, Captain. Megmadors have enhanced our technology in the past. The last one was a wine expert. You're the most technologically advanced of them all. Thanks to you, we're ready to explore the next galaxy."

Sedo materialized two glasses of wine. She raised her glass and toasted him. "Beltese will remain the most advanced species in both galaxies," she said.

He gawked at her. "How did you do that?"

"Do what?"

He waved a hand at the glass before him.

She shrugged. "I just think about it and it happens."

"I understand that if a Megmador materializes something, it comes from some other place. So someone is missing two wine glasses and a portion of their stock?"

"There's no proof of that," Sedo said.

"If it's true, then you're a thief," he accused.

Sedo placed her glass back on the table. "I usually don't do it."

"Return them," Rota ordered.

Sedo thought about replacing the items, and they disappeared.

"What about the force field?" he asked.

"I can choose to generate it, but it automatically protects me when I'm threatened."

Rota picked a dead leaf from a plant on his desk and threw it into a trash container. "Your mind detects danger, even during rest?"

"Yes. I'm not a monster, just a simple female with superpowers."

"Well, you do have us worried."

Captain Sedo considered herself a very patriotic Beltese, accustomed to only their traditions. "This is my home, my planet, and I won't do anything to dishonor or jeopardize it."

Rota said, "Promise me you'll use your powers only when necessary."

She smiled at the inferior being before her. "I promise." Sedo didn't just see his fear diminishing, she felt it.

Rota's skin gradually returned to its normal color, and he leaned back in his chair. "Our engineers have studied the data you presented, Captain. They're very impressed with your calculations. I'm putting you in charge of the Human Planet Project. Work with Reiser."

"Reiser thinks the project will take fifteen years. I believe it can be completed in less than three."

Rota interlaced his fingers and rested his hands on his desk. "We'll try to make the three-year deadline. Where do you see yourself in the future, Captain?"

She took a deep breath and smiled. "I want to become fleet commander, like my father."

His head jerked. He frowned and pushed his chair back. "Fleet ... I ... what?"

"After you, of course. Is that an impossible wish?"

He rapidly blinked his eyelids. "Well, I—"

"You seem baffled."

"Surprised. Yes," Rota admitted.

Sedo cleared her throat. "A Megmador isn't good enough to be fleet commander?"

He combed his hair back with his fingers and repositioned himself in his chair. "I suppose it's possible. Once you've proven yourself worthy of the position."

She leaned forward in her chair. "Good, because that's my goal."

Rota didn't answer. He seemed to be in deep concentration.

"I have a request," Sedo said.

"What?" Rota asked.

"Dr. Kaen and I would like your permission to become lifemates."

Creases on Rota's forehead deepened. "Lifemates? Husband and wife?"

As Rota digested the information, Sedo went to the door and beckoned Jogen. He entered the office and stood next to her.

Rota's face turned pale again. "Dr. Kaen, you wish to become lifemates with a Megmador?"

"Yes," Jogen said. "We need your authorization."

Rota drummed his fingers on his desk. "I don't think that's a good idea."

"Megmadors in the past have had wives," Sedo protested. "So why can't I have a husband?"

The commander addressed Jogen, rather than her. "They are known to dominate their spouses, and she'll do the same to you. Do you realize that when you reach Naconda, she'll not have aged and will outlive your offspring?"

Jogen said, "I realize that, Commander, and I still want to spend the rest of my life with her."

Sedo stood her ground. She wanted and needed Jogen

in her life. "I love him, and there are great differences between me and the average Megmador."

Rota stared into the distance. "Give me time to think about it."

Jogen shifted his weight. "We want your approval now."

Rota touched his computer keys and studied his screen. "What's the rush? I want you two to discuss this matter with ah ... Dr. Fea. If he agrees, I'll require monthly reports from him and you, Dr. Kaen."

Jogen said, "Anything that appears unusual or against Fleet Command regulations, I'll report directly to you."

"I agree with Jogen—ah, Dr. Kaen. As my husband, he'll be very close to me always. I approve of monthly reports," she said, reluctantly.

"That'll be all, Captain. Doctor."

Sedo and Jogen didn't speak until they stepped out of the building.

"What did you say to him? He looked so pale," Jogen said.

"He asked where I saw myself in the future."

He stopped and smacked his forehead with his palm. "Not your Megmador fleet commander idea?"

"Yes. He couldn't get his words out." Captain Sedo burst into laughter.

***

When Sedo approached Reiser's office, his door stood open. She entered and stopped at his side, but he failed to acknowledge her presence. Leaning back in his chair, he concentrated on a stationary, three-dimensional computer projection of the human planet. Deep blue water covered three-fourths of the sphere, and ice covered the north and south poles.

He kept his gaze on the object, sulking. "Fleet Command engineers think you can complete this project within three years."

Sedo suppressed her annoyance with this childish adult. She knew she had to spend many hours working with him. "I've reviewed your calculations, and I'm impressed. I commend you for making a habitable planet for humans."

Reiser's eyes didn't move from the projection. "Fleet Command also said you'll oversee my project."

Sedo sensed a faint energy level radiating from Reiser, but he wouldn't realize it himself at such an early stage. Ten years in the future, she might have competition as a Megmador. She couldn't imagine a pout like him with powers.

He was to be the next Megmador in the Beltese society, not her.

"This is a charitable project. You asked for this assignment. I've only improved it," she said.

Reiser kept his gaze on the projection. "A Trazod ship

is moving a piece of lithosphere as we speak, and I wasn't informed."

"You're a scientist, not a Fleet Command officer. You've done your job. Stop behaving like a child whose treat has been taken away."

His slender frame became larger as he swelled with anger, rising from his chair. He stared at her with menacing eyes, pointed a stiff finger at her, and growled, "You took over my project after I did all the work."

"You volunteered to create a habitable planet for humans, and you're about to accomplish that goal. What else do you want?" She stepped in front of his desk and into the middle of the projection, disrupting the image.

He seated himself again.

"Because of your work, it's still considered your project. The *Volpus* will be more involved than other ships. Are you ready to travel?"

He jumped to his feet, as if his chair were ablaze. His words flowed faster, and his voice became high-pitched. "I'm allowed to go on this voyage?"

"You did all the calculations, but remember I found the two planets."

Reiser's right eye twitched. "How many ships?"

"Six. The *Volpus*, the *Eliptus*, two Camagon, and two Elgon. Each will tow one of the largest plates."

"I'll need to inform you of my plans," he blurted.

"Reiser, your meeting with the Galactic Committee was documented. I've reviewed your proposal."

He glanced around his office. "When we bring the water up to the added lithosphere, the planet will cool. Then the large body of water will become blue."

Sedo wanted to slap the babbling idiot back into reality. "Yes, I know."

He muttered, "There are frozen rivers, lakes, and streams on each lithosphere. I'll add the microorganisms and bacteria from each clan's original environment. Introduce flora, fungi, and insects first, and give them time to multiply." He waved his hands back and forth before her, as if he were a god, creating life. "Next, I'll add the herbivores and give them time to expand their herds. Later, I'll introduce the humans, then the carnivores." He extended his arms toward the ceiling, as if trying to catch a huge ball and bellowed, "I'll build an entire ecosystem."

Reiser was really trying her patience. "Reiser, calm down. We should be ready to move the last plates within two months."

"That soon? When do we leave?" he asked.

"Tomorrow."

Reiser stared into space. "Tomorrow, but—" He glanced around his office again.

"Yes, tomorrow."

***

Sedo rushed into Jogen's laboratory, her hearts racing. "We've been approved to become lifemates."

Jogen grabbed Sedo around her waist, lifted her off her feet, and swirled her about. "Let's do it now."

She felt like a child at a birthday party. "I've never been so excited."

Sedo and Jogen transported to the central government complex on Tandon and presented their marital documents.

A female wearing a long white robe, who was nearing Naconda, shuffled toward them. The old employee touched keypads on her counter. "Yes, you two have been approved to become lifemates. Would you like a ceremony?"

"No," Jogen said.

"I suggest you think about it a few days, then return. Lifemating is permanent. The bond can only be broken by death."

"We're leaving Tandon tomorrow. We want to unite now," Sedo insisted.

The female hit more keys and gazed from Sedo to Jogen. "Dr. Jogen Kaen, do you acknowledge your mating with Captain Sadera Sedo will be for life?"

Jogen beamed. "Yes, I do."

"And do you, Captain Sadera Sedo, accept Dr. Jogen Kaen as your lifemate?"

Sedo's hearts fluttered. "Yes, I do."

"Then I pronounce you two lifemates."

Jogen embraced her and squeezed the wind out of her. He kissed her hard on her lips. "Now we can hold hands in public."

The fragile assistant reached over the counter and physically separated them. "You're not allowed to do that here. Touch your index fingers on the pad, and off with you."

They left the building holding hands.

"Now we qualify for larger living quarters," Jogen said. "At least we'll have two bedrooms."

***

The *Volpus* towed the second largest plate.

A dark green glow appeared on the lithosphere, where the electromagnetic field locked on. The light dimmed in both directions and faded from the contact point to nonexistence.

Ahead, a Camagon warship towed the largest plate, and a distant star lit the load. The lithosphere resembled part of a cracked eggshell, and the curvature of the plate concealed the ship.

Ferrus said, "Captain, my computer has detected a large object headed straight toward us, an asteroid on the port side. At present speed, it'll make contact with the plate in twenty minutes."

The object appeared on a vektren. "Release the load." She closed her eyes, pressed the fingers of both hands to her temples, and concentrated on reducing the impact of the asteroid. She couldn't stop the asteroid—but did slow its speed.

Ferrus said, "Captain, the asteroid is decelerating, and I can't determine why."

Sedo didn't respond but concentrated on saving the plate.

She felt Ferrus's gaze. "Release the plate, Ferrus."

"Now the asteroid just rotated its position in space. What we've witnessed here is impossible. An unknown force controls it. Captain, did you hear me?" Ferrus asked.

Eyes closed, she responded, "Yes. Strange things happen in space, Ferrus."

Excitement stirred in Ferrus's voice. "It doesn't make sense. It appears that something is deliberately protecting the plate."

The plate continued to move forward as the oblong, spiked mass embedded into its crust, creating a cloud of dust. Then, rebounding, the asteroid decelerated and spiraled away.

Ferrus quickly stroked his keypad. "According to my computer, the plate is still intact. Look at the hole that asteroid left. If it had impacted at its original speed and position, the lithosphere would have severed into many pieces."

Sedo had saved the second largest lithosphere from destruction. Each time she used her powers, she felt an elevated drive to go above her potential. Her gift exhilarated her.

"Where's the asteroid now?" she asked.

"It separated from the plate. We can't see it because of limited visibility, but my computer verifies it."

"Catch up with the lithosphere," Sedo said.

Ferrus sped the *Volpus* toward the target. "I'm slowing it down, Captain, and locking on again."

***

Sedo sat in her captain's chair with Reiser standing behind her, breathing down her neck.

The *Volpus* and multiple warships hovered in space above the exosphere of the human planet. Twenty-five Camagon warships, gigantic spheres with huge domes, were equally spaced above the largest plate.

On another vektren, Sedo saw elliptical Elgon ships spaced out at equal distance, controlling the third largest piece.

Ships of other Beltese allies controlled the remaining five pieces of lithospheres. All seven pieces surrounded the planet, aligned like the projected prototype.

Reiser's hands gripped Sedo's headrest. He constantly shifted his weight as overwhelming excitement emanated from him.

Ever since she'd found out about the human clans, Sedo had wanted to find them a permanent planet. Pride and relief struck her, and she felt just as excited as Reiser. The Galactic Committee had claimed the planet and promised to allow humans to live in peace, and to safe-guard them from other alien species.

Sedo said, "Have a seat, Reiser. Use Khyla's desk."

"I can see better from here, and I don't want to miss anything," he said.

Sedo resisted the urge to swat him like an insect. "This is Captain Sedo from Command Control. Are all ships ready to descend?"

All ships acknowledged.

"Turn on your force fields."

Dotted lines of anti-gravitational force fields attached at each ship, causing the lithospheres to glow purple.

"All ships, standby," Sedo said.

She tapped a button on her desk, and her computer started a ten-second countdown. At zero seconds, every cluster of ships towing a lithosphere entered the human planet's atmosphere at the same speed.

The anti-gravitational force field slowed the load but caused the *Volpus* to vibrate as it resisted the planet's gravity.

The lead Camagon captain rocked in her chair. Her skin had changed to the color of her surroundings: the gray background of her walls. "Command Control, we're moving faster than predicted."

"What's the problem?" Sedo asked. "We checked our calculations at least a dozen times."

The Camagon captain shouted back, "The anti-gravitational force field on ship four is too weak. The lithosphere is tilted downward on that side, and we can't stabilize it."

Captain Sedo concentrated on the lopsided plate headed for the human planet. "All ships, increase your speed to that of the Camagon fleet. At least the surfaces of the lithospheres will make contact at the same time. Remain within the established coordinates."

Reiser clung to Sedo's headrest with both hands, struggling to remain on his feet. "Oh no, we're moving too fast."

"This is Command Control," Sedo yelled. "Captains, as you see, a Camagon ship is out of control. We must remain on course."

Turbulence caused Reiser to fall to the floor. "Stop it, Captain," he shouted. "We must slow down. The impact will be too great."

As the speed of the *Volpus* remained constant, Sedo gripped her armrests and planted her feet firmly on the floor, fighting to stay in her chair. "Reiser, we can't terminate this project. It's too late."

The Camagon captain summoned Sedo. "We're still out of control."

"Have you determined the problem with your fourth ship?" Captain Sedo asked.

"Yes, but we don't have time to repair it," the Camagon captain said.

Sedo mentally reached out to the runaway Camagon ship and concentrated on decelerating it.

"Captain Sedo, the speed of the runaway ship has

decreased," the lead Camagon captain reported. "I can't understand why. We didn't do a thing."

"We'll figure it out later," Sedo said. "Release the load once it contacts the surface and exit as planned."

It didn't take long for Sedo and the other ships to reach the surface of the planet, superimposing the plates at exactly the same nanosecond. The lithospheres hit the planet with a thunderous bang, and a dust cloud mushroomed over the planet.

The *Volpus* sped away and joined the other warships at a safe distance.

"We won't be able to see anything down there until the dust settles," Sedo said.

"I've performed analyses, Captain," Somgu said. "Computational results show that everything went as planned."

"This is Captain Sedo at Command Control. Excellent job. Now our ships will travel back and get the smaller plates. Each ship can probably tow two masses."

Chapter 21

The Baby Megmador

The Galactic Committee contracted the Agoorons to assist with introducing life-forms into the human environment—a selection of millions of species housed in pre-assembled laboratories and facilities.

Sedo left Reiser and a few of her scientists on the planet to complete the life-ecosystem process. The Agoorons hated working with Reiser, and Sedo couldn't blame them.

When Sedo transported from the planet, the rivers, lakes, and streams had begun to thaw. She would monitor the relocation of the human clans from the *Volpus*.

***

Jogen worked at his computer as Sedo massaged his neck. She debated telling him what was on her mind, even though she didn't want to keep secrets from her husband. "Jogen, remember how we decided to wait five years before we had a baby?"

"Against my wishes, yes," he said.

"Well, I'm expecting."

He jumped to his feet, picked her up, threw her on the bed, and straddled her. "I hope it's a male. How long have you been pregnant?"

"Two weeks."

"Why didn't you tell me earlier?" he asked, his eyes excited.

"We can't keep him."

"Him. You know how much I want a son. He won't interfere with your captain's duties. I'll take total responsibility. You won't have to do anything."

"No," she said.

Jogen grabbed her shoulders and shook her. "This is not just your decision. He's my son too."

"It's a Megmador. I've already discussed this with Dr. Ohma. His nurse will terminate the pregnancy tomorrow morning."

"How do you know? Maybe he doesn't have powers." Jogen scanned her stomach with one of his instruments. "He is a Megmador. His energy level is high."

"He'll be deadly to everyone aboard the *Volpus*, except me."

"This is a medical phenomenon. We can keep him." He threw his hands into the air. "He'll have parents to love and nurture him. I want to keep my son."

"What would the Beltese think if we had a baby? How will we explain it?"

"We can admit that you're Beltese now. Since your

incident on M-7, the Velekans have already started rumors about you having powers. Sooner or later, everyone will know," he said.

"I'd prefer later. A baby Megmador can't control his powers. If we conceive a normal boy, we'll keep him." She kissed his lips. "The safety of my crew comes first, and you are crew."

***

The next morning, Captain Sedo found herself sitting in Dr. Ohma's office, discussing the termination of her pregnancy.

Dr. Ohma said, "Captain, allow me to incubate the embryo for two months."

"Why wait?"

"I'd like to study it. An offspring like this may never occur again. It's too small to analyze now, but a fetus of four months will make a big difference. I want to know everything about it."

"You said two months. Now it's four. No." Sedo was adamant.

"Just two months then. Please, Captain," Ohma said. "I'll do extensive research, instrumental only, and I promise he won't suffer. Do you know what this will mean to medical science? Your son holds the key to how Megmadors obtain their powers."

"He's my son, not a research project—the way I was. I won't allow him to be treated as such."

"I'm sorry about what happened to you. You were an experiment," Dr. Ohma admitted.

"Maybe our powers should remain a secret."

"Please, just three more months," Ohma said. "Don't dispose of it yourself. Allow my nurse to incubate it."

"I guess it really doesn't make any difference. Two months," she agreed.

Ohma put a hand on her shoulder. "All right, two months. Come with me."

Sedo followed him into another room, undressed from the waist down behind a curtain, and donned a clinical gown. When she stepped back into the room, Dr. Ohma's nurse was the only one there.

The nurse had set up equipment for the fetus transfer. She never asked how Sedo had become pregnant or who the father was.

"I'll need fresh blood for the fetus. You have less than six months to decide whether to keep the baby."

The human gestation period was nine months, not six. The nurse never commented on this discrepancy.

"There's nothing to think over. I can't keep it," Captain Sedo said.

The procedure didn't take long. Rid of the foreign entity, Sedo was glad to go back to her normal life.

***

Ohma entered Jogen's laboratory with a wide, serpentine grin on his face. "Come with me. I have a surprise for you."

Jogen stood, pushed his chair back under the desk, and followed Ohma. "What?"

"You're going to love it," Ohma said.

They walked into the infirmary and entered a back room where incubators lined the center of the room. He saw six fetuses at various stages through transparent containers.

Ohma stopped before one and waved his hand. "Surprise."

Jogen stood over the incubator and saw a fetus at almost fullterm. "So, it's a human baby."

"Look closer," Ohma said. "He's not just any baby."

The incubator label read: KAEN/SEDO. Jogen froze in his tracks and stared at his son in shock. He then turned his attention to Dr. Ohma, who seemed pleased with himself. "What have you done?"

Dr. Ohma checked the fetus with his Z-2 scanner and beamed. "It's almost six months. Can you imagine? A baby Megmador?"

"You promised Sadera that you'd terminate him after two months."

Ohma smiled. "Just ten more days, and you'll have the son you've always wanted."

Jogen couldn't betray his wife's trust. "You must terminate it. He'll be too dangerous."

"You may not be able to control him, but his mother can. She can nurture him, just like any other child."

Jogen pondered the issue for a few seconds. "No."

"Just a few more days," Ohma said.

Jogen folded his arms and shook his head. "It's an evil trick."

Ohma tapped a finger on the container. "It'll be murder if she destroys him after he leaves the incubator. I know how much you want him. The next one might be a female."

"We'll abort it and try again," Jogen said.

"But you have one now. No one needs to know he's a Megmador."

"What if Sadera can't control him?" Jogen asked.

"She has powers that you don't," Ohma said.

Jogen said, "She'll be very upset. We've never had a fight."

Ohma touched his shoulder. "She'll get over it."

Jogen felt proud to have a son. He smiled. "All right. I'll keep him."

"Good." Dr. Ohma smiled. "You've made the right decision."

***

Sedo responded to the incubation room at Ohma's request. When she arrived, Jogen held a baby and flashed a broad smile. She felt the energy level in the room, and it emanated from the baby. She froze in horror. Now she understood why Ohma had taken huge amounts of her blood over the past few months.

Sedo pointed a stiff finger at Ohma. "You haven't changed. You are, and always will be, corrupt. You experimented on me—and now my son."

Ohma took a few steps backward. "Calm down, Captain."

She then turned her hostility to her husband. "How could you do something so stupid?"

"I only found out ten days ago. It's too late to terminate him. His name is Kutru." Jogen hugged the baby and kissed his cheeks. "Isn't he cute?"

Pressure from the energy that flowed through Sedo's body, wanted to explode from within her. She took several deep breaths, trying to control her rage, and for a moment, she hated her husband. "Jogen, we're no longer lifemates," she shouted. "I may not be able to sever our unity, but no one can make me live with you. You take care of your son and don't speak to me again, ever."

Wrapped in a green blanket almost the color of his eyes, the baby kicked his little feet, gave her an adorable smile, and his chubby hands reached out for her, enticing her to grasp him. The bond between Kutru and her was strong. She resisted the urge to reach back—to hold him—to feel the warmth of his body and the softness of his skin against hers. He had that newborn baby smell.

It was her job to protect, not destroy, him.

Captain Sedo turned her attention back to Ohma. She grabbed him by the collar of his blue lab jacket and threw him across the room. The back of his head hit the wall with a thud, and he slithered to the floor. Yellow blood spattered the wall where his head had made contact. "You are fired. When we reach Tandon, I want no sign of you left on my ship."

Jogen rushed to Ohma's aid.

"My head," the doctor whimpered.

Jogen tended to Ohma's injury as Sedo rushed back to their quarters. She passed crew members in the hallway, but she never acknowledged them. The mistrust of her mate saddened her to a point of uncertainty. Over the past few days, she had sensed something deceitful about him, but she'd never imagined this.

Back in their quarters, she dumped her personal items onto their bed, stuffed two bags, and closed them.

Jogen entered the room and stepped into her path. "Dr. Ohma has a concussion."

She threw more things onto the bed. "I wanted to kill him."

"Wait, Sadera." He fidgeted before her. "What are you doing?"

"Don't speak to me, you deceitful idiot."

"Where are you going?" Jogen asked.

Sedo threw him aside with her mind as she continued to gather more of her things. "Back to my old quarters.

You and Kutru can share this extra bedroom. I refuse to live with a mate I can't trust."

"Sadera, you can't do this. We have a baby to care for."

"You promised to take care of him, and you will," she shouted.

"Stop yelling. Others can hear you."

Sedo shouted louder. "I don't care."

She rushed out of the room as if it were on fire, her arms loaded with personal items, dropping some as she went.

Jogen ran after her, picking things up behind her. "Don't go. We can talk this out."

She shouted back at him, "Stop following me."

She passed a few crew members. They stepped aside and hugged the walls, as if she might attack them.

Entering her old room, she threw things onto the bed. Jogen dropped his load as well.

Sedo felt tears rolling down her cheeks, but when she looked into the mirror, she saw none. As she walked back down the corridor, Jogen trailed behind her. "Sadera, please don't leave me."

Sedo turned and slapped his face. "I never want to see you again." She wanted him gone, forever.

It took three more trips to retrieve all her belongings, and he followed her each time. Crew members stared at them, but Sedo was too angry to care. After her last trip, she threw Jogen into the hallway. He crashed into a crew member, and they both landed on the floor. Then she closed the door and locked it.

Sedo sat in her room and cupped her face in her palms as her mind whirled over the new entity in her life. She pounded her desk with both fists. She was responsible for a living being, and it wasn't going away.

She punched in Starco's code from her computer station.

"Yes, Captain. You're in your old quarters again?" Starco said.

She wanted to give Starco a piece of her mind. She knew the gossip about the scene between Jogen and her had spread across the *Volpus* like a wildfire. "Contact Commander Rota. Put him on a vektren in my old room."

"Yes, Captain," Starco said.

Seconds later, Rota came into view. He sat in the living room of his residence, wearing a dark robe.

"Captain," he acknowledged.

Sedo's throat was dry, and she had trouble getting her words out. "Commander, I have a very serious situation here." She sighed. "I was expecting, and I asked Dr. Ohma to terminate my pregnancy. Instead, he kept the fetus until fullterm. My son is a baby Megmador, and I'm the only one who can control him. The baby is too dangerous to society, and we must euthanize him at once. I have terminated Dr. Ohma's service aboard the *Volpus*."

Rota didn't seem to fear her anymore. "I'm afraid I can't allow you to do that. Dr. Ohma knows more about your anatomy than anyone else. It's not wise to bring in a new doctor at this point. You can file charges of insubordination against him, and that's all. I'm sorry, Captain, but the doctor stays."

She blurted out, "Within two months, everyone aboard this vessel will know we have a baby Megmador. Our laws mandate the abortion of all abnormal fetuses. What he did was criminal."

"I've already discussed this matter with the doctor. I understand that your husband disagrees with you. Both said you can easily control your son."

"How can you trust Dr. Ohma after he falsified my medical records for over thirty years? My son will be a great danger to everyone aboard the *Volpus*. It's my job to protect my crew."

"Captain, we don't kill babies."

She felt her voice tremble. "But you don't understand. A baby won't be able to control his powers."

"Do you want your son destroyed because you think he's a danger—or because he's an inconvenience?"

"I know what he's capable of. I've envisioned him killing some of my crew. He's deadly and—"

Rota crossed his legs at the ankles. "Captain Sedo, do you love or want your son?"

"That's not the point," she said.

"Answer the question: yes or no?"

She shook her head frantically. "I can't allow myself to get attached. In the near future, he must die, and I'm the only one who can terminate him. Think of the position you're putting me in."

"Captain, calm down," Commander Rota said.

"I'm tired of being told to calm down," she shouted.

Rota disappeared.

Sedo lowered her gaze to the floor. "What am I going to do?" she said aloud. "He's my son."

***

The *Volpus* still orbited the human planet when Jogen walked into Navigational Control. Bruises covered his head and neck, and Sedo knew their son was responsible for his injuries. He dropped Kutru in her lap, turned, and walked away.

Sedo jumped to her feet. "Jogen," she called, but he rushed out the door.

Unlike the few human babies Sedo had seen, Beltese babies had better motor skills at an earlier age.

Her son was smartly dressed in the same Beltese uniform as the other crew members, with a white collar.

Sedo held the baby as if he were so fragile she might break him. He smiled up at her. She held him close, and he touched her face with his soft hands.

"Mommy, Mommy. Why don't you live with us?"

He was so cute, cuddly, and innocent.

"Somgu, take over until I can get this situation under control."

Somgu flashed a smile at Sedo. "Sure, Captain. Cute baby."

Her crew had started rumors about her and Jogen having a child. She quickly scanned Navigational Control.
Immediately all eyes left her and turned back to their
own stations.

Starco decided to be the brave, outspoken one. "Where
did he come from, and why is he calling you Mommy?"

Sedo was abrupt. "You have a child of your own, and
you don't know where babies come from?"

"He looks human, but they can't talk at that age," he
said.

"Starco, mind your own business," Sedo snapped. She
turned and looked around the room. "And that goes for
the rest of you."

Sedo left Navigational Control, carrying Kutru in her
arms. On the vertical lift, she caressed her face against
his. She held him tightly and didn't want to let go. His
eyes, hair, and complexion were exactly like hers, but
other than that, he was 100% Beltese. She couldn't block
her strong motherly bond.

"Do you love me, Mommy?"

She squeezed him and kissed his cheeks. "Yes, dear.
You're so precious."

"Then you'll come live with us?" Kutru asked.

She kissed his cheeks again. "Yes, Mommy promises."

When Sedo reached Jogen's quarters, she buzzed the
door, and it opened. Upon entering the room, she saw
destruction and knew Kutru was responsible. She sat on
the sofa next to Jogen.

Silence stretched between them.

At last, Jogen spoke. "He's beautiful, isn't he?"

"Yes, but he's dangerous. Did he do this?"

"He's only four months old, and I can't control him."

"Jogen, it's only going to get worse. We can't keep this hidden. Where do you leave him each day?"

"In my office. I'm so exhausted. I need a break. I took him out of the nursery, because he used his powers to throw things around."

"I've heard rumors."

Jogen reached out and ran his fingers through her hair. "I'm sorry I listened to Dr. Ohma. I need you to move back in."

"Kutru starts school next month. Maybe I can get him under control by then," Sedo said.

"Are you moving back? Only you can discipline him."

"Yes, I'll move back," she promised.

Jogen took the baby from her arms, stood him on the floor, and moved closer to her.

Meanwhile, her son ran to a chair and tried to climb into it. When he couldn't, he threw it across the room with his mind, smashing it against the wall.

"Fortunately, we only have one neighbor, but they have been complaining about the noise coming from our room," Jogen said.

"What does Ohma think?" she asked.

"He fears that Kutru will harm others, and soon."

Sedo picked up her son, took him into his bedroom, and mentally confined him in one corner.

"Mommy," he whined.

In a soft voice, she said, "Behave. You know what that word means."

Over the next month, Sedo disciplined Kutru and tried to make him understand why he shouldn't use his powers.

***

On Kutru's first day of class, Lieutenant Bago summoned Sedo. He rushed out his words. "Captain, get down to classroom nine, and hurry."

The carnage she envisioned shocked her tremendously. "Oh, no."

"We have nine casualties here," Bago said.

Sedo gasped, "I'll be right down."

She leaped from her chair and hurried to the vertical lift, then took the horizontal route to the classroom.

Bago stood in the hallway next to her son. His words flowed with fear and fury. "Walk inside and see what this human has done. Records show that he was born on the *Volpus*. How can that be?"

Sedo didn't respond to Bago's question. She peeked inside and saw the teacher and eight students dead, their heads twisted off.

"The only survivor ran from the classroom and said he did this." Bago pointed at Sedo's son. "Who or what is he?"

She went down on one knee. How would she punish him for such a horrific crime? "Kutru, why did you do this?"

"They said I wasn't Beltese. They said you're not my real mommy—that I'm human and don't belong."

"When you look in the mirror, you don't look like your father, but me."

"They said I was adopted," Kutru said.

"That's not true. You recognized me the first time we met. Why did you listen to them?"

"They said I was different, so I showed them, didn't I, Mommy?"

"Why did you kill your teacher?" Sedo asked.

"Because she started it, talking about me being human. She said humans are inferior."

"Do you know what that word means?"

The boy's face was calm. Too calm. "Yes, she told us, and everyone laughed. So I stopped them."

"How does he have the power to do something like this?" the security officer asked.

"Let me handle him," Sedo said.

Bago stepped forward. "It's my job, Captain."

Kutru suspended Bago in midair.

She picked up her son and landed Bago back on the floor. "Unless you want to end up like them, you'll stay back."

Bago's eyes grew larger. "How did he do that? What is he?"

"A baby Megmador—who can't control his rage," she said.

Bago's hands went to his throat. "Megmador? Did you say Megmador?"

Sedo hugged her son, ignoring her lieutenant's question. "You've killed. Do you know what this means?" she asked Kutru.

Kutru smiled and nodded. "It means they can't tease me anymore."

"Understand that you'll be punished for this," Sedo said.

Her son folded his little arms and stuck out his chest, his lower lip protruding. "Just let them try."

Bago raced from the area.

Sedo shivered at the thought of terminating her own son. It would have been easier when she first saw him, but not now.

Dr. Ohma's voice rang from her collar communicator. "Captain, please bring Kutru to my office."

She knew that meant death for her son. "Dr. Ohma, don't think of doing what's on your mind. It could prove fatal."

"I'll be walking along a secluded beach," Dr. Ohma said.

The news was out. As the captain walked down the corridor, she felt her crew gawking at the strange human boy.

When Sedo arrived at Dr. Ohma's office, Bago was there.

"Hello, Kutru," Ohma said. "I understand you've disposed of nine Beltese, most brutally."

The boy bragged, "They're dead, all right."

Ohma held a syringe in his hand. "So, you understand death."

Sedo loved Kutru and wanted to save him, but she knew that was no longer an option.

"Dr. Ohma, don't," Sedo warned.

Kutru's eyes never left the doctor's hand. "Yes, I do. I also know you plan to poison me."

Sedo gasped, "Kutru, no. Don't hurt—"

The syringe left the doctor's hands, and its contents were emptied into his neck before Sedo could react.

The doctor fell limply to the floor.

"He was going to hurt me, kill me," her son said.

Jogen panted as he rushed into Ohma's office. "Are you all right, Kutru? What happened in your classroom?"

"He killed nine Beltese, because they teased him about being human," Bago said. "Now he has taken Dr. Ohma's life."

Jogen stopped in his tracks, reeling.

Bago peered at Jogen, his eyes crazed. "Apparently, he enjoys twisting crew members' heads off."

Jogen looked down at his son. "Kutru, did you do that?"

The boy said, "Yes, they deserved it. You don't like me anymore, Father. You think I'm a monster."

Jogen scanned Ohma's body with an instrument from

his belt. "I'm disappointed in you, because you don't mind me. Sadera, what are we going to do?"

Kutru's cold eyes scrutinized his father. "Now you're thinking about killing me."

Sedo said, "Jogen, for your own safety, think about something pleasant." She looked around the area. "Where did Bago go?"

"I don't know," Jogen replied.

"He's contacting your commander," Kutru said.

"Captain, Commander Rota has requested to speak with you in private," Starco said.

"I'll speak with him in Conference Room B, Deck One. Kutru, wait here with your father."

Captain Sedo entered the conference room farthest from her son and took a seat in front of Rota's grim face.

"What's happening on your ship, Captain?" he asked. "I've heard that your son has murdered ten crew members."

"That's correct, Commander. Dr. Ohma attempted to euthanize him, but—instead—Kutru injected Dr. Ohma with the poison."

"I understand that he twisted the heads off of the others."

She placed her arms on the table, the fingertips of both her hands touching, her hearts thumping. "Just as any baby Megmador does who can't control his powers."

"I know it'll be difficult, but you're the only person who can end this."

She wanted to choke the life out of Rota. "At least Dr. Ohma told you that much. I'll take care of it, Commander."

He pointed a finger at her. "You'll destroy him now. I'll not allow him to murder any more of my crew."

She shouted back at Rota, "I warned you this would happen. Now you're ordering me to kill my own son. This is Ohma's fault. He got exactly what he deserved: death."

Rota leaned in and gave her a menacing glance. "What did you say?"

She yelled, "This entire episode is Dr. Ohma's fault."

Rota growled, "You calm down, Captain. I'll not deal with insubordination from you. Eliminate the problem, now. And I want extensive analyses of the body, especially the brain."

"My husband is the only research doctor on this ship. Do you actually expect him to anatomize his own son? Are you mad?"

"Then preserve the body and bring it back to Tandon."

Commander Rota disappeared.

Her collar communicator went off. "Captain."

She yelled, "What now?"

"Captain. Let me talk to your son," Fea said.

She tried to control her anger. "Do you realize he just killed Dr. Ohma? He can read your mind."

"I pose no threat to him," Dr. Fea said.

Sedo said, "All right."

On her trip back to the infirmary, she met Bago. He rushed into the lift before the doors closed. "Commander

Rota told me everything—in confidence, of course—about you being a Beltese and a Megmador. Captain, you must put an end to your son."

Sedo didn't respond, just stepped off the lift when it stopped.

She retrieved Kutru from the clinic. "I'm taking you to see another doctor. Hurt him, and you'll be sorry."

"If he has bad thoughts—" Kutru said.

"I don't care what he's thinking. Do you understand?" Sedo asked her son.

"I won't hurt him, Mommy," he promised.

When they walked into the waiting room, Dr. Fea immediately summoned them into his office. He sat behind his desk, the fingers of both his hands laced together, as usual.

"Hello, Kutru. Have a seat," Dr. Fea said.

Sedo helped her son climb into a chair in front of the doctor, and she took the one next to him.

"There's talk around this ship about what you did to your fellow students. I'm a psychiatrist. Do you know what my job is?"

"You try to complicate my mind, my thoughts, and behavior," Kutru said.

"No, I don't try to complicate them, just understand them," Dr. Fea said. "You know what you did today has a great impact on your parents."

Kutru cocked his head. "I didn't mean to cause problems for them."

"You're a very intelligent student, I understand."

"Smarter than anyone on this ship, except for Mommy."

Fea smiled and ran his fingers through his graying hair. "And at such a young age."

"That's because I can read minds," Kutru bragged.

"Like you're reading mine at this moment."

"You think I should be eliminated too," Kutru said.

"Crew members—and you are a crew member—don't kill each other. We find other ways to work out our problems. What do you think would happen to me if I killed everyone I didn't like? What you did is against the law. Crew members fear you, and they think you should die like the ones you've killed. You have no compassion or empathy for life. Did your mother talk to you about this?"

"I have powers that the Beltese don't."

"Your mother also has powers, but she hasn't killed anyone. She's captain of the *Volpus*, respected by all. Ones with such powers must have respect for those who don't."

"I enjoyed killing them, seeing their faces twisting, their eyes rolling around in their heads, and their yellow blood splattered all over the place. My blood is red like Mommy's."

"How do you know her blood is red?" Dr. Fea asked.

"I don't know. I know lots of things."

"You inherited your powers from your mother," Dr. Fea said.

"Father doesn't have powers. He's just a Beltese. He has bad thoughts about me."

"Do you want to hurt him?" Dr. Fea asked.

"Sometimes."

"Fathers want to feel proud of their sons, and you're a part of him. He's a doctor, and he would never hurt anyone. His job is saving lives and making patients feel better. If you were angry with your classmates, why not tell them to stop?"

"Because I wanted them gone," Kutru said.

"Why did you twist their heads off?"

He chuckled and kicked his feet. "Because it was fun."

"It couldn't have been fun to kill," Fea said.

Kutru giggled. "It was to me."

Sedo's son was far more dangerous than she had imagined. He was a threat to everyone aboard the *Volpus*, especially Jogen. Kutru wanted to kill his own father, and she had to stop him. Destruction had become the most satisfying thing in his life. He felt no remorse, only pleasure.

"Do you think that in the future, if someone is rude to you, you can resist killing them?" Dr. Fea asked.

Kutru scooted to the edge of his chair and leaned forward. "No. They must die."

"Even if your parents are against it?"

"Yes. When I kill them, I don't have to look at them again."

"Do you realize that what you did caused others to fear and dislike you?"

"They already hate me, so why should I care?"

"Kutru, is there any way your parents or I, can stop you from wanting to hurt others?"

"No. Why do you feel sorry for me?"

"Because you're just a child and shouldn't have to be confronted with such fatal decisions."

Kutru lowered his head, the first and only time he had shown remorse.

"Well, that's what I wanted to talk to you about. Is there anything that you want to ask me?" Fea asked.

Kutru shook his head.

When Sedo picked up her son and carried him from the doctor's office, his mood had turned sour. Everyone they passed stared at him and gave them a wide berth. When they stepped on the lift, three crew members stepped off.

"Would you like something to eat, Kutru?"

"No, Mommy."

The pain in her hearts went to her stomach. "Not even dessert?"

Kutru tightened his grip around her neck. "They're staring at me. I hate that."

"I'll take you up to your room, then I'll bring you some food."

"Mommy, why can't I read your thoughts?"

Sedo held him tighter. "Because I'm like you, and I'm an adult."

When Captain Sedo entered their quarters, she stood Kutru on the floor. He ran into his room, climbed up the steps, and jumped onto his bed.

"I'll be back shortly. I have an errand to run." She locked the door.

When Sedo stepped into Jogen's lab, she found him sitting behind his desk, staring into the distance.

"How are you?" she asked.

He didn't make eye contact with her. "How do you expect me to be?"

"I need poison, enough to kill a hundred Beltese," she said.

He rubbed his face with both hands. "To kill my son."

Starco's voice rang on her communicator collar from Navigational Control. "Captain, where are you? The commander wants to know if the special job has been completed."

"Tell him I'm working on it," she said.

Jogen stared up at her with sad eyes. "I must see him one last time. I need to hold him."

"That's not possible. He can read your mind," Sedo said.

"Will you take his body back to Tandon, as Rota ordered?" he asked.

Jogen had conspired behind her back once. Had he done so again?

"How do you know what Rota said?" she asked.

"I talked to him after you did," he admitted. "I apologized for my ignorance."

"I'll transport his remains to the human planet," Sedo said.

"What will you tell Rota?"

She hugged Jogen. "That his body disintegrated, like all Megmadors do at death. If I had remained with you and Kutru, maybe I could have controlled him better."

"It wouldn't have made any difference," Jogen said.

"It's my fault for keeping the fetus."

She sighed. "Let's not dwell on the past."

An awkward silence fell between them. He didn't say another word, just gave her a syringe and small vial.

When Sedo entered Kutru's room, she found him asleep. She sat on his bed, holding the syringe, watching his little chest rise and fall with each breath. He looked so peaceful and adorable. She couldn't take his life—not now, not ever.

Sedo walked back into the living room and sat in a chair. She was still sitting there when Jogen entered their room and stood before her.

His eyebrows went up in question. Their eyes met for a moment of uncomfortable agony.

She suddenly realized she was trembling and had been for quite some time. "I couldn't do it. He's asleep."

Jogen said, "Kutru is vulnerable in that state. Dr. Ohma should've waited until he had fallen asleep."

Her son's bedroom door stood open. Jogen took the syringe, walked into the room, and stopped. He slowly turned, gazed back at her, then proceeded. He returned shortly thereafter, carrying their son in his arms.

Sedo sat with her feet together, her fingers digging into her thighs.

Kutru's head lolled back and his arms dangled at his sides. Jogen placed his body in her arms. "I'll give you a death certificate."

Sedo didn't move. Her hearts tightened, and she lingered on the edge of a scream. "We'll claim that he went up in flames. I'll contact Chedzer and transport his remains to the human planet."

Jogen asked, "Why not disintegrate him?"

"We can't. Each time the chamber is used, the ship's computer automatically documents the data, and I can't override it."

When Captain Sedo cradled her son's lifeless body, his hair fell back. His muscles were relaxed, and he still felt soft and warm. "Are you sure he's dead?"

Jogen placed a hand on Kutru's face. "I'm a doctor. He's dead."

She said, "He may be in some kind of suspended animation. After all, he's a Megmador. I think we should keep him for a few days, just to make certain."

"We need to dispose of him now," he said.

Sedo didn't feel an energy field or any signs of life emanating from their son, but she still had doubts. As she made her way down the corridor, crew members stared at what appeared to be a sleeping boy.

When she entered the engine room, the chief engineer approached her. "Captain."

"Chedzer, I need to dispose of this body."

He stared at Kutru. "Is he dead?"

"Yes, and I don't want anyone doing research on his remains. As far as everyone knows, his body went up in flames. Is that understood?"

He stuck out his chest and leaned back on his heels. "Well, Captain, if a certain incident on my record would disappear—"

Sedo stepped closer to Chedzer and stared him down. "Are you trying to blackmail me?"

He lowered his eyes to the floor. "Ah, no, Captain. It was sort of a joke."

"Am I laughing? I'm holding the body of a child—and you're cracking jokes?"

"I'll take him up to the incineration chamber. The stairs will be faster and secluded."

"No. Prepare a ventilated container strong enough to prevent scavengers from getting to his remains. I'll transport his body to a desolate place on this planet."

"What size container?" Chedzer asked.

"A large one."

"Are you sure he's dead?" Chedzer asked.

When she held Kutru to her chest, she felt that his body was still warm, and she detected a faint heartbeat. "Yes. He's dead."

"How did he die?" Chedzer asked.

"Does it matter?"

"Why such a large container?" he asked.

"Because that's what I requested."

She had only two choices: kill her son or send him into exile.

Sedo went to the transporter room and placed containers of food in the box, enough to last Kutru for a year. With his powers, within a year he would be able to function as a full-grown Beltese. She placed Kutru's body in the container and set the coordinates, and it disappeared. Sometime in the future, she would meet him again.

***

The next day, Captain Sedo found herself standing before seventeen of her lieutenant commanders.

"Who called this meeting?" she asked.

"We all did," Somgu said.

"Usually I'm the one who calls meetings. Why would all of my ranking officers wish to speak to me at the same time?"

Somgu stood. "I've been chosen to speak for this group. Your officers would like answers to many questions. We respect your privacy and realize you don't have to respond."

Sedo took the chair at the head of the table and held her head high. "First question, Somgu."

"What was Kutru, and whose son was he?"

"He was a Megmador. Dr. Kaen and I were his parents. Kutru is dead and cannot harm anyone else."

Starco gasped and gazed around at the others. "Human and Beltese genes are incompatible."

"My genes were altered by my parents. I'm now 100% Beltese, and a Megmador. This meeting is adjourned."

***

When Sedo transported down to the human planet, she found tall, lush grass and flourishing herbivores. Babies frolicked about, and their mothers nursed them. She stood next to Reiser. "It's exactly the way you projected."

Reiser's eyes twitched. "It's perfect."

Sedo's species now had a home, their own planet. "The ecosystem is perfect, and it's so beautiful."

"What about the Velekans?" Reiser asked. "They've turned the humans on Kodas into slaves."

"When we transport the humans here, they'll be protected forever," Sedo said.

"Our jobs are done here. All we need to do now is transport the rest of the humans," Reiser said.

Sedo felt the surge of energy emitting from Reiser, now slightly stronger.

CHAPTER 22

REVENGE

Planet Onupa in the Quadra 6 Solar System
When Ming reached his old village around midday, the sky was as black as night.

Thunder rumbled, and with each flash of lightning, his old family house came into full view. A wave of nostalgia swept over him, and his heart raced at the first sight of the place. He stood frozen in front of the house as angry tears mixed with the downpour and ran down his face.

Except for the lush, green garden, the place looked as gloomy as the weather. His mother's face washed before his eyes like the surrounding wall of rain. He expected to see his father open the door and check the weather as he usually did during storms, but no one stirred. The love and security the house had once offered were distant memories. Ming bit his lower lip and tasted blood. The fury inside him had risen to a penchant for revenge. Today he would kill those who murdered his family. The guilt and nightmares that had haunted him over the past five years would finally cease.

Tao, second-in-command, approached Ming and shouted over the pounding rain, "Why are we stopping here? Do you know this place?"

Ming forced his eyes from the house. "No," he shouted back and moved on.

Pelted by midsummer rain, he splashed through muddy water, slowing his pace as they neared Cong's village. The soldiers carried kulls—sharp, flat rocks affixed to straight tree branches by pieces of leather.

The smell of food permeated the air and enhanced hunger pains deep within the pit of Ming's stomach.

Eastern villagers usually hid at the first sight of soldiers from the West, but the pouring rain had already forced them inside.

Ming approached Cong's house and knocked on the door.

It took an inordinate amount of time for someone to open the door a crack and then slam it shut again. Ming heard a barricade being forced behind the door.

"Open up," Ming yelled.

Cong shouted from the other side of the door, "You have no dealings here."

Using their body weight, Ming's soldiers rammed at the door without success. After many strenuous attempts of kicking and shoving, the door yielded and Cong stood before them, gripping a stick with both hands. His face was frozen, and he stared for a long time, as if seeing a ghost.

Ming broke the silence. "I'm here to avenge the murder of my family. You took my family's life, now I'll take yours."

"But you took advantage of my daughter. It's a father's duty to defend his daughter's honor."

"Clear the house and bring everyone out back," Ming ordered, and his men obeyed.

Lin was among the group. No man had married her. She wasn't the pretty fifteen-year-old girl he'd remembered, but a woman. She locked her eyes on the ground, not on him or his soldiers.

Ming saw no beauty, only evil, and he wondered what he'd ever seen in her.

When he addressed Lin, he stood directly over her. "So, you lied about me, whore, and got my family killed."

She hissed at him, and for the first time her savage eyes peered into his. "I had to do something. I would've been beheaded."

Cong turned and stared at his daughter. His bushy eyebrows furrowed in disbelief. "You weren't forced?"

Ming scrutinized the woman he had once loved—and now hated. "No, she wasn't."

His wet hand slapped Lin across her face, and she fell to the ground. "Admit to your father that you're a whore and a liar."

Cong lowered his voice. "Lin, did you lie to me? Please, tell me the truth."

She sat up slowly but kept her head down. Her silence spoke for her.

Cong clasped his hands together, and his voice came out grimly. "I'm sorry, Ming. Please, forgive me. Lin's punishment is death. Kill her, not my family."

Ming screamed, pain lacing his every word, "Never. You all must die."

"Ming, you've joined the West," Cong said. "You're ... a traitor."

Ming lowered his voice. "You murdered my family, and I'm the evil one?"

"Please, kill her, but spare the rest of my family."

It pleased him to hear the man who had haunted him for five years beg for his family's life. A fiery and sinister laugh erupted from Ming's throat. He had the upper hand and could sense Cong's terror, his desperation over the situation at hand. "You and your sons murdered my family."

Cong waved a hand toward his family. "Let them live."

"They must die," Ming said.

Cong continued to beg. "Please, Ming."

"Kill them." He'd waited five years to give such an order. "Kill them all," Ming roared. He pointed a stiff finger at Lin, then Cong. "Except them."

Ming would've allowed his men to toy with Lin, but they had ventured deep into the Eastern Dynasty and didn't have time for pleasure.

With a mighty thrust of his kull, he attempted to stab

Lin's throat where she sat. Her right arm blocked the blow, tipping the kull to one side, and the weapon penetrated her shoulder instead. Unable to control his rage, Ming stabbed her repeatedly in the chest, stood over her recumbent form, and watched the blood ooze from her body. Her vacant eyes stared up at him, and her face twisted in pain as life wilted from her mutilated body.

Cong was the last to die. Ming first wanted him to witness the death of his entire family.

Groaning with each thrust of his weapon, Ming stabbed Cong in the throat twice before he fell to the ground. He hovered over Cong's body as he repeatedly stabbed his neck, until he severed his head.

Tao gripped his shoulder. "Ming, he's dead."

Ming yanked up his kull and turned to find Tao staring at him, his face wrinkled.

"What's wrong?" Ming asked.

"You told us you left home because you refused to marry the girl your father picked. You brought us here to kill these people for revenge?"

Ming said, "I'm the leader of this group. You'll kill whom I tell you to. Don't ask questions." He straightened up, his bloody hands still gripping his weapon, his muscles tense.

Ming left the carnage of Cong's family and went in search of his next victim.

A lone man approached them with his head down, leaning into the strong wind, his shoulders hunched against the deluge. He didn't notice Ming and his throng of a hundred men until he had almost stumbled into them. At first, he stopped in his tracks, but then the man attempted to flee.

"Stop," Ming ordered.

The man turned, faced the soldiers, and coughed his words out. "I have nothing. I'm just a peasant."

Like the soldiers', his clothes were soaked, and his hair ran down his forehead with the rain.

Ming bellowed, "I'm seeking one called Bojing. Do you know where he lives?"

The peasant didn't appear to recognize Ming, only the colors of the West. The man pointed a shaky finger in the direction from where he had come. "He lives in the last house on the left, just before the lake."

As the soldiers trooped past, the man ran.

Ming marched his men in silence. When they arrived at Bojing's house, he pounded on the door, just as an angry mob had done at his home five years earlier.

A cautious voice croaked from the other side of the door, "Who's there?"

"Open up," Ming roared.

The muffled voice came louder. "I don't know you. Please go away."

Ming motioned to his men. "Break it in."

Soldiers thrust their shoulders into the door while others kicked at the bottom. The door crashed open, and Bojing stood before him, chewing a mouthful of food.

Bojing spat out his words. "Please leave us alone. We have nothing to offer you."

Ming studied the man's expression. "You don't recognize me, do you?" He didn't remembe Bojing either, until he stood face to face with him.

Bojing's voice echoed inside the room. "I know no one from the West."

"Five years ago, you joined Cong and slaughtered my entire family in the forest. Perhaps you should get to know a man before you murder his family."

Bojing frowned and shook his head. His jaw dropped, his eyes narrowed, and his face twisted. "But you took advantage of Cong's daughter. He asked for our help. We had to uphold our traditions."

"Bring his family outside," Ming ordered.

The frightened man dropped to his knees and begged. "No. Please. Not my family."

Ming's soldiers jerked Bojing to his feet—just as Ming's family had been beaten and forced outside, so was Bojing's family.

The man pleaded, "Spare my family."

"My father begged for his family's lives that night. Don't you remember?"

Bojing sobbed, "But it was Cong and his sons."

Ming didn't share his grief. "It was also you and your sons. Kill them," he ordered.

His men showed no mercy. Kulls penetrated flesh and crushed bones, and blood flowed in the pouring rain.

After the slaughter, Ming's soldiers washed the blood from their hands and faces in the rain.

The hungry soldiers reentered Bojing's house and ate all the food. Then, as they had at Cong's house, his men stuffed their pouches with uncooked rice, meat, and vegetables.

Ming and his men slaughtered another family and moved on to the next house, and the next, until most of the villagers were dead. The hate that had festered within him all those years still lingered.

Killing the families had not satisfied his thirst for revenge.

The rain had turned to a drizzle. They walked until dark and stopped in a small village.

"Split up," Ming said. "Ten men to each house. Eat, get plenty of rest, and meet me here tomorrow morning in the early light."

As the men roamed off in groups of ten, Ming pounded on the door of the first home.

"Who's there?" asked a young girl.

Ming spoke in a gentle tone. "Open the door."

Once the girl recognized they were soldiers from the West, she tried to close the door, but Ming blocked it with his foot. They forced their way into the dimly lit house.

"We need food, and quickly," he demanded.

"We have none," she said.

Ming slapped her with a backhand swing, and she landed on the floor.

Her scream summoned her mother, who rushed in and hugged her daughter in fear as the soldiers searched their house.

Ming addressed the mother. "Get us food, woman. Where are your men?"

"They're soldiers," the mother replied.

By the light of the fire, Ming got a good look at the young girl, who was about sixteen. She reminded him of Lin, and he hated all women who resembled her. He grabbed the girl by her hair and shoved her into his group of men.

"Here, you deserve some company," he said.

The mother spoke through sobs. "Leave my daughter alone. Please don't." She fell to her knees before Ming. "Stop them."

Ming pressed his kull to the woman's throat and drew blood. "Cook us food, or we'll kill you both."

The soldiers forced the girl into the next room and muffled her screams.

***

The next morning the weeping mother cradled the body of her lifeless daughter, her eyes filled with tears and hatred.

Ming picked up his kull and left.

He took the same path he'd taken years earlier, past

distant ramshackle homes: some in clusters, others standing alone.

The sun stood high in the sky when his soldiers and he approached two men. The youngest one fled into the forest, but the older man continued creeping toward them. At a distance, the fleeing man resembled his ex-brother-in-law, Sheng, but Ming dismissed the thought.

The wood carver was a short, bony man who had wrinkled skin that was tinged with reddish-brown spots. A pointed straw hat that was tattered and soaked in sweat crowned his head. Long, tangled silver hair fell down his back, and a scraggly matching beard fluttered in the gentle breeze. His clothes were dirty and rancid, and he stood barefoot.

The old man cocked his head and blinked several times, as if trying to clear his vision. His vigilant eyes scanned Ming's blood-soaked clothes. He took a deep breath and exhaled loudly, shaking his head in disgust.

"Ming, is that you?" the man asked.

Ming wondered why the old man was so far from home, but he didn't ask. "Yes."

The man scratched his chin, and the expression on his face grew grimmer. "Why are you with these soldiers?"

Ming stuck out his chest. "I'm their leader."

The old man squinted. "So, it's you who's raiding our villages and killing our people?"

Ming didn't respond. His mind flashed back to the death of his family.

The man wrinkled his nose and spat on the ground near Ming's feet. "The Western Dynasty, your dynasty, has claimed our land. I've heard how vicious your soldiers are." He wiped sweat from his wrinkled forehead with the back of his hand and continued his stone-cold stare.

"I'm a soldier," Ming said. "I do what my ruler tells me to."

"I'm sorry about your family, but that's no reason for you to kill, steal, or force yourself on women."

Ming leaned on his kull. "You helped them kill my family."

The old man shook his frail head. "I've never killed anyone."

Ming remembered the old man as an excellent wood carver. He had made toys for children, combs, spoons, bowls, and plates. "You were at the pit that night when the others murdered my family."

The old man shook his head again. "I only held a torch. I never touched anyone."

Ming said, "Holding a torch makes you just as guilty."

The old man's eyes went to the ground.

Ming said, "I've heard the East is planning to fight us, rounding up all the men and training them."

The old man raised his voice and clenched his fists. "The Western Dynasty has invaded our land. We're peaceful people who just want to live simple lives."

"I was once peaceful, like you." Ming lifted his kull

and thrust it into the old man's chest. His victim let out a low gurgle and folded to the ground, his knees buckling as blood spilled from his mouth and nose.

***

Ming and his men continued westward and veered off the well-worn, sandy trail flanked by flat fields and then by high grassland.

"Where is everyone?" Tao asked. "We've passed only five peasants, and all carried heavy loads."

Ming said, "The population of the Eastern Dynasty outnumbers us three to one. It's like the woman said last night, their men are training, and the women and children are hiding in their homes."

Tao chuckled. "Easterners are cowards. They'll never fight us. One of our soldiers can easily kill ten of theirs."

"Perhaps they're—" Ming stopped talking and pointed. "A man just hid behind that bush. Let's see what he's carrying."

When the soldiers surrounded the peasant, he had wedged his pouch under some branches.

"What do you have?" Ming demanded.

The man stuttered. "Nothing."

Tao retrieved the pouch and dumped its contents on the ground. "What's this?"

The peasant's nervousness intensified. "Ah, stones for cutting."

Thin, sharp stones used for cutting were among the pile, but most were longer, like those used for weapons. The corrugated stones ranged from light brown to dark brown: some had black stripes, others were solid black.

"Why are you carrying so many weapons?" Ming asked.

"To trade for food," said the man.

"You're trading with the East," Ming accused him. "These stones are found only in the mountains in the West, and that makes you a traitor."

"They're for hunting," the peasant said. "And for cutting meat and vegetables."

"Our stones are going right past us," Ming said.

Tao was the first to spear the man in the chest, then two others joined in.

The group then divided the stones and continued their journey westward.

***

The sky was clear, and the moon hung low and large. Ming gazed up into a perfect sky, mesmerized by the starry night. As he marched in the soft light, labored breaths and tromping footsteps drowned out the sporadic chatter of birds, insects, and frogs. A gentle breeze rustled the leaves and cooled the air.

Ming targeted another village for food and shelter. Chickens scurried away, and piglets squealed and raced about as they neared.

"Split up," Ming said. "Meet up here at dawn."

His men drifted into the village, seeking shelter for the night.

A baby wailed behind the door of the home Ming knocked on.

Like the previous night, Ming and his soldiers forced women to cook for them. They ate and fell asleep on the floor. During the middle of the night, a loud thud and a groan woke Ming. He jumped to his feet and saw his guard falling over from a sitting position, while two men beat him with rocks.

Ming stabbed one of the intruders with his weapon and yelled, "On your feet, men." A heavyweight landed on his back, and he reeled forward and lost his balance.

Tao thrust his kull into Ming's attacker, but more enemies entered the room.

An injured villager staggered and fell backward, blocking the doorway. He let out a low moan and covered his wound with both hands, trying to stop the flowing blood.

"Western pigs," one of the intruders yelled.

Shouts came from outside the house. "Murderers."

Three enemy soldiers trampled over the bodies of their fallen comrades to reach Ming and his soldiers. One tripped at the door and fell. Ming attacked him before he regained his balance.

One man opened a window shade and scrambled through it, and Ming heard his cries of death. His own soldiers stumbled over the mangled bodies in the doorway and rushed outside.

One of his soldiers fell to the ground, groaned once, and rolled on his back. Ming nudged him in the side with his foot, but the man didn't respond.

His other men fled houses and ran toward him, seeking comfort in numbers.

Tao stabbed two Easterners, freeing one soldier. Ming and the others fled, with Tao at their heels.

They joined the few remaining soldiers and raced from the village, and their attackers didn't follow.

Near dawn, Tao stopped, bent over with his hands on his knees, and sucked in air. "Ming, we can't keep up with you."

"Let's get off this trail." Ming led them into the forest, where he fell to the ground, thankful to be alive. Moments passed, and the only sounds were deep breathing.

Ming sat up and counted his men. "Seventeen? A hundred men, and only seventeen are left."

Tao still gasped for air. "There were so many of them, and they attacked so quickly."

"I'm the only one in my group who escaped," said another soldier.

Tao rushed out his words. "Not only did they kill most of us, but they now have our weapons. It'll be daylight soon, and they'll be searching for us."

"We need to keep moving. If we take a shortcut through the forest, we should reach the West in less time, and we'll be safer. Let's go." Ming led his men into a trot.

CHAPTER 23

MING'S FAMILY

Planet Onupa in the Quadra 6 Solar System
When Ming reached the territory the West had once claimed, intense fighting was waging between the two dynasties.

He and his men were now behind the Eastern line.

Ming peeked over a bush, watching the battle, and saw that the West was losing. "Look at how many there are."

Tao whispered back, "Only half have kulls, but we're outnumbered."

"We need to get around them. Stay behind the bushes and grass." Ming squatted close to the ground with his kull in his right hand, and his men followed.

Ming sneezed, but with the intense fighting no one noticed. He tucked his tie inside his shang. "Hide your red ties. We can walk right past them."

Ming and his men ran through the enemy lines and joined the West. They fought hard and powerfully, but so did their opponents.

After four days of intense fighting, the East had forced the West from their territory.

Ming's remaining soldiers fell one by one. After Tao's death, he only had four men left. "Let's get out of here," he said.

Ming's men refused to give up. One said, "Ming, you're asking us to run. We'll fight till the death of us."

Another man forced Ming's hand from his arm. "We never thought you were a coward. Killing defenseless families? That's your way, not ours."

Ming fled the battlefield and rushed home, knowing the Eastern Dynasty wouldn't stop until they had conquered the emperor of the West.

It was midday when he pushed the door of his house open with such force that his boys—Jing, three summers old, and Fai, two—jumped to their feet. The odor of lunch still permeated the air.

His wife, Suylin, let out a frightened gasp. She sat on the floor sewing, with the two boys at her feet. The wall shade was open to allow sunlight into the room.

Ming carried a large rag. "Pack your things. Take only what you need," Ming ordered. "Quickly. You and the boys must leave here."

She jumped to her feet and followed Ming into their bedroom. He divided his loot into two smaller rags.

"Where are we going?"

"We're losing the battle, and the East is only days away. They'll kill the emperor and his loyal subjects," he yelled back at her.

"But we're winning. The emperor said—"

Ming turned, holding a bundle in each hand. "Our ruler doesn't know what's going on. I'm a soldier. Trust me, we've already been defeated."

"What about our house?" Suylin asked.

"Your brother can take care of it. He's a cripple and poses no threat to the East."

"Where will we go?" Suylin asked.

"Take the boys and go to my old village in the East," Ming said.

She froze. "You're from the East?"

He placed one of the rags into her hands. "Travel to the East. To the old Chi Chang home near Gong Ho," he urged. "You'll be safe there. Tell no one you're from the West. My soldiers will escort you around the fighting. After that, you're on your own. Stay on main trails. Travel only during the day and spend the night with peasant families."

Her brow wrinkled. "What about you?"

"I'll come later. I have things to do before I leave."

"But traveling with two small children?"

"I'll catch up with you tomorrow." He pointed at the rag in her hand. "Keep them hidden."

Suylin untied the bundle to reveal pieces of opaque white and light green precious stones. Their religious Pi and Tsung carvings. They were priceless and sacred, belonged only to the rich or high spiritual leaders.

"Ming, where did you get these? Did you take them from our emperor?"

"I'm going to get more. If anything happens to me, remember the large tree at the edge of the backyard. More will be buried on this side."

"But Ming, we can't keep these. It's wrong. We'll anger the gods."

He grabbed her shoulders and shook her. "Put these in with the children's things. Remember what I told you about traveling."

Suylin rushed about and gathered clothes, as Ming had instructed. "Yes," she repeated. "Travel only during the day and spend the night with peasants."

"Change your clothes, wear one of the peasant dresses, and get rid of your head ornament. Do you remember the name of the village?" he asked.

"Gong Ho. But what if I'm caught with these ..."

"Don't argue with me. Collect your things. I'll explain more as we walk. Hurry," he urged.

Suylin shook her head. "I've heard that soldiers take advantage of women. I won't be safe."

Ming picked up his youngest son. "Eastern soldiers will not harm you."

"So it's our soldiers who are doing those horrible things?"

"I don't want to discuss this now. I promise you'll be safe," he said.

Ming led his family to the edge of the village, where two soldiers met them. The men helped him tie cloth and animal skin between two sticks.

He hugged both boys goodbye, then embraced his wife. "Remember, I'll catch up with you tomorrow unless something goes wrong. If I don't, keep traveling."

Ming placed his sons on top of the structure and watched his wife drag the makeshift litter.

***

At sunrise, Ming set out for his old village, disguised as a peasant. An exhausted army from the East brought a cloud of dust with them. He leaned on a stick and waited for them to pass.

"Hey, peasant, where are you from?" the lead soldier asked.

"A village near the East," he said.

"Why are you here if you're not a soldier?"

Ming faked a limp. "My leg."

"What are you carrying?" a man near Ming asked.

With dirty hands, he opened a pouch, exposing stones.

"Weapons for our soldiers," a man in the crowd said.

"What's in that other pouch?" the soldier asked.

He extended the filthy thing to the nearest soldier, who refused to touch it. "Toy carvings for my children."

"Have you seen any Western pigs?"

Ming said, in the utmost humble voice, "No, this trail is deserted because of the fight. I've met only two travelers, peasants like me."

A soldier pulled out a greasy rag from his pouch and

tossed it to Ming. "Dried rice and fish. It's men like you who have helped us win this battle."

"I'm most grateful for your kindness," Ming said.

The cloud of dust moved on.

Ming thought of many deserters, like himself, in search of far and distant kingdoms. Chaos among the soldiers of the West had erupted like a threatened beehive. Some took refuge in the land of the dragons, taking all the valuables they could find.

***

Ming walked along a deserted trail that had once thrived with travelers. The only indication of life was smoke rising from a few scattered homes. He saw no one and seemed to be the only man in the world.

He studied the ground and saw drag marks, hopefully from Suylin's litter. He hastened his pace, and the drag marks became more pronounced. He hadn't met soldiers that day, but kept his walking stick.

He caught up with his family the next afternoon.

"Suylin," he yelled.

His boys jumped off the wooden rack their mother pulled them on and ran to him. "Father, Father," they cried out.

Suylin laid the litter on the ground and rushed to him. "I thought something had happened to you. What's wrong with your leg?"

He hugged his boys. "Nothing. Soldiers kept stopping me. That's why I'm late."

"I haven't seen any lately. I think they're all behind us."

"When we arrive home, Sheng, my once brother-in-law, and his brother will be there. I must account for my whereabouts over the past five years."

She scowled. "Why didn't you tell me you were from the East?"

"A young girl claimed I forced myself on her in order to save her own life. She was two months with child. We were to be married, but my father found me another bride. I was away when my entire family was killed."

"You met her without a chaperone." She pointed a stiff finger at him and yelled, "You lied to me about your family, where you were from. And now, I find out that you have another child?"

Ming placed his hands on her shoulders. "Her father promised to kill the baby as soon as it was born, and I'm sure he did." Ming gritted his teeth.

Maybe Cong hadn't killed the child.

What if he'd murdered it when he killed Cong's family?

His wife's eyes welled up. "I want to go back to our home. We won't feel safe in the East."

"Everyone involved is dead," Ming assured her.

"How do you know?"

"My soldiers killed them," he said.

"You had your men kill these people. How many?"

"Lots. I had the power to order it, and I did. Don't you see? They deserved to die," he said.

She turned and started walking back the way she had come. "Our sons and I are going back home."

"No, we'll continue east," he demanded, grabbing her arm.

"How will you explain where you've been all these years?"

"I'll tell them I started a small farm and bartered like my father. I built a place on a lake near the West and lived simply. Shortly afterward, we met and married. After the West claimed that land, they took all our vegetables and pigs. Like most people, we fled and moved farther east, we lived with an old man and his wife, who had no sons."

Suylin was adamant. "I'll not risk the lives of my sons. Go if you please, but without us."

In a rage, Ming raised his hand to slap his wife's face. Suylin closed her eyes and cowered.

"You'll go where I tell you." Ming had never raised a hand to his wife before, and he saw pain and confusion on her face.

They walked for days, and she remained distant, rarely speaking to him. Ming worked for food, doing farm labor. During the nights, they gave cutting stones to peasants in exchange for refuge in their homes.

***

When Ming knocked on the door of his old family home, Sheng answered, holding a toddler. He flashed a broad smile. "Ming, welcome home. Are you here to stay?"

"Yes, this is my wife, Suylin, and our sons."

"Please come in. My wife is cooking," Sheng said.

Ming admired Sheng's child. "It's a boy?" he asked.

"Yes, and we have another, a newborn."

"Good," Ming replied. "I'm glad you remarried. We both have two sons. Where's your brother?"

Sheng closed the door and took a seat on the floor. "He doesn't live here. He remained with my parents."

Ming took in his familiar surroundings. The old house brought back good memories. His mother's bamboo boxes were just as she had left them, and he wondered if they still contained her comb and head ornaments. Bowls and cooking items, and even the aroma of the house, remained the same.

Ming and Suylin sat across from Sheng and told the story they had rehearsed while their boys explored their new home. For a brief moment, Ming remembered how the man traveling with the toy maker had resembled Sheng.

Again, he dismissed the thought.

***

The next morning, Suylin sat on the floor at the edge of the table eating her morning meal with Ming, Sheng, and his wife. Her sons were asleep, along with Sheng's children, when half a dozen soldiers stormed into the house, leaving them little standing room.

Four men jerked Ming to his feet. "Come with us."

"Why?" Ming protested.

Suylin ran to her boys to protect them. The men stared at her, then at her sons. "Are those your children?"

Suylin cradled them in her arms. "Yes."

Two men retrieved the sleeping boys. "They must come with us."

"No, don't take my sons," she pleaded. Suylin lurched for her boys, but two soldiers held her back.

One of the men poked Ming's chest with a kull and drew blood. "Traitor."

The men dragged him outside.

In a soft voice, Sheng's wife said, "I'm sorry, Suylin, but Ming is a killer."

Sheng said, "I saw Ming kill a man with my own eyes."

Suylin thought about what the East would do to her sons. With shaky hands, she pressed fingers to her temples, hoping it would ease the sudden pain. Her legs buckled, and she collapsed onto the floor.

***

Later that morning, Suylin knelt at the feet of Manchu, the leader in her new village.

Another man sat in the room. Manchu did not

introduce the man, nor did he speak. He quietly sipped his tea and stared at her.

A nervous sweat saturated Suylin's body.

Manchu had white hair and a face filled with lines of wisdom. Even sitting, she could see he was small and short.

His home was almost exactly like Sheng's, apart from the two soldiers who stood directly behind her.

A baby wailed in the next room, and it reminded Suylin of her children. A sweet odor she didn't recognize permeated the house. She heard hens clucking outside, and the sound of children's voices filtered through the walls.

"Do you understand the charges against your husband?" Manchu asked.

"Yes," she said.

"When everyone in Gong Ho involved in the Chi Chang family's deaths were killed, we first suspected Ming. Sheng witnessed him killing the toy maker. I'll spare your life, because you didn't know about Ming's past. He admitted that he lied, deceiving you like the rest of us."

Manchu's words tortured her. He already knew the truth, so why antagonize her. "Please, return my children."

"Ming will be killed tomorrow morning. And, as you know, the father's bad blood flows through his children, so they must die as well."

She wailed and bowed at Manchu's feet. "No, not my sons. Please have mercy on them."

"This is our custom," he said.

"They're just children," she cried out.

"Evil children shall not be spared. You'll witness their deaths," Manchu said.

"Please, don't." She rocked back and forth as she wept. "They're just babies."

"Ming was innocent of the crime Lin accused him of doing. Sheng told us what happened. The girl was not forced. She lied to save her own life. It's our custom for a father to avenge his daughter's honor. But, if that daughter lied, it's she alone who shall be punished. Ming had the right to take the life of the girl but not the others."

"And me?" she asked.

"You must return to the West. Your life is in danger here."

She took a long pause, wiped tears from underneath her chin, and cleaned her cheeks. "Kill me too."

"I've spared your life," Manchu said.

Suylin stared at the floor. "Without my children, there is no life."

"When did Ming become a soldier?"

"When I met him, five years ago, he had just joined the army," she said. "He learned quickly and moved up fast."

Manchu shook his head. "Ming's father was my friend. It hurts my heart to have his son killed, but as leader of this village, it's my duty."

"Where are my sons?"

Manchu said, "They'll remain with the soldiers tonight."

"My Graciousness, please. May I see my children?" she begged.

"You may see your husband, but not your sons. It'll only add to your grief."

She collapsed on the floor. The soldiers carried her outside and escorted her to Ming.

Suylin's strides were too short to keep up. During the brief walk, she fell far behind.

She hated Ming for lying to her and causing the death of her children, but her heart pounded at her first sight of him.

Ming sat on the ground, his hands tied behind a tree in the center of the village, with leather straps secured around his waist. Villagers surrounded him, staring at him, as if seeing a strange, wild beast for the first time. They taunted him with threats of death and spat and threw stones at him. Two soldiers were present, but they did nothing to stop the abuse.

The soldiers who escorted Suylin to her husband chatted with the two who guarded Ming.

"Ming, they know everything," she said.

"Sheng told them all about me. He saw me kill the last man responsible for murdering my family."

"Sheng told Manchu you were innocent of the crime the girl accused you of," she said.

"He knew—but never told anyone else until now," Ming said.

She wiped her eyes. "He's a coward."

"I'm sorry for not being a good husband and father, for causing you shame and dishonor. I'm sorry I won't be there to help raise our sons, teach them about life, honor, and how to become men."

Suylin stared up at the tree above his head. "But Ming, they're going to kill our sons. I'll never forgive you for causing their deaths."

Ming's face twisted. "No," he bellowed. "They can't kill my sons. I must speak to Manchu. Soldier, bring me Manchu."

One of the guards yelled at Ming, "Our leader has made his decision, and it will not be reversed. The villagers won't allow it."

Suylin dropped to her knees and sobbed. "Tomorrow I'll see my family for the last time."

"We entered people's homes and took things. I let my soldiers force themselves on women. I'm a thief and a murderer. How did you think we lived so well?" he asked.

"What?" she asked, her face still in shock.

"Forgive me, Suylin."

Her voice quivered. "I can't forgive you. They won't let me see my children. They're forcing me to be here in the morning, but they can't stop me from closing my eyes."

"Don't let our sons watch," he said.

"They're going to kill you first. They have no choice."

"You must return to the West, Suylin."

"I'll be leaving after—" she sobbed.

"Come closer," he whispered.

She wiped spit from his face with her sleeve and pressed her ear to his mouth.

"Remember, buried near the giant tree at the edge of the yard, you know the one?" he asked.

She nodded.

"On the side of the tree trunk, nearest the house. Be careful of how you dispose of them. Take them to another dynasty. I want you to have a good life."

"Stop that," a guard yelled. "No whispering."

Suylin continued sobbing. "Ming, I can't live without you and my children. I begged Manchu to kill me too."

"You'll manage. I know your brother will take good care of you. Goodbye, Suylin. You'll find a more suitable husband."

"Ming," she whimpered.

He lowered his head. "Please go. Please."

Suylin stood.

She didn't say goodbye but turned and walked away.

***

The next morning, soldiers escorted Suylin to the center of the village. More people than she could count, adults and children, crowded the area. She knew bystanders from both villages would be there, but she hadn't expected the place to be so packed. She felt their eyes groping her. Their stern expressions couldn't hide their hatred.

"Let us through," one of the soldiers said.

"It's her." A woman pulled Suylin's hair and another tore her dress at the shoulder. A rock smashed her forehead and blood ran down her face. She covered her head with her hands and arms.

Her escorts forced the crowd back and stopped her directly in front of her husband, who stood strapped to a large tree. Her boys hugged Ming's legs.

"Mommy, Mommy," her sons called out to her.

Suylin rushed for her children, but the soldiers restrained her. She struggled like a wild beast to break free, and her stomach knotted and churned. "No. Not my children."

The fear and emptiness that surged throughout her body couldn't overpower their hold on her. She could manage life without her husband, but not without her children.

When the huge executioner wobbled up to Ming with a kull in his hands, the crowd roared in anticipation.

Manchu stood. His clothes hung loose on his small, fragile body. The crowd fell silent. "Ming Chi Chang, you are guilty of treason, murder, theft, and forcing yourself on women. One of the children you killed at Cong's house was your own son. Would you like to admit to your evildoing before being put to death?"

Suylin was shocked to discover that her husband had forced himself on women. She dropped to her knees. She had never known the man she'd married.

The crowd remained silent and waited for the guilty party to speak.

Ming held his head high. Blood covered his face and clothes. Another rock hit him above his right eyebrow.

"Stop that," Manchu insisted. "Let him speak."

Ming tilted his head to prevent blood from spilling into his eye. "I killed the ones who murdered my family. I didn't realize my child was among those in Cong's house. I did my duty as a soldier of the West. I fought for my emperor."

Shouts erupted from the crowd. Some pounded fists into the air. Voices from strange faces chanted out anger and contempt. An old man shook his walking stick into the air. "Traitor."

A woman screamed, "Baby killer."

An elderly woman wept. "You murdered my entire family."

The man Suylin saw at Manchu's house yelled, "You slaughtered most of Gong Ho."

A man about Ming's age stepped through the crowd. "Ming, you were once my friend. If you were killed with the rest of your evil family years ago, many others would be alive today."

Someone kicked Suylin in the side, and she fell to the ground, face first. She sat up, but didn't turn around.

The executioner stood on the right side of Ming. His massive arms swung back, and his muscles tensed as he tightly gripped his kull. With a mighty force, the weapon struck Ming in his throat, then again. The third blow severed his head. It tumbled to the ground and landed in front of Suylin.

She covered her eyes and screamed.

The crowd cheered. Women joyfully cried and babies wailed.

Blood spattered on the executioner as Suylin and her sons, Jing and Fai, wailed. As their mother, it was her job to protect and take care of her sons, but she could do nothing to comfort them.

The crowd grew silent again.

She yelled, "Please don't kill my boys."

When she opened her eyes, the executioner had targeted her oldest son, Jing. The man didn't restrain him but stood Jing against the tree. He swung the kull back, and Suylin closed her eyes.

Men yelled and women screamed.

Suylin heard disruption throughout the crowd as someone tripped over her. When she opened her eyes, everyone was fleeing for their lives, and her boys ran into her arms. Surrounding the area were many giant, bug-like beasts. Most of the men now had glowing green collars around their necks, and the Bugs were herding them like livestock.

Demons had taken over the East.

Suylin took her boys and fled back toward the West.

Chapter 24

Earth

The Saxons

Weeks after the Saxons discovered their new world, Burle and three men scouted the area through scattered fog, a half a day's ride from their village.

Headed for a snow-capped peak, they spotted a large lake in the distance and galloped toward it through thick grass in the early dawn, while the air was still cool. Willows swayed in the wind as they scanned the area. A harmless fox scurried away as the men approached, then it disappeared into the vegetation.

"Why didn't the gods move us here?" Mace asked. "This is a perfect place to live."

"We can move here later. Let's learn the lay of the land first," Burle said.

They had found a variety of berries, onions, and potatoes growing in a meadow near a large lake, but their journey would not end there.

Burle's new land frightened and intimidated him. He couldn't allow his clan to detect his fear. Although he remained the Saxons' leader, he lacked the courage of Sax.

First, the gods had provided them with weapons to defeat The Lords; now, they had moved them to a lush land away from the Velekan devils. Burle galloped his horse through a grassy meadow where he saw a huge herd of strange animals too large and fast to be goats.

Mace moved his horse in closer, but the long-legged animals leaped farther away. "What are those?"

Burle stopped his mount next to Mace. His heart pounded, and beads of sweat ran down his face. He wondered if his men were as frightened and confused as he was. "I don't know, but let's try to get one. They might be good eating."

Mace sat lean and tall on his horse as he studied the herd. "Look at the horns on the males. They branch out like tree limbs."

Burle pointed at the largest male. "That's probably their leader." He galloped his horse around to the front of the herd, and his men surrounded the animals.

The lead animal seemed confused, unsure of which direction to flee.

Mace's arrow penetrated the animal's neck, and another arrow pierced its side. The wounded animal went down on its front legs, and then on all four, gasping for air.

Burle galloped to the incapacitated animal, praising his men. "Good shots." He slid off his horse and slashed the thrashing animal's throat with his sword.

Mace grabbed its hind legs. "I can't wait to see what it tastes like."

"Put it on your horse," Burle said. "You can ride double with me."

The four men lifted their prize and tied it to Mace's horse.

As they prepared to leave, six men approached them on foot through thin fog. Burle squinted to make out the shape of them. Fur covered their genitals, and their chests were bare, except for the wooden medallions that hung around their necks. They were barefoot. They had no beards, but their hair was long and ungroomed. But the most amazing thing of all was their bright orange skin. He pointed. "Another clan. Look at how they're dressed."

Mace jumped on Burle's horse. "This is a strange place, and they might be enemies."

An arrow penetrated Mace's back, came out his front, and pierced Burle. Mace fell to the ground.

A sharp, burning pain throbbed in Burle's side. He slid to one side of the horse, barely hanging on. He yelled, "Let's get out of here."

John's horse pranced and then hesitated. "What about Mace?" he asked.

Burle rode behind his group. "Head for the village."

The man kicked his horse in the side and galloped away, towing the horse that carried their kill.

Burle followed, barely able to stay upright.

"Can you make it?" John yelled back at him.

"Yes. Ride ahead and gather the men," Burle said. A crowd had gathered when Burle rode into his village. He fell from his horse and into the arms of a group of men. He had never been so relieved to see his village.

***

Burle lay on his back while his wife patched him up.

"Find out where their village is," he said to five of his council members, who had crowded into the small room.

"We'll go back to where they killed Mace and track them from there," John said.

"I don't think they have horses," Burle coughed out.

"When you find them, check the size of their village before attacking. Make sure we're not outnumbered."

"We're Saxons. I plan to attack, even if we're outnumbered." John leaned in and studied Burle's wound. "It doesn't look deep."

"It's deeper than it looks, and it hurts something awful."

"You rest and get well," John said. "We'll take care of our enemies."

"No," Burle said. "Rest the horses. Leave at dawn. You should reach the place where they attacked us before the sun is directly above."

"We'll leave some men here to protect our villages, just in case they followed us." John headed for the door. "Let's get organized, men."

***

John led the throng, but only about 20% of the men had horses. The men were loaded down with arrows hanging in pouches over their shoulders, and each carried a sword. The remainder trotted behind, taking turns riding.

John galloped back toward Mace's body. When they arrived at the place where Mace had fallen, he lay dead.

John slid from his horse and studied the man on the ground. "Mace didn't have a chance. Let's bury him."

It was near dusk when the enemies' trail led the Saxons straight to their village. Smoke billowed from four fires that blazed in the center, surrounded by crude huts, as women cooked. Children ran around naked.

The village was larger than the two Saxon villages combined, but the Saxons had revenge on their minds and blood in their eyes.

"Doesn't look like they're expecting us," John said. "I'm afraid we're going to intrude on their last meal."

The Saxons surrounded the village on foot while hiding in the tall grass. When the horsemen stormed into view, a young boy spotted them and yelled out in a strange tongue. Women rushed inside the huts as men ran for their weapons.

The Saxons entered the village, attacking from all

sides and killing everyone they saw. Having no mercy for women and children, they slaughtered everyone. Then they returned to their village, proud of their victory. They had lost only two men, and only a few suffered minor wounds.

The Saxons became so paranoid about their new world, they posted guards day and night and only traveled in large groups.

The Western Dynasty

In Suylin's new world, a mountain range separated the Eastern and Western Dynasties. Trapped soldiers from the East were quickly defeated, and the West regained their territory.

She hugged her sons at the sound of pounding on her door. When her brother answered, six soldiers stormed in.

"Are Eastern soldiers here?" one asked as the others hastily searched the house.

"No," Suylin's brother replied. "We've heard lots of fighting. We're afraid to leave our home. What's going on?"

"We're searching for Eastern soldiers. How long have you lived here?"

"Five years," Suylin replied. "My husband was killed by Eastern soldiers."

***

Suylin knelt in front of the new emperor of the West with both of her sons at her side. The items that Ming had stolen were on a small table beside him.

"Why do you have these items?" the emperor asked Suylin.

"My husband hid them before he was killed by Eastern fighters. He didn't want them to take them, so he buried them near our home. I was instructed to return them when we regained our territory."

The new ruler smiled. "He must have been a good man."

"Yes," Suylin said as her last sight of Ming flashed through her mind.

The Wombas

Thabo woke in the early dawn at the sound of the goats making a ruckus.

He heard a woman scream, "A lion. A lion."

Eight men rushed outside with their spears, then attacked and killed the beast, but the goat it had been pursuing was already dead.

The woman stared around the area in confusion. "We're not in the same place. The gods have moved us again."

"Where is the jungle?" Kobe asked, his eyes searching the landscape.

"Why would they move us to such an awful place?" the woman moaned.

"Did we do something to anger the gods?" a man asked.

In the distance, Thabo saw herds of gazelles grazing in lush, green grass. He held his youngest brother. "There's a lake."

"And it's probably filled with crocodiles and hippos," his father said.

Kobe passed his second son to his wife. "Quickly, let's fill the space between our huts with brush to keep the animals out."

Thabo worked with the other men, trying to protect their village, as he remembered from the old days. The Nubian and Yoruba villages were nearby, and they were setting up barricades as well.

"Children, get the goats into the center of the village," Kobe yelled.

The tribes carried tree limbs and bushes and piled them up densely between each hut, so the lions couldn't enter.

Two men pulled the dead goat into the village.

"They put us back in our old world or one like it," Kobe said.

In the distance, they heard the Zulus' war drums.

Palmnut vultures sat in nearby trees, waiting to pick the remains of any kill.

The tribe's huts and belongings were there, but the place was surreal.

***

The Zulus accused the three tribes of angering the gods, because they had traveled through the jungle. They led a surprise attack on the villages, just as they had two years earlier. The three tribes, however, still outnumbered them. They chased the Zulus back to their village, slaughtering most of them. The remainder fled south, and never returned.

Chapter 25

The Wrath of the Velekans

"Captain," Starco said. "The commander would like to speak with you in private."

Sedo moved from her computer station. "Put him in my room."

Rota appeared on a vektren in front of her desk. "Captain Sedo, I've just promoted you to Beltese Fleet Ambassador. Bonuve will assume captainship of the *Volpus*."

Sedo was at a loss for words. This was her stepping-stone to become fleet commander. Her Megmador instincts had never warned her of such a glorious occasion. She felt flushed, and her hearts throbbed out of control. "Ah—"

"We've been very impressed with your work, Ambassador. Not just the Human Planet Project, but other advanced accomplishments in technology as well."

Sedo said, "I'm also working on seven more projects."

"You'll travel to the next galaxy on the *Volpus* and report your findings to me. I'm especially interested in this species known as the Tewils. So that you'll not be out of touch with Fleet Command, we're contracting the Agoorons to set up a communication station near the next galaxy."

She tried to maintain her composure. "I can't wait to venture there."

"I want you and Bonuve at my office in two weeks. Can you make it to Tandon by then?"

"Yes, Commander. I'll contact Captain Bonuve now."

Sedo waited until Rota sounded off, then raised her fist and punched air. "Yes."

Sedo immediately contacted Captain Bonuve.

He stared back at her from his captain's station on the *Eliptus.* "Captain Sedo."

"Captain Bonuve, I've got some wonderful news. It's a good thing you're sitting down."

A smile dented his cheeks. "It must be good. You're glowing."

"I have a reason to beam. You're now captain of the *Volpus.*"

He frowned and seemed to ponder the idea. "The *Volpus*?"

"Isn't that wonderful?"

"But what about you?" Bonuve asked.

"Captain Bonuve, I've just been promoted to Ambassador of the Beltese Fleet. You and I are trekking the next galaxy."

His mouth gaped open. "The next—"

"We'll meet with Commander Rota on Tandon in two weeks. That is, if you're available."

Bonuve displayed a proud grin. "I'll be there."

"Since your ship is slower than the *Volpus*, you need to leave now."

I don't know if I can remain on the Volpus and not interfere with the captain's duties.

After Sedo's conversation with Bonuve, she called a special meeting with her lieutenant commanders.

She mingled among the crowd before addressing them.

"Chochu wine. What's the occasion?" Somgu asked.

"Quiet, please." Sedo held up her glass. "I have three special announcements to make. First, the completion of the Human Planet Project. All humans are prospering as well as expected on their own planet, thanks to Reiser."

Everyone cheered when she presented Reiser with a galactic plate for excellent workmanship.

Reiser flashed a crooked smile, and his voice croaked. "Thanks to you, Captain."

Sedo smiled. "Bonuve is now captain of the *Volpus*."

The group fell silent.

"I'll still be aboard as ambassador for Fleet Command. We're traveling to the next galaxy. We may be there for years."

Everyone congratulated Sedo, and the crowd erupted into murmurs.

"Ferrus, we must reach Tandon within two weeks."

Ferrus moved closer to her. "A special congratulations, Captain—uh, sorry, Ambassador. I'll make sure we get there in one week."

Sedo's pride in her crew overwhelmed her.

They didn't fear her anymore.

***

Sedo and Bonuve met with Commander Rota at the Fleet Command complex on Tandon. She proudly wore the *Volpus* emblem on the chest of her new uniform. Her blue collar designated her top position in the Beltese Fleet, just as Assistant Commander Colas.

Sedo took the chair on the right side of Rota's desk with Bonuve on the left.

Commander Rota tapped a key on his desktop, and the Mantus Solar System appeared on a vektren between Bonuve and her. "This is the information I received from you, Ambassador." Rota then addressed Bonuve. "I expect the *Volpus* to visit every planet in this solar system before moving to the next. Determine what life-forms exist on each planet and their intellectual levels. Even if life doesn't exist, I want a detailed analysis of minerals, metals, and gases. I want to know about all species, hostile or friendly. Contact us immediately with your findings."

Bonuve studied the projection.

Sedo said, "We have no idea how long this voyage will take. We were informed that the beings on Neptus were the only hostile species in the first solar system, but we may encounter others."

Rota pressed another button, raised the vektren above their heads, and increased its size for a better view. Turning to Sedo, he said, "Ambassador, I chose you for this job because of the progress you've made, and your special powers. We'll not make the same mistake your father did."

That brought back sad memories. Her father had once been a highly honored commander: now all Beltese hated him. "When shall we leave, Commander?"

"In a week. I will meet with you two again prior to your departure. That's all for now."

Bonuve stood, but Sedo remained seated.

"Captain Bonuve, do you mind if I speak with the commander in private?"

"I'll wait for you outside, Ambassador." Bonuve threw a proud glance over his shoulder as he left the room.

"Commander, I have some very disturbing news." She sighed. "Reiser is becoming a Megmador."

Rota gasped and sat up sharply. "What? You can't be serious."

"He has a faint energy level radiating from his body, and it will increase with time."

Sedo had seen the same expression on Rota's face when he'd first learned of her powers.

He drew a deep breath. "How long have you known?"

"I suspected it shortly after I started working with him on the Human Planet Project."

Rota stiffened his shoulders. "Reiser is unstable and won't be able to control his powers. He'll behave more like your son." His hands clenched into fists, and he raised his voice at her. "Why didn't you tell me earlier?"

She searched for a logical explanation. "Well, I—"

"How can we have two—no—three Megmadors? Historically, only one exists at a time."

"That was probably my parents' fault. They made a mistake by reengineering my genes. Reiser was intended to be the next Megmador, not me."

Rota paused. "Does he know?"

"No, but he'll start to gain powers in about ten years."

"Does anyone else know?" he asked.

She tugged at her itchy new collar. "No, not even my husband."

"For the sake of the Beltese and the galaxy, he must be terminated. Give me a few days to discuss this with my officers. Don't ever keep anything like this from me again. Good day, Ambassador."

When Sedo approached the vertical lift, Bonuve waited in front of the open doors.

He stepped inside, and Sedo followed him. "A private conversation. I hope it wasn't about me."

She turned and stared at herself in the mirror and loosened her collar. "No. It was a Megmador ordeal."

When Sedo and Bonuve walked from the Fleet Command complex, a gigantic dark circle appeared in the western sky. The wind strengthened, and the spot turned into a whirling mass. It spun faster and faster. Tree limbs swayed, and dust flooded the area.

A young couple huddled together, dropped to the ground, and hugged each other. A female wrapped her legs around a tree, gripping her young baby in both arms. Sedo reached out with her mind and helped the woman into a building.

An elderly man's white robe whipped in the wind. He covered his head with his arms, flattened himself against a building, and edged his way toward an underground shelter.

Others dashed into buildings to avoid the strong winds, but most took shelter underground.

All around her, Sedo felt the fear and confusion of nearby Beltese. Like Bonuve, she sensed something tragic and surreal lurking above them.

Sedo's Megmador instincts kicked in. For the first time since obtaining her powers, she was afraid.

Sedo grabbed Bonuve around his waist and used her powers to keep him afoot. She had never seen anything like this on Tandon, or any other planet. "Let's get underground."

As the wind died down, the circle stabilized. Sedo searched the eerie sky, but she didn't realize what was happening until many warships emerged from a wormhole.

Bonuve stumbled, and she caught him. "What's happening?"

"It's the Velekans. They're back." Sedo punched

in Somgu's communication code. "I'm with Captain Bonuve. Transport us up. Now."

Within seconds, they were in Navigational Control on the *Volpus.*

Somgu's voice quivered. "Captain, what's out there?"

Sedo jumped into the captain's chair. "The Velekans have discovered a wormhole, and they've had years to improve their warships."

"I need to get to my crew," Bonuve shouted.

The Velekan warships were larger than their former model but still small, compared to the *Volpus.* The *Eliptus* hadn't activated its barrier. Four Velekan warships targeted it and fired multiple blue beams. The rays pulsed like wind whistling through space. The *Eliptus* split in half before shattering into inflamed, flying debris.

Bonuve's eyes widened and resentment showed strongly on his face.

He froze in place and watched the remains of his burning ship litter space.

Somgu activated the protective barrier and started firing on the enemy ships.

Bonuve regained his composure, jumped behind Khyla's vacant station, and started firing.

As with the *Eliptus,* most of the *Volpus's* crew members were taking leave on Tandon. Some Beltese warships activated their barriers, but most were too late. Blue rays of light from enemy warships lit up the area, destroying Beltese ships. A Beltese warship exploded near the

Volpus, and the rubble left from the exploded ship and others floated in the space over Tandon. Beds, chairs, crew members, personal items, and crumpled metal floated into space.

On three vektrens, Sedo watched enemy ships target Tandon. Numerous strikes hit the planet, collapsing buildings and cutting down citizens. Within minutes, Tandon fell into ruins.

Their enemy had caught them off guard, attacking during midday and focusing on the most populated areas on Tandon.

A shocked, almost bewildered expression still clouded Somgu's face. "Their weapons are just as powerful as ours, Captain, but their protective barriers are slightly weaker."

All Sedo could do was watch the destruction. She felt defeated, helpless, and confused. What good were her powers if she couldn't save Tandon? She shuddered. "Get my crew up here," she demanded.

"Not without deactivating our barrier," Somgu yelled.

Sedo's mind raced, like the chaos around her. She concentrated on the wormhole, forcing it to shrink. Ships traveling through it crashed into each other and exploded. Within seconds, the wormhole totally disappeared, leaving the wreckage of ships floating in orbit.

Sedo couldn't take her eyes off the destruction on Tandon. She contacted Fleet Command, surprised by the panic in her own voice. "Commander Rota, are you there? Please, respond. We're under attack."

When she received no response, she rushed to Starco's communication station. The barrier protected the *Volpus* from four powerful, shattering blasts that would have devastated the ship. Still, it felt, as if the ship had hit an asteroid, throwing Sedo headfirst over Starco's desk. She stopped herself in mid-flight and landed on her feet.

She opened all communication channels from Starco's station and anxiously punched the keys on his desktop. "This is Captain Sedo of the Beltese Fleet. Tandon is under attack by the Velekans. We need immediate help from any nearby warships."

Twelve other Beltese ships acknowledged their presence.

A Trazod captain came into view. "You're breaking up, Captain, but I received your message. We're almost there."

"Captain, use your powers," Bonuve shouted.

"I just closed the wormhole," she growled at him.

He pleaded, "Can't you destroy their ships?"

"If you allow me to concentrate," she snapped.

"The Bugs and the Velekans have joined forces," Somgu said.

The Velekan warships were now a smaller version of the Beltese's and larger than their old ships. The Bugs' warships resembled various insects.

Enemy ships came after the *Volpus*, and equal numbers surrounded other Beltese warships.

Bonuve fired on a ship, and it exploded. Somgu hit another, and it shattered.

Sedo closed her eyes and concentrated on the enemy's zircolon cores, which produced an infinite quantity of neutrinos, just as the *Volpus*. If she paralleled the neutrino spinning action, the ship engines would explode, but she also feared destroying their own ships in the process. She changed her approach and concentrated her powers on their weaker barrier. Sedo contacted the remaining Beltese Fleet. "Fire on them. Their protective barriers no longer work."

Somgu immediately took out more enemy ships. "Good job, Captain. They're now defenseless."

Another strike shook the *Volpus*. Since it wasn't as devastating as the first hit, the ship only rocked and trembled.

"Destroy the others," Sedo ordered. "We need to help our citizens."

Sedo had been concentrating so hard on keeping the enemy barriers deactivated, she hadn't realized the other Beltese ships had destroyed the remaining enemy vessels, with the exception of the two that got away. Four Beltese ships followed them. One of the captains appeared on a vektren. She said, "Don't worry, Captain, we'll get them."

If Sedo had not been so distracted when it all started, she could have closed the wormhole earlier, thus saving Tandon. "Deactivate the barrier and transport my crew aboard, Somgu."

"Some of our crew have been located, and I'm transporting them, Ambassador," Somgu said. "Most are not responding."

Three crew members showed up in Navigational Control. Except for Starco, their uniforms were dirty and tattered. Only a third of the *Volpus* crew reported for duty. Some had suffered minor injuries.

Ferrus jumped into his chair as soon as he arrived. "They've destroyed Tandon."

Nedra didn't make eye contact with Sedo or anyone else in Navigational Control. She assumed the position at her old workstation.

Sedo was baffled. "Nedra, why are you here? Where is Khyla?"

Somgu sounded more under control. "I couldn't locate her or the other weapons engineer."

The *Volpus*, as well as other warships, operated with only a skeleton crew.

Sedo needed a weapons expert, and she even welcomed Nedra.

"Somgu, can you locate Dr. Kaen?" Sedo asked.

"Just a minute, Captain."

Bonuve asked, "How could they create a wormhole?"

Sedo said, "The Bugs have been working on the theory for a century."

A Trazod captain appeared on a vektren. "I believe they came from the Quadra-6 Solar System. There has been a lot of activity on Onupa over the past few years."

Confusion flooded Sedo's thoughts. "Why didn't you report this activity to the Galactic Committee?"

The Trazod captain shrugged. "We weren't concerned, because the Bug species had mined the planet in the past."

"I warned Fleet Command that the Velekans may be secretly making warships, but Commander Rota didn't take me seriously," Sedo said.

The Trazod captain focused on the devastation displayed on Sedo's vektrens. "We have two more warships nearby. They should be here soon."

Sedo stared at him. "Thank you, Captain. Your fleet can help us defeat the remainder of our enemies."

Somgu said, "I've located Dr. Kaen. He has organized a medical emergency staff on Tandon."

Everyone in Navigational Control fell silent as the crew studied the projections on the vektrens. Hatred for the Velekans surged through them like the burning flames that lit the area.

The enemies had destroyed the Fleet Command complex, along with Rota and all highest-ranking officers, and Sedo felt the weight of Tandon on her shoulders. "Starco, try to contact Tandon. Anyone."

"I'm trying Fleet Command," he said.

Sedo said, "They're all dead."

She didn't see Starco's eyes but felt them. "I gave you an order, Starco."

Starco jumped straight up in his chair. "Yes, Captain—Ambassador."

***

Postrow, ruler of the Tandon Empire, communicated with the Beltese allies from the *Volpus*.

He was short and thin, and his face was haggard and grim.

The most miserable things in Sedo's life had been the deception of her parents, then the secret birth of her son, and later his exile. Now, she felt far worse than she had through all three tragedies combined. Millions of lives had been lost because of her negligence, her failure to respond quickly. She should have seen death and destruction coming to Tandon, but the excitement of her promotion had clouded her judgment.

Nowe expressed his condolences. "No one could have predicted such a disaster, especially from the Velekans. How many warships did the Beltese lose?"

Sedo slumped in her chair and stared into the distance. "Forty-seven. Fortunately, most were in space."

"Citizens?" the Trazod commander asked.

"Over fifty million," Postrow answered.

Nowe gasped and seemed to be at a loss for words.

"So many innocent Beltese, murdered by two inferior species," the Trazod commander said.

Sedo corrected him. "They're no longer inferior."

Nowe asked, "What about the injured?"

Postrow's wrinkles grew deeper. "The remainder of our citizens are in underground facilities. We're transporting the injured to warships and treating and returning the less critical ones back to Tandon."

The Camagon captain's face was as white as her workstation. "What shall we do about the Velekans and the Crustans?"

Postrow looked from one vektren to another. Hatred beamed from his face, and his voice growled with revenge. "Obliterate both species. I don't want a single one left in this galaxy."

"You're asking us to wipe out two species?" Sedo asked.

"I'm not asking, I'm telling you, Ambassador." Postrow's voice boomed loud and strong for such a small man.

"At the moment, we're all filled with rage. Why wipe out two species because of their leaders' stupidity?" Sedo asked.

Postrow shouted, "It's not rage, but justice and retribution. This is no social event. This is war."

She had a job to do, and Postrow left her no room for debate.

The Trazod commander volunteered his fleet. "We'll attack the Crustans first. We don't have the authorization to wipe out the entire species."

"No." Tandon's leader was adamant. "Take out the Velekan planet first, then destroy the Bug planet."

"I must accompany the annihilation of each species. I can deactivate their barriers, and they'll be defenseless," Sedo said.

Postrow clenched his jaw. "And how do you know this?"

"I have powers," Sedo said.

"Yet you didn't predict this disaster." Postrow's words came out cold and harsh. "What good are your powers?"

"Commander Rota instructed me to use my gift only in life-or-death situations. The more I use my powers, the more alert I am to threats. Rather than pondering, I should have immediately closed the wormhole."

"You have my permission to use your powers at will," Postrow said. "Get rid of our enemies, and get our planet back to normal."

Ambassador Sedo said, "There'll be warships here to protect Tandon."

Postrow turned to her and pounded a fist on her desk. "Protect us from what? There's nothing left."

Sedo sighed. "When I return, I can help rebuild Tandon."

"You're wasting time," Postrow yelled. "Transport me back to Tandon. My citizens need me."

Sedo contacted Jogen on a vektren from their room. She watched him reattach a severed arm on a patient. She zoomed in on his hands. With small, delicate instruments, he joined nerves and veins. He glanced up at her. "I can't talk to you now, Sadera."

Dr. Mano had replaced Ohma, and he was working on another patient in the background.

Will Tandon's citizens hate me?

If Sedo could, she would have changed those few minutes she had hesitated before closing the wormhole.

Unfortunately, Megmadors could only alter the future, not the past.

Jogen concentrated on his work. "My old hospital is gone. So is the research center."

Sedo said, "I'll be back as soon as I can."

Jogen didn't respond. He just continued working on his patient.

Sedo summoned half of the Beltese Fleet to help rebuild Tandon.

***

Sedo led a fleet of thirty-two warships, which moved in a cluster.

Other allies joined her convoy along the way as she headed toward the Velekan planet. When the *Volpus* arrived at Numus, Sedo's number of warships had increased to eighty-seven.

She now had more confidence in her powers and leadership skills, and she controlled an assertive fleet of warships.

Sedo confirmed forty-three Bug warships and thirty-seven Velekan warships in orbit around the planet.

"Captains, spread out," Sedo said. "Seems like they're expecting us. Surround the planet."

Her ships put great distance between each other. The enemies did the same thing.

An Elgon captain sat straight up in his chair. "They're approaching, Ambassador. Our barriers are activated."

Blinking lights surrounded the Bugs' warships. They maneuvered behind the Velekans' fleet.

The two caravans slowed their pace, as if sizing up their enemies prior to battle.

Ferrus said, "Here they come."

Sedo communicated with her fleet on a secured network. "Let them get closer. We have a surprise for them."

Savage energy surged through Sedo's body like never before, and she had trouble remaining in her chair. Her body heated up like a star but was absent of perspiration. Her nerves tingled, and her two hearts throbbed out of control. She wondered if anyone in Navigational Control noticed.

Somgu's voice rose. "They're within firing range, and their protective barriers are deactivated."

Sedo smiled. She had outsmarted her enemies once again. "We'll surprise them again."

Sedo's convoy approached the cluster head-on. Suddenly, the enemy ships scattered and fled in various directions.

Bonuve asked, "Why are they leaving?"

What Sedo had thought would be an easy defeat was now a more difficult task. "They've figured out their protective barriers don't work. Our ships are faster. Outrun them and cut them down."

All around, the Beltese and their allies took out one enemy warship, then another, until none existed.

"There might be more in space," Sedo said. "Destroy them on sight."

"Captain, the Velekan commander has summoned us," Starco said.

"Ignore him," Sedo snapped. "Captains, destroy all facilities and every Velekan on this planet."

Everything stood above ground on Numus due to its high aquifers. Unlike Tandon citizens, Numus citizens had few underground shelters.

Nedra and Bonuve fired, destroying homes and other structures and cutting down fleeing citizens. Fires erupted all over the planet, and debris and dust clouded its surface.

Sedo felt remorse for the destruction she was inflicting on the innocent. After an hour of turmoil, all Beltese convoys ceased fire. Then they bombarded the planet with a biological chemical, raising a cloud of pink gas above the surface that killed only the Velekan species— by clotting their blood and causing instantaneous death.

After thirty minutes, the chemical dissipated, leaving no trace.

The Trazod captain appeared on a vektren. "Ambassador Sedo, there are seven Velekan children alive on this planet. I don't think we should finish them off. With all their technology destroyed, it would take centuries for them to excel."

She pondered. "How did they escape the gas?"

"They are sealed in a compound." The Trazod captain shook his head. "I don't agree with wiping out an entire species. That decision should only be made by the Galactic Committee."

Sedo placed both hands on her armrests and leaned back in her chair. "Are they old enough to survive on their own?"

"The oldest one is fifteen," the Trazod captain said.

"Leave them," Sedo ordered. "I'll deal with Postrow."

"Thank you, Ambassador," the Trazod captain said.

Sedo said to the Trazod captain, "Please, help our citizens back on Tandon. I'll have other ships waiting for me at our final destination."

Bonuve shifted in his chair and bellowed, "We were ordered to kill them all."

"I've made my decision. Ferrus, take us to Onupa."

***

Sedo went to her quarters, hoping to contact Jogen.

The captain of the ship that he worked on appeared on a vektren, his uniform covered in dirt.

"Hello, Ambassador, I understand your fleet destroyed the Velekans."

"Yes, Captain. I can't locate my husband," Sedo said.

"He's on Tandon and can't be reached. When he transports up again, I'll have him contact you."

"No, that's all right. Seems like he's too busy," Sedo said.

"The doctors rarely get rest here," he said.

"How are things on Tandon?" she asked.

He shook his head. "Terrible. We're looking forward to your return."

"I hope this battle will be as easy as the one on Numus, Captain," Ambassador Sedo said.

***

When Sedo reached Onupa, a fleet of sixty Beltese and ally warships decreased their speed and eased toward the enemy.

Flangus, a Beltese captain, winced. "We've seen the devastation on our planet. It's not Tandon anymore."

Sedo's voice roared with confidence. "We'll rebuild it."

"Ambassador, our leader wishes to speak with you," Starco said.

"Put him on a vektren," Sedo said.

Postrow was drenched in perspiration and covered in dust, and he gasped for air. "Ambassador Sedo—"

"Speak up. I can hardly hear you over the machinery," Sedo shouted.

He turned and ordered the noise to stop. "I said we have very few leaders left, and you're the highest-ranking officer. I promote you to fleet commander. I trust your decisions, even though you disobeyed my orders and left a few Velekan children alive."

Fleet commander.

Those were the words Sedo had wanted to hear all her life, but not at the expense of so many lives. This saddened her, and she no longer felt worthy of the position. She said, "I didn't protect Fleet Command and the Tandon citizens."

"Commander, you're our only hope," Postrow said.

She not only had superpowers but was now the leader of the Beltese Fleet. "I'll do my best, sir. Thank you for this honor."

Her mind went to Jogen. She hadn't consulted him concerning her promotion to ambassador and now fleet commander.

Postrow sneezed. "We've started recovery work here. Adults are working twelve hours per day, adolescents eight."

"I can be of great benefit when I return," Sedo said.

Somgu interrupted. "Captain-Ambassador Commander, three Bug ships are trying to outrun us."

"I must go, Leader. Our work has just started here. I'll contact you after we've completed our mission."

Sedo could still see the desperation on Postrow's face after communication had ceased.

"Captains Coma, Lugo, and Flangus, catch up with the enemy ships. Their barriers are deactivated," Sedo said.

"We'll get them, Commander," Flangus promised.

The three ships fell out of formation and sped toward the Bug ships shaped like spiders.

"Look, there's another wormhole, and they're headed for it," Ferrus said.

"Don't follow them inside," Sedo said to her captains. "Return."

Sedo downloaded an in-depth analysis of the wormhole in her computer. She noticed that Bonuve had done the same.

The three Bug ships entered the wormhole, and it vanished.

"It would have been suicide if we had followed them," Flangus said. "Our ships would have ended up over their planet."

Bonuve said, "Now they'll alert the others."

Flangus said, "Commander, they have more warships than we do."

"We can defeat them. Keep advancing," Sedo ordered. "We need to get this matter over with and get back to Tandon."

"You warned Fleet Command about the Velekans," a Camagon captain said. "Why didn't they listen?"

"They didn't believe the Velekans could advance so quickly, starting from scratch. And they certainly didn't anticipate them joining with the Crustans."

The Camagon captain said, "The Agoorons are terrified."

"The Velekans are more concerned with the Beltese than the Agoorons," Commander Sedo said. "We destroyed their production facilities."

"It's a good thing the humans were removed from this planet," Bonuve said.

Sedo had confidence in her premonition. She envisioned the destruction of the remaining enemy ships. "It doesn't matter. They're doomed."

A Trazod captain shouted, "Here they come."

In the *Volpus* Navigational Control, a 360-degree view of the enemy warships appeared on vektrens.

Tension stirred Sedo's superpowers, which guided her to a point of relentless victory. "All captains, turn off your zircolon cores."

She received numerous complaints from other ships. Had she not been a Megmador, she wouldn't have been able to decipher all the negative feedback at once.

"We'll not have protective barriers."

"It will be suicide."

"What's the purpose of this?"

"We cannot comply with the Beltese orders, Commander. We need to know why."

"Trust me," Sedo said. "Our enemies may have tapped into our communication system. Turn off your engines. Operate your barriers using your solar power system."

"You know how quickly our systems will drain," an Elgon captain said.

"That's an order," Sedo shouted. "I'm not asking for opinions or comments. We'll only need a few seconds."

"Commander, we volunteered for this mission," a Camagon captain said. "You can't command us to commit suicide."

"If you don't deactivate your cores within the next minute, your ships will self-destruct. I don't have time to explain. Just do it. Now."

Her convoy shut off their engines and drifted into space, as their enemies moved in.

Sedo closed her eyes, and a more powerful force than in the past took control of her mind, reaching out like an invisible tentacle, clutching the weakness of her enemy ships, and causing the matter-antimatter to spin parallel, rather than opposite each other. All at once, the enemy's ships exploded, and so did two mountains on the planet. Her powers had increased exponentially since closing the wormhole.

She had never felt so invincible.

The *Volpus* shook from the pressure surges of the exploding enemy ships. She opened her eyes and saw the wreckage collide with her fleet. Their temporary barriers had protected them. She gripped her armrests with her feet flat on the floor as chunks of the wreckage hit the *Volpus* barrier. "Now activate your engines and destroy all alien life on this planet."

Things she had once feared now excited her: more like a power game. She knew the Beltese would not only win this battle, but also remain the most intellectual and powerful species in the galaxy.

"Thirty-six Crustans just took cover in a cave," Bonuve said.

Sedo thought about the Bugs living as her human clan

had, without any modern conveniences or technology. "Then they'll have no means of leaving this planet, ever."

If they survived, it would take centuries for them to regain their technical knowledge. They wouldn't be a threat to the galaxy anytime soon.

Somgu frowned at her. "What about the three Bug ships that escaped into the wormhole?"

Sedo felt very pleased with herself. "They're headed for their home planet. We'll catch up with them there."

Somgu's voice faltered. "They know how to generate wormholes, and we don't."

Sedo smiled. "We do now, and it won't take long for us to reach their planet. Trust me, they won't be expecting us so soon."

Bonuve glanced at Sedo. "I copied their wormhole data, Commander. It makes no mathematical sense. I've distributed it to all engineers aboard the *Volpus*, and they can't decipher it either."

Sedo chuckled. "I understand it. We should be able to create a wormhole within minutes. Ferrus, set coordinates from here to the Bug planet."

He touched keys on his desktop. "Course has been established, Commander."

Sedo worked her fingers with speed and accuracy at her computer. "Now enter this data into your vector dimensions."

Ferrus complied. A wormhole appeared above Onupa— a huge gray circle.

A dark invitation into the future.

Ferrus gasped, "How did you do that, Commander?"

Sedo felt everyone's eyes on her. They trusted her, looked up to her as their leader and savior. She would use her powers to do good for the Beltese and the galaxies. "How did the Bugs create something so technologically advanced?" Sedo asked.

"Commander Sedo." Bonuve jumped to his feet and walked closer to the view screen. "This is astronomically amazing."

Sedo said, "Once we're inside, we can only communicate with our ships. Ferrus, increase the size by changing the space vectors."

He did as she'd instructed, and the hole grew large enough for their ships to enter.

"Increase its size a little more," she said. "Give us room to maneuver once we're inside."

Another Beltese captain asked, "Commander, is it safe to enter this thing? We have limited technology."

Adrenaline surged through Sedo's body as her anticipation grew. "It worked for the Bugs and the Velekans."

"How long will it take us to get there?" the Elgon captain asked.

"Let's find out," Sedo said. "Just follow the *Volpus*."

Ferrus hesitated. He turned and gawked at her. "But Commander—"

"Ferrus, continue," Sedo said.

Reluctantly, Ferrus advanced toward the mysterious abyss.

"Speed up, Ferrus," Sedo urged.

The *Volpus* entered, and the other ships followed.

The wormhole was exactly like space but absent of stars, planets, or other objects.

It contained only eerie darkness.

Sedo said, "Increase the speed to maximum."

An unexpected acceleration wedged Sedo to her chair, and she hoped her crew had been sitting when the velocity jump occurred.

Ferrus's voice shook. "Commander, we're traveling faster than the speed of light."

Bonuve turned his attention to Sedo. "That's impossible."

"Strange things happen in space," she said.

"Captain, time has stopped," Ferrus said.

"We're not traveling in time, Ferrus. That's why it's called a wormhole." She announced to her fleet, "All captains, put great distance between each ship. When we exit, we'll slow to normal speed, and we don't want to crash into each other."

Navigational Control fell silent. Everyone concentrated on the viewport, mesmerized by its darkness.

"All captains, prepare to exit," Commander Sedo said. "Quickly spread out and hit the enemies fast."

The *Volpus* automatically decreased its speed as it shot out of the wormhole with its barrier activated, ready to fire. Sedo estimated that it had taken them about two hours to reach the other side of the galaxy. There were only twenty-three Bug ships in orbit, far less than the number Sedo had expected.

Bonuve immediately reported his scan of the Bug warships to Sedo. "Their ships are operated by a skeleton crew. They're not expecting us, probably thought it would've taken us months to reach their planet."

Nedra and Bonuve fired on three enemy ships, reducing them to flying debris. Blue pulses whooshed through space, as Sedo's captains hit other enemy ships. A few tried to scramble away, but her warships destroyed them.

"Where are all of their warships?" Bonuve asked.

"I think we destroyed most of them on Onupa," Sedo replied. "We'll destroy any we meet in space. There may be more on the other side of this planet, so let's surround it. Close the wormhole, Ferrus. Two enemy ships are fleeing in that direction."

Ferrus panicked. He threw his hands into the air and shrugged his shoulders. With glazed eyes, he said, "I don't know how."

Sedo disappeared from her workstation and instantly reappeared at Ferrus's side. She pressed a few keys, and the wormhole closed.

Ferrus froze. "You can teleport?"

"Concentrate on your workstation, Ferrus. Review the data I entered," Sedo ordered. "Nedra, Bonuve, destroy all structures and Bugs on this planet."

Sedo watched from vektrens. It reminded her of Numus all over again. Her crew chemically bombed the

Bugs' planet as well. "If any survived, they don't register on the ship's computer," Bonuve said.

Commander Sedo said to her captains, "Our jobs are finished here. I'll create wormholes and send all ally warships back to your home planets. The Beltese will remain here until you all safely reach your final destinations."

From her workstation, she created four wormholes, one for each ally. The ships entered and started their journeys home.

Then, after the dust cleared, Sedo transported down to the planet. She had never seen a battle other than on vektrens, and she wanted to see everything up close. She waded through the rubble. Dead bodies, some half-covered with debris, littered the area. Small fires still blazed here and there, leaving the planet sizzling hot.

First, a silhouette of Bonuve appeared beside her, then his body. He gripped a Rex-7 and anxiously studied the surroundings. "Why transport down here, Commander?"

Particulates floated in the air and tickled Sedo's nose, and she coughed out her word. "Curiosity."

Bonuve must have sensed her desire to be alone, or perhaps the heat discouraged him. He transported back to the *Volpus*.

She saw bodies, innocent ones like babies. Even if they resembled bugs, Sedo loved all babies—animals, humans, aliens, it didn't matter. Unlike in the destruction of Numus, here she felt more remorse. The Bug species had never been a threat. Why did they join forces with the

Velekans? Was it because she had forced them to free the human slaves on Onupa?

The pungent odor of Crustan blood reminded her of stale, stagnant water in the rain forest on Tandon. As she walked among the ruins of the desolate planet, she thought about her life, her future. *Am I becoming cold and callous, like past Megmadors?* She had two things the others didn't: Jogen and her position as fleet commander. Jogen made her happy and gentle, and she hated being away from him.

She couldn't imagine life alone again.

When Sedo returned to Navigational Control, she verified that her allies had reached their final destinations and closed the wormholes.

"Bonuve, you are now captain of the *Volpus*. Our coordinates have been established." Sedo left the captain's station. "The wormhole is just there. Take us home, Ferrus. Tandon needs us."

Made in USA - Kendallville, IN
44421_9781985859173
03.29.2022 1438